Crowning Glory

Crowning Glory

Pat Simmons

www.urbanchristianonline.com

Urban Books, LLC
78 East Industry Court
Deer Park, NY 11729

ISBN 13: 978-1-60162-897-8
ISBN 10: 1-60162-897-8

First Printing April 2011
Printed in the United States of America

10 9 8 7 6 5 4 3 2 1

Distributed by Kensington Corp.
Submit Wholesale Orders to:
Kensington Publishing Corp.
C/O Penguin Group (USA) Inc.
Attention: Order Processing
405 Murray Hill Parkway
East Rutherford, NJ 07073-2316
Phone: 1-800-526-0275
Fax: 1-800-227-9604

Crowning Glory

By Pat Simmons

Acknowledgments

Acknowledgments include, but are not limited to the following people who took my phone calls and e-mails or took time away from their busy schedules to invite me into their offices. I hope I have crossed my t's and dotted my i's. Please make sure you read my author's notes at the end of the story.

Ella Brand and family
Peggy Tyson, Crime Victims Advocacy Center St. Louis
Jessica, Victim's Advocate
John Devouton, St. Charles County Prosecuting Attorney
Jacqueline LaPine, Missouri Prison System public information officer
Renee Williamson, Evangelist
Raoul William, Senior US Probation Officer
Author Steve Haymon, PhD
Robert Eastern III, East St. Louis Alderman
Lois "Cookie" Garmany Berryman

To my countless family members who have supported me since book one:
Coles, Carters, Scotts, Thompsons, Wades, Sinkfields, Simmons, Sturdivants, Thomases, Bethesda Temple Church family, St. Louis Glory Girl book club, Barnes & Noble (Florissant) whose booksellers are my biggest cheerleaders and make me feel important.

Acknowledgments

To the descendants of Winnie Jordan Scaife and Ephraim Scaife from Arkansas. Winnie was my great-great-great grandmother—Manvera Wade's six-year-old half sister. Manerva was fifty-four. It's true. I have the 1880 census to prove it. LOL.

To Sister Juana Johnson and Dr. Marilyn Maxwell for their suggestion on naming a future book. LOL.

To Bishop Johnson for the informative Bible classes and soul-stirring preaching.

Fellow authors and the village people.

Freelance editor Chandra Sparks Taylor for holding my hand, and UC editor Joylynn Jossel for always seeing the vision God gave me.

To literary attorney Elaine English for working out the details in my contract.

To my dear husband, Kerry. I am so blessed!

Thanks, Jared, for your vote on the cover. To salesperson extraordinaire, Simi, who finally talked someone into buying my book. LOL.

My mother, Johnnie, and sister Kim.

FINALLY to the four generations of Rossis in my life:
Ross Cole (my grandfather 1915-1998)
Rossi Cole, Jr. (my father 1935-1995)
~~Rossi Cole III (brother)~~
Rossi Cole IV (nephew)

PRAISE FOR NOVELS BY PAT SIMMONS:

"*In Guilty of Love*, Simmons' sometimes whimsical approach to delivering the message of salvation is anchored by opportune scriptures. The author boldly tackles issues like abortion, child abuse and anger toward God, adeptly guiding readers into romance, reconciliation and restoration as this novel flows effortlessly from haunting pasts to delectable happiness."
— *Romantic Times Book Review*****

"Simmons has written her best work with this sequel to *Guilty of Love* (*Not Guilty of Love*). The richness of the characters and foundation of the word not only bring the story to life, but will encourage you while renewing your faith in God. This is a Christian fiction work of art."
— *Deltareviewer*****

"*Still Guilty* was a really good and powerful story. Pat Simmons brought it to the line. As I read this book, it was just what I needed. I was going through my own personal struggles and all of the scriptures that Cheney and Parke recited I jotted down for my own personal use. I have told SO many readers about this series and I'm looking forward to reading more books by Pat Simmons!
—OOSA Online Book club****

Praise For Novels By Pat Simmons

"In *Talk to Me*, Pat Simmons weaves together a love story from the perspective of each of the main characters. However, one of the main themes involves the struggles and hardships that Noel faces as a member of the deaf community. While reading this novel, I began to take note of the fact that my church doesn't have a deaf ministry and how that may seem unwelcoming to members of the deaf community. I also began to think about other things, such as phone conversations without an intermediary, the ease in hearing my child should he cry out at night and other things I simply take for granted as a hearing person. Ms. Simmons does a great job of bringing awareness to issues facing the deaf community, while at the same time, telling a wonderful love story."

— RAWSISTAZ Reviewer****

CHAPTER 1

Without a test, there can be no testimony, Karyn Wallace reminded herself five minutes after she agreed to a date with Levi Tolliver. She wasn't Cinderella, and Karyn doubted the widower would be her Prince Charming.

Yes, she was affected by the most beautiful dark chocolate eyes she had seen in her lifetime. They were hypnotic, even camouflaged behind designer glasses, which were angled perfectly on his chiseled nose. Levi's skin was a blend of chocolates: dark, milk, and white, which created a creamy undefined tone. His thick, wavy black hair and thin mustache were nice touches, but it was Levi's dimples that seemed to be on standby, waiting for his lips' command to smile. Buff, at—she guessed—about five feet, eleven inches, Levi's height didn't intimidate Karyn as he towered over her petite stature.

"You might as well surrender to what God has stirred between us," Levi stated as if he had sealed a business deal after his seventh-and-counting visit in a month to Bookshelves Unlimited, where she worked as a specialist in children's books.

Suspicion set in. What did he know about God in her life? At twenty-seven, Karyn was too old to play games. Sometimes the devil injected the word *God* into conversations as bait to Christians so they would believe they'd found a kindred spirit. Where was Levi's spiritual allegiance? She didn't have time to test the waters to see if she could survive another relationship gone awry. The memories of one bad relationship had a way of lasting a lifetime.

When he moved intimately closer, his lashes mesmerized her, catching Karyn off guard. "Deny the attraction, Karyn."

She hated dares. Bluffs got people into trouble, hurt, or sometimes killed. Karyn blinked. Now she was getting carried away. Anchoring her elbows on the table in the store's café, Karyn nestled her chin in her hands. She took pleasure in delaying her response. After all, he was interrupting her dinner break.

"I'm attracted to flashy cars, white kittens, black-eyed peas, and—"

"Me," he interjected as a fact.

Karyn refused to confirm or deny his assumption, but she silently admitted she was enjoying their banter. There was something intoxicating about a person who oozed confidence. Despite her outward boasting, building her self-assurance was, at times, an inner struggle. Shrugging, she continued as if she hadn't heard him. "Although I don't own a flashy car or a white kitten, I can put away some black-eyed peas."

"Your preferences are noted." Levi lifted a brow and held it in place to make sure he had Karyn's attention. Only after she became impatient did he soften his features and smile, offering his sidekick dimples for her pleasure.

"My Buick LaCrosse is new, but not flashy. My daughter is allergic to cats, and my mother can throw down on any beans, peas, or greens." A dimple winked as he stretched his lips into a lazy grin. "For the past four years, my spirit has laid dormant, waiting on a word from God. Now, all of a sudden, with no warning, I got a message plain enough that even a caveman could read it." He snickered.

Karyn smirked. "I've seen those GEICO commercials, and I'm not impressed."

"I couldn't resist saying that."

"Maybe in the future . . ." She paused and lifted a finger. "But not any time soon." Her refusals were solely based on experience with one man, which she knew wasn't fair.

"Hmmm." He nodded. "At least it's not no again." As he snickered, Levi's dimple performed an encore. "After all, with God all things are possible."

She nodded. Karyn knew the scripture—Mark 10:27. That was the first thing she uttered every morning when she prayed after waking up. Levi had been relentless in his pursuit. Why? Her appearance was simplistic: tan pants, a white polo shirt bearing the store's logo, and tennis shoes. A French braid, dipping inches beyond her shoulders, was her trademark hairdo. To some customers, she resembled a teenager, and the pay seemed to fit the description.

Whenever Levi strolled through the door, he received more than a passing glance, whether modeling a tailored dark suit or dressed in business-casual clothes: his pants were creased, shirts starched, and shoes polished. When Karyn first noticed him and the wedding ring, she envied the woman who had a wonderful blessing from God: an adorable little girl and a father who doted on his child, calling her sweetheart or darling. He exhibited more patience than the average man.

After that initial distraction, Karyn had sobered during the subsequent visits. She reminded herself that God was an equal-opportunity blessing giver. She referenced Matthew 5:45, where God provided the sun to rise on the good and evildoers while He allowed the rain to fall on the just and unjust.

Tonight, Levi had entered the bookstore with a suspicious, determined stride. His presence was too bold to ignore. Even mall security officers went on alert, but backed off when it was apparent that Levi's intentions were harmless. Strangely, Karyn's busybody coworker, Patrice Lucas, who saw everything and everyone, didn't seem to notice him. She was the poster child for the O'Jays' old song "Back Stabbers." Patrice was the type to be a good friend one day and the worst enemy the next. Karyn was still trying to figure out where she placed on Patrice's list. It really didn't matter. Patrice would never be one of Karyn's confidants.

What is he up to? she wondered. He never came to the bookstore alone. From day one, Levi's precious four-year-old daughter, Dori, enchanted Karyn. The child had a ready-made smile, minus the dimples. Her skin was a few shades darker than her father's. Her hair was thick, long, and sometimes wild. One and two ponytails seemed to be the only doable options for the widower. With the recent chilly temperatures in the last days of October, Dori was always dressed with matching multicolored hats and gloves.

As Bookshelves Unlimited's children specialist, Karyn enjoyed interacting with the little ones, helping them choose games and books that were age appropriate. In Dori's absence, Levi clutched the handle of a large gift bag as he roamed the aisles. Confident she was his target, Karyn waited patiently until they made eye contact, then he kept approaching.

"Do you have a moment?" He didn't wait for an answer to his summons as he turned and headed to the elevated platform that claimed to be the café's territory near the entrance. It was the only spacious area in the cluttered bookstore.

Already, Karyn's fist was fishing for a comfortable resting spot on her hip as she formed an attitude. *If I do, am I supposed to jump?*

Marking his spot at a white round parlor table, he laid his bag in a black wood chair with a black vinyl cushioned seat. The buzz in the coffee shop didn't miss a beat as he unbuttoned his black suit coat and claimed an adjacent seat. If he wore a coat, he must have left it in the car. Levi crossed his ankle over one knee and leaned back. His demeanor was relaxed and carefree, as if this were his designated VIP seating.

She hadn't planned to follow, but curious as a feline, Karyn set aside the new shipment of stuffed animals that recited bedtime stories when they where squeezed. She strolled to where Levi was camped out as if he were royalty. He met her eyes with tenderness. Levi's simmering smile was ammunition to detonate a romantic explosive in some poor woman's life.

For a fleeing moment, Karyn felt unworthy in his presence with her red canvas apron smeared with dust from opening boxes that had been sitting in warehouses. "What's going on?"

"It's a late birthday gift. Happy birthday, or it could be an early Christmas present—merry Christmas. Whichever works in my favor," he explained, patting the bag with a Macy's logo.

Speechless, Karyn fretted with her braid as her heart pounded wildly. She indulged in a secret moment of excitement. The contents represented anything but a birthday or Christmas present. It was a bribe gift. Karyn knew it and was flattered—confused but thrilled.

"But I . . ." She grasped for an excuse not to accept it, although her birthday, which was two months ago, and Christmas, which was a month away, were ideal reasons.

Levi remained focused as he stood and pulled out another chair as if she were adorned in a ball gown. Karyn scanned the store. Besides the few pockets of café customers, it was a slow night, easily managed by the supervisor and two other employees. Patrice could stretch any small task into an eight-hour shift.

"Let me go clock out first," Karyn stated.

Suddenly, Patrice appeared, arms folded and eyes suspicious as Karyn signed out for a ten-minute break. Patrice didn't smile or frown, but her eyes hinted she was waiting to be fed juicy tidbits to spread—true or false. Karyn always felt uneasy around the unkempt woman. Patrice spoke her mind without fear of censure. Fellow employees called Patrice harmless, but Karyn was wary of the woman's best intentions. *Beware* was written in invisible ink on her coworker's forehead. Since jobs were hard to find and Karyn didn't want any rumors floating back to her boss to find fault with her, Karyn gave an unnecessary explanation. "It's quiet, so I'm taking my last break."

"Sure, go ahead. I've got your back," Patrice encouraged with a wink, then added over her shoulder as she walked away, "Watch it. That guy is way out of your league."

Karyn knew that, but Patrice didn't have to bluntly voice it. Ignoring the small stab to her heart, Karyn headed for the café.

Levi waited at his post in a military stance. She stole a deep, brave breath as she obliged his invitation at the table and rested.

Retaking his seat, Levi inched his face closer to hers. "Do you remember the first time I asked you to go out with me?"

"Yes."

"Me too." He grunted, amused, and shook his head. "How about the second?" After she nodded, Levi recounted word for word each instance she had turned him down. "To an ordinary man, you would've crushed his ego. I'm not one of them. I'm calling your bluff after your last textbook recital of 'I don't have anything to wear.'" He presented his offering. "Problem solved. I happened to be in the mall this weekend, and you weren't working." Disappointment briefly brushed his face as his words mildly scolded her. "Dori and I made a special trip to buy a book from Miss Karyn. When you weren't here, I thought I was going home empty-handed. My little girl had other ideas for my wallet, so we shopped until I practically dropped."

Karyn laughed. Levi possessed a wonderful sense of humor. He often appeared serious—until he smiled. He was a handsome man.

"When I saw it on a mannequin, I imagined you in the outfit. I don't know why," he teased with a shrug. "Here's the deal: Since we're both Christians—God drew me to you—I know honesty won't be an issue. When you get home, try it on. If it fits, then you've just agreed to dinner with me on Friday night."

This time Levi didn't ask for a date. He already had one orchestrated as he gathered his car keys. Levi shook his head as if he could hear her formulate another ridiculous excuse. "I'll pick you up at seven, and I'm always on time."

Not only had Levi outwitted her, he had removed his wedding band. Karyn wondered at the meaning. On his first visit, thanks to his chatty daughter, Karyn learned his status.

"Daddy's a widow. Sometimes he's sad. I think he needs someone to play with." Dori babbled on and on as Levi stood nearby, seemingly unfazed by his daughter's assessment. A few visits later, he confirmed his daughter's biography with his ring finger still bearing signs of his bond to his deceased wife.

Karyn looked away, hoping for a customer who needed her attention despite the fact that she was on break. When there were no diversions, she swallowed. Accepting whatever was in that bag meant more than a simple dinner. He was challenging her. Again, she hated dares.

Once Karyn found her voice, she shoved doubt aside. She never gambled, but she hoped she was wearing a poker face. She couldn't wait to tear open her present. She knew his taste in men's clothes and little girls' outfits, but what did he envision for her? She beamed anyway. "I agree with your terms."

"I'll cherish your smile until Friday." He winked then adjusted his glasses.

"Don't you need my address?"

"Nope. I followed your bus home a while back," Levi said, unashamed, then he exited the store more conceited than when he first entered.

She didn't register his last remark as she peeked into the bag, but the gift was protected with an army of colored tissue. "Yep. This is definitely some kind of test," she whispered to herself. She had mapped out a schedule for school, work, and church. How was she going to make room for a man?

CHAPTER 2

"You stalked the woman?" Rossi Tolliver asked incredulously over the phone. "Have you lost your mind? There are laws against that . . ." He rattled on, advising Levi of the repercussions.

Annoyed with his cousin's scolding, Levi gritted his teeth and huffed. Although his intentions were genuine, leave it to Rossi to overreact. What was stalking anyway, a misdemeanor? "Call it what you want, but it was for her protection."

Satisfied with his own explanation, Levi finger-combed the fine hairs of his mustache. At thirty-one, Levi had retired his thrill-seeker fixes the day after he hit twenty years old.

"Is it okay to be angry with God? Does that make me less of a Christian?" Levi had braced himself, fearing the answer. Some might have considered his questions juvenile, but his state of mind at the time was anything but logical.

After the death of his wife, the counsel and prayers of Rossi, who was a youth minister, had cushioned the blows to Levi's distraught spirit. Levi thought back to the day forty-eight months ago that changed his life forever.

When Rossi didn't comment, Levi had rambled on. "The Lord allowed the devil to steal the most important person in my life. He allowed it to happen." It was a bold accusation.

Levi sniffed as they sat in matching chairs, facing each other in the bedroom Levi had shared with Diane. It was the night—a nightmarish day—before her funeral. A closed door separated the cousins from the crowd of comforters who did everything but console. Laughing and eating mocked the sad occasion.

Nodding, Rossi clasped his hands. His weary expression was a reflection of Levi's. "God has grace for all emotions, but in the end, God is God, and He doesn't make any mistakes.

"Whatever you do, don't sin against God, man. Our thoughts aren't God's thoughts, so we'll have to wait until we get to the Holy City for answers. Maybe then the Lord will explain all this to us." Rossi swept his arm in the air for dramatics. "Remember, God never takes anything away without replacing what you lost. Our hope is to believe Psalm 116:15: *Precious in the sight of the LORD is the death of his saints.*"

Levi didn't know what he had expected from Rossi, but yet again, he wasn't finding any comfort. "Look, man, I've got a little girl in there"—he paused, pointing an unsteady finger at the door—"who is two months old. Dori won't have a mother when she begins to talk and walk, or a mother to take snapshots at her first birthday party. She'll never know Diane . . ."

Levi turned away as his shoulders began to shudder. He grabbed the first available item—a baby's blanket—to muffle his tears of agony. Rossi never pulled the "men don't cry" macho line. Levi was grateful.

Once Levi had regained some composure, Rossi gripped Levi's hands and prayed in a hushed whisper, "Lord, you left us with a Comforter. We need help right now to trust you through this stormy time in our lives."

The days faded into weeks, and his friends and family were growing impatient with his slump. It was as if they were counting down to a magical moment when he would be fine. By the third month, most folks expected Levi to accept his fate, get his act together, and move on, but Levi was trapped, struggling with his emotions where he couldn't move forward even if he wanted to. Grief was not a pre-existing condition that had a three-month waiting period in hopes that one would feel better. Levi learned it had to run its course.

Frustrated, people threw up their hands in defeat and abandoned Levi, accusing him of self-torture. Maybe so, but it was his prerogative. Not only was he not prepared for the early death of a spouse, but the senseless act of the crime kept the hole in his life enlarging. Levi did what any other grief-stricken man would do: He secluded himself and Dori inside their home, rarely leaving except for necessities.

"I'm not sure sitting in a room, forming a circle, and sharing my pain with a group of strangers in exchange for listening to those competing for who suffered the worst tragedy is going to help me move on," he had vehemently warned his family.

Rossi never questioned Levi's behavior. Rossi had picked up the slack at their office when Levi didn't have the mental strength to go into work. Time wasn't healing all wounds. The second year after Diane's death was worse for Levi. It was a reminder that the previous year had been the first. It had become a cycle of heartache.

When Dori turned three years old, life had caught up with Levi, forcing him to make changes, whether it made sense to others or not. He uprooted his daughter from their North St. Louis city home and moved across the Mississippi River to the bordering state of Illinois. He had to put some distance between him and the neighborhood reminders, yet he was still less than fifteen minutes from downtown St. Louis.

Reluctantly, Levi ate his words when he agreed to seek grief counseling. He quit after the first meeting because it was as he had predicted. Talking to a group of unknown faces didn't advance his healing. Surprisingly, one-on-one sessions with a professional did help, along with counseling from their pastor.

"I hope Karyn will interpret your stalking as protection," Rossi said, pulling Levi back into the present-day phone conversation and a promising future.

"Listen." Levi pushed aside a proposal on his desk for the revitalization of a business district in downtown East St. Louis, Illinois. It was a historical area that had become neglected for decades. The cousins had planned to rename it Tolliver Town. The strip would house classy boutique stores and small businesses without charging the merchants Wall Street rent.

"Role play with me, okay, Rossi? What would you do, man? I'm driving off the parking lot at St. Clair Square Mall. I thought I saw Karyn sitting on a bench. She told me she liked flashy cars, so I assumed she had one. Maybe not flashy, since she worked at a bookstore, but something on wheels. I don't know what made me glance at the bus stop anyway, but I'm glad I did." Levi leaned back, rocking his office chair, almost tilting it over because it wasn't on wheels. He grabbed the edge of his mahogany desk.

"The woman is hot. That simple uniform she wears can't hide it. At first that braid down her back gave me the impression she was barely twenty." Levi took a deep breath and smiled. "God, was I wrong." Just the thought made him grit his teeth in appreciation. "Her shapely hips would make any man think twice about dismissing her as a budding juvenile.

"I haven't touched her yet, but I bet Karyn's skin is unquestionably soft from every angle. I guarantee every male species on that bus wanted to ask her out. My job was to make sure that didn't happen." Levi sighed with satisfaction. His testosterone came alive with a thunder. Instead of his world remaining in black and white, it turned into living color.

As Levi steadied himself in his chair, he made eye contact with a beautiful set of gray eyes. It was projected from a photo on his desk, no bigger than a wallet size. His deceased wife, Diane, smiled at him. He stared. The picture was taken before they knew she was expecting. Sometime during the past year, he had swapped the eight-by-ten portrait for the smaller photo now on display. He couldn't remember why. Maybe it was a sign of someone coming into his life.

Diane's image was swallowed up in a shrine of Dori's pictures at different stages in her young life. Diane might have been hidden from sight, but Levi knew he would always feel her presence. Blinking, Levi pushed his glasses back on the bridge of his nose. He took a deep breath, not only to rejoin the conversation, but to participate.

"What was she doing catching a bus anyway? Maybe her car is down," he mumbled. "As I drove closer, an SUV blocked my view. The bus came, and the next thing I knew she was in line waiting her turn to climb on. I started honking my horn, and everybody stared at me but her."

Rossi didn't control a wayward yawn. "Classy woman. Why should she give a crazy man an audience?"

"Yeah, right." Levi ignored Rossi's dig. "Since it was dark and the lights were on inside the bus, I noticed

Karyn was outnumbered by male riders. As far as I was concerned, it was a call for action. I trailed her until she got off—at a distance, of course. I wanted to make sure she got home safely."

"Of course. Although I'm not sure whether Karyn would appreciate your gallivanting efforts, you should've at least gone through the motions of taking her address, so she wouldn't think she was about to go out with a criminal or insane person."

Levi grunted. His cousin was most irritating when he was right.

"So, you finally asked her out—"

"Correction: She finally said yes. That woman hustled me, probably without knowing it." There was no way Levi would disclose how he eliminated more of Karyn's excuses.

While shopping for Dori, Levi had gone to Macy's to pick up a suit. As he walked through the women's section, Levi devised a plan after a dress caught his eye on a mannequin. He envisioned Karyn's face and body.

Turning on the Tolliver charm, he approached three unsuspecting ladies—probably another act of stalking—and asked if they wouldn't mind helping him out. They eagerly agreed to model outfits until they learned it was for a woman who wasn't his mother, sister, or cousin. After telling them the sad story about his wife, two ladies relented. They tried on several dresses until one held his attention. Although another woman modeled it, Levi envisioned Karyn Wallace enhancing it. He guessed the woman was about Karyn's size.

Besides his daughter, Levi had never bought a woman a piece of clothing before. Not even for his mother, Sharon, who preferred cash, or Diane, who enjoyed the thrill of ordering out of catalogs. On the rare occasions when

Diane did venture into the malls, she never deviated from her routine: Go into a store with a mission, come out with it completed.

"Seriously, Rossi, it's something about Karyn that makes me want to jump into the water whether I can swim or not. There's a certain level of mystique about her, and that fascinates me."

Rossi barked out a laugh before sobering. "Sounds like a Tolliver man talking. I just hope she lives up to your hype."

Levi removed his glasses and rubbed his eyes "Although I wasn't actively looking for a lady, it's as if God placed her right before my eyes, sorta like 'Here, Adam, take Eve.' "

"I hope Jesetta will see that as divine intervention."

"I doubt it." Levi grunted. "Jet vowed to be mad at the world for eternity about the loss of her sister. That type of anger was robbing me of my life. I had to make the decision to move on."

"Jet needs Jesus to put her out of her misery, but she doesn't tolerate close encounters with church folks. She cautioned me not to even think about laying hands on her for prayer. She's too young to let bitterness ruin her life." Rossi paused. His tone changed as he continued. "But I'm not in her shoes. Diane was her baby sister for twenty-six years, and you were married to her for almost two years."

Levi's fiery sister-in-law stirred up tornadoes where there wasn't any wind. She made no excuses for taking prisoners. That's just how devastated she was over her sister's death. If Jet felt like lashing out, she didn't care about the victim.

Dori was the exception. His daughter could wrap her aunt around her pinky. At the time of Diane's sudden death, Jet's attempt to usurp her authority about Dori's proper upbringing fizzled. In the calmest Holy Ghost spirit God gave Levi, he put Jet back in her unsanctified place.

Still, Levi respected Jet's anger. He had learned how to mask his grief until he was behind closed doors. Around others, he had a pre-set smile in place, but if one looked closer, his sadness was undeniable.

Dori was Levi's sunshine and rain. Her generous smile and curious eyes filled him with laughter. Her expressions, similar to Diane's, made him ache for his daughter, who was left without a chance of knowing her mother.

Levi's life started to change months ago when he and Dori were leaving the mall after attending a Disney movie marathon. They were almost out the door when a larger-than-life poster of a clown in the window of Bookshelves Unlimited captured Dori's fancy. If it weren't for the guidance of Levi's mother and father, Victor and Sharon Tolliver, Dori would be a spoiled brat, getting everything she wanted, instead of a well-mannered and an exceptionally bright child. He had caved in to Dori's whim that day and allowed her to drag him inside. As Karyn weaved tales, Dori and Levi were instantly caught up in her web.

"I like pop-up books," Dori had informed Karyn.

"They're my favorite too. You can play with them as you read." Karyn squatted to Dori's level. The beauty of Karyn's hair was hidden in a fat, single braid.

Before long, other children swarmed around Karyn as she lined them up to see the live clown whose image was in the poster. Levi tried not to stray far away as he scanned the shelves but couldn't recall one title.

Karyn played several games while the clown blew up balloons then twisted them into odd shapes, supposedly resembling animals. When the other children dispersed, Dori remained at Karyn's side. She trailed Karyn to the café where treats were available. Before Levi realized it, they had been in the store an hour.

By the time they made it to the register, Dori wore some type of a balloon crown and carried five pop-up books. Reflecting on that day, the true magical moment happened in that bookstore for Levi, not in *The Princess and the Frog*, one of three Disney movies they had seen that day.

After that impromptu visit, he and Dori returned to the bookstore every Saturday morning. Levi couldn't tell whether Karyn noticed him or she did an excellent job of ignoring him. Oddly, that was his motivation to make his presence larger-than-life.

Although Levi wasn't conceited, he knew he was a good catch. His sister-in-law had warned him countless times about vultures ready to eat him alive. Those were Jet's words, not his, and Levi didn't ask for an interpretation.

"You've talked about her beauty. You've mentioned her charm, but what about Christ in her life? Any evidence that she is committed?" Rossi quizzed.

"I know that's your focus as a minister, but, man, what do you expect me to do? Walk up to her, introduce myself, then ask a list of questions, which include 'are you saved and sanctified, been baptized in Jesus' name, what church do you attend, who is your pastor' and on and on?"

"It works for me, man."

Levi huffed. "Yeah, well, I prefer a woman who lives it, not just professes it. That's what going out to dinner is for. I've never seen her have a bad day, even one time when a coworker was giving her grief about something. I went on alert, ready to intervene and distract."

"You mean defend," Rossi interjected.

"If necessary. The woman had to be five-nine, a giant over Karyn. Not only was she rude, but loud."

"Hmm, reminds me of your sister-in-law. You sure it wasn't Jet?"

"Funny." Levi glanced at his desk clock then at the plaques on the wall, recognizing the company's accomplishments and noting the time. "We have a business to run. I don't have to go over plans for the Jones development—"

"You have my attention," Rossi stated in a serious tone. "But you left me hanging about how Karyn handled the situation with the woman. That's a true test of a person's character—how she reacts in conflict."

"Karyn didn't cow." Levi didn't know why he grinned as if he were the one responsible for her tact. "She retained her professionalism and walked away. I trailed her to make sure she was okay—"

"So that was the start of your stalking addiction," Rossi said.

"Yeah, right, but get this: I'm sure she didn't think she had an audience when she pulled a Bible off the shelf and flipped through the pages. She mouthed a few verses, took a deep breath, and returned the Bible to its place. It wasn't for show. She didn't know she was being watched."

When Levi had left the store, he had a higher opinion and greater admiration for the beautiful bookseller who seemed to apply Christian principles during times of stress. Suddenly, Levi wanted to know more about her: age, boyfriend, and favorite color. His daughter served as a great source of information, providing those answers and more, such as Karyn and Dori sharing September birthdays. He stored that fact in his mental notebook. Besides that and the apartment building where she lived, Levi had a running list of questions.

"Cuz," Rossi said, breaking into Levi's reverie, "I don't want to deflate your fascination, but you're right. Christians do more than quote scriptures. It's how long they stay in the ring with the devil before they take him down that's the true test."

"I want this. I want to get to know Karyn, and if I have to put on boxing gloves to make that happen, then bring it on," Levi boasted.

CHAPTER 3

Rossi was one of the most sought-after youth ministers at Living for Jesus Church where two sets of the Tolliver family fellowshipped. He knew how to pray, and at times, God allowed him to discern demonic criminal activity around him. Levi was also the most sought-after bachelor at the church.

Rossi relaxed and smiled as he closed his Bible. "Levi, you have really moved on with your life. You have been emotionally healed," he spoke to the wind in his quiet third-floor condo.

He lived in an upscale building that was the brainchild of Tollivers Real Estate and Development. Business partners, Rossi and Levi had overseen the renovation of the sixty-five-year-old former warehouse. The six-story building featured multi-level lofts, condos, and a penthouse. Several of their family members were residents.

The cousins were often referred to as the comeback construction kids. The Tollivers had an eye to discern when to renovate or when rebuilding was the only way. They were known for transforming long-forgotten black neighborhoods into majestic masterpieces. If an area was blighted, their crew gave it a facelift. If they couldn't resuscitate a building, their demolition crew took it down.

As a teenager, Rossi, who was two years older than Levi, was the ringleader of seven cousins. As men, the bond between Rossi and Levi never waned, and their bloodline had little to do with it. When Rossi repented for his sins, he set a standard for salvation that most of the young Tolliver men followed.

Rossi and Levi were alike in many ways. They worked in the same profession. Where Rossi enjoyed buying up large tracts of land in depressed areas, Levi had the vision to develop them. Both were diehard college football fans; Rossi cheered for the Baltimore Ravens, while Levi was behind the Philadelphia Eagles all the way. The Tollivers believed in strong family ties. Levi and Rossi would take soul food over barbecue any day, and had the same taste in clothes—stylish but conservative.

Most times they shared the same taste in women—physically appealing, not necessarily outright stunning, and a healthy dose of temperance in their response to situations. They had to know how to hold it together when things didn't work in their favor. In the past, Levi and Rossi had a close enough relationship that sometimes each could guess what the other was thinking. They didn't agree on everything, and that was the source of heated debates. Still, they loved each other and had each other's backs.

Levi and Rossi Tolliver were also distinguishable. Where Levi was barely six feet, Rossi made up for it at six five. Levi wore glasses; Rossi had perfect vision. Levi was too light-skinned for Rossi's taste, considering Rossi was a degree away from being called midnight black. Levi could thank his Jewish mother for that one. Rossi appreciated his sole African heritage.

It was argued that the Tolliver clan included cousins in every state. Rossi never challenged the assertion. With a Pentecostal upbringing, the Tollivers spawned babies as if they were in a race to see what the end would be. It was the norm for their households to have five-plus children. However, Levi and Rossi's parents didn't make the cut. Levi's father, Victor, had three sons. Rossi's father, Ross, had four sons. Neither brother had daughters.

Before Diane came along, Rossi often joked, "If she has a sister, hook me up." Well, Diane did have a sister, but the woman was crazy. Jesetta wasn't a bad person or bad looking. She was a born dictator and expected everyone else to line up behind her without question. Following the death of her sister, her mood swings were almost unbearable.

Over the past four years, Rossi never left Levi's side—always a phone call away. Levi had a massive hole in his heart and life. Rossi had silently prayed for his cousin to get out of his personal purgatory where the past seemed to have a steady grip. It would never close, but the right woman, the right circumstances, and the right blessings from God could keep it from growing. Was the time now?

"Jesus, I'm not privy to what's going on in Levi's heart, but let me be a vessel for him," Rossi prayed. Shutting his eyes, Rossi rolled his neck. Most folks didn't understand the responsibilities of a youth minister and the burdens they carried, especially when some hardships were close to home. He ministered to teenagers struggling with drugs, young girls who were sexually active either by their choice or force. He had to pray for those who had given up hope and were ready to accept the consequences of suicide. God gave him a yoke for souls.

Finally, it appeared grief had to run its course, but Levi's haunting words stayed with Rossi even after four years.

At one time, in addition to Levi carrying his wallet, he carried Visine and a face towel. "Kleenex isn't sturdy enough to hold my tears," he had said.

That's when Rossi started praying like he never had before. Just because Levi finally had a new lady in his life didn't mean it was time for Rossi to stop praying.

CHAPTER 4

"Where does it say in our parole manual that ex-felons can't date?" Cynthia Williams, better known as Buttercup, asked and then twisted her lips in a challenge. She was referring to the pocket-size booklet that was designed to instill terror in parolees or probationers.

Karyn observed Buttercup. She was the only woman Karyn knew who wore two lip colors at the same time and made it work: pink on the upper lip, red on her full bottom one. When the mood hit, Buttercup experimented with bold shades of brown, orange, or purple and burgundy lipsticks. Somehow, Buttercup could pull it off among her other quirky fashion statements.

For the past twelve months, Karyn and Buttercup had shared a living space with a common area for watching TV, a bathroom, plus a kitchenette. For privacy, their suite had separate bedrooms. Buttercup had been at New Beginnings for two months when Karyn moved in. It was one of twelve women's traditional centers in the state approved by the Illinois Department of Corrections.

"Umm-hmm." Buttercup clicked off the TV and in a mocked frenzy reached for her backpack. Methodically, she began to search through its compartments.

Karyn was convinced her roommate was a self-proclaimed member of somebody's Indian tribe. Buttercup meticulously maintained her thirty-inch-plus hair weave in stringy cornrows, then crowned her forehead with wide headbands—a different color for each day of the week. Retrieving a worn pocket-size book from the jungle of her personal belongings, Buttercup used her extended nail tips, lavished with art décor, to shuffle through the Illinois re-entry booklet.

Physically, Karyn's skin tone had a butterscotch hue, where Buttercup's skin was like a rainbow. She was fair enough to turn red when she was heated, a yellow tint when she was sick, and blue from bruises when she bumped into something, which she did regularly.

"Page three," Karyn said absentmindedly to annoy her friend as payback for nagging her about the date. Karyn hadn't tried on the dress because she was too busy memorizing its every detail.

When she arrived home from work a few days earlier, Karyn had practically shredded the colored tissue paper to get to the gold-foil gift-wrapped box. Once opened, the contents were like a jack-in-the-box where the garment sprang from its confines to shout for Karyn's attention.

With gentleness, as if it were a newborn baby, Karyn had cradled the black velvet dress as she lifted it up and laid it on her pink-and-brown paisley print bedspread. She fingered the dress's accent, a white chiffon border that extended past the hem at least an inch. The sleeves were also made of chiffon—black—with black satin ribbons that tied at the wrists. Now the exquisite gift was still tempting her to "come on, try me on."

Buttercup's *tsk*ing caught Karyn's attention.

"I haven't found it, and you know I can't afford another violation." Buttercup gnawed on her lip, mumbling. "That chick who was shoplifting at the grocery store was trying to set me up. It's a good thing God had my back on that one, because if I was going back to prison, I would've insisted she be my cellmate." Snapping her fingers, Buttercup shook her head. "Wait a minute. That's the old me talking crazy, isn't it?"

Praise God the parole officer believed Buttercup was innocent of any involvement. Karyn couldn't fathom how a six feet two–inch woman with a quick temper earned such a sweet, non-intimidating nickname.

If people knew their situations, which Karyn preferred they didn't, they would pin manslaughter—involuntary—on Buttercup and forgery on her. Karyn smothered a bitter chuckle. Looks were deceiving. Who could pinpoint a sinner and a saint? Thank God for Christ being the Master Forgiver of sins.

She was twenty-two years old when she made an irreversible, life-altering mistake. When the trial was over a year later, the consequences of her actions caused her to serve four years and fifteen days in prison. She vowed never again to break any more laws. Karyn knew a vow to God couldn't be taken lightly. The Lord meant business, and so did she.

Karyn believed in the truth-setting-people-free scripture, but John 8:32 had a special clause. A person had to first discover the truth. The past was just that— the past. The blood of Jesus had washed her slate as clean as Dove soap.

Slapping the booklet closed, Buttercup squinted at Karyn. She took great pleasure in taking a deep breath before speaking in a soft tone. "Hmmm. Maybe I can't find it because . . ." She shouted, "It's not in there!"

"Isn't it?" Karyn shrugged, not one bit repentant that she had put her friend through the needless search.

Buttercup huffed. "Game over. We have enough rules to follow. Why would you want to put another yoke around our necks when it comes to going out?"

"I feel like we're operating on the Don't Ask, Don't Tell policy. It was hard enough to find a job. If it wasn't for the government's Work Opportunity tax credit or WOTC, I don't know if employers would be willing to hire us ex-offenders, and we wouldn't have a chance. I won't mention housing discrimination, and then add dating to the mix. I don't want a man who feels he has to watch his back, his wallet, and his woman. What was I thinking? It's too soon for me." Karyn couldn't keep the dejected mood from descending on her.

"Wrong. Jesus is the one who gave us second chances. You better remember that, because no one else will." Buttercup's game face meant she had no patience for an argument.

She and Karyn were protégées of the Crowns for Christ Church prison ministry. Without the church's mission, neither woman might ever have turned to Christ.

It was during a prison visit that an evangelist prophesized the Lord was calling five women to redemption. Karyn, Buttercup, and three others who believed the message, had come forward with repentance in their hearts, not only seeking God's forgiveness, but receiving something so powerful it gave them hope behind bars. Not long after Karyn and Buttercup's conversions, the Crowns for Christ Church family adopted them. They became the beneficiaries of monthly donations of inspirational books, plus prison necessity items of undergarments, toiletries, and money orders for other incidentals.

Karyn gnawed on her lips. She had too much on her plate without worrying about a romantic entanglement. "I'm not going," she decided.

"Oh yes, you are." Buttercup squinted.

"No, I'm not. I should've never encouraged him by accepting his gift. He said if I tried it on, it was a yes. Since the tag is still on it, I'm giving it back."

"Well, I guess it's settled."

Something wasn't right. Buttercup never backed down and rarely agreed with her. Karyn became suspicious as Buttercup towered over her. She walked out of Karyn's bedroom, through their shared sitting area to her bedroom, and then returned.

Karyn recognized her roommate's on-a-mission expression. Karyn swiped the garment off the bed. "What do you think you're doing?"

In a swifter action, Buttercup snatched it out of Karyn's arms. With one yank, Buttercup tugged on the tag until it came off. "Oops. Sorry, but scissors are prohibited. Hope I didn't rip a seam." She grinned.

"Give that back!" Karyn frowned at her vain attempt to wrestle the dress from Buttercup. Karyn was hot with disbelief.

"Sure." Unzipping the dress, Buttercup produced a marker and scribbled something on the inside before tossing it back on the bed.

"Are you crazy? What did you do that for?" Karyn raced to her bathroom. "You're nuts," she yelled over her shoulder. She came back with a wet hand towel. "I hope I can wipe off those marks, or you better keep one eye open while you sleep, crazy."

As long as Karyn had known her suitemate, Buttercup had never done anything without thinking it through since her release. Clearly, Buttercup's blood sugar was low or something.

"I doubt it will come out. Permanent usually means permanent," she said smugly. "And hey, I'm a jailbird. You know I know how to sleep with one eye cracked." Folding her arms, Buttercup struck a pose that reminded her of the stereotypical Indian stance.

Rolling her eyes, Karyn deciphered the messy inscription: *Gift from God.* "What is wrong with you? Now I can't return it. I don't even know if it's my size."

"You better believe it's your size. If not, you're missing dinner tonight and breakfast tomorrow. Don't make me withhold water to squeeze you into that beauty."

Tears of frustration temporarily blinded Karyn as she flopped on the bed. "This won't work." She covered her face with her small hands.

"Listen, Wallace, you're a new creature. Jesus died on the cross to redeem us." Buttercup pointed. "Old things are passed away. All things are new. Can't nobody pin anything on us." She thumped her chest then joined her friend on the bed. "This Levi guy sees something in you God has shown him . . ."

Karyn temporarily zoned out. Hadn't Levi said something similar? Buttercup's raving snapped her out of it.

"People go on dates all the time—except for me, of course. Halo and I are just biding our time. Once we complete our parole, look out. But for you, a date could mean dinner, dancing, or a movie, not a marriage proposal or a contract to bear his children."

Karyn gave her a murderous glance, then replayed 2 Corinthians 5:17, which Buttercup had quoted from: *Therefore if any man be in Christ, he is a new creature. Old things are passed away; behold, all things are become new.*

"It's just one dinner that came with a dress. It's no different than a prize that comes in a cereal box." She frowned. "You still can get prizes in a cereal box, right? Anyway, you get the point. I love God." She sighed with a worshipping expression as she clasped her hands. "He doesn't withhold blessings."

"That's just it, Butter. I don't know if Levi or a free dinner is my blessing."

"Think of it this way: If he keeps inviting you out and you keep accepting, you'll have a complete wardrobe before you know it. Just think of Michael Jackson's 'Bad' hit—you know, the black leather jacket, the tough look, and the strut. You're bad, you know it." Buttercup sang it note for note. In contrast, Buttercup's dance steps were off beat.

Leaving her bedroom, Karyn paced their common room. "There are several problems." Karyn started counting off her fingers. "I'm on parole. I have a curfew. My job barely pays more than minimum wage. I don't have a stash of clothes. I'm paying for my class—"

"Karyn! We are not the victims here, remember?" Buttercup followed. "But you're starting to sound like one. Unless you want my size eighteen-and-a-half to snuggle up inside that dress—and I will break some seams—then I suggest you check your doubt at the back door and welcome faith in at the front, and I don't mean Faith Hill either.

"Now I'm hungry. Spaghetti at dinner is never filling. All this brainstorming worked up my appetite." Buttercup dragged her feet into their kitchenette. She began slamming cabinet doors. Karyn knew she was in search of peanut butter, honey, and bread. Once the stash was found, Buttercup grinned over her shoulder. "Of course, you don't have to worry about your hair or nails. I'll do those for you for free."

Karyn groaned. This was becoming a big to-do about nothing. "Of course," Karyn mumbled to the experimental beauty queen.

Buttercup was known for mixing concoctions with plant extracts and basic food staples to make enriching hair and skin conditioners. Buttercup had earned the respect of many of the residents and a few staffers as an eccentric fashion consultant, since she graduated from cosmetology school while serving time in prison.

Picking up the dress, Karyn walked back into her bedroom and grabbed a hanger from her closet. After slipping it inside the delicate sleeves, Karyn hung it up. When she returned to the common room, Buttercup was relaxing with a sandwich in one hand and the TV remote in the other.

Karyn leaned against the door frame and folded her arms. "Do you think it's a coincidence that he gave me a present that was too early for Christmas, too late for my birthday, but right on the one-year anniversary of my release?"

"John 8:36 is my last word on the matter until the next time: *If the Son therefore shall make you free, ye shall be free indeed.*"

CHAPTER 5

Karyn marveled at Levi's ability to guess her size, plus give her some breathing room to enjoy dinner. Once Karyn had stepped into the dress, it was as if an imaginary wand circled her from the bottom of her feet to the crown of her head, transforming her into a princess, as if she were the main character in a Disney movie. Buttercup *ooh*ed and *ahh*ed as Karyn strutted across the room's impromptu runway.

Somehow, Levi must have known she would confirm the date. Karyn had to admit she was curious about their magnetism. Buttercup threatened to put her in a choke hold if she didn't admit she was willing to at least dispel or confirm an attraction.

Buttercup sniffed and toyed with her headband. She dabbed her eyes before accidentally popping her forehead with the headband. "Ouch." She rubbed her forehead. "You remind me of the night of my prom. Can you believe the cutest guy in my senior class asked me out? Percy Atkinson was fine—short, but fine. I'll never forget that night."

Clearing her throat, Karyn tapped her foot. "Is this about you or me?" she teased.

"You're right. Sorry."

They ended the night praying for their new beginnings. Karyn reflected on the message of Lamentations 3:22–23: God's compassions are new every morning. Waving good night, they retreated to their bedrooms.

Friday morning at work, Karyn began counting down the hours before she saw Levi. She was as excited as a school girl after learning that the cutest boy in her class had a crush on her. Karen knew she didn't deserve a fairy tale moment, but she was thankful God was merciful to allow her to experience one.

In the six months since Karyn had worked at Bookshelves Unlimited, she prided herself on never missing work, calling in sick, and thanks to an on-time bus schedule, she had never been late.

It was bad timing that her first date happened to fall on a busy day for the bookstore. Karyn was nervous about asking to get off early. Although her case manager had approved her request to go out on a date—forgoing the required one week advance notice—that didn't mean she wouldn't have to explain why her paycheck was short. One of New Beginnings Center's rules was that a counselor had to verify residents' pay stubs in order to withhold thirty percent to establish and build a savings account for each woman. How the mighty fall. Coming from an influential political family, she never wanted for anything. That was before she broke the law.

Is this worth it? she asked herself more than once that day. Karyn didn't have the same liberties as other ladies who would say yes to an evening out. She didn't have a disposable income to lavish on outfits, or a carefree lifestyle to enjoy the company of a good-looking man until after the clock struck midnight.

Karyn's musings were interrupted when one of her many favorite customers labored to clear the bookstore entrance. Karyn hurried to assist. "Good morning, Mrs. Harris. How are you today?"

The woman's elongated huffing was Karyn's answer. "Considering I woke up this morning," Mrs. Harris said then paused, gathering a deep breath before she continued, "I'd say I'm off to a good start. Don't you think, baby?"

On the first Friday of every month, they exchanged a carbon copy of the previous month's conversation. It appeared Mrs. Harris was as tall—maybe five feet five—as she was wide. She was a butterball without the distinguishable bust, waist, and hips.

Mrs. Harris's clothes were a uniform of dull colors, but rain or shine, heat or snow, she always topped off her look with a hat bearing fruits, flowers, feathers, or something odd that defied people not to take a second look.

While shopping at Bookshelves Unlimited, the woman never strayed from her usual purchase: one magazine of crossword puzzles for her and two books for her grandson, Sonny. Karyn looped her arm through Mrs. Harris's to guide her to the customer service counter, but the old woman waved her off.

"I didn't bring my walking cane along because I doubled up on my vitamin B tablets today. I've got plenty of energy. Just give me a few seconds for my blood sugar to catch up."

Her few seconds actually turned into lengthy minutes. In the interim, a young boy approached the desk needing help, so Karyn tapped on the store's computer keyboard to search for a book for him. Mrs. Harris inched closer. Karyn squinted, wondering if she should offer Mrs. Harris help again, but three ladies intercepted, wanting a recommendation for their book club.

Finally, Mrs. Harris dragged her body to the customer service desk and practically collapsed against the counter for support. "Whew." She beamed. "I feel those vitamins working. Now, Sonny wrote me and is asking for the book *The Hood Game Plan*."

The boy to whom she referred was thirty-five years old and serving twenty years for charges stacked against him, including probation violation and carrying a firearm.

"Mrs. Harris, you know we can't ship any books to your grandson that depict or glorify violence or abuse toward women."

"Humph. I don't care what he's reading as long as he's reading. Sonny can't do nothing locked up anyway. If that's what he likes, I say let him have his enjoyment."

Karyn never budged, and the elderly woman always relented. The following month, they were back to square one, arguing over another inappropriate book not approved by the prison system. The biggest blessing for Sonny was that he had someone on the outside who loved him.

"Sure you don't want to try some Christian fiction thrillers? And we have them in paperback. They'll scare the devil out of anybody and make them beg the Holy Ghost to come in," Karyn offered, believing that one month Mrs. Harris would take her suggestion and start a Christian revolution in Sonny's life.

"Nah. Jesus can't get him out of prison, so he won't want that stuff."

For the next ten minutes, Karyn suggested other choices. Surprisingly, the elderly patron splurged on three Manga comic books in addition to her regular purchase.

As Mrs. Harris headed for the register, Karyn turned around and jumped. She patted her chest to slow down her erratic breathing. "You scared me."

"Sorry," Levi said, but he didn't look convincing. "My intention was to take you to lunch."

"Don't we have a dinner date?" Karyn frowned. She could smell his cologne. She tried not to blink as she dared to inhale. Although Karyn hadn't taken the time to appreciate the male population, she doubted another man would be as handsome as Levi in a black leather cap with a black jacket. His tie was a Crayola print against a black background. Karyn lifted a brow, questioning his fashion statement, although she guessed Dori had something to do with it.

Levi twisted his mouth in amusement. "I'm glad you remembered and accepted." He paused, making Karyn impatient. "Why wait for dinner when we could share a pre-dinner snack together?"

She folded her arms. "Really? I agreed to dinner, not breakfast, lunch, and dinner."

"I could've brought you breakfast," he said with an arrogant shrug.

Karyn was beginning to second-guess her decision to finagle her way to leave early to get ready for her date with Levi. She prayed their personalities didn't clash.

It was undeniable that Levi Tolliver was a gentleman, but he also seemed overly confident. Tonight she would watch for any telltale signs of him being controlling or possessing unchristian-like characteristics. If so, the night would end with "Thanks for dinner. I'll see you at the bookstore."

Karyn snapped out of a game plan she was formulating before their possible relationship's first pitch, coin toss, or the drop of the punt to start. "Today will be extremely busy. If I take a break, I may not get off on time, which means we may need to reschedule—"

"That's not going to happen, since it took a year for you to agree to go out with me." The teasing dimmed in Levi's eyes. He frowned in displeasure. "We're not rescheduling, Karyn. Not now. Some blessings only happen once—twice if God speaks it."

His words were eloquently spoken, and they had the desired effect, because Karyn's heart muscles danced. Karyn smiled and he matched hers. She liked hearing him put God in control of things, because at times, she struggled with that.

"It did not. I've only been out—I've only worked here six months."

Whew. Karyn barely recovered. Just that quick, the devil had arrived, acting as the middleman between them. He almost had her ready to spill the beans. Satan's mission was to keep adding interest to a debt already paid. Her past was hers—and private.

Levi wasn't aware of her internal battle, but Karyn rebuked the devil. *He who the Son has set free is free indeed.*

Mrs. Harris returned, rescuing her by clearing her throat. "Karyn, you're getting to me. Throw in one of them religious books you were talking about. Maybe it will scare some of the devils out of that place."

"I've got to go," Karyn whispered to Levi, dismissing him as her heart leaped with excitement that Mrs. Harris had caved in for once, not realizing she was planting a tiny seed in Sonny's life. "I'll see you later."

He didn't move.

"Promise," she hissed, frowning.

His dimples stood at attention. Levi nodded and began his swagger out of the store.

Karyn exhaled as she watched his gait. She swallowed. His confidence scared her and excited her. She had to get off early. She needed more time preparing her heart than getting dressed.

Returning to Mrs. Harris, Karyn addressed the paperback books—since hardcovers were not allowed—to the correctional center in Centralia, Illinois, writing Sonny's full legal name and identification number on the label. Hours later, as expected, the first day of the month brought in a steady line of mothers, wives, and girlfriends ordering care packages of books for their loved ones behind bars.

It was a bittersweet service. Although Karyn didn't know the inmates, she now worked in the community where a high number of offenders once lived. She didn't need to read the newspaper or watch the news to know what areas had unsuccessfully tried to nurture law-abiding citizens. The book orders shipped to prisons said it all. It was a bustling middle-class neighborhood with sturdy homes, good schools, and thriving businesses. So, what happened? The devil tricked them.

Her shift ended an hour early at three when two employees showed up for work at the same time because there was a mix-up in schedules. The boss gave Karyn the option to leave, and she jumped on it. Her bus was pulling up seconds after she got to the stop. Karyn experienced a fleeting moment of nervousness. Was God orchestrating the day's events so she would be ready for her date?

Okay, Lord, what are you trying to tell me?

CHAPTER 6

Six-forty. Levi tapped his finger on his watch and exhaled. He was parked in front of Karyn's apartment building, debating. Twenty minutes early was a first for him. When he and Diane dated, Levi's reputation was, at a minimum, five minutes late. Diane, who possessed an easygoing nature, charged his offenses to the male species.

Another first, let Rossi tell it, Levi had broken dating protocol with his unrelenting pursuit of Karyn. Levi smirked. He was actually proud of himself. God had given him a new focus.

While Levi was deciding if he should get out and knock on the door, God whispered into his ear to look, listen, and learn. Karyn was a soft-spoken woman with a spirit that seemed to mirror Christ's requirements. What Levi really wanted to know was why her and why now? God never answered.

Levi's spiritual life had been a journey where the valleys shifted like quicksand and any attempts to scale the mountains had too many booby traps. When Diane was alive, he was a practicing Christian. After her death, he stewed in rebellion against what he perceived as Christ's injustice. Now, fast forward four years and a day, and Levi's self-description would be the reconstruction of a Christian.

"Seven minutes." He continued his countdown. Enough stalling. If there was a test for impatience, Levi would top the charts. "Early is better than late, right?" he convinced himself.

Getting out of his car and slipping on his cashmere coat, he armed his car alarm. Levi didn't have the patience to walk to meet his date. As he jogged up the stairs, he took in his surroundings. Surprisingly, the block was quiet, somehow escaping the horns from Route 159, a busy thoroughfare blocks away. He hadn't noticed any of that the night he followed Karyn's bus. His sole purpose had been to make sure she was safely behind closed doors.

Actually, he wasn't familiar with this side of town. It appeared safe, but looks could be deceiving. The apartment building was free of excessive shrubbery. It had just enough landscaping to show visitors that even renters knew how to pamper it as if they were homeowners. Before he could knock, the door swung open, and Karyn appeared.

"You're early," she accused. "Good thing I was ready."

Her smile was his incentive to release his greeting. "I couldn't wait," Levi whispered.

The daintiness of her beauty was so overpowering that he fought not to collapse. If he thought Karyn was pretty in her unappealing bookstore uniform, then he wasn't prepared for the vision before him now. Her eyes sparkled, her lashes seemed to have grown, and her curls . . . Where did she get all that hair? The little black dress added to her allure. This was definitely not the vision he imagined when he saw the dress on the hanger.

Levi stuttered as his lips tried to get in sync with his heart. "Karyn," he said in awe.

She shivered. The black sweater draped over her shoulders was no match for the chill. "Here." Levi shook off his coat and whipped it around her like a magician's cape.

Closing the door, she stepped out on the landing and welcomed his gesture. "Thank you," she said, barely audibly.

"You look absolutely beautiful," he complimented and then ushered her to the car.

Tonight she smelled like flowers, a contrast from her usual Zest soap scent. "I guess we should've expected the falling temperatures instead of being fooled by today's warm weather, since it's the first week in November."

She nodded as he disarmed his alarm and opened her passenger door. As she slid into the seat of his sedan, he gawked at her molded legs supported by high-heeled sandals—a little exposed for the night air, but nice—and healthy calves. He exhaled, fingering the ridge of his nose to push back his glasses, only to remember his vision was intensified by his contacts.

Levi closed her door and hurried to his side, not motivated by the chill, but the yearning for her company. He felt like beating his chest like King Kong. Levi was a thirty-one-year-old father and widower, not a teenager new on the dating scene. He chided himself as he masked his jubilation with an in-control, nonchalant shrug and climbed inside.

Turning the key, Levi blasted the heat for her comfort and quietly assessed her. Karyn's after-work transformation was mesmerizing.

"I realize now that I made a mistake when I chose that dress."

Facing him, Karyn sucked in her breath. Her expression appeared guarded as she waited for him to explain.

"You are the most gorgeous creature God has ever made. Karyn, to be honest, you're twisting my self-control in that dress, and that's saying a lot. Only a body cast will keep my eyes off you tonight," he mumbled.

Lashes—whether hers or borrowed—lowered. Blushing, she teased, "Levi Tolliver, the clock is ticking on our date."

"Say no more, Miss Wallace. Buckle up. Reservations await us at Andria's Restaurant."

The drive to O'Fallon, Illinois, was surreal. Levi felt as if his unsettled spirit had discovered a parking spot. While en route to dinner, contemporary gospel floated between them, overriding their silence. One thing was for certain. He would not rush the night with Karyn. He planned to take his time and get to know her.

Less than thirty minutes later, Levi almost passed by the restaurant with a black-and-white-striped awning that was nestled between two striking evergreen trees. He hadn't a hint that beyond the door awaited a degree of charm to romance its patrons. The recommendation came from a friend.

A woman greeted them as if she were the lady of the house. After Levi removed the coat that he had placed around Karyn's petite stature again when he helped her out of the car, they followed the hostess.

They were seated at a table for two draped in white linen with burgundy cloth napkins folded in teepees. The tables were lined up against a soft beige wall. Dainty sconces shed a faint light on the patrons, giving Karyn a subtle spotlight. He half listened as the woman recited the night's specials, placed menus on their plates, and waited dutifully for their drink selections.

With ice water already at their place settings, Karyn ordered a glass of Sprite. Levi dittoed.

"I thought she would never leave," Levi teased, winking. He gave Karyn his full appraisal, ignoring the menus. He stared unflinchingly and appreciatively.

As if the quaint table weren't intimate enough, he slowly inched his face closer, coaxing her to meet him halfway. At first, she hesitated, but then took a chance. Levi withheld his sigh of contentment. He missed the building of intimacy in a new relationship. He enjoyed watching her. The cozy ambiance created the enchanting night he had envisioned.

Karyn's skin glowed, reminding him of a cup of coffee with a generous drowning of cream. She had blemish-free skin—no beauty moles or dimples. Her teeth were a few shades away from ultra white, and when she smiled, the sincerity reached her eyes. A mass of weak curls with a dusting of shimmer replaced her girlish braid. He counted a few wild strands of premature gray, but it didn't distract from her beauty.

As he lingered inches from her face, Levi broke the trance. He mouthed, "Thank you for spending your Friday evening with me." Levi was in no rush tonight. He didn't work on Saturdays, Dori was sleeping over at her aunt Jet's house, and Karyn had mentioned she only worked two Saturdays out of the month because she had a class and need to study. They had plenty of time to get to know each other.

"Levi, you didn't have to bribe me with a dress to go out with you." She pinched the tablecloth as if she had told a lie. No movement went unnoticed by him. Plus, she didn't sound believable, but the clarity in her eyes revealed she was telling the truth.

Still, Levi wasn't buying it. "Oh, so you would've gone out with me, huh?"

"Eventually," Karyn said, tilting her head and appearing to give it some thought. "Okay, maybe." Unfortunately, that answer didn't sound convincing as she anchored her elbows on the table. She smugly rested her chin on top of her linked hands.

His nostrils flared as if he smelled a challenge. "Hmmm. And it's that percentage of doubt that I had to eliminate." He blinked first. "So, tell me about Karyn Wallace. Who is she? What does she like? What church does she attend? Tell me all the preliminary stuff that I'll file away as a keepsake." His renewed confidence made him proud. Levi Thomas Tolliver was swimming back to shore.

"Here are your drinks," their hostess said, returning. "Are you ready to place your orders?"

Karyn looked guiltily. Levi shrugged. When Karyn suggested he order for them, he nodded and opted for the easy way out. "Okay, the special sounds good, but with Caesar salads. Oh, just in case we become distracted, we'll share a slice of cheesecake for dessert."

The hostess smiled at his choices and left to do his bidding. Levi returned his focus to Karyn. "As you were about to say, Miss Wallace?"

Karyn took a deep breath and relaxed. "I just turned twenty-seven, so I guess you can say I'm wearing my late birthday gift."

Levi liked the sound of that, but didn't interrupt.

"I'm taking one business class at Southwestern Illinois College in Belleville, I work at Bookshelves Unlimited, and I'm an active member of Crowns for Christ Church." She tapped her finger on the tablecloth as if she had just typed a period at the end of a story. Her hands looked soft, but her misshaped nails hinted at a self-manicure. Either way, the polish was evenly brushed on each finger.

Levi read between paragraphs of what she wasn't saying. Karyn Wallace was humble, ambitious because she was advancing her education, and concerned about her salvation.

"I'd rather talk about that adorable little girl of yours," Karyn said, turning the subject matter away from herself.

It didn't take much coaxing for Levi to sing the praises of his daughter. Before Levi knew it, the aromas of their meals ceased their budding conversation. Their steaks arrived bathed in the legendary Andria's Steak Sauce. Karyn closed her eyes and stole a generous whiff. Levi stretched out his hands, waiting for hers. He squeezed her fingers a couple of times, verifying his earlier assumption that her hands were soft, but not as moist as his late wife's, his mother's, or other women he had known.

He dropped his head and refocused to concentrate on his prayer. Normally, he allowed Dori to bless their food.

"Lord Jesus, thank you for bringing me joy in the morning," he began, referencing Psalm 30:5. He silently praised God that his drought and anger were gone. Joy had seemed to elude him for so long.

Rubbing Karyn's fingers, Levi continued the prayer, "Please, bless and sanctify our meal and the hands that prepared it." He was about to close with "Amen" when, thinking about the popular reference to the fifth chapter of Daniel, he added, "Lord, I need a handwriting on the wall." He needed a clear message on how to proceed with Karyn.

Ending the prayer, Levi indulged in one delicious bite after another of his sirloin strip steak. He only took his eyes off Karyn when he was forced to cut a piece. What was going through Karyn's mind?

Karyn surprised him when she cracked their silence and asked about Dori again. She didn't seem to have the same inquisitiveness as the handful of other women about the circumstances surrounding his late wife's death, and how they were qualified to fill his loneliness.

"Aren't you curious about her mother?" He lifted his glass and took a sip.

"I already know Dori's mother was a blessed woman. Besides, curiosity not only killed the cat, it sometimes can kill dreams. I believe that everybody has the right to keep their thoughts private about unhappy moments and mistakes from the past."

Did that mean she didn't want to pry, or that she was uninterested? When had he become so analytical? *"Enjoy yourself, nut,"* he could hear Rossi say. He finally decided she probably already knew about the story and didn't want to the spoil the night with him reliving the memories.

Shaking his head, Levi chuckled. "My little pride and joy is doing extremely well. She's spending the night with my sister-in-law. As a matter of fact, my daughter gave me instructions before I picked you up. She told me to be on my best behavior, eat all my vegetables, and not to talk with food in my mouth."

Karyn's engaging laugh pulled Levi into the amusement. For the next few minutes, Karyn shared nothing but accolades about Dori's politeness and intelligence. She even complimented his parenting skills.

"I have a lot of needed and uninvited help in that area. That's what happens when someone is suddenly thrust into widowhood."

Levi paused and gave Karyn space to quench any curiosity she had about his status with questions, but she didn't bite as they finished dinner. He wanted her to have a glimpse of his open wound.

While waiting for dessert, Levi gathered Karyn's hands again. "Thank you for sharing this evening with me."

"You made it hard for me to say no . . . again." She grinned sheepishly.

"Mr.Tolliver, is that you?"

Levi dragged his focus from Karyn. Ready to release his displeasure for the interruption, Levi peered at the stranger. Initially, the man with the long, unkempt blond hair and beard strained Levi's memory. Finally, recognition flashed. The intruder was the son of a woman killed in the same store robbery as Diane.

Jonathan Gleason hadn't been a teenager then, maybe ten or eleven, but it appeared youth had skipped over him, forcing him into adulthood. He seemed mentally lost, a contrast to the snapshot of a happy family the media posted during its extensive coverage of the victim left behind.

Standing, Levi hugged him. "Jonathan," he whispered then pulled away. "What are you doing here?" He momentarily forgot about Karyn. "How have you been?"

He shrugged. "The owners were friends of my mother. Sometimes when I'm hungry or need a place to stay, one of them will come and get me."

Whirling around, Levi remembered his date. "Oh, Karyn, I'm sorry. I didn't mean to be rude. This is Jonathan Gleason. His mother and my wife were—"

"Murdered," Jonathan mumbled as he turned and stalked out of the dining room.

Levi wanted to go after him and ask what was going on with him, but it wasn't the time or place. He couldn't keep chasing the past. Every victim of crime had a season. Jonathan was in the middle of a storm, while spring was about to bloom in Levi's life.

Clearing his throat, Levi decided to add the teen-ager to his prayer list as he retook his seat. Sighing, he gathered his thoughts and met Karyn's eyes. In order to explain Jonathan's odd behavior, Levi first had to disclose his hurt.

Karyn frowned. "Is he all right?"

Levi shook his head. "I don't think so, and it's been four years. . . ." Shoving his plate aside, he no longer had an appetite. "Karyn, I'm ready for a new beginning, and I don't want to wait until New Year's to begin that quest." He took a deep breath. "You can't imagine how many people have waited for me to say that. I don't even know how long I've wanted to say that. " Glanc-ing over his shoulder, Levi randomly squinted at other patrons until their faces seemed to fade. He looked at Karyn again. "I've been torn the last four years between scared to move on without the mother of my child and afraid to stay in limbo. It appears Jonathan's still in limbo, and he's so young."

Karyn's gorgeous, sparkling eyes softened. Her ex-pression gave nothing away—no green light to go or blaring red to stop. Not even a yield. It was as if she were holding her breath, waiting for him to explain.

Reaching across the table again, Levi opened his hands. When Karyn placed her hands in his, Levi trapped them.

"I don't know when I planned to share this with you, but it definitely wasn't tonight." Levi swallowed. He looked away and inhaled, breathing in the subtle scent of a sweet perfume. "I've lived through the saying that the day isn't promised to us. Almost four years ago,

Diane walked out our front door. It was a quick trip around the corner for a few things. How would I know she would never return?

"Less than an hour later, she was killed in a botched robbery at a grocery store in North St. Louis." He bit his bottom lip. "A gunman killed Diane. I should've gone to the store, but she insisted she needed to get out for a few minutes. For a long time, I had a case of the what-if-I-had-done-this or what-if-I-had-done-that-differently guilt. I second-guessed those last minutes of her life."

The hostess appeared, and Levi nodded for her to remove their plates. She left and returned minutes later with a doggie bag and a chunk of cheesecake. Clearly the news was making Karyn uncomfortable as she squirmed in her seat.

"I woke up one morning a happily married man. That night, I closed my eyes but couldn't sleep, digesting the fact that I had become a widower with an infant. I knew little about parenthood and practically nothing about widowhood.

"Next thing I knew, everybody wanted to chart out my life, giving me advice when I didn't ask for it. My sister-in-law fussed when Dori's hair wasn't combed to her liking. I finally told Jesetta if I wanted and needed help, I would call my momma, which I never did."

For four years, he had managed without any complaints from Dori about her hair, until she admired Karyn's intricate braid and wanted one just like it. He held in a snicker. That was a pleasant moment he would savor later.

"It didn't take long for the subject of Diane Tolliver to become taboo. On good days, I want to ramble on about Diane—how we met, etc. On bad days, I would snap if her name was mentioned. I know it sounds like I had lost my mind, but for a long time, I had. I stayed angry, sad, lost. Sometimes, I retreated into my private shrine of her."

"Levi, I don't have the right words to say to make you feel better." Tears filled Karyn's eyes.

"You." He pointed. "Your presence is like a balm to my soul. No other woman has done that. I've attracted more women than I could've exchanged the attraction. The constant phone calls and the visits were beginning to suffocate me. It was as if the world was keeping track of my days of mourning, and when a particular number was called—bingo. My grief was supposed to disappear, and I should carry on as if nothing happened.

"That's when I took the first step. I gathered my belongings and the best gift Diane left me, Dori. I sold the house I was renovating and moved across the river into St. Clair County. I've been in Illinois ever since. To remain in the neighborhood seemed to be an active crime scene, even though the Thomas Foods chain eventually went out of business."

"Sometimes starting over means everything is new," Levi heard her say in the distance.

"Those demon-possessed criminals lined up seven people and shot them execution style. Those who did survive played dead to describe the ghastly scene. One person escaped to the rooftop and flagged down the police."

Karyn gasped and her brown eyes watered.

"Yep. Three teenagers disguised themselves as part of the cleaning crew. It was in all of the papers. I'm sure you've read or heard about it." He frowned. "When the whole world knows your pain, where is your hiding place?"

She shook her head.

"It doesn't change anything that two of them were caught, prosecuted, and sentenced to so many years that they better not get out. They destroyed seven lives and their families. What does matter is that one who got away." Levi's nostrils flared. "I live to see that lone animal caught. I breathe to watch him or her die by lethal injection. Crime does pay. A life for a life. I don't feel sorry for anyone behind bars."

The venom in Levi's voice made Karyn stare as if she were a deer caught in headlights.

CHAPTER 7

Did I kiss Levi good night or thank him for a lovely evening? Karyn couldn't remember. *What did I order? What was Levi wearing? What day is it?* For the first time since her release, Karyn was thankful she had a curfew.

Whew! Karyn shook her head. Levi had dropped an atom bomb. His loss tugged at her conflicting emotions after witnessing the ever-present pain crime victims sometimes hide from view. There was no standing on the outside with her taking a peep. Karyn was inside, staring face to face at Levi's pain caused by a thoughtless act.

"God bless you, Levi," Karyn whispered as she dragged herself up two flights of stairs in heels she had purchased for five bucks at the church's thrift store. Buttercup talked her into them, stating four-inch heels were a piece of cake

You aren't good enough for him, the devil taunted. Funny, Karyn had just thought the same thing, but it made her mad that the devil said it.

The entire scenario had to be a joke. Levi was attracted to her? What kind of trick was Satan trying to play with both of them? Now, any future relationship was more doubtful. It would only serve to remind her of a crime she had committed. *What fellowship can light have with darkness?* That scripture was making a strong case against her. She tensed.

Karyn doubted she exhaled until she turned the key to her living quarters.

She entered her apartment and found it quiet and dark. Karyn relaxed. With any luck, Buttercup was already asleep. She didn't feel like talking.

"How was dinner?" Buttercup perked up from her makeshift napping area on the couch and turned on a lamp.

Startled, Karyn almost leaped in the air. When her heart beat stabilized, Karyn closed the door and squinted at her friend.

On the hardwood floor lay a messy stack of hair and beauty magazines. Buttercup was neat, as required by the housing staff, so the haphazard pile could only mean she was anxiously awaiting details about Karyn's date.

"Depressing," Karyn mumbled as she headed for her bedroom.

"Hold it. That's the wrong answer for someone who gave up an hour of sleep for you, which means I lost valuable time for producing new skin cells. . . ." She ranted about the latest health and beauty tips as she waved her hand. "Never mind. Anyway, you've got a hunk, a free dinner, and a new dress. If you brought a doggie bag, then I would say the date was a success."

Karyn stopped and faced Buttercup with tears swimming in her eyes. Her voice shook as she struggled to form a sentence. "I can't do this. He hates criminals."

Twisting her lips, Buttercup sighed as she adjusted her baby blue knit headband that matched her pajamas. "No surprise there. The only people who have arms wide open when we're released are family members—well, some of them—and of course, God. Hmmm, so was this before or after you told him about your time served?"

Buttercup stood and steered Karyn away from escaping into her bedroom. She guided her to sit on the worn but clean plaid sofa. Karyn toyed with her poorly shaped fingertips, unconsciously scraping off the thin layer of polish as Buttercup knelt in front of her.

"Stop that!" She swatted at Karyn's hand. "That was the best manicure I've done yet."

"Right. You said that last week after Terri's manicure when you left a trail of pink polish to her knuckles."

"I turned that into the latest fashion statement. Besides, how was I to know that it was a cheap brand? It's supposed to bond to the nail, not drip all over the place."

"The biggest hint was it was five bottles for a dollar." Karyn rolled her eyes before dropping her head into her hands. Who cared about dead skin cells or cheap fingernail polish when she was having a crisis?

Maybe she didn't think this dating thing through. Maybe she was beguiled by Levi's fascination with her. Maybe she was having a nightmare. Maybe she was going to drive herself crazy. Karyn groaned. Maybe she already was.

Buttercup struggled to get up from her squatting position, tugging at Karyn's hands in the process. Karyn looked away, her eyes bouncing from one object in the room to another: the lone picture, coffee table, and two recliners. "Scoot over so I can give you a hug. Now, tell your sanctified fairy godmother all about it."

"There's no room for your plus-size hips," Karyn said, upset she was falling apart. "My past is off limits, right? I paid for my offenses, right? Christ paid for my sins, end of story, right? What's the creed we recite at church? Behold all things are new. I'm not obligated to tell anybody anything. I'm obligated not to lie, but that's the extent."

"Karyn!"

"What?" She gave her roommate an annoyed frown. She massaged her scalp; her fingers tangling in the mass of curls piled high.

"Having dinner with a man couldn't be freaking you out like this. What really happened?" Buttercup's voice was soothing and encouraging.

"Levi's wife was murdered along with six others, execution style."

Karyn could tell Buttercup was struggling to substitute her previous choice curse words for more Christian-correct phrases as she attacked her bottom lip with her teeth. When she quieted, they stared blankly at the TV as if they were watching a reality show instead of a black screen.

"Not all of us behind bars are violent offenders. Some shouldn't be there because they aren't guilty, and some of us make bad choices—stupid mistakes. People need to stop lumping us together."

Of course, Buttercup was right, but Levi's raw emotions made Karyn shiver as if she had pulled the trigger on the gun that killed his wife. The scenario frightened her. She hurt for him. "I couldn't keep myself from feeling so guilty. I might as well have been one of the killers. I paid for my poor judgment, and I don't want to take on another man's sin."

Buttercup folded her hands. "Can you imagine that's what Jesus did? He took on every one of our sins, from lying to killing to stealing to the most unthinkable, and nailed them to the cross with him. Girl, we've been redeemed. We knew the devil was going to try to burden us with our past sins, but by Galatians 5, I refuse to let him."

"What about 2 Corinthians 6:14? *What fellowship can light have with darkness?*"

Rolling her eyes, Buttercup smacked her lips. "Girl, the devil must have your mind twisted, because he's known for quoting partial scriptures. Verse fourteen says, *Be ye not unequally yoked together with unbelievers: for what fellowship hath righteousness with unrighteousness? And what communion hath light with darkness?* You are not an unbeliever. Is he?"

Karyn shook her head.

Buttercup stood, rolled her neck, and jabbed her side with her fist as she searched for a resting place on her hip. "Karyn, you know the devil is the master of half-truths. That snake," she hissed. "Pastor Scaife says when the devil talks, instead of listening, argue back with fast balls, like a baseball pitcher, of scriptures. What you should've done when the devil called you unworthy was quote Acts 11:8–9. What God has cleaned, don't call it unclean. Take that, Satan," Buttercup said, stomping her heel into the floor.

With Buttercup around, Karyn always got a dose of preaching, teaching, and testimony—when Buttercup wasn't complaining and arguing. And Buttercup made it plain. Karyn did feel better. She knew she was cleansed, but Levi may not see it that way. What Levi needed was prayer and healing—and he would get it from her, but Karyn planned to do it from afar.

CHAPTER 8

It was early Saturday morning. Levi should have been at home, enjoying the extra hours of sleep in Dori's absence and dreaming about Karyn. Instead, he stood outside someone's front door, knocking. Since Rossi was less than fifteen minutes from Levi's Metro-East home, Levi didn't bother calling him in advance. Levi figured if he couldn't get a good night's sleep, neither would Rossi.

Surprisingly, his cousin opened the door within minutes, alert and full of energy. Rossi's refreshed look just grated at Levi's nerves. Levi should have come in the wee hours of the morning. That would have given Levi some satisfaction—misery with company.

Rossi sported a white Mizzou college sweatshirt—short for University of Missouri at Columbia—creased black jeans, and socks thick enough to lift dust off the glossy mahogany wood floors. To complete his casual, no-worries look, he held a hot cup of coffee.

"What happened to you? It's barely sunrise." Rossi checked his watch, giving his cousin a critical once-over. He groaned. "Do I want to know?"

"Probably not . . . but here it is. I'm not ready to move on," Levi admitted as he removed his dark glasses and crossed the threshold without an invitation. He knew one wasn't coming. His destination was a black sofa, where he collapsed flat on his back, jacket and all.

"Whew. You had me concerned with the dark glasses, but seeing the dark circles under your eyes, I'd say put them back on, brother." Rossi took a long, noisy sip of his coffee.

Levi ignored his snide remark and continued, "Don't start the praise party yet after last night's date." Levi rubbed his face, frustrated. "Karyn was so beautiful. I couldn't keep my eyes off her. A couple of times, I had to remind myself to breathe. The dress I bought her fit to a T. Her perfume was sweet—"

"Hold up. You bought her a dress? Since when do you buy women's clothes?"

Again Levi shut out Rossi as he closed his door. "I can't believe how tangible my vibes were with Karyn, then all of a sudden memories from four years ago came rushing back when I saw Emma Gleason's son. Of all places on earth and last night at that time, Jonathan was there. He called me by name. I remembered him because of all the victims' families, only three of us had children under the age of ten who were left with one parent or none. Jonathan had none, and he looked so lost and much older than his possible early teens. It freaked me out. I hadn't seen any of the other victims' families since the one-year anniversary of the shooting. Next thing I know, my mouth started talking about Diane, and before I realized it, I had let my mouth run rampant."

A frown began its trek across Rossi's forehead. Levi wondered if his cousin had heard him.

"I've messed up, man," Levi confessed. Blinking, Levi stared up at the ten-foot ceiling. He wasn't admiring the open lighting design plan.

Rossi stood over him, peering down at him with a confused expression. "Should I get a pillow and blanket?"

Levi didn't respond. He didn't want Rossi to ask any questions. The best thing his cousin could do for him at the moment was to listen and begin praying. Levi exhaled loudly. "You should've seen her . . . the blood draining from Karyn's pretty face when I told her how Diane was murdered. The clarity in her expression scared me—shock, compassion, and condemnation before she mumbled softly she was so sorry, as if she had pulled the trigger." Levi turned on his side. He anchored his arm so that he could rest his chin in his hand. "Once I started to pour out my heart, I bled, Ross, profusely."

Setting his cup on an end table, Rossi took a seat across from Levi on a four-piece leather ottoman/ makeshift coffee table. "I hate to mention this, but . . ." He paused, twisting his lips. "That was definitely a date buster." Leaning forward, Rossi rested his elbows on his knees. "The way I see it, we have two options: Give her some space so she can digest what she's getting into, or act stupid and force your drama on her."

"Yeah," Levi agreed sarcastically. *There Rossi goes again with the "we" speech. When it boils down to it, it's always me,* Levi thought.

Now, Levi was ready to listen, waiting for Rossi to impart some wisdom as he did when counseling young adults and teenagers. The swishing of the washer, crushing of the refrigerator's ice maker system, and the traffic below filled in the gaps of silence.

"Cuz, this is your first sign of life in years. There's no doubt you're interested in her. Karyn went out with you face value. From what I understand, she accepted you as a widower with a daughter. Now, give her time.

"She probably had already read about the story in the newspaper, watched the TV coverage, or learned about the outcome on the radio. Everybody in St. Louis and across the country—and probably in the world—heard about the grocery store massacre," Rossi said. "It wasn't that long ago. The most important thing is that she listened. Have you talked to her today?"

Levi shook his head. "She said she has to study for a mid-term."

"Oh. Was this before or after you told her?" Rossi stood and reached for his cup. He drained the contents. He retook his seat in front of Levi and waited.

"After."

"Ah, man." Rossi gritted his teeth. "We may have to scratch everything I just said. Okay, let's start from square one. Tell me about Karyn. What did she share with you about herself?"

Maybe Rossi was hoping to learn something Levi might have overlooked. "Not much. She's twenty-seven, has a younger sister, works full time, goes to school part time. I guess I was doing all the talking. I know she likes white kittens and flashy cars."

"Cats, huh?" Rossi said.

"Kittens. There is a difference."

"Kittens grow up, man. Is that all? You could've gotten that off Facebook." Rossi held in a sarcastic chuckle. "Was she not talking, or was it you weren't listening?"

"She attends Crowns for Christ Church near down-town East St. Louis," Levi said as if he had checkmate.

Rossi whistled. "Every church leader in the Metro-East is well acquainted with Crowns for Christ's work in the community. If she belongs there, it says a lot about her walk with the Lord. The congregation is known for its Holy Ghost busybodies for the Lord. The members focus on outreach and its prison ministry. They put mega churches to shame.

"I think Karyn's church routinely collects and stocks food pantries year round. Last year I read they sponsored youths to summer camps, and their prison ministry is a proven model for reducing recidivism."

"Humph. As far as I'm concerned, murderers, thieves, drug users, sex freaks, gangsters and every other low scum of the earth should never be released. Those are hardcore sinners. They can never be trusted. Two of the men who gunned down Diane and the others had already served time in prison."

"Wait a minute, Levi. We're talking about this wonderful woman named Karyn, remember? Like I was saying before, you listed your grievances, Karyn's out on the battlefield, getting her hands dirty for the Lord. If that is the case, I doubt if you shocked her. Maybe she's God's healing balm for you. My word of advice is get rid of the 'tude, because you don't want to chase your blessing away. Understand?"

Levi mulled over what Rossi was saying. Shifting on the couch, Levi seemed to struggle with a response as he took sudden interest in Rossi's interior design. Sitting up, Levi slipped off his jacket and then stretched his arms on the back of the sofa.

"Understood, minister." With a ceasefire reached, Levi massaged his stomach. "Hey, what ya cooking me? I'm a guest."

"Cheerios."

They laughed. Rossi seemed relieved that he had walked Levi through another type of crisis. As Rossi headed for the kitchen, Levi stood and trailed him.

Levi stayed for breakfast and lunch. Finally before dinner, Rossi kicked him out of his condo. It was hard to tiptoe around Karyn's name as they talked about a variety of subjects.

"Okay, that's fifteen times Karyn's name has popped up. How can a man connect a woman with toothpaste to Dori's homework is a stretch. Go home. Have some quiet time with God while Dori is with Jet. Just don't stress yourself. Karyn sounds like a sweet lady. There's no rush in getting to know her. You're already old and about to get your AARP card in the mail."

Levi barked out a laugh. "Right. Considering you're two years older than me, you would have to activate yours first." He left, feeling the world was his to conquer.

CHAPTER 9

Buttercup's pep talk with Karyn—although it felt more like a scolding—helped a little. Saturday, Karyn had to force herself to study her principles of management notes from her business class. Her mind drifted back and forth to the unimaginable, horrific torture Levi and his family had undergone. Karyn actually chided herself for judging the offenders as if she hadn't been one herself.

Although she and Buttercup prayed every morning before Buttercup left for work at an insurance call center, Karyn yearned for Sunday morning services. She thrived on the much-needed hugs coming from the saints: prayer warriors, children, and mothers. They treated former prisoners with dignity, respect, and shameless love. She wanted to breathe in God's Word that was preached from her pastor's lips.

The Crowns for Christ Church van pulled up in front of the New Beginnings building. Buttercup and Karyn were ready before the driver could park. It was the only time the roommates could associate with each other outside their shared suite. The only exception was living under one roof in a halfway house or residential center.

To do so would violate the conditions of their parole. Even if ex-offenders were kin, approval would still be required. If an ex-felon was trying to remain an ex, the person had to distance herself from temptation. Parole was one foot away from prison and two steps away from freedom. Rules were enforced to the letter. If there was ever any doubt she could be penalized, Karyn recalled one line from the Bible. She didn't think God would mind if she used a portion of Romans 14:16 out of context—*Let not then your good be evil spoken of.* It just seemed to fit every situation.

After the driver stepped out of the van to assist them, Buttercup and Karyn were welcomed on board with the customary good mornings, praise the Lords, and how you doin's. Minutes later when the Sunday chauffeur drove off, quietness resettled around them.

"Stop thinking over there," Buttercup warned. "You're hurting my head." She massaged her forehead then adjusted her white faux fur headband.

"I'm not even talking to you. How am I giving you a headache?" Turning to face her, Karyn lifted a brow, perplexed. After shaking her head, Karyn returned to gazing out the windows across the aisle.

"You always talk to me, and when you don't, scenarios are running through my mind until they become a blur. They start screaming until my head starts pounding for clarification, but there are no answers in my brain."

"Are you having a breakdown?" Karyn asked dryly.

"Humph. You know God gave me a sound mind." She wiggled in her seat to stir Karyn. "Are you still bummed out over Levi?"

"No . . . Maybe . . . Okay, yes, a little." Karyn sighed. Eventually the Holy Ghost did get the truth out of her.

Buttercup shoved her face within inches of Karyn's. "Reality check, oh saint of God. Again, you didn't commit that crime that killed Levi's wife. Jesus saved us from being one of Satan's regular puppeteers. Our job is to pray he and his cronies remain bound. We no longer have a rap sheet."

Karyn didn't respond, forcing Buttercup to sit back. Her roommate's accusation made her reflect on a scripture in 1 Timothy 2 about intercessions. What would have happened the day of the shooting if a mass number of God's people were praying to bind the demons sent to kill Levi's wife and the others? Maybe their lives would have been spared, she mused as the chatter picked up in the van.

More than once, Karyn wished someone had been praying for her during her crisis, but there had been no one. Her mother had died of cancer the previous year. Her father's grief included lashing out. His emotions had become so raw that they spiraled out of control. Her only sister, who was almost five years younger, wasn't interested in finding fault with Karyn. When Karyn was sentenced for manslaughter, Nalani broke through security detail and hugged Karyn until the bailiff pulled her off.

"I'll always love you, Karyn. No matter what." That declaration was made more than four years ago, but Nalani's words stayed with Karyn every day. She missed her family.

Despite Karyn's wrongdoing, Nalani had reached out to her. Their father, Senator Nathaniel Wallace, harshly scolded Nalani after intercepting a letter from prison. From that moment on, he restricted her from ever communicating with a convicted felon again, even if it was her sister. Strong-willed, Nalani risked one last contact.

Karyn,

Whatever you do, don't write back, please! Daddy went ballistic when I got your letter. I thought he was going to kill me. Actually, I'm afraid he will if he finds out I wrote you again, so please, please don't write back. He threatened to change our phone number if you call here collect one more time. I love you very much and I wish we could talk. I will miss my big sis, but we'll talk soon. I don't know when you're supposed to get out, but I'll be there. Promise.

Love you always,
Nalani

P.S. I'll pray real hard for you.

Karyn had memorized every word of that letter that carried a warning not to respond. Eventually, Nalani's letters slowed then stopped coming the last year of her incarceration. Karyn figured her dad made good on his promise about any contact. Her eyes misted. Most people thought the worst thing that could happen behind bars was getting raped or assaulted. The biggest punishment, above all, was being cut off from the outside—completely—forgotten by everyone in the world except the victims, and hopefully not God. For so many, incarceration meant a repeat of the day before, the month before, and the year before. There was no future.

Even in prison, Karyn had to earn her keep, a mockery of her previous lifestyle where Karyn's housekeeper earned more per hour than she made in one month. For forty cents a day, Karyn cleaned up after meals, wiped off tables, and washed dishes under heavy security. If she worked every day, then at the end of the month, her productivity could yield her $12.

Nalani must have kept her promise and prayed for her big sister because Karyn entered the penal system at security level three, where level five was maximum security. Good behavior and time served eventually elevated Karyn to minimum security, until finally, the parole board approved an early release with the stipulation she would live in supervised living quarters for seventeen months.

Karyn closed her eyes. She didn't even want to think about that dark period in her life. She was redeemed by the blood of Jesus. Besides, once she had saved up enough money and gotten permission from her caseworker, she would catch a train back to Joliet, Illinois, and visit her sister and father, if he would see her. She had no idea what kind of reception awaited her. She hoped forgiveness was a big part.

She sniffed. An elbow in the side caused Karyn to shut off the memories.

"What is your problem today?" Karyn gritted her teeth.

Buttercup started massaging her temples. "My head is hurting again."

"I've got some aspirins in my purse," Mother Caldwell offered, sitting a few rows in front of them. Karyn heard the woman unzip compartments in her purse in search of them.

"No, no. That's okay. I'm sure it will go away once Karyn and I start praying over some things," Buttercup sweetly replied while squinting at Karyn.

"Okay, I'll pray too," Mother Caldwell said. "You know, you young people think too much today and pray too little. When I was your age, my mother always told me to pray without ceasing whenever I was in doubt about something. That's what you two need to do. I often wondered how a person can pray without stopping. As I grew older, I learned it isn't a marathon. It's all about keeping your mind on Jesus."

"I heard ya, Mother Caldwell," Deacon Deacon echoed from behind the wheel of the fifteen-passenger van. Regardless of how loud the gospel music blasted or how muffled the conversations, the sixty-nine-year-old, whose first name was Deacon, heard everything. Karyn learned from his joking that he strived in his salvation walk, so that he could become a deacon in somebody's church, and the Lord sent him to Crowns for Christ.

As the two friends fussed, Mother Caldwell changed seats. The other three occupants chimed in, testifying how God had revealed answers to them. Deacon Deacon backed everything with scriptures.

By this time, Mother Caldwell had gotten up and moved closer. "Who's Levi? You know that's a good Jewish name. One of the twelve tribes of Judah. Did you know God set the Levites aside to serve in the Holy Temple because they refused to bow down to idols?" Mother Caldwell nodded. "That's right."

Buttercup grinned. "See, he's a winner."

"But . . ." Mother Caldwell frowned in thought, tapping her lip. "Levi had a dark side. He was ruthless when it came to his sister, Dinah. He and his brother Shechem took down an entire family because their sister was raped. As a matter of fact, they sold another brother into slave—"

"Ah, that's enough, Mother Caldwell. Karyn and I will go back and read the story ourselves."

"Of course, baby. The Book of Exodus got some serious studying in it." She patted her hat and moved her mouth as if she was adjusting her dentures. "Sister Buttercup, you need to focus on one subject and stop going off in another direction. Anyway, you listen to me, Sister Karyn. You're such a sweet girl. I can tell you're doing right by God, but you can add some sanctified spice in your life. You need more than work, church, and school. Even a puppy has gourmet treats every once in a while."

Deacon Deacon burst out laughing as he shrieked to a halt at a stop sign. "You can't compare people to pets."

They held on to their seats when the deacon made a whiplash turn then came to another stop to pick up more churchgoers. Mother Caldwell tapped her cane. "If any young man has a problem with you, tell him to come see me."

"Who has a problem with Karyn?" Hanson "Halo" Ramos's booming voice announced his presence as he took center stage down the aisle, heading toward them.

The three women screamed their pleasure at his sight. Like Buttercup, Halo's angelic nickname was another mystery that would confound anybody. Six feet three, with bulging tattooed-covered biceps, the Puerto Rican pretty boy was anything but sweet. After violating an earlier probation sentence for a gang-organized shoplifting spree, the judge sent him to prison for two years when Halo was caught with less than one hundred dollars of merchandise in his possession.

Halo had earned his nickname not because he was a sweet and kind person before he came to Christ. It was just the opposite. He was a hit man—highly paid.

While the young men were behind bars, Crowns for Christ ministered to them and made a commitment to help them once released. The church had made good on their promise, and Halo had become a changed man, receiving the baptism in the name of Jesus and the Holy Ghost with evidence of speaking in tongues. Today his nickname conjured up a whole new attitude. He was willing to represent Christ even if he was the one who had to do the dying this time around.

Halo was serious about preaching the saving grace of God. He refused to return to hell on earth inside the prison walls, or the hell waiting for sinners—the fire and brimstone stuff. He was also Buttercup and Karyn's unsolicited bodyguard. Together the trio formed a pact to encourage one another.

He kissed all three of them on the cheek and sat across the aisle and stretched out. The clean-cut look was the best makeover Karyn had seen on a man since she was released. Although Karyn, Buttercup, and Halo couldn't socialize outside the church walls for fear of parole violation, they enjoyed the time together at church.

Sunday was an all-day-experience that started with Sunday school, followed by morning worship. The church provided dinner before the evening testimony service.

Since Halo was the last pickup, the van was less than ten minutes away from Crowns for Christ. Inside the church, Karyn could breathe in some liberty where she wasn't a woman on parole, but another member of the body of Christ who was saved by grace.

"Praise the Lord, ladies. Now, I repeat, who has a problem with Karyn?" Halo asked.

Karyn loved Halo. He was like the brother she never had, the ideal boyfriend, and the father figure in a younger version.

"No one, Halo," Karyn answered.

"That's not exactly true," Deacon Deacon said over his shoulder. "There's some guy who likes Karyn, but knows what she did."

Buttercup and Mother Caldwell laughed, clapping their hands. Karyn wondered exactly how much the man had heard.

"Deacon, you know that's not what was said," Karyn said defensively.

Halo yawned. "Why don't you tell me what was said so I can read between the lines?"

Karyn gave Halo an abbreviated version of her dinner date with Levi. The bus was quiet as they waited for Halo to respond.

"Do you like him?" Halo asked quietly. His piercing brown eyes warned her to answer honestly because he would know from her expression, which always gave her away.

Before Karyn could answer, Mother Caldwell blurted, "She may have a love connection."

Besides her scriptures, Karyn had learned five little words perfect for any conversation or situation: "I neither confirm nor deny."

"Humph. That means yes," Buttercup teased.

"Karyn, you have to decide if you want to be with this guy. Personally . . . never mind. I'll keep my thoughts to myself." Just as quick, Halo held up one finger. "Remember Jesus paid the price for all our sins—the ones from the past, the ones we make today, and the ones that are coming up. You've cleaned your house, legally and spiritually; therefore, there is no condemnation for those that are in Christ—"

The van came to a screeching halt again. Deacon Deacon shouted over his shoulder, "That's right, Brother Halo. *There is therefore now no condemnation to them which are in Christ Jesus, who walk not after the flesh, but after the Spirit.*"

"Now, Deacon, please drive this van and get us to church with our hats on our heads," Mother Caldwell scolded, referring to herself, the sole hat wearer.

"Yes, madam. I'm just quoting Romans 8:1"

While the others chuckled, Karyn continued to ponder what to do. Maybe she was making a big deal out of nothing. Levi said he was attracted to her. She liked the sound of it. Yet, she realized she had better tread carefully and listen to how God wanted her to proceed. She hadn't planned for personal entanglements.

"I am a new creature in Christ," Karyn whispered to herself.

"You better not forget it," Buttercup reminded her.

Karyn frowned at her lack of private thoughts. Did the van have amplified speakers with mini-microphones embedded in the seats or what?

CHAPTER 10

The Sunday morning message at Levi's church, Living for Jesus Fellowship, challenged him.

"There are benefits to those who overcome adversities. You have to work at getting past your fears to move on." Pastor Tillman Nance laid down his handheld mike and walked to the pulpit. "I'm just going to tell you like it is. If I don't, I'll be in trouble. The Lord demands that I feed His flock in 1 Peter 5. See, when it's test time, if you earn an A, then that's my score.

"Verse four says, *And when the chief Shepherd shall appear, ye shall receive a crown of glory that fadeth not away.* You can do it. Make yourself teachable, because God wants us to pass. But God will resist the proud, stubborn, and downright foolish hearts. They are too much maintenance," the pastor said with a disapproving shrug.

"Here's the formula, church. . . ." He paused as if expecting the congregation to pull out paper and a pen. "Clear your head by casting your cares on Jesus, add prayer for a humble attitude. That equals an overflow of God's grace," the preacher summarized with a nod. Dressed in all black, he grinned, displaying white teeth that matched his white collar. "For your homework this week, reread the passage. Be an overachiever for the Lord. Be an overcomer."

Levi, along with his younger twin brothers, stood for the altar call. Pastor Nance's appeal for souls to repent was never rushed. He would not close the call for discipleship unless one person willingly walked to the front for prayer or a desire to be baptized after repenting.

The words *cast your cares* kept revolving in Levi's head. *Lord, that's so much easier said than done, but I'm going to trust you with this new situation in my life. I believe whatever you have started between Karyn and me, you're going to finish*, he silently prayed.

On the other side of the sanctuary, two young women slowly made their way to the altar. Neither appeared dressed for church, but their hunger for salvation seemed to be raw. They lifted their hands in the air as Rossi, who was posted in the front with the other ministers, laid a hand on each of their foreheads. One released a tormented scream, yelling without censure, "Lord, have mercy on me! Jesus . . ." then fell to her knees, overcome with emotions. Levi had never seen such open, shameless repenting.

Rossi continued to pray as another youth minister assisted him. The spirit of the Lord began to move. Levi strained his ear. He thought he heard what sounded like an engine of a train. The next thing he knew, a loud thunder seemed to vibrate across the sanctuary until it landed. It was as if there were a zap and the power caused an indisputable explosion of unknown tongues.

I save who I will. Man looks at the outward appearance. I look at the heart. God spoke the message of 1 Samuel 16:7.

Again, looks were deceiving. Levi chided himself for judging the women's hearts based on their attire. The Spirit continued to stir the congregation as a missionary worker came to assist the tear-stricken lady to her feet.

Once the women requested to be baptized, they were led away to change into white garments.

Levi continued to watch the Spirit move around him, until he glanced at the baptismal pool. He hadn't noticed the others who had repented and joined the women.

Adorned in white swimming caps, hospital-type gowns, pants, and socks, the women quietly entered the pool and went to the waiting ministers. They crossed their arms over their chests as instructed.

"My dear sisters, you have confessed your sins unto the Lord and exercised your faith in Him to cleanse your soul. By the promise we have in the blessed Word of God concerning His death, burial, and grand resurrection, we indeed baptize both of you for the remission of your sins in the only name under heaven by which men can be saved—Jesus."

Simultaneously, they were dipped back until the water covered them, and then quickly pulled up. One practically danced her way out of the pool, while tongues exploded from the other woman's mouth. The baptism was repeated seven more times, until all who wanted to be saved had come.

After the benediction, the crowd lingered. Levi's parents, Victor and Sharon, crossed the aisle of plush brown carpet. At first glance, the pair was a contrast. Victor was tall, dark-skinned, and a bear of a man. Levi's height was a cross between his mother's five feet three inches and his father's six feet three inches.

His mother, at fifty-five, was still a beauty as she opened her petite arms for a hug. Levi didn't disappoint.

"I feel refreshed." Sharon sighed and patted her chest in worshipful awe. "I love Jesus. I'm glad I didn't miss this service and the wonderful evidence of God accepting our praise and worship."

Sharon Tolliver was biracial and a religious oddity. She had delicate skin and features. Short and soft-spoken, Sharon could get lost in a crowd, but when she wanted to be heard, she would roar, and others took notice.

Born of a father who was African and African American mixed heritage and a Jewish mother, she was identified as a Jew. Although she acknowledged her Jewish heritage, she converted to Christianity after attending a Jews for Jesus crusade years before she married.

Sharon's mother, Leah, said her decision to marry outside the Jewish race was of ignorance and fear. Levi's maternal grandmother was a carrier of a defective gene that caused Tay-Sachs disease. If she had married another Jew who was also a carrier, they had a one-in-four chance their offspring would develop it. The disease predominantly strikes babies of Jewish descent, and they usually die before they reach their fifth birthday.

His mother, on the other hand, wasn't completely detached from her Jewish roots. The evidence was giving her three sons Hebrew names: Levi, the oldest, and twins Seth and Solomon.

"You're coming to the house for dinner, aren't you? You don't have to eat alone since Jesetta has Dori until this evening," Sharon told Levi.

Hungry or not, at the moment, his urge was to swing by Karyn's apartment to talk. Levi grimaced. That had been his problem on Friday night. He had dominated the conversation. Karyn had politely listened as if she identified with his pain. He wondered if she had also lost a loved one in a tragic way.

"Not this evening, Mom. I have other plans." He brushed a kiss on her cheek, shook hands with his father, and left.

Not an hour later, he was almost at Karyn's apartment building. He abruptly scratched his mission when he admitted she might not welcome a surprise visit. Women were known for the curlers in the hair and the face mask thing going on behind closed doors.

He started to press on when God spoke: *What I start, I finish. I need no man's help. Be patient.*

Levi had headed home and warmed up leftovers. While he waited for Dori to get there, he read passages from his Bible. The quiet encouragement calmed his spirit until he dozed off. It didn't seem long before the doorbell buzzed, announcing Dori's arrival and whatever storm Jet was stirring up. His sister-in-law always had a complaint about something.

Opening his door, Levi hugged his daughter and then Jet, but he didn't invite her inside. "Thanks. I better get Dori ready for bed."

Jet didn't take the hint as she tried to widen the gap, but the door wasn't budging. "Hold on, Levi. I wanted to chat with you about that Karyn woman Dori keeps bringing up."

"We'll talk." Levi kissed her cheek, signaling good night, and then added a little pressure to close the door. Jet stomped her foot and walked off. He loved Jet, but at times, he had to make a mental appointment to deal with her.

An hour or so later, Levi had tucked Dori in bed. Her room was decorated in a crayon box of colors. The angled ceiling gave her bedroom an attic feel with its white planks. He had picked out the white Catalina bedroom set. The toy-inspired lamps, animal murals on the walls, and other accessories were Jet's idea. It was a bit busy for him, but Dori loved it. That was all that mattered to him—his daughter's happiness.

"I like Miss Karyn," Dori said without prompting.

"Me too." Levi grinned as he sat at the foot of the bed and sank into the layers of comforters. Jet had made her a fan of animal prints. Dori even had dozens of flannel pajamas with giraffes, monkeys, even Winnie the Pooh.

"Did she look like Cinderella in her shoes, Daddy?" Her expression was hopeful.

Levi shook his head. He had bought Karyn a dress, not shoes.

"How about the princess in the movie?" She referred to *The Princess and the Frog.*

"Nope."

Dori sighed, clearly frustrated. She sat up in her bed. He was about to rub her hair, then thought twice about it. His sister-in-law had his little girl's hair washed, her scalp oiled, and then styled with four long and twisted ponytails. Levi had to give Jet her kudos sometimes. If he didn't remember to put a satin scarf on it, Jet would have a fit. Dori did look adorable, like a younger version of her mother.

She also had that same determined look as her aunt. Dori wanted to know and now. "Daddy, how pretty was she?"

"She was as beautiful as an angel." Levi recalled her perfect smile, long lashes, curls galore, and the misshaped nails—yet she was a glorious sight to him.

"Daddy, do you think she likes me?" A worried expression and tearful eyes took over the happiness in Dori's face.

Levi scooted closer and pulled his daughter from under the covers. He squeezed her without crushing her small frame. "Here's a secret," he whispered in her ear.

"Okay." She waited with widened eyes.

"She likes you better than she likes me."

"Really?" Dori jumped on her father's lap and clapped her hands in glee.

"All she wanted to talk about was Dori, Dori, Dori." *And stupid me, I couldn't stop talking about your mother.* That tidbit earned him a squeeze around his neck.

"Yay."

"The next time you have a date, can I go?"

What? Are you kiddin' me? I need to earn my own brownie points. . . . Who knows? Maybe Dori was his brownie point.

"I don't think Miss Karyn will mind, but we'll see. Now, go to sleep, my little butterball."

"That's a turkey, Daddy."

"I forgot how smart you are. Anyway, you have pre-school tomorrow." Standing, he lifted her in the air and turned her around as if she were a fairy about to take flight. Dori laughed as she stretched out her arms. He brought her down and smacked a juicy kiss on her cheek. Levi tucked her back under the cover. "Good night." He turned off the lamp, leaving a night light to guide her way to her bathroom during the night

"Daddy?"

He was near her door when he stopped and turned back around. "Huh?"

"I'm real smart because Miss Karyn gives me all the big kids' books."

"Umm-hmm." Miss Karyn put a dent in his wallet every time he walked into Bookshelves Unlimited, but that bookstore was the biggest investment he had ever made.

CHAPTER 11

Squatting, Karyn was stocking shelves for the bookstore's Black Friday sale when she felt a presence then recognized a deep voice behind her. The cologne was unmistakable. Standing, Karyn turned around. Through Levi's designer glasses, Karyn connected with his clear brown eyes. She didn't linger there, as she looked for and wasn't disappointed to see his twin dimples outlining a tentative smile.

It was their first contact since the doomed date a few weeks ago. They sized up each other. In the end, she silently confirmed she missed him and denied she was going to play coy about it—only if he asked.

She wondered why he was there. It wasn't Saturday, and he didn't have Dori. The other times he had been in the bookstore alone were of a personal nature, and usually it centered on her.

"Do you have plans for Thanksgiving?"

No "how are you" or "sorry I haven't called"? Then Karyn slightly remembered his request for her number on the way home from their dinner, when she was too distracted to respond. Although she heard herself confess with her lips that she didn't think they would be a good fit, her heart held on for signs of life that some type of relationship could be formed.

"Hi, Levi."

Breaking eye contact and looking away didn't cam-
ouflage his embarrassment. It was the same soft, vul-
nerable side he leaked the night of their date. Since
meeting him, Karyn had never seen him lack confidence. He was always patient with his daughter, polite
to the staff, and complimentary toward her, and he let
it be known he loved Jesus but struggled sometimes.

Even when they were on the date, Levi didn't shy
away from his hurtful past. She liked that in him—being human, acknowledging his pain, but pressing on.
Without Levi knowing it, he was teaching her a lesson.

He grunted. "I got ahead of myself. Forgive me?" He
held a straight face, but somewhere a tease was hiding
in his words.

Karyn nodded, mesmerized by his overwhelming
presence. She missed him.

Clearing his throat, he clicked his heels and stood at
attention. There was the tease. She wanted to laugh at
his playfulness. They both wrestled to keep blank faces.

"Good evening, Karyn. How are you?"

"I'm well." As she returned his smile, she inhaled
his cologne. She wondered how much he was wearing
because it was so faint, but his closeness allowed her
to indulge. "I'm sorry, but I do have plans. My church
is sponsoring a soup kitchen near downtown East St.
Louis. I volunteered a long time ago to help. I've been
warned to be prepared to collapse on my bed in my
clothes and shoes at the end of the day; then I'll have
to turn around and be back at the store at five the next
morning for the pre-dawn early bird specials."

Karyn was getting exhausted just thinking about the
upcoming hectic schedule in twenty-four hours. She
shook her head, amused, which opened the door for
Levi to smile. "I can't believe people really get up at
that hour."

He didn't appear too happy with her news. Stuffing his hands forcefully in his pants pocket, Levi leaned against a shelf. He focused on her without blinking. "Not me, but my brother's girlfriend has a two-hundred-mile radius limit for staking out a bargain. She never goes gorilla hunting alone. She always has her contingency of backup shoppers ready to go at a wash-your-face, brush-your-teeth moment."

His eyes twinkled before silence drifted between them. "Since you won't accept Thanksgiving dinner, I would think a foot massage from a spa or someplace else is what you need, but I have a feeling you wouldn't accept that from me either."

"No," Karyn whispered. She withheld a moan at the thought of such an extravagant service. Although the personal attention from Levi would be a fantasy, the intimacy would be too much of a temptation. Plus, she was ticklish, and if he touched her too close, she was sure she would forget who Jesus was.

"How about a ride home?"

Karyn hesitated. What did she want from Levi? More importantly, what did he want from her? She reflected on her scolding from Halo, Buttercup, and the van riders who ordered her not to excavate the past, but to move forward. Plus, any change of plans, including transportation, needed approval.

"Thank you, but I'm working a double shift." It wasn't an excuse. She volunteered so others could go home to get a jump-start on their Thanksgiving dinners. Karyn was not about to tell him she needed the extra money.

Levi didn't appear to be backing down when they were interrupted.

"Excuse me." Patrice shoved herself between them with her back to Levi, obstructing Karyn's view. "I'm not about to stock the shelves all by myself. If you're not going to help, why don't you clock out? Isn't that what a break is for?" Patrice stormed away, scowling and cutting her eyes at Levi. "They let anybody work here."

Levi leaned in. "She's mean. Is she your boss?"

"She thinks she's everybody's boss. Today she's having a good day. I've learned to pick my battles." Karyn felt naughty. "Besides, she has friends in low places."

On the surface, Patrice was kind, concerned, and cheerful, but she was also self-absorbed. She could manipulate any situation to her benefit. Although she was working a double shift along with Karyn, she complained she was too tired to stay on the register and her back was aching so she couldn't pick up crates of books. Finally, the manager, desperate for help, assigned Patrice to assist customers. All Patrice did was point them in the right direction, or sometimes the wrong direction, which meant Karyn would eventually have to help them.

"What time do you get off?" he whispered, glancing around. "I don't believe in letting a woman push my buttons, but if she keeps acting like that toward you, I may have to consider fighting her like a man."

"Stop it." Karyn lifted her hands as if to push him back. Levi cupped her fists inside his. They stared. She blushed. His nostrils flared with his determination.

"What time?"

"Closing." Karyn held her breath, not knowing how she wanted him to respond.

Levi checked his watch and nodded. "That's in six hours. I'll be back." He didn't wait for her confirmation as he left the store.

Karyn was stunned silent. That was the second time he had told her what he was going to do and left before she could put up an argument.

Karyn sucked in her breath, flattered. Now she had to get permission to catch a ride home instead of catching the bus. "Maybe this will work," Karyn mumbled as Patrice returned.

"I don't mean to be a grouch, but I—"

Ignoring her sometime—no, most of the time—nemesis, Karyn hummed a tune she had heard at a recent testimony service, tuning out Patrice.

The evening progressed with no further interaction with Patrice, so Karyn clocked out for her last break to call her counselor. She walked out into the mall as she tapped in the number to the center on her cell phone.

"New Beginnings," her counselor answered.

"Hi, Monica." She bobbed her head and rushed on before the woman drew any conclusions. "Yes, everything's fine. I was hoping you would okay for me to get a ride home from Levi Tolliver." Karyn held her breath.

"He's the man who took you out to dinner a few weeks ago," Monica stated after a long pause. "I'll okay it this once since you're working overtime, but don't make this a habit. We have to follow the center rules of advance requests with no favoritism."

Karyn exhaled, thanked her, and disconnected.

By the time Karyn clocked back in, the customers had thinned and the bookstore was peaceful. She walked over to an older woman strolling through the kids' section.

"Hey, Karyn, do you think you can get this customer? I'm on the phone. Man, I've got to do everything," Patrice yelled rudely from across the store in front of a teenage girl.

Karyn cringed with embarrassment. Patrice was unprofessional, tacky, and crazy, all for the price of one. "I can't. I'm helping this customer," she mouthed, shaking her head so as not to duplicate Patrice's bad example. A few minutes later, with her task completed, Karyn headed to the customer service desk.

"Look," Patrice snapped, "if you want to ship something to your daddy in prison, you're going to have to know his prison badge number. Go ask your momma and come back after the holiday."

In tears, the teenager was about to turn away. Karyn considered violating parole just to knock Patrice's eyes crossed and then back straight again. Jesus was the only thing stopping her. When He returned for professing, practicing Christians, Karyn didn't want to be left behind.

The other small fact was that Karyn needed the job. Checking the *yes* box on applications which revealed she was a convicted felon wasn't a plus. Jobs were hard to find, especially when a person was starting over.

On Bookshelves Unlimited's pre-employment assessment test, Karyn remembered the question about turning in an employee if he or she was caught stealing. *Yes* was the right answer, but what could she do when Patrice's crime was simply being rude? Karyn couldn't fathom how Patrice would treat her if she knew about Karyn's past. Probably not well.

It had been months since Karyn reached out to Patrice when she was having a bad day. "Jesus's sole purpose of coming, dying, and rising from the dead was to keep everyone from hell."

Patrice had grunted, "Hell can't come fast enough."

God spoke firmly to Karyn not to cast His pearls before swine. That had frightened Karyn, so she shut her mouth and walked away. Patrice was on her own.

"Excuse me," Patrice's badgered customer said to Karyn, sniffing back tears.

The girl was a few inches taller than Karyn and couldn't be any more than twelve or thirteen. She had big, expressive brown eyes. "Yes, sweetie? I'm Karyn."

"I just wanted to send my daddy a book of poems. I thought if I told y'all the jail, you could send it. I can't ask my mom because she's in jail too."

Karyn's heart broke for the young victim who was the remnant of sin. She wondered if the girl meant prison instead of jail, which was most likely a shorter stay. "Come on. Let's see what we can find out."

Wrapping her arm around the teenager, Karyn gently guided her to the other end of the customer service desk, where a computer was located. Typing the web address for the Federal Bureau of Prison homepage, she waited then clicked on the inmate locator. "What's your daddy's name? You can't ship hardback books because of prison regulations, but I'm sure we can find something else."

"David King," she whispered.

She entered it, and sixteen men with that name popped up. Most had been released, including an eighty-one-year-old man. Sadness descended on Karyn. A soft melody of a song swept through her head. *I once was lost, but now I'm found.* She smiled. God not only allowed her to be set free, but the icing was He picked her out to save her. "I think I found him. He is in Menard Medium Security Unit."

The girl nodded and her eyes sparkled. "Yeah."

Karyn reached for a pad and pen to jot down David King's prisoner number and mailing address.

"Can I see him?" Her expression was hopeful.

"What's your name?" Karyn wasn't sure that was a good idea. Prison ID photos weren't glamour shots. The only person Karyn knew who smiled when processed through the system was Russell Simmons' former wife, Kimora Lee. The woman had money and clout behind it. She could afford to smile.

"Tiffany."

"Your daddy's not going to look happy. It might make you sad," Karyn tried to warn her. The man looked as if he had been roughed up during and after he landed in prison. Karyn wouldn't wish for anybody to go to sleep with that image stuck in their mind.

"Oh, I've seen his picture before whenever I can sneak and use the computer at the library. It's cool. That's why I want to send him some poems to make him happy."

"You can't see him this time, hon. Now, let's see if we can find another book that's paperback, so we can order it."

Tiffany twisted her lips in disappointment. That was too bad. Karyn wasn't budging. She didn't want the child going to sleep with that image. There was nothing to smile about in prison.

Politicians argued people were sent away as punishment, not to be punished. The truth was that anybody caged in a cold cell, sometimes taking a cold shower, with twenty-four hours a day to think about why they did what they did and to ask if it was worth it, was being punished. It was punishment for Tiffany King, who was growing up without her mother and father. Karyn silently prayed the cycle would be broken.

"Thank you, Miss Karyn, and happy Thanksgiving." Tiffany grinned and turned to leave a while later. She found Patrice and stuck out her tongue before racing out the door.

CHAPTER 12

What a difference a couple of weeks, sermons, and prayers made. Rossi was honored to witness Levi overcoming any doubts about a new relationship. As a matter of fact, his cousin had more gusto toward Karyn than a double helping of jalapeño peppers.

Downtown living always enchanted Rossi as he stood at his window, overlooking the city. There were just enough snowflakes to cover the grass. As the lights went out in business windows, announcing the closings for the holiday, Washington Boulevard's night life came alive. The bowling alley, eateries, and bars began to bustle as if the patrons were clueless that Thanksgiving was a day away.

He backed away to relax in front of the fireplace when a knock at his door delayed his planned tranquility. As a youth pastor, Rossi wasn't a stranger to unexpected visitors, but this time Rossi hoped it was a neighbor wanting a stick of butter or whatever else people borrowed.

Rossi opened the door. Levi stood cocky in a larger-than-life stance even though he was shorter. Amused, Rossi suspected the cause—or rather the person—behind the radiance oozing from Levi's face.

"What's up?" Levi asked as he crossed the threshold.

Rossi smirked, as Levi came in, removed his jacket, and tossed it absentmindedly on a chair. "Hey, didn't

I just see you a few hours ago at work, across the hall from my office?" Rossi frowned. Where's Dori?"

"Yep, you recently saw me, and Mom picked up Dori from school so she could help with the baking."

"Umm-hmm."

Levi performed a slow turn as if he were at the end of a runway. That's when Rossi noticed that Levi had changed out of his white shirt and tie into a dark turtle-neck, blazer, and slacks. This was not a man dressed for an evening at home.

"You're seeing me again until I have to pick up Karyn." Levi meticulously adjusted his glasses on his nose.

"Oh." Rossi closed his door and strolled to his fire-place, where he stirred the logs until the flames danced higher. Glancing over his shoulder, Rossi silently ob-served his cousin. Levi was leisurely inspecting one piece of art decor after another and handling family photos as if he had never seen the snapshots before. He lifted a stained-glass vase off a pedestal, scrutinizing it as if he were about to make a purchase. Finally at the end of his journey, Levi prepped himself in front of an oval mirror in the foyer.

Turning around, Rossi squinted and folded his arms. "So does that mean I'm babysitting you?" he asked sar-castically.

"Funny. I happen to want to spend time and chill with my cousin." Levi grinned.

"Listen. Don't take this the wrong way—scratch that, you can take it the wrong way. I spent six hours with you today, beginning at seven this morning. It would've been longer if we hadn't closed the office early. I don't want to see you again until after Thanksgiving, like . . . say, Sunday morning worship. Is that soon enough for you?"

Levi chuckled and sighed. "You are way too uptight. You need a little lady around here."

"Really?"

"Umm-hmm. A woman could do a brother good. Forget the milk."

Levi seemed bored with his reflection as he helped himself to a seat and stretched out his arms on the back of the couch. Crossing his ankle on top of his knee, Levi waited expectantly for Rossi to grill him.

Let him stew, Rossi decided as he strolled across his wood floor to the open kitchen floor plan. "Hey, do you want some eggnog or juice?"

"Nah, I'm good. Karyn may want to stop and grab a bite to eat."

Karyn again. His cousin looked ready to burst with information, but Rossi would wait him out. Opening the refrigerator, he grabbed a carton and then poured eggnog into a mug. He took a sip to sample the flavor before placing the carton back on the shelf.

Taking his time returning to the living room, Rossi eased into his recliner near Levi. Rossi reached for the remote, ignoring his cousin's presence. Before he could peruse the programming, Levi stood swiftly, grabbed the remote, and clicked off his flat-screen TV.

"Are you crazy? What's wrong with you?" Levi was starting to grate on his nerves. Rossi snatched back his remote.

"Do you want to hear this or not?" Levi balled his fist at his side.

"I have no idea what you're talking about." Rossi returned to his recliner.

"Now I know God's going to get you for lying."

"Okay. You're right. Lord, forgive me. What, or should I say whom, would you like to talk about? No, don't tell me. Let me guess: Karyn."

"I've got some time to kill, so I figured you needed some company—"

"Levi, I've got a high-def flat-screen TV with a remote in my bedroom. If you don't get to the point, either I will put you out, or I will leave you out here by yourself." He gulped down his eggnog.

"I can't believe we're related," Levi grunted. "Yes, this is about Karyn. I went to see her at the bookstore. Evidently, I hadn't struck out when I ruined our first date. When she gave me one of her pretty smiles, I relaxed. We chatted a few minutes, and Karyn accepted my offer to give her a ride home. Funny, I still don't know if she owns a car or if it's in the shop. Regardless, I don't like her on that bus."

Leaning forward, Levi made eye contact with Rossi and held his stare. "It's those little things I want to know about her. Wait until you meet her. Karyn also has the backing of one other special lady in my life."

"Dori." Rossi loved his little cousin, who seemed more like his niece. She was the only little girl in the family, since he and his three brothers weren't married and didn't have any children.

Rossi relaxed and put his sock-covered feet on his coffee table. He scowled at Levi. "Don't you even think about it."

Levi huffed. "You're worse than a woman. And speaking of the female species, I don't think I told you about Jet's reaction when she found out about Karyn. I think she had been stewing and decided to boil over when she brought Dori home. Jet's face was distorted as she readied herself to fire one question after another at me, but I was in no mood."

"What did you do? Jet can be like an unleashed mother Rottweiler."

"I accepted my daughter and her belongings and thanked her for bringing her niece home."

Rossi whistled, impressed. "No Q and A?" Rossi grinned and bobbed his head. He loved Jesetta as he would anybody else, but she was too opinionated, domineering, and sometimes rude. After Diane died, she became pit bull, boxer, and Rottweiler personified.

"Man, I'm a Tolliver." Levi patted his chest, claiming his dominance. "At times, I may come across like I don't have it together—"

"A few weeks ago, you didn't. But I'm glad Karyn kissed it and made it feel better," he teased.

"Not yet, but she will. Anyway, back to Jet. I have two things working for me: Jesus, and my dad didn't rear his boys to let any woman run over us."

Leaning forward, they exchanged fist bumps. Rossi was glad that Levi held his ground. "So, tell me about Dori's reaction."

"We had one of those daughter-dad talks as I got her ready for bed. Without knowing it, she was my inspiration to basically get it together. In the past, it was okay to be weak at times because that's when I was riding on God's strength."

Rossi nodded. "Second Corinthians 12:9."

"Right, but God broke down verse seven to me. Despite the devil's torment, God allowed it to keep me in check. In my case, my grief was keeping me in a place that God wanted me in for a season. It seemed like the devil tried to turn the tables and crank up the heat, but that's when God seemed to say enough is enough."

Levi glanced at his watch and shot up. "Hey, man, I've got to go. I need to do a few things before Karyn gets off."

Rossi also stood. "Well, by all means, don't let me hold you hostage."

"It ain't goin' to happen. I've got this." Levi thumped his chest, opened the door, and walked out.

CHAPTER 13

Only a few cars remained in the parking lot at St. Clair Square Mall when Levi pulled up to the curb. Karyn was standing outside the glass doors at the entrance. He didn't like the scenario of her waiting for him by herself. Levi didn't believe any location was one hundred percent Satan-free, especially after Diane was killed in a public place.

Shifting his LaCrosse into park, Levi hurried out and barely slipped his arms into his jacket before he jogged to her. Masking his concern with a smile, he looked down into her face. "Next time, wait inside for me," he ordered.

"I'm fine. I catch the bus all the time by myself." She shivered with her down jacket zipped to her chin. Her head was covered by an unsecured hood, and her single braid peeped out.

"Umm-hmm. Yeah, I don't like that either." He scanned his surroundings. The place was nearly deserted. "Do you own a car?"

She shook her head. If Karyn was really his—his woman—he would buy her a car. He would also change her place of employment.

Wrapping an arm around her shoulder, he steered her to his vehicle then opened her door. Levi assisted her inside, remembering the first time she was a passenger, when he saw her gorgeous legs. This time, tan uniform pants blocked his view. Skirts and dresses were definitely his preference on a woman, but since that would cause him to lust, it was better he was distracted.

Once Levi climbed back into his seat, he adjusted the temperature for her. Stealing a glance at Karyn, he saw her blush under his examination then turn and face the window. Before that, it took Levi only a few seconds to take a snapshot of her features. Gone were the curls and makeup. Remaining was her natural beauty, plus the dark circles under her eyes.

He concentrated on her body language and expression. "Did Patrice give you any more problems?"

"Not directly." Karyn closed her eyes and shook her head. She sighed. "I'm just thinking about a customer."

"What happened?" Levi didn't know what her job was paying, but he was sure it didn't pay extra for stress.

"Patrice lashed out at a customer who wanted to send a book to her dad who is in prison. Books have to be shipped directly from the bookstore warehouse with the prisoner's identification number, and the young girl didn't know it. I also learned her mother's in prison."

Levi whistled. Wow. He would never have thought working in a bookstore would have that type of mental torture. "I'm sorry."

"She was so sweet. I think a little mischievous, but who is raising her? Her grandmother," Karyn answered her own question. "What type of hope will she have?"

"Maybe she's better off. Depending on what crime sent them to prison, she and society may be better off," he snapped before he softened his words.

This time her sigh was very audible.

Okay, Tolliver, don't mess this up, Levi coaxed himself. "I'm sorry."

"Once I located him, I scanned his release date," she continued as if she didn't hear his sarcastic remark or apology. "By the time he's scheduled to be released, it's possible his baby girl will be a mom, and I'm not talking about a teenage mother."

Levi shook his head in disgust. "What a waste of life. Did you look to see what crime he committed?" he asked, turning the corner.

"Yes."

"Well?" He glanced at her. When she didn't say anything, he wondered if the information was confidential and he had overstepped his boundaries.

Karyn changed the subject, allowing him to save face. "Thank you for offering to take me home. I'm sure you had other plans."

"I more like demanded to be your chauffeur." They chuckled. "I was hoping you were hungry and we could grab a bite to eat before I drop you off."

Karyn checked her watch. "I'm hungry, but I don't have time."

"Sure we do. There are a few places that haven't closed early for Thanksgiving." He scanned across Route 159 at a strip mall. One fast food restaurant's drive-through lights were still on. Checking for traffic, Levi turned onto the street, and hoping a light wouldn't snag him before they made it there.

"No, you don't understand. Levi, let me explain something about my lifestyle: I'm single."

"I know." He grinned. "And I'm loving it."

"I'm serious." Karyn didn't return his smile, and she appeared a bit flustered. "I live in a very secure building where every precaution is taken for the protection of every woman. To ensure my safety, I have a set schedule. If I deviate from it, people get concerned and may send help to find me to make sure I'm all right. I'm starting over from a bad situation. Until I save up enough money to move, I have to honor those rules. I don't have the flexible schedule you're probably expecting."

Now some things were becoming clearer. She was on a tight budget—the reason why she didn't have a car—but what circumstances would cause her to have to start over? The first thing that came to his mind was whether she had been in an abusive relationship. What other reason would there be for tight security? If some loser had touched her and Levi got a name and address . . . Levi took a deep breath. He was getting carried away. Whatever the reason, Levi hoped one day Karyn would feel comfortable enough to talk about her past.

"You don't owe me an explanation, but thanks for sharing that with me." He frowned as he struggled to convey his thoughts. "I'll hold it close to my heart."

He pulled into Boston Market's drive-through lane behind another car. Within a few minutes, he ordered them two meals. He wasn't necessarily hungry, but he didn't want her to eat alone. "So, Cinderella, what time do I need to have you home?" he teased.

Blinking, Karyn sucked in her breath.

He didn't expect a stunned reaction. Did he offend her in any way? "Karyn, should I apologize? Did I say something wrong?"

She stiffened. "What makes you think that?"

"I watched your expression change."

She blushed. "I'll confess. I never expected to be anybody's Cinderella. Are you my prince?"

Levi's cockiness was in full force. She was definitely a boost for his confidence. He toyed with the best mack-daddy reply, but then God brought him down a notch. "You're the princess, Karyn. I can't be a prince without you."

Her eyes watered as he inched to the window and exchanged money with the clerk for their food and wished him a happy Thanksgiving. He passed the bag to Karyn for her inspection. Once she nodded that their order was right, he drove off.

"Karyn, I want us to spend as much time together as you will allow me. It's as if God gave me a rose. You open slowly and become more beautiful at every stage."

"Ha! Me, beautiful?" She chuckled. "No wonder you wear glasses."

Biting his lip, Levi nodded. "Let's just say I can see clearly now that my rain has gone."

CHAPTER 14

Karyn was convinced that Levi Tolliver was a prince. He just wasn't hers. It was because of her self-reproach that she had ignored his innocent query about the father's crime.

God spoke bits of Romans 8:1: *There is no condemnation to you which are in Christ Jesus, who walk not after the flesh, but after my Spirit.*

That boosted Karyn's confidence as Levi pulled up in front of New Beginnings. She saw her temporary home as a blessing, but also a hindrance to any type of romantic entanglement. What would passersby think of the female ex-convicts who were living behind closed doors in their neighborhood, trying to transition back into the community? What would Levi think?

Karyn blinked and faced Levi, who appeared to be watching her. The aroma of their meals interfered with Levi's cologne, frustrating Karyn. She liked the way he smelled. Lights on the dashboard pierced the interior's darkness and allowed Karyn to glance at her watch. Twelve minutes. Not a minute more or the staff would lock the door for the night.

What was Levi's purpose in her life? Karyn didn't know if she could stand the answer as she chanced reaching out to massage his chin.

"Levi, you asked me about the little girl's dad in prison. He stabbed someone to death. It doesn't list details." She focused on his eyes. If Levi could easily read her expressions, then she wanted his skill.

"God is just, and He will judge every one of us. Everyone in prison shouldn't be there. For those who are, well . . . well . . ." Karyn shook her head. "Levi, you are entitled to your hurt and anger. Let no one, including me, make you feel guilty for who you lost." She softened her voice. "As you move on, remember to forgive so you'll be free."

Listening, Levi rubbed his mustache as he anchored an elbow on the steering wheel. Oh, how she wished to see the dimples. They had a calming effect on her. He bit his bottom lip.

"See, that's the thing. None of those scums at my wife's trial asked for forgiveness. They didn't even try to explain why they committed such a hideous, cowardly act. It would be hard—very hard— if one in that bunch had asked for my forgiveness." Patting his chest, Levi added, "God would have to force my lips to say yes." He looked tortured. "Lives were changed forever."

Karyn could feel his internal struggle. *Lord, you made a mistake sending me. Please help him to overcome his torment,* she prayed.

"Sometimes," he struggled with his words, "when I read Luke 17:3 about forgiving whenever or whomever asks, I don't recall anyone one of them asking." He choked.

Maybe Karyn was asking him to do the impossible. "Sometimes people don't. When we pray The Lord's Prayer, we're telling the Lord we'll forgive whoever trespasses against us. In exchange, He will forgive us when we trespass against Him. I've learned something these past twenty-seven years on this earth. Patrice, for example, may never apologize to me or anybody until the day she dies, but what gives me peace is I can forgive her. Sometimes it's hard, but I want God to forgive me for all my sins. It's a trade-off."

Levi closed his eyes. "Where did this precious woman come from?" he whispered loud enough for her to hear. "Karyn, I want to test the waters then stake my claim. Is it too soon to say I'm in love with you?"

She caught her breath. Surely Levi Tolliver was teasing. He wasn't a bit more ready to fall in love than she was. "You're so silly, Levi Tolliver. Of course it's too soon. You don't even know me—"

"Oh, so you're saying if we took the time to get to know each other, I would definitely fall in love with you?" he asked, smirking.

That sounded like a dare, and she didn't do dares. "Good night, Mr. Tolliver." As Karyn reached for the door handle, Levi stopped her.

"I'm sorry. You just do something to me. When I'm around you, I feel everything is all right in my world. I'll get your door."

Levi strolled around to Karyn's side. Once he assisted her out of the car, he carried her bag as he escorted her to the door. What if he asked to come in for a while? Karyn became nervous about what to say. When she stepped up on the porch, he didn't.

"Look, I know you're tired and have a long day ahead of you tomorrow. You go eat and get some rest. Let the other meal be a leftover."

She exhaled, not realizing she had been holding her breath. *Lord, I owe you so much, especially this small blessing.* Karyn felt emboldened.

"Levi, never tell anybody you love them unless you really do, because true love means unconditional love like Christ gives the church."

He reached out and pulled her chin closer. Karyn knew what was coming. When his lips were inches from her mouth, she covered his mouth with her hand and captured his kiss in her palm. She placed her kiss in her palm and returned her hand to his lips.

Levi lifted a teasing brow. His expression said it all. If she thought she was going to get away with that, then she should think again.

"I really need to go," she softly pleaded.

He stole a kiss, then a second, and grinned with his dimples saluting her. Turning around, he whistled his way back to his car. Suddenly, he whirled around. "Hey, I need your number!"

Karyn giggled. The image of the cool swagger was shattered at his near-panic mode. She shouted the seven digits, hoping he had sonic hearing, and ran into the house. Maybe she could be a princess for a day.

She had made her curfew, breathing heavily. She signed in at the desk and climbed the stairs to her suite. She found Buttercup watching a show on TV that was demonstrating beauty tips. Once she saw the Boston Market bag, her program was forgotten as she jumped up.

"Finally, a doggie bag." Buttercup clapped.

CHAPTER 15

Jesetta Hutchen's presence was a reminder of Diane's absence.

Because she was Diane's older sister and Dori's only auntie, the Tollivers continued to embrace her as family, and family tradition was Thanksgiving dinner at Levi's parents' house.

It was a home where Tollivers Real Estate and Development had replaced pipes, floors, electrical outlets, and anything else Levi's mother would okay, from the roof to the basement. In essence, it was practically a new house on the same old lot in Fountain Park. The city neighborhood was known for its stately two- and three-story brick houses that had been in the possession of black folks, some for more than three generations.

As they all linked hands around the table, Levi's father, Victor, began the traditional holiday blessing. "Jesus, we are blessed today not only because of the meal you have provided and the hands you sanctified to prepare it. I thank you for each member around this table and for our ancestors before us. Help us to continue a legacy of a strong people."

Levi's mother, Sharon, picked up the grace, "Lord, we worship you because we are healthy. Our sons have prospered even as their souls have prospered. . . ."

The prayer chain continued until it was Jet's turn. She cleared her throat. "I'm thankful for the Tollivers and my precious niece. Help us never to forget my younger sister, who has gone on before me," she mumbled and choked.

Next in line was Rossi, whose tradition was to make pit stops at several Tollivers' homes after spending time with his own parents. He couldn't resist his aunt Sharon's turkey with apple stuffing.

Standing next to Rossi, Levi knew his cousin would speak soothing words to comfort Jet. Holidays were hard for Levi too.

"Jesus, we thank you for the memories you give us of the family gatherings and fun times. We especially thank you for the blessings you haven't released. Help each one of us to receive them." Rossi paused for the next person.

Levi continued, "Jesus, thank you for the special people in my life. I thank you for the place you have me in this stage of my life. I'm grateful for your blessings and trials."

Finally, as was customary, it was the children's turn. Gathered around a miniature veneer dining table reserved for young children, which included Dori, a few cousins, and three neighborhood children, Dori shouted, "Lord Jesus, I'm hungry, and thank you for Grandma's food, my auntie Jet eating with us, my daddy, and Miss Karyn. Amen." The adults added their Amens, clapping.

Levi held his breath, waiting for someone to rib him about Karyn. It was as if they didn't want to make a big deal out of his new relationship in fear of him suddenly shutting out the world again. He had been hush-hush except with Rossi, who knew about the failed first date and the new details.

Jet stood and fixed her niece a plate before returning to her own seat. The conversation was lighthearted and changed every five minutes. Eventually, gravy stains marked a few spots on the white tablecloth as Levi's brothers, paternal grandparents, parents, and a couple of neighbors showed the turkey no mercy. As the dessert was about to be decimated, Sharon started her fishing expedition.

"Levi, I thought perhaps we would have an extra guest today. I was looking forward to meeting Karyn." She lifted a brow and stared at her son. "The only thing I know is what my grandbaby tells us, which is she's pretty, nice, and pretty. Is there anything you would like to add?"

Dori stopped eating and whipped her neck around to the main table. "She likes kids, too, Grandma." Nodding, Dori returned to her glass of milk.

Jet's expression became stoic. Levi already knew she was itching to get answers as well. Her argument would be it was too soon for him to move on. "I didn't know you were dating—seriously. Levi, I would sure want to get to know her."

I bet you would. He ignored his sister-in-law. There were a lot of reasons why the request wouldn't happen. The main one was that Jet would eat any woman alive who she even thought was interested in her late sister's husband and niece. The second was that Jet was plain evil—well, since Diane's death anyway.

"I did invite her, Mom, but Karyn and her church are serving Thanksgiving dinner at a homeless shelter." Levi felt proud of a woman who was busy with the Lord's business instead of busy in other folks' business. Karyn was like a jewel that Levi wanted to keep hidden as long as possible.

"How convenient," Jet said snidely.

"How humbling," his father complimented. "I guess if President Obama and his family can pass out Thanksgiving turkeys, we as a family should look for ways to bless others," Victor suggested.

Levi relaxed when the pending inquiries about Karyn turned into an open discussion of performing charity work. It was agreed the family would look into it for the following year. Then the clinking of a spoon against a crystal goblet got everyone's attention.

"We have an announcement," Levi's brother Seth said, commanding the room as he stood. He was Harvard educated and on the faculty at Washington University, a prestigious St. Louis university known for its medical research. Seth saw the good in everybody.

Seth and Solomon were six feet one, two inches taller than their big brother. Where Seth was easygoing, Solomon was quiet, almost sinister—if a person didn't know him. Solomon was a master at keeping his thoughts to himself; then at the midnight hour, he would show his hand. Solomon wouldn't trust anybody until he did a mental assessment on an individual's assets versus pitfalls.

Lifting a champagne glass of sparkling white grape juice, Seth smiled at Tia Rogers, his girlfriend of two years. She blushed. "Tia has finally agreed to marry me."

The congratulations exploded around the table. The men pushed back their chairs and started the ceremony of slapping Seth on the back. Sniffing, Sharon Tolliver smiled through joyful tears as she shoved the towering Tolliver men out of her way to get to her soon-to-be daughter-in-law.

"Hold on," Seth said firmly, lifting his hand. He snarled at Tia then winked. "It appears my woman wants a winter wedding as close as possible to Christmas next year." Seth appeared tortured. "That's twelve months, three hundred and sixty-five days—"

Tia shrugged. "What can I say? I'm into the white fur look."

Everyone chuckled, including Seth. "Although this woman is testing me to wait a year, if I need a snow plow to get to her, I'll put my order in now."

Not only did Tia and Seth complement each other physically, but they were each other's confidant. A few years after Levi lost Diane, he envied their relationship, but he couldn't begrudge them the once-in-a-lifetime happiness. They were Levi's inspiration to find happiness again.

He still couldn't believe he had told Karyn he was in love with her. Women held onto the L word as ransom. Not that it couldn't happen, but if it did, it had to be a woman as sweet and special as Karyn; but still, it was too soon for Levi.

In the midst of all the hoopla, Jet quietly stepped back and gave the future Mrs. Seth Tolliver a critical eye, as if Jet were born a Tolliver and had the right, instead of being Levi's late wife's sister—in essence, no blood relationship.

The family had learned when to tolerate Jet and when to ignore her. Since it was a day of thanksgiving, they tolerated her, knowing her loneliness was real.

Reluctantly, Jet embraced Tia. "Well, we'll have to spend more time together."

Seth huffed, Rossi smirked, and Levi adjusted his glasses. They all were thinking the same thing. Once again, Jet was sticking her nose in someone else's business, but Tia was the epitome of a strong black woman, and she could tangle with the devil and put up a good fight without the boxer Laila Ali, daughter of Muhammad Ali, as backup.

CHAPTER 16

Jesetta was hurt, upset, and downright mad. Depression and holidays were co-conspirators in her life. Her last good memory of Thanksgiving Day was at Diane and Levi's home in North St. Louis city five years ago. The couple had purchased the fixer-upper in an area on the verge of a rebirth. They had already sanded most of the hardwood floors and removed decaying wallpaper. It seemed so long ago.

Once dinner was finished at the Tollivers', the kitchen restored, and leftovers put away, Jet said her good-byes with a smile to mask the hurt that wouldn't heal. Driving back across the bridge into Illinois, Jet returned to her upscale, 2,500 square feet house.

Walking through the garage door to the kitchen, she disarmed her alarm. Jet flipped on every light en route to her bedroom. She changed into sweats before strolling into the adjoining media room, which had theater seating for twelve. Jet dropped the remote as soon as she picked it up.

She wandered through her house until settling into the living room, where she turned on her gas fireplace. Anchoring her elbows on the mantel, she rested her head on folded arms and stared into the instant flames. Without the Tollivers, Jet wouldn't have any family at all. Her parents, who were only children, were deceased. Her younger sister—her only sibling—who was now deceased, meant everything to her.

"I can't let the Olympic torch go out on Diane's memory." She wiped away a tear. Although she had an upper management position at one of the largest banking institutions in the area, a luxury car, two minks among her size twelve clothes, and the looks of a darker version of the once popular movie diva—turned author Pam Grier, anger woke her up in the morning and kept her going throughout the day—especially since one person involved in Diane's death had yet to be caught. Jet lived her days to see all of them die.

The bitterness that had consumed Levi was dissipating, which meant she would have to turn hers up more than a notch. Yes, Levi had the right to have another wife, but where did that leave Jet? She couldn't get another sister. She relocated from North St. Louis to Illinois to be close to her niece and to help Levi pick up the pieces.

With genuine love, she had driven thirty minutes one way into suburban downtown Clayton for work on a good day—fifty minutes when she was trapped in a traffic nightmare on others—for more than a year, until the bank officers noticed her commitment and performance. After that, the CEO created an impressive position with all the perks at their satellite location in the Metro-East area.

Lifting her head, Jet stared at her image in the deco-art mirror. Her face was pretty, but her heart sad. She had a curvaceous body endowed with the black-woman hips, and her height of five feet ten inches turned men's heads. Most of the time, she preferred her long hair to be natural and carefree. Jet could put Diana Ross to shame. Yet, her life was so empty that she might as well have no future.

Before her death, Diane had discussed all the dreams she had for Dori. Diane's happiness was so contagious that Jet was hoping to find a man as loving as Levi. She met men, but none had captured her heart. Jet even considered artificial insemination, so the sisters could be new mothers together. Their plans were dashed.

As Diane's lifeless body was lowered to the ground, Jet made a promise to fulfill all the dreams for Dori that Diane had planned. It wasn't just the fact her younger sister died before her, but her life was stolen, snatched away as if God didn't have any control over how Diane was to die. That was Jet's torment, knowing Diane had no say on how she left this earth.

"It's not fair," Jet whispered.

Months later, she even sought counseling from her former pastor.

"Reverend Joe, do I really have to forgive?" She held her breath, wondering if she really wanted to know. Regardless of the answer, her life wouldn't be the same.

He was trained in grief counseling. At Diane's funeral, he had given her a copy of Janice Harris Lord's book, *No Time for Goodbyes*.

"Forgiveness comes from the heart. If it's not in yours, Jesetta, then they're meaningless words. Right now, you need to cope, do whatever it takes for you to get up in the morning and go on with your life. I pray that your heart does find forgiveness, but be realistic. It may take a while, even years, so if anger is your coping skill, be angry."

Jet couldn't remember what else he said, but he gave her permission to be mad, establishing her new mission in life. She was angry that Thomas Foods stores didn't have night security, angry that Levi let Diane go out at night instead of going himself, angry that Levi and Diane wanted to live in a depressed area that was under rehab, angry that some people survived but her sister didn't. She was angry period.

To fuel her rage, she became an active member of the Victims' Advocate Crime Survivors. In the past four years, she hadn't missed an annual National Crime Victims' Rights Week.

Why did Diane die before her? Jet was the oldest. People didn't understand death had many definitions: natural death versus violent murder. Four years was four years. She wished she could move on, but how could God replace what the devil stole?

Tears stained her face. She wiped them away. She had made progress. Instead of having crying spells every day, she could hold out for weeks. One time, she made it to three months. Levi had fared better. Once Levi officially moved on past the grief, others would expect Jet to fall in line and let go emotionally. At least he found interest in another woman. No man could tolerate her crying binges.

The phone's insistent ringing interrupted her self-induced depression. She wasn't in the mood. TOLLIVER flashed on the caller ID. Clearing her throat, she sniffed before answering.

"Hello." She plastered a smile behind the words to pull off a lighthearted mood.

"I'm checking up on you," Rossi said cautiously. "You okay?"

Jet lifted a brow. The man seemed to know when she wasn't okay. "Didn't I look okay when you saw me a few hours ago?"

"Looks are deceiving. Your prayer around the table confirmed that you are still struggling. When Aunt Sharon mentioned Karyn, you almost broke out in a sweat."

"How observant, Minister Tolliver. If you want to pray for me, please do it when I'm not around. It's hard for me to talk to God when I know God allowed Diane to be murdered."

The line was quiet. Jet knew Rossi hadn't hung up on her. Maybe he was offering up a prayer on her behalf anyway. Did he and everyone else think she enjoyed living in misery? She wanted to be released from the cage she was in, but no one seemed to have a key that fit her lock to open the door.

"Jet, you know you're like a sister to the Tolliver men. If you need me, I'm here. I'm accessible twenty-four hours a day by cell—"

Sighing, Jet cringed. Rossi was starting to sound like those who had offered their condolences at the funeral and then went missing in action a month later. "I know, Rossi. I know."

"Okay, you can brush me off if you want, but you know Aunt Sharon will be calling next to check up on you."

Jet's eyes teared. "I know," she whispered, touched by their abundance of love as she said good-bye and disconnected.

Jesetta Hutchens would cross over one day. In the interim, she had two things to look forward to: an all-day shopping spree the next day on Black Friday, and meeting Karyn, Diane's competition.

CHAPTER 17

A decision had to be made. Levi's late wife, Diane, would always have a part of his heart. What remained of his life was fighting for fulfillment, happiness, and love. His eyes were set on Miss Karyn Wallace. Something about her made him utter the premature words *I love you*. Why? Could he fall in love again? It was a question he asked during his nightly prayers.

He considered himself a meat-and-potato man, even in pursuing a relationship. The bookstore meet-ups with Karyn weren't going to cut it for Levi. Salads were meant to be appetizers only, and seeing Karyn at work was just that. If she needed another dress, he would open a store charge account for her. Levi wanted Karyn.

The day after Thanksgiving, with Dori in tow, Levi returned to the bookstore, braving the weather, the sparse parking spaces, and the lunatics that apparently would fight over underwear for a bargain. If it was Victoria's Secret, he might agree, otherwise, Black Friday was a day for the crazies.

Worming their way through the store, the two searched for a petite woman in the thick of the customers. Levi spotted Karyn first. His heart shifted. That was going to be his woman. Levi tugged on Dori's hand. Although their joint mission was to surprise Karyn, Christmas toys and gifts distracted his daughter.

Squatting, Levi put a finger to his lips then pointed to where Karyn was stationed. Dori's eyes widened with excitement. Grinning, she was about to break away, but Levi gently restrained her. "Shhh. Let's surprise her. Okay?" He nodded.

"Yeah," she shouted, dancing in place.

Before Levi could stand, Dori yanked on his hand, almost dragging him forward. When they were within a foot of Karyn, Levi began to tiptoe and Dori mimicked.

"You missed some good cooking," Levi whispered in Karyn's ear as he and Dori snuck up behind her. Startled, she jumped, losing a few books to the floor. Levi steadied her before picking up the items. When she recognized her intruders, a beautiful smile weakened a frown that was sprouting on her forehead. Her eyes confirmed that she was glad to see him.

"Boo." Dori giggled, covering her mouth.

Dismissing Levi, Karyn knelt and gave Dori her full attention, welcoming his daughter's hug. Levi's mind clicked a mental picture. The affection was so thick he felt it.

As their embrace ended, Dori fingered Karyn's hair. Levi envisioned Karyn braiding Dori's hair somewhere in the near future.

"Miss Karyn, I read all the books you gave me," Dori started.

Gave? Levi grunted. Karyn sold him every last one of them.

"Mmm, and my momma's black-eyed peas were 'licious," Levi teased, vying for her attention as he rubbed his stomach. Through pockets of people, Levi eyed the approach of Karyn's archenemy. He wondered if the woman was ever in a good mood and what she had against Karyn.

"Come on, Karyn, we're swamped." Patrice's best imitation of a mug shot was the real thing. "I guess your boyfriend doesn't see we're swamped. I wish I didn't have to work the register and find books for the customers at the same time while you flirt. Can't you two—"

With his nostrils flaring, Levi gently moved Karyn to the side. Levi had enough. "And who do you have a problem with today? Me, Karyn, or my little girl?" Levi didn't want to act a fool. As a child, he didn't tolerate bullies—mainly because there were too many Tollivers—and he definitely had no mercy for them as adults.

She scanned him up and down. "Right now, I have a problem with my feet doing the job of two people," she said snidely. "I have diabetes and don't get good circulation. I've been diagnosed with arthritis in my lower back. Sometimes, I get heart palpitations. . . ."

Levi could hear God's voice reaching out to him, but he was shutting it out. He was about to exercise his free will, and he didn't want to hold his tongue. "If Karyn quits and walks out of this store, you're going to wish you had four people to replace her. Doesn't the store have a policy, the customer is always right? Right now your rudeness is offensive. My purchases—and I spend a lot of money—pay your salary."

As Patrice stormed off, he faced Karyn, who was holding Dori's small hand. He didn't know how Karyn would respond to him stepping in to defend her honor—being her protector—but hero worship was not shining in her eyes. She didn't appear to be impressed.

"What?" Levi hoped his face shone innocence.

"I believe in the Lord fighting my battles, Levi."

"He sent me."

***

One day, Patrice was going to mess with the wrong person. Karyn prayed she was not that person. It would be a test Karyn couldn't afford to fail. Maybe God would dispatch a person to give Patrice the whipping she was begging for. Buttercup wouldn't have any qualms about it, but the line was fine, and they had to keep their distance. Patrice wasn't worth violating parole and going back to jail.

Karyn's back was aching from being on her feet nonstop, helping one customer after another. Only in Levi's presence did Karyn seem to relax and every ounce of pain to cease.

Whatever was developing between her and Levi, if God didn't step in, Karyn wasn't sure she could stop it. Levi was becoming the next best thing after Jesus's salvation.

"Are you okay?" Levi's face was etched with concern.

"Yes."

"It's wild in here. Do you get a break?"

"If I can get out of here on time, it will be my break," she said.

Levi's adoration was tender. She couldn't believe she was the object of his affection.

"Miss Karyn, will you make a braid in my hair like yours?"

"Absolutely, but I can't now." Karyn squatted to Dori's level again. "Who combed your hair today?"

Dori was decked out in a candy apple–red corduroy jumper with a white turtleneck sweater splattered with printed red puppies. To finish her ensemble, she sported red Mary Jane shoes. The attempt to part her hair down the middle was a wasted effort.

"Daddy. When my auntie Jet doesn't wash and comb my hair, Daddy does it, but he lets me pick out my clothes." She grinned, sticking out her belly in pride.

Karyn glanced up at Levi. He shrugged and suddenly became interested in a book on a nearby bookshelf.

"The next time I see you, I'll do it." She stood. "Listen, I'd better go. It isn't fair to slack off. It's a madhouse."

"Okay." He leaned forward for her ears only. "How about dinner later? You know you ate my meal."

Karyn laughed, thinking how Buttercup had wolfed his food down. She then sobered. One day she was going to run out of excuses for why she didn't have the freedom of changing her plans. "Sorry. I promised my roommate that we'd do our own version of a girls' night out, but we're staying in. It's movies and popcorn tonight."

Levi's dimples appeared. It wasn't from a genuine smile. Clearly, his mouth was stretched in frustration. He nodded, seemingly accepting her answer. "Tomorrow?" he pushed.

"I'm studying at the library."

"Are you avoiding me?" Levi challenged. He folded his arms as a customer bumped him, trying to walk around him.

"Would I do that?" She managed an innocent smile. It didn't work.

"It doesn't matter, Karyn. We can't stop this wheel from rolling." He winked then glanced down at his daughter. "Tell Miss Karyn good-bye." After Dori waved, they turned, and Levi swaggered out of the bookstore with Dori skipping at his side.

CHAPTER 18

On Saturday morning, Levi woke with a smile on his lips. In his heart, he knew Karyn wasn't being coy—though maybe she was being cautious about a relationship with him. He surprised her with a wakeup call. He had memorized her phone number as she shouted out the digits. He had ached to talk to her the night he dropped her off, but she looked wiped out. He refrained Thanksgiving morning and then Thanksgiving night. Now, let the games begin.

"Good morning, Karyn," he greeted her as soon as she answered.

"Levi?" she said drowsily. "You remembered my number?"

He was still in bed with his back propped against the pillows. It wouldn't be long before Dori would wake, ready for breakfast. He chuckled. "I never forget things I want to remember."

After a few moments of silence, Karyn said, "Oh."

"Did you enjoy your girls' night out?"

"We stayed in, and I did."

"Good, because today you'll enjoy the Tollivers."

Her voice revealed she was fully alert. "Levi, I told you I have to study at the library."

"Which one?"

"Fairview Heights. Why?"

"Would you like for me and Dori to pick you up?"

"That's sweet, but I have a few stops to make before I get there."

"Tolliver's taxi service." He saluted as if she could see him. "You can enjoy the comfort of leather seats at no charge." That got a laugh out of her, and he joined in.

"It's tempting, but no thank you. Maybe next time."

"Watch what you say to me, Karyn, because there will always be a next time."

Karyn didn't respond, which was fine. Levi was using shock treatment to the max. He had been in a drought, until God opened the windows of heaven. It wasn't a drenching, but the sprinkles gave him new life by way of Karyn. She wasn't going to get rid of him.

"What time are you planning to arrive at the library?"

"About noon. Why?"

"Dori and I will be waiting for you." *Click.* Levi grinned.

Before he shaved and showered, he slid to his knees. Closing his eyes, he concentrated on what to say to the Lord. "Jesus, it's been so long since I've done my morning routine of thanksgiving. Please forgive me. Lord, thank you for the season in my life. . . ."

Levi didn't realize he had been in prayer for almost an hour until he opened his eyes. Dori was in his bed, quietly waiting for him to finish.

"Hi, Daddy." Dori rubbed her eyes. "I'm hungry."

"Already? I just fed you," he teased.

"But that was last night. It's gone." She sat up.

Laughing at her innocence, he scooped her up in his arms as he stood. He swiped his glasses off the nightstand and placed Dori on her feet. Taking her hand, he led her to her bathroom to wash her up. It was time to start a new day.

After breakfast, television occupied Dori as Levi showered and dressed. He kept checking his watch. Whatever time Karyn got to the library, he and Dori would be waiting. Count on it.

Levi finished dressing Dori. Like any man, he wanted his daughter to have long hair, but her length was, at times, too much to handle. Thank God he had mastered one ponytail. He added three colorful barrettes to her hair for decorations in no specific pattern.

"Daddy, can I bring my books to the library?" Dori asked, trying to balance a stack that reached her chin. Minutes earlier, he had told his daughter about an impromptu field trip to Fairview Heights Library. Dori could barely contain her excitement. When she learned they were meeting Karyn there, she was ecstatic.

"You don't have to." He grinned, sharing her enthusiasm. "They'll have plenty of them for you to read."

"Can I bring them all home?"

His little bookworm. She was as perfect as any child could be. Dori preferred books over video games. Her interest was piqued once she had met Karyn. "Some, but not all."

"Do you think she'll braid my hair if I bring my comb, Daddy?"

There was no guessing who the "she" was. Levi had become accustomed to Dori's rapid subject change. Plus, he knew Dori couldn't talk about books without adding Karyn's name somewhere into the conversation. That's how his parents had come to know of Karyn, though they had yet to put a face with the name. After cookies and milk, story time at his parents' house had become an enlightening event.

"I think she would do it with her fingers if you ask her."

"Yay."

Within minutes, father and daughter were bundled up as they walked out of the house to brave the November temperatures and got into the car. Dori was a ball of bright colors in her purple coat and multicolored cap with matching scarf and gloves. Jammed inside one pocket was a large, wide-tooth plastic comb. Levi chuckled at his baby girl. She was just as enamored with Karyn as he was.

Dori climbed into her booster seat and fastened her strap. Levi double checked it before driving off.

Dori's excitement about Karyn was somehow different from that of seeing his mother or Jet. Dori loved her grandma and expected to see her aunt on alternating weekends, but the anticipation about seeing Karyn trumped everything.

It took Levi less than seventeen minutes to drive to the library on Bunkum Road. He had passed the one-level modern brick structure many times, and it never dawned on him to take Dori there. Their weekend activities were basically movies, toy shopping, visiting relatives, and church when they didn't stay in. As he turned into the side parking lot, he checked his rear-view mirror. No buses were in sight. He had timed his arrival to be early.

Getting out, they looked for a bus stop sign near the library entrance. It didn't take him long to realize something was definitely wrong with this scenario. The CEO of Tollivers Real Estate and Development was standing in the cold, waiting on a bus that his woman—almost his lady—was using as transportation. It was so unbelievable that Levi had to chuckle. This was different.

He whipped out his cell phone. If she wasn't right around the corner literally, he was taking Dori inside. Levi punched in Karyn's number. "We're waiting." Karyn laughed. He loved the sound. "It's cold out here." His teeth chattered. "Brrr."

"Welcome to my world. My bus was late. We're turning the corner now. Hey, I see you. You shouldn't have Dori out in the cold," she fussed.

The bus driver, who was manhandling the number twelve St. Clair MetroBus like a reindeer, came to an abrupt halt. Levi blinked and pushed Dori back as a precaution. Truck drivers didn't own the roads; they lost that honor to the bus drivers. The doors opened, and Karyn began her descent.

"Hi, Miss Karyn. Hi!" Dori shouted, jumping up and down, impatient for her attention.

Her smile was the first thing that touched Levi's heartstrings. Using a firm grip, he helped her off the bus and retrieved the backpack dangling from her shoulder. "Hey, you."

"Hey yourself."

"Miss Karyn, I brought mine too." Dori grinned and lifted her pink-and-brown vinyl Snoopy backpack.

Karyn *ooh*ed over it, causing Dori to deepen her giggles. Levi captured the scene with his mind's lens, admiring Karyn's worn jeans, which outlined God's perfection. She enhanced her look with a multicolored striped turtleneck. She wasn't in anything dressier than when she wore her work uniform. One thing that didn't change on her crowning glory—the single plait. When Karyn shivered in her functional jacket, Levi gathered his party and guided them up the stairs to the entrance.

After opening the door for the ladies, Levi took in the inviting atmosphere. The gray carpet, fuchsia padded chairs, and the sporadic placement of plants seemed to nourish the pleasure of reading. "This is nice. I've never been in here before."

"You should've. It's your tax dollars working."

"Wow, Daddy," Dori said in awe. She looked at Karyn. "Did they buy all these books from your store, Miss Karyn?"

Levi and Karyn exchanged an amused expression.

"No, no." Karyn shook her head. "The books at my store you have to pay for—"

"Humph. Tell me about it," Levi mumbled.

Karyn squinted, then finished. "These books are free—once your daddy gets you a library card."

Dori's eyes widened. "Can you, Daddy?"

He nodded as they wandered through the aisles. Dori released his hand, but not Karyn's.

He smirked. The day would give him plenty of Kodak moments. "Hey, why don't we get her settled with some books, then I can watch you do your homework. As a matter of fact, I might even help you."

"Right." Karyn murmured, shaking her head.

Slipping out of her coat and yanking off her hat and scarf, Dori left them in Levi's care; then she rested at a round, bright yellow kiddies' table with four chairs. She folded her hands and waited expectantly for Karyn to pick out books. Levi lounged nearby. Stretching his legs, he admired Karyn doing her thing as she scanned through books as if she were in a kitchen, looking for recipes.

A few minutes later, Karyn chose her selections. "Okay, Dori, I think you'll like these," Karyn decided, squatting next to the table. Dori fingered Karyn's locks "Would you like me to braid your hair?"

Dori nodded and leaped off the chair. She ran to where Levi was sitting and sifted through their coats. Grinning when she found her comb, Dori danced in place. When she was about to yell, Karyn put her finger to her lip to shush Dori. "Remember, we have to be quiet in here."

Levi absentmindedly shoved their coats aside, creating space for Karyn to sit and perform her magic. Dori dragged a kiddies' chair to Karyn's legs and sat expectantly. Unsnapping the hair barrettes, Karyn began to finger-comb long strokes through Dori's hair. Dori remained quiet and content.

Bored from lack of attention, Levi scooted closer and stretched his arm on the back of Karyn's chair. Of their own volition, his fingers began to play in Karyn's hair. Within minutes, Levi twirled loose strands from her braid around his finger. "I'd like to see your hair in curls again. They were beautiful."

Turning, Karyn tilted her head and met his stare. Whatever she was thinking and about to say, she held her tongue. Lifting his brow, he smirked. He wished he were privy to her thoughts as he tried to read the emotions playing out in her eyes—she was affected by him. Good. When he fiddled with his mustache, Karyn returned to Dori's hair.

A calm feeling seemed to settle around Levi. He had Karyn Wallace all to himself. Even if she had to study, her presence gave him peace. In record time, Karyn was finished and his little girl was a miniature version of her idol.

"Daddy, you like it?" Dori asked, grinning as if his opinion didn't count.

"You've never been more beautiful," Levi said with adoration.

"Like Miss Karyn?"

"Yes," he whispered. "Just like Miss Karyn. Now, you'd better get started reading all those books. We're going to move to that table." He pointed to a section that offered him some privacy, but was close enough to keep an eye on Dori.

Five minutes into Karyn opening her book and organizing papers, Levi knew he wouldn't be satisfied just watching. It was selfish to disturb her, but he would make it up to her.

"How many more credits do you need before you graduate?" he asked her.

"Six," Karyn answered, followed by a sigh.

Levi pushed back his chair from the table to relax as he crossed his ankle over his knee. "Congratulations. You're almost there."

She smiled. "Yeah."

Evidently, Karyn wasn't easily distracted, and her one-word responses proved that. Then she revealed she was a business major. "I'm tweaking my SWOT."

He grinned, recalling his SWOT analysis: Strengths of his real estate and development company; potential weaknesses, opportunities, and finally threats. "Really? Mind if I see?" Levi glanced over his shoulder at Dori. She was gripping her single braid as if it were an anchor. Smiling, Levi pulled closer to the table, invading Karyn's space.

She slid the clipboard in front of him. She had scribbled several notes and had revised her business proposal. Her mission statement was clear, her projections realistic, and costs conservative. Karyn was thorough.

He was impressed. Levi laid his hand on top of her work, as if he were safekeeping her document. "Okay, beautiful. Clearly, you rank high on the intellectual stage, so why are you working at the bookstore? Benefits with an entry-level job in Corporate America would finish paying for school."

Karyn gazed at their surroundings as she struggled to answer. She checked on Dori a couple of times and began to fidget. "Levi, it's a long story."

"I'm in no hurry, and by the stack of books Dori's collected, she isn't in a rush either. At least those books won't cost me." He grinned and nodded toward his little girl. "Look at her. I wonder if she'll let go of her Karyn Wallace braid. Now, back to you."

"I have a saying: Just because I'm not at the place where I want to be doesn't mean I won't get there. It should be obvious that I don't have a lot of money. Does my not working in Corporate America make me any less—?"

He lifted his hands. "There is nothing about you I would change. You are the most humble woman—no, person—I've ever met. Okay, sell me on this Crowning Glory venture." Levi smirked. "Hearing that name reminds me of your hair stacked in a mass of curls. Lord have mercy, you were gorgeous in that dress on our first date, and I lost it."

"You needed someone to listen, and I didn't mind." Her expression was tender, not judgmental. Her hands covered his. "Your last statement is typical. Men think—and some women too—that hair defines a woman. She is so much more than that, and her needs are more than a shampoo. Inspired by our church's prison ministry, my two business partners and my goals are when a customer leaves our shop, we want her to glow with a physical crown backed up by spiritual authority, reminding her of her royalty status because of her connection with Jesus.

"My roommate and I have been saving money, and we've already been looking for a start-up location. We figure we might get a deal if we do some sweat equity on a former storefront business. We would set up an area for product applications, such as hands-on makeup demos, individual bath soaps for every mood, trendy hairstyles, and facial massages. The final touch is a brief ceremonial placing of a tiara on every woman's head before she leaves; then we'll present her with a small gold-foiled book with a scripture for every day of the week. Crowning Glory is more than a business."

She held Levi captive. He was caught up in her excitement.

"Our target audience is those who are trying to make positive changes in their lives and need second chances to prove their worth." She finished her impromptu presentation with a deep breath.

"Sounds like you're reaching out to those who have been hurting." Again, Levi thought that maybe she had been in an abusive relationship. How could he ask her about it without making her feel uncomfortable? Levi decided to bide his time and wait for her to know she could trust him with anything.

Tilting her head, she thought about it and then nodded. "I guess we are. Who knows? We might be able to get a nonprofit status if we achieve our goals."

He wanted to be her benefactor. He believed in her dreams. "Karyn, I have some property you and your group might be interested in."

"Levi, I accepted the dress and a ride, but certain things I can't accept, period."

His suspicions were growing. Something happened in her life and she didn't want it to happen to her again or someone else. *Lord, help her to open up to me.* He had other questions he could ask. "I see. Well, tell me about Karyn Wallace. What about your sisters, brothers, parents? Are you close?"

Dori picked the worst time to become restless. Still clenching her braid, she abandoned her table for theirs. She was heading to Karyn when Levi scooped her up. When he was about to tug on her braid, she protested.

"Don't touch it, Daddy. You'll mess it up."

"Yes, madam." He glanced over at Karyn, who had the nerve to giggle while he was reprimanded.

"I'm getting hungry. Can we have McDonald's?"

"Sure. Why not? Go back to your table and give me and Miss Karyn a few more minutes, okay?"

"Why can't I sit with you and Miss Karyn, Daddy?"

Before he could answer, Karyn stood and stole her off his lap and onto hers when she sat. "Sure you can." Dori shifted until she was comfortable.

Lifting a brow, Levi folded his arms. "I'm waiting, Karyn. Tell me about your family."

She lowered her eyes and took a deep breath. "My relationship is strained ever since my mother died while I was in college. She was a good woman. My younger sister, Nalani, and I took it hard. My father was devastated."

That explained Karyn's compassion. She had dealt with loss. He prayed it wasn't tragic.

"Dad's grief consumed him until it overpowered him. I couldn't wait to leave for college."

"Which school?"

"Northwestern in Chicago."

"Good choice." He nodded in approval.

"Anyway, my father and I separated on bad terms. I haven't seen him and Nalani in years. In a few months, I hope to take the train to see them."

A few months? A train? "Karyn, I have a car and I would be more than happy to drive you. I know your money is tight."

"Thank you, but—"

"Don't tell me thank you but no thank you. When I offer you anything, there are no strings attached."

"There are always strings attached. What about that dress?"

Levi gritted his teeth. She called him on his own words. "I wanted you to go out with me. I preferred it to be my sooner rather than your later. I'm sorry I interrupted your study time, but I'm not sorry I'm here with you. Little by little, I learn more about you. I want to know about your happy times and sad times. Fill in the holes."

"Daddy, I'm really getting hungry." Dori's stomach growled to prove it.

"Okay." Levi stood and grabbed their jackets. "Spend the rest of the day with us, Karyn."

She checked her watch and grimaced. "Ah, I better not."

"A man has only so much tolerance for rejection, Karyn. Don't wear me down." Levi reached for their coats. It was a struggle for him to put Dori's hat back on. She was on the verge of becoming hostile as she fussed about messing up her hair. Finally, Karyn assisted him. "Okay, break my heart, but don't disappoint my little girl. You know she's expecting you to come."

Karyn stood, gnawing on her bottom lip. She had a slight panicked expression. "Let me use the bathroom."

"Can I come too, Miss Karyn?"

"Sure," Karyn said after a brief hesitation. She grabbed Dori's hand and her cell phone off the table, leaving her purse.

Levi always thought a woman's handbag never left her sight, especially on a trip to the ladies' room. A few minutes later, Karyn walked out, ending a call. "Okay, McDonald's it is."

His heart pricked again.

CHAPTER 19

Hours later, Karyn was exhausted when Levi parked in front of the New Beginnings building. Besides taking Dori to McDonald's, they had attended a Disney movie in the same shopping complex—against her better Holy Ghost judgment and in spite of the consequences.

"I've had a good time today, Levi." Karyn couldn't put words to her feeling of contentment.

"Next time, let's plan something more upscale, just me and you." He lifted a brow in a silent challenge.

Karyn thought Dori—who had started dozing since leaving the theater—perked up when the car came to a stop. "You're supposed to kiss her good-bye, Daddy. That's what the frog did to the princess."

"That's right," he drawled out. Levi formed a mischievous grin, showcasing his dimples. "Are you calling me a frog?" he had teased his daughter.

Dori giggled. "No. Miss Karyn is a princess." She began to unbuckle the strap on her booster seat. "But we have to walk her to the door like in the movies," she cheered.

Levi performed his daughter's bidding by getting out of the car. He then helped Karyn and Dori. So many emotions were going through Karyn's head. This was not ten o'clock when the center was about to be on lockdown for the night. It was early evening when other questionable people could be entering or leaving, or a police cruiser could pull up at any minute. The scenarios were unlimited. She knew the probability of them having a long term relationship was not good, but she didn't want it to end in front of other ex-convicts. She swallowed and stopped them before they got to the door. "Well, thanks again."

"I'll close my eyes, Daddy, so you can kiss her real good like the frog." Dori did just that. It was so cute. Seconds later, Dori asked with her hands covering her face, "Did you kiss her yet, Daddy?"

Karyn stared at Levi. She didn't know what message he was reading in her eyes: pleading for him to go, or preparing for his sweet kiss. Their stare was longer than the kiss, but Levi didn't disappoint her, mumbling afterward.

Dori, who had been peeping, giggled. "See, Daddy. I told you that's what the frog did."

Laughing, Karyn said good-bye and went inside with her heart pounding. Today was the first time Karyn had ever gone somewhere unauthorized. That could never happen again. Her caseworker had cleared her for McDonald's, not a movie. She had come too far, and she wasn't about to violate her parole for Disney or any other character.

Karyn opened the door to her suite to find Buttercup experimenting again. Her roommate was rummaging through a freezer-size Ziploc bag containing lipsticks and eye shadow cases.

With black eyeliner, Buttercup had drawn a raggedy circle on the right side of her face, encompassing her eyebrow, eye, and upper cheekbone. She had shaded one area grass green. Now, she was about to add pink. Karyn shook her head. Buttercup was back to her salute-to-sororities kick. Karyn had grown accustomed to her creative nature.

"Hey, the library must have had a reading marathon. You've been gone almost the entire day."

"I did go to the library, but I wasn't alone." She placed her apartment key on a wall hook.

"And?" Buttercup squinted, leaning forward for an explanation. "Where's your backpack? I thought we were going to go over the Crowning Glory proposal this afternoon."

"Oh, no." Karyn collapsed against the wall. She let go of her purse, which spilled its contents once it hit the floor. Groaning, she stomped her foot in frustration. "I must have left it in Levi's car."

"Levi?" Buttercup grinned. "Yes!" She took spirited Indian powwow steps. Within minutes, she came to a complete halt before lifting a pink brow and wiggling it. "Hmm. So what's the Levi latest?"

"Forget the update. I need that backpack."

"Forget that old proposal," Buttercup argued. "I need details."

Karyn paced the floor. "You knew he called me this morning before I left."

Buttercup nodded.

"Well, Levi offered me a ride to the library. I declined. He said he would be there when I arrived. Levi made good on his promise. He was waiting for me in front of the library when I got off the bus." Karyn smiled. "Actually, it was charming."

Buttercup sighed. "Ah, how romantic. That man really likes you, and you like him. See, it's not so bad to take a chance, but this is getting serious."

"You're telling me." Karyn matched Buttercup's sigh and wrestled out of her jacket. She flopped on the sofa. "Just so you know, I got little done at the library, thanks to Levi."

Buttercup mumbled, "Levi will get no thanks from me on that."

"Anyway, we left the library and took Dori to Mc-Donald's, then we went to Weinberg Theater to see the latest Disney movie."

"Wait a minute." Buttercup bucked her eyes. "Your caseworker allowed you to alter your schedule? She must've been feeling generous."

Karyn gritted her teeth. "I kinda pushed my luck going to the movie. Otherwise, I was going to have to come up with something to tell Levi that was close to the truth without telling him the truth. Maybe I could ask Monica about wearing an ankle bracelet." Karyn laughed.

"Nope. Those things definitely aren't fashionable. Remember Madea?" She shrugged. "Be careful. Violating parole is easier than getting out of prison."

"Noted." Karyn had never been so scared. She'd lost count of the number of times she discreetly looked over her shoulders.

"Now, get to the good stuff. Did the man kiss you?" Buttercup asked. "He blew it on the first date. You reported the other night when he dropped you off there was no smooching, so I'm hoping the third time is a charm."

"Yes, and he whispered it was not the best he could do."

"Whew." Buttercup jumped up. "Girl, let me get my church fan. As Nelly, the rapper, said years ago, it's getting hot in herre."

"Yes. My lips"—she paused—"still tingle. It was chaste, but I almost cried. I felt so wanted."

"That's because maybe you are wanted." Buttercup lifted her voice then softened it. "You've got to tell him, Karyn."

"I gave Levi the perfect opening today at the library when he asked me about my business plan. We discussed Crowning Glory and how the name reminds him of my hair. I told him our business would be a ministry for giving second chances to those who fell by the wayside."

"Some people aren't smart enough to get the hints, especially men. God is fighting your battles. You should've told him."

"He rambled on about the mass amount of property his company owns and how basically he was willing to help me with no strings attached. There are always strings."

Buttercup lifted a hand, showing off her fingernails, which were painted in high-gloss red. "No strings are good. Cross out everything I just told you. Don't tell him."

That was too easy for Buttercup to agree with her. Karyn squinted. She knew her reasons, but what was her roommate withholding? "Why?"

Buttercup stood and began to pace their cubbyhole. "Remember the pact?"

"Yeah, the book about some thugs who went on to become doctors. I read it. It's a bestseller."

"Not that. Our pact—you, me, and Halo. Crowning Glory will not only provide jobs for ex-offenders, but will encourage newly released convicts physically and spiritually. We've been praying that God will make a way. I'd say Levi Tolliver is our way."

Shaking her head, Karyn stood. This was adding too much pressure to her so-called simple life. She headed to her bedroom door to unlock it. She didn't lock it because she didn't trust Buttercup; it was another one of the house rules. Karyn sighed. "No way. Forget it."

"It was a self-serving thought, huh?" Buttercup claimed Karyn's vacated spot and grabbed the TV remote. "We don't have to shout to the mountaintop our sins, but isn't there at least one relationship you value that is good enough to share a secret? I say be prayerful. Maybe fifteen years down the road when you're a successful business owner of several chains, your past will be a testimony. Until then, you've got a series of tests."

"You are really irritating me. You aren't in my shoes. You served time for check fraud. I served time for manslaughter. You're dating Halo undercover until you're both off parole. There are no secrets between the two of you. Levi lost his wife to violence. That makes me and Levi on opposite sides of the fence."

Karyn's cell phone chimed a soft rendition of the gospel song "His Eye Is on the Sparrow." She checked the ID: LEVI. "I'll talk to him later."

"You better be talking to him now and think hard about crossing over to the other side of the fence."

Pushing on, Karyn drowned out Buttercup's guilt trip. She walked into her bedroom and closed the door. "Hi."

"You've lost something, and I found it. Imagine that." Levi chuckled.

"Yeah, I realized that when I came inside my apartment empty handed. I'll get it from you," she said, wanting to get off the phone. Levi had other ideas.

"I really enjoyed you, and Dori is in bed determined to sleep in one position so she won't mess up her hair."

Karyn smiled then cleared her throat. "I've got to go. I'm almost out of minutes."

"Now, that I might believe. Good night, Karyn, and sweet dreams, baby."

CHAPTER 20

Wake up. Wake up, Rossi, and pray.

Moaning, Rossi stirred then did the opposite and snuggled deeper into his pillow. He pulled his comforter over his head to block out the antagonist.

Wake up, Rossi, and pray! God thundered.

Rossi's spirit quickened. He sat up with his heart pounding as if a drill sergeant had shouted orders. Fully alert now, Rossi heard nothing. He blinked, disoriented, waiting for further instructions. God didn't disturb his sleep for nothing. It had happened a few other times when something big was going down, as Rossi always told himself.

Sliding to his knees, Rossi dared not lay his head on his mattress. Not only was he a light sleeper, but when he was tired, he would fall asleep immediately. "Lord, what should I pray for?"

With force and speed, the Lord cut him off, filling Rossi's mouth with an explosion of tongues. The prayer was intense and exhausting. What Rossi heard and his mind interpreted astonished him.

Levi is blind and cannot see. I speak to him and he cannot hear. Therefore, you are his shepherd. Lead him.

"Me?" Rossi's heart pounded with concern for his cousin. Intercessory prayer was one thing, and living an exemplary Christian life was another. What kind of stuff was Levi getting himself into that he needed help to get out?

The room was quiet, but Rossi knew he was still in God's presence, so he called out to Him. "Lord Jesus, I am your servant, but yet a man. Give me spiritual strength, discernment, and guide me because you are the Great Shepherd."

Staying on his knees, Rossi whispered and talked to God until he felt his confidence return. Opening his eyes, he worshipped God by lifting his hands in praise and thanksgiving. Standing, Rossi danced before the Lord in victory. Finally, he laughed. "Satan, you are already defeated." Rossi glanced at the clock: five o'clock on Sunday morning. He was too keyed up to return to sleep, so he sat on his bed and turned on the lamp.

Rossi believed God always backed up his message during prayer with scriptures from His Word. Reaching for his Bible, Rossi opened it to a folded page he had previously marked with notes: Proverbs, the third chapter. He scanned the passage until verse five leaped off the page: *Trust in the LORD with all thine heart; and lean not unto thine own understanding.*

He continued to read the entire chapter and then meditated on verse five as he closed his Bible. After stretching his muscles, he crossed the room and walked down the hall to his home gym. As he worked out on the treadmill then lifted weights, he didn't allow his mind to stray from the morning's events. One thing was for sure: It was the unknown that had Rossi concerned.

Forty-five minutes later, he headed for the shower. Once the warm water beamed on his back, he began a congregational song, "Oh, the Blood of Jesus." He repeated the chorus until the water cooled.

Finished with his shower, Rossi continued humming as he prepared to shave. He didn't wait for the steam to evaporate on his mirrors as he grabbed another towel to wipe a circle.

He stared at his dark reflection, admiring the richness of his black skin. He wiggled his brows. Grinning, he noted his healthy teeth, which he whitened at least once a year. Rossi was six feet five and maintained a healthy weight of 225 pounds. It would be 228 pounds soon if he didn't stay away from his mother's homemade peanut butter cookies.

The sisters at his church often commented that he had the body of an athlete—push-ups and boxing did wonders for his cardio. At thirty-three, he still had a head of thick, African-textured hair. He was blessed, considering some younger men's hair had started to thin, and some, to his horror, felt they had no other option but to sport the bald head.

Rossi was determined to hold on to every strand as long as he could, but with that came gray strands. He wondered how many more would be added after this morning's prayer. "I have the victory," he said to himself, accepting Levi's trial that he didn't ask for; but he loved his cousin.

As he foamed up his jaw to shave, he contemplated whether he wanted the hassle of growing a beard. "Nah." Minutes later, after he performed his task, the phone rang. He picked up the wall extension in the bathroom.

"Hey," Levi greeted.

Rossi raised a brow. His slow-waking cousin was too chipper for an early Sunday morning. Plus, Rossi knew Levi had spent the previous day with Karyn. On alert, Rossi mentally clocked in for his spiritual bodyguard duty. "What's up?"

"I'm just giving you a heads up. Dori and I are visiting Crowns for Christ today."

"Karyn," Rossi deducted with a smirk. It was time for him to meet her.

"You know it."

Rossi imagined Levi's jubilant expression.

"I'm going along with you."

"You? Why? You never miss our church service, even when you're sick, believing by faith that God could heal you, which Jesus has on many occasions."

Rossi was already on God's clock regardless of the location. "I'm good. I've wanted to visit Elder Scaife's church for a long time."

They agreed to meet at Crowns for Christ at eleven in the lobby. Rossi had plenty of time to fix breakfast and relax. An hour later, Rossi was dressed in his charcoal-gray suit. After checking his watch, he still had a few minutes. Rossi strolled over to his office-size windows, which offered a magnificent view of the Cardinals' ballpark village and the St. Louis Gateway Arch.

A blizzard of snowflakes drifted in the air, but none seemed to stick to the ground. Looking out of his window always gave him the sense of being larger than life—a man who had God's favor and salvation, disposable income, and the potential for a lavish lifestyle if he was foolish enough to chase it.

Rossi was reminded he didn't have anyone special in his life. He reflected on the church sisters—young, his age, and a little older—waiting for his call. There was something about those pickings that made him think he would probably never call any of them.

Rossi Tolliver dated for keeps. He just hadn't found the right combination of looks and tempered spirit. Most of the sisters' agendas were snagging a minister, but God hadn't shown him the right woman. Huffing, he checked his watch one last time and pushed off the wall, whispering, "Remember me, Lord."

CHAPTER 21

Karyn believed in prayer, but she hadn't been praying about her involvement with Levi. She was scared what God would say about the matter. Some women had said God always told them the opposite of what they wanted to hear—basically, give the man up. For some reason, Karyn had an inkling that wasn't the direction God had for her.

What if the Lord said Levi was her destiny? Why couldn't her emotions be in sync with her heart? She wasn't prepared for a relationship.

Trust me, God spoke. *Unlike man, I make no mistakes.*

Karyn sighed. What did that mean? Suddenly, Buttercup elbowed her right before they reached the foyer of their transitional home to wait for the church van.

Annoyed, Karyn frowned. She had to crane her neck higher since Buttercup was sporting her new stilettos. "What did you do that for?"

"Stop thinking over there. I told you, you make my head hurt when you're too quiet," she complained, struggling to balance on the four-plus-inch shoes.

Thinking? Karyn was trying to talk to God. She didn't respond. They signed out at the desk when they heard Deacon Deacon honk the horn. Buttercup hurried and used the door handle to steady herself. Once she cracked it open, a gust of wind pushed them back.

"Whoa. Of all the days for it to snow, why today?" Buttercup griped. "These are three-hundred-dollar suede boots," she shrieked in horror.

"You got them off the clearance stack for twenty bucks," Karyn said.

"That's not the point, okay?" Buttercup said.

Residents at the center were only allowed a certain number of personal items, including clothes and shoes. Buttercup's new boots made her two pairs over the limit. Karyn rubbed her forehead in mock pain. "Now you're going to give me a headache if you don't stop fussing. Anyway, it's only flurries."

"Ha! Right. We'll come out of church and just my luck, there'll be a foot of snow."

Usually Karyn had to take extra strides to keep up with her friend's long legs. This morning, it was the opposite as they made their way down the walkway and greeted Deacon Deacon.

"Sister Buttercup Williams, do you need a cane? I'm sure Mother Caldwell will let you use hers." He grinned.

"'Okay, Deacon Deacon, you can joke, but if I fall, guess who has to pick me up?" Buttercup responded.

Deacon rushed to her. "Can't let that happen."

Drama. Buttercup's drama never ceased, even in her sleep. On more than one occasion after Buttercup had retired to bed early so her skin cells could rejuvenate, Karyn overhead Buttercup yelling in her sleep, apparently having a nightmare. Before Karyn could check on her, Buttercup had awakened and laughed at herself, then fallen back asleep.

Although the snow wasn't accumulating, it was creating a few slick spots. Since Deacon Deacon and Buttercup were moving at a snail's pace, Karyn beat them to the waiting van. A teenager inside the van descended the steps to assist Karyn. A chorus of "Praise the Lord" greeted her, and the energy of the van riders' love warmed and embraced her.

"Good morning, sugar," Mother Caldwell said. "I see your roommate is trying to look cute again. I hope she doesn't hurt Deacon, because he's the best driver—well, sometimes—that the church has had." She patted the space next to her. "Come sit by me. Buttercup can sit by herself until Halo gets on."

Karyn obliged and kissed the woman's powdered cheek.

"Don't you look pretty this morning, and I like your hair in curls. Red is your color." She leaned closer. "I'll have to tell you about another thrift store. They get designer clothes, and everything is under ten bucks."

Between Buttercup experimenting with Karyn's hair on the weekends and Mother Caldwell's fashion suggestions, Karyn was gaining more confidence.

Once Deacon Deacon made it to the van, he released Buttercup, who appeared to be supporting him. Climbing the stairs, Buttercup stood taller. In her heels, the crown of her head touched the ceiling. Deacon brought up the rear, rubbing his back as he slid behind the wheel.

"Praise the Lord." Buttercup addressed everybody as she flopped into an empty seat.

When the deacon pulled off, Mother Caldwell didn't waste any time snooping into Karyn's business. The elderly woman's eyes sparkled with mischief; her dentures aligned perfectly as she smiled. "So, how's that young man of yours?"

"She's scared," Buttercup answered from across the aisle before Karyn could respond. Winking as if she had checkmate, Buttercup reclined in her seat, resembling a wild turkey with her headband made of dark feathers.

"Well, as Luther Vandross says, there is the power of love," Mother Caldwell said.

"But we aren't in—" Karyn had started.

"It's just a matter of time!" Buttercup interrupted, changing places so she could elbow Karyn.

"We're pulling for you, Sister Karyn. Nothing stands in the way of a man in love. Ask my wife." Deacon Deacon laughed as he stopped for his next pickup.

Halo stepped on. He spoke to every person then lingered at Buttercup's side before taking his reserved spot next to her. It was a routine he developed to disguise his interest in Buttercup, since they were both on parole. Everyone on the bus knew Halo and Buttercup loved each other.

At least Buttercup had somebody. The pair had no secrets. Soon they would be starting over together, once they were released from parole.

CHAPTER 22

Levi smirked as he pulled into Crowns for Christ's parking lot. Rossi was already there, standing inside the church's lobby, alternating between speaking with some unknown brother—although Rossi seemed to know everybody—and peeping out the door for Levi.

"Figures he's early," Levi mumbled under his breath. "The man doesn't have a daughter to primp."

A few minutes later, he located a space near Rossi's vehicle. The building was an intimidating, long, one-story edifice with multiple steeples. Once he parked and made sure Dori was bundled up, they got out. The snow had ceased and left behind a thin dusting.

With a firm grip on Dori's tiny right hand, Levi guided her to the glass double doors with Karyn's backpack in the other. Immediately, the Tolliver men embraced while Dori vied for Rossi's attention.

"See my hair, Cousin Rossi. Miss Karyn did it." She smiled and added a curtsy. Her eyes sparkled with excitement as she practically ripped off the buttons on her coat to show him her dress.

He lifted Dori into his arms. He kissed her cheek and tickled her neck. "You'll be the prettiest girl in church."

"And Miss Karyn too." Dori nodded.

Levi shrugged as he shook out of his wool trench coat. Rossi would soon see for himself why Levi's recovery seemed so instant. "Come on. Let's find us a seat," Levi said.

Crowns for Christ's ushers, men dressed in black suits and white gloves, stood nearby, waiting to lead them inside the sanctuary. Peering through a ceiling-to-floor clear wall, Levi noted the congregation wasn't as large as his church, Living for Jesus—maybe three or four hundred compared to his thousand-plus membership, but without an usher, Levi didn't see how they would find a seat, because practically everyone was standing during praise and worship.

The lobby floor was a coordinated effort of mahogany and bleached-white wood planks. As they opened the door to the sanctuary, they almost had to step up to the plush carpet.

Levi smiled at the eagerness on his daughter's face. When she learned they were visiting Karyn's church, she couldn't get ready fast enough. She put her red patent leather shoes on the wrong feet. She had forgotten to brush her teeth. Levi corrected those oversights, but she wouldn't let Levi touch her hair.

At least he had learned the trick of tying a satin scarf around her head at night. Once Dori was ready in her red velvet dress, white tights, and red shoes, she asked Levi to snap a big red suede bow at the end of her braid. That, he could manage.

After the usher found them a vacancy, Levi thought he should have asked where Karyn was sitting, but decided against it. The church wasn't that big. If he didn't see her during service, he would ask once it was over.

Inside the pew, the trio got on their knees and briefly prayed as a sign of respect in entering God's house. Afterward, Levi and Rossi stood to join in with the praise. Dori sat down and yanked a kid's picture Bible from her purse.

Time escaped Levi as the music quieted, and a short man dressed in a black minister's robe with bold red trimming approached the pulpit.

"Thank you, praise team, and good morning, church, and welcome visitors. I'm Pastor Ephraim Scaife. Along with my wife, Dr. Winnie Jordan Scaife, and the Crowns for Christ fellowship, we welcome you today. We won't ask our visitors to stand, because we don't want to 'peep you out,' as our young folks say. We want you to feel comfortable so that you will come back again. If we have any visiting ministers, please come and sit with us on the pulpit."

With a smirk, Levi exchanged looks with his cousin. Levi was reminded of what God had called Rossi to do—work in the ministry. Standing, Rossi stepped over Dori and Levi. Smoothing down his printed tie and buttoning his suit coat, Rossi walked confidently toward the front, carrying his Bible. Two other ministers in the sanctuary followed.

"Is Cousin Rossi going to work, Daddy?" Dori's eyes followed Rossi.

"Yeah, he is, sweetheart. Be good, okay?"

Satisfied, Dori nodded and began flipping through the pages of her Bible.

Pastor Scaife continued. "I want to speak from two passages today: the Old Testament and the New. In the second book of Samuel, chapter twelve, I want to focus on verses one and seven. The Lord sent Nathan to King David to let him know there were no secrets with God. I'm sure you've heard of the saying, 'Your sins will find you out.' If God ain't happy, nobody's going to be happy. Remember that." He made a few more comments on the passage then referred his audience to read Numbers 23. "See the repercussions of David's sin of taking another man's wife and then ordering the killing of that man to cover his tracks. Despite David becoming a murderer, adulterer, and a hypocrite, yet God loved him and had mercy. Stew over that for a few minutes."

A hush came over the congregation. The pastor silently read the text then looked up. "That's messed up. David was a king, he was after God's own heart, and David messed up. Humph. Just when you thought you've done the unthinkable, God is ready to forgive you. Now let's go to 2 Corinthians, chapter five. Again, this is a Bible-reading church. If you can think to put your shoes on before you leave home, grab your Bible too."

"Daddy," Dori whispered loudly, "I got my shoes on and my Bible."

"I know," he mouthed then put his finger to his lips to shush her. A few adults around them chuckled.

Pastor Scaife continued, "You're going to have to read the entire chapter for yourself, but there's hope and victory in verse seventeen: *Therefore if any man be in Christ, he is a new creation; the old has passed away. Behold, the fresh and new has come!*" He closed his Bible. "This sermon is a no-brainer. God wants to save us."

Levi lost track of time while he listened to the pastor's intensity to accept God's salvation. Breaking his concentration, Levi did a quick sweep of the crowd for Karyn. There was no sign of her.

As Pastor Scaife walked away from the podium and descended down the pulpit's steps, he concluded his sermon with the altar call. "You may not have a good track record, but God can turn it around for you. You can't beat drugs, but He can. If you've sold your body for sex, yep, God can clean you too. If you've stolen, killed, and sworn against God, Jesus has the authority to fix it. Come today. Everybody in this building, please stand and pray for our brothers and sisters. Give God the power today to change your life. Repent and ask God to forgive you. After you make up your mind, walk to me.

"Ministers on the pulpit, please join me on the floor. We are here to serve you. Let us pray for you. The second step is to be baptized in the name of Jesus. No detergent can get you cleaner. We have clothes for you to change into. And finally, God knows your struggles. That's why He's ready to fill you with His Spirit. Will you come?"

Levi was moved by the sermon. People began flocking to the front. Some were dressed well, others were unkempt, but they came. Some seemed too thin, maybe sickly.

So, this was the church everybody was talking about, the congregation that reached out to the community to save folks.

A crowd began to swell at the altar, and Rossi was there doing his thing, working as a vessel for Jesus as if he were at Living for Jesus Church laying hands on people and praying. Levi smiled. His cousin was never on vacation.

When a couple across the aisle near the back left their seats and headed for the front, Levi thought he saw Karyn. The woman wore a red fitted jumper with a white turtleneck. She was about the same shape and height as Karyn, but the curls threw him off. Maybe it wasn't her.

He refocused on the service as he glanced at Dori, who had fallen asleep. Levi propped his daughter's body against the back of the pew so she wouldn't get a crook in her neck, then eyed the spot where he thought he saw Karyn. He still wasn't sure, so he turned his attention back to the pulpit, where overhead lights danced off and over the water tank used for baptisms.

The water stirred as three ministers dressed in white descended into the water then faced the congregation. Within minutes, candidates also dressed in white followed them into the pool.

Once the candidates' arms were crossed, the ministers raised their voices in unity. "Our beloved brothers and sisters, upon the confession of your faith and the confidence we have in the blessed Word of God, concerning His death, burial, and grand resurrection of our Lord Jesus Christ, we baptize you all in the name of Jesus Christ as instructed in Acts second chapter. God shall fill you with His Holy Spirit and give you evidence by speaking in other tongues. Amen."

One by one, each candidate was dipped under the water and brought up again once they had been completely submerged. The congregation cheered loudly as if they were in a stadium. The power swept through the air and moved the new converts to join in the spirited praise. Levi heard several explosions of those speaking in tongues from the microphone above the pool. The evidence had come.

Not long after that, Pastor Scaife gave the benediction, advising everyone they could leave their free will offerings with any usher holding a basket. Some members acknowledged the conclusion and began to leave, others continued their rejoicing. Levi chanced another look in the section he had monitored for a few minutes during the sermon. When the woman in red turned around, his heart pounded wildly. As she looked up, their eyes locked. Levi's mind flashed a picture at her startled face. Karyn Wallace was a knockout in red.

CHAPTER 23

"Another great message," Buttercup said with a sigh, crossing her arms over her chest.

"I loved it too, because despite what we've done . . ." Karyn chatted absentmindedly as she turned to grab her purse and Bible. She paused. She felt it—the same sensation whenever Levi was in the bookstore. His cologne would assail her, and then his voice would arrest her. Could she miss him so much that . . .

"Levi?"

Blinking, she saw that his image hadn't vanished. Levi was handsome in another tailored suit with a Tide-bright white shirt and a red tie. In a *GQ* pose, Levi stood with one hand resting in his pants pocket. She couldn't see his eyes behind his glasses, but she knew he was reading every emotion across her face. Once his smile appeared, it didn't leave. They stared at each, not distracted as others scurried around them.

"Girl, you must have that man on your mind, because . . ." Buttercup's voice faded as Karyn walked toward Levi.

It was as if her steps were choreographed. Drawing closer, Karyn recognized the mischief that flashed in his eyes through his designer glasses. The dimples were there, too, waiting for her.

As if he were cued, Levi began his waltz toward her. In the pew near him, Dori was knocked out. Karyn and Levi were within touching distance when someone blocked their view and wouldn't budge.

"Karyn," Halo, her fellow ex-convict and self-appointed body guard said, bending and brushing a kiss on her cheek. "Are you ready to eat?" Either Halo was unaware he was in the way or he purposely intercepted. When Levi's nostrils flared, Karyn thought it was best to make an introduction. Levi beat her to it.

"I'm Levi Tolliver, and you are?" Sizing up Halo, Levi extended his hand.

Levi didn't appear to be intimidated by Halo's height or muscles. The man oozed confidence. It was only on their first date that he had exposed Karyn to the crack in his shield. Since then, the man proved to draw on his weakness for his strength.

Halo accepted the shake, pumping Levi's hand. Levi retaliated with his own firm grip, and his biceps seemed to flex under his suit sleeve. Halo didn't answer.

"I hope you enjoyed service today. Visitors are invited to come back at any time," Halo recited as if he were part of the welcome committee.

Karyn separated the two with an elbow to Halo's side, which she was sure he barely felt. Levi reached for her hand and she accepted it. His squeeze was gentle and confident of her loyalty. *Men.*

"Levi, this bodyguard here is my friend, Hanson Ramos, but we call him Halo."

After a nod, Levi drew her closer, shutting Halo out of the picture. Her friend left, but Karyn knew Halo would return—and not alone.

"What are you doing here?" She smiled and allowed her eyes to worship God's creation.

"Besides coming to praise God with you? I brought you something." He brushed a kiss against her cheek. To any church observer, it was a friendly brother to sister greeting. Between Karyn and Levi, the vibes were undeniable. Levi stepped back and seemed to watch his handiwork take effect as Karyn's skin tingled. She blushed.

"My backpack." She couldn't believe she had forgotten about it just that quickly. "You didn't have to do that, but I really appreciate it."

He winked. Turning around, Levi walked back to his pew and Karyn followed. Dori stirred, but didn't wake. Karyn knelt and smoothed back the loose strands from her braid. Dori had called Karyn a princess, but his sleeping beauty was the true princess. She was a doll.

"You better be glad she didn't bite your hand off, because she wouldn't let me touch her hair."

At that moment, Dori's eyes popped open as if she had heard a code word. She blinked her recognition and almost slipped on the seat, but Karyn steadied her. "Miss Karyn!" She wrapped her arms around Karyn's neck, and Karyn returned the affection then pulled back.

"Hi, sweetie. Don't you look pretty?"

"Umm-hmm." Dori reached out and fingered Karyn's curls. "Will you comb my hair like that?"

"She can't even comb her own hair like that," Buttercup said. "I did her hair and her nails too."

Startled, Karyn glanced over her shoulder. Halo had returned with Buttercup, padding in her stocking feet. Her stilettos were dangling from her hand. Behind them, Mother Caldwell hurried to catch up with the aid of her cane. A few other van riders followed.

"This must be that young man we've been hearing about. He's nice looking, but I'll take that little cutie pie home with me," Mother Caldwell teased, nodding toward Dori.

Dori shook her head and squeezed Karyn closer. Leaning in, Levi whispered, "A fan base. Nothing like the support of the saints."

One by one, the group made introductions and invited Levi and Dori to stay for the church dinner. Karyn relaxed as her friends vanished as fast as they had appeared, except for Halo.

"I'm watching you, brother," Halo warned with a smile then rolled his shoulders and walked away. Shoeless, Buttercup fell in step.

"That bodyguard—you don't need him. There's a new sheriff in town, and you're under my protection. I've got you." Levi smirked.

Karyn's heart leaped at the sound of possessiveness in Levi's voice. Karyn sat down and lifted Dori on her lap. Although the crowd was thinning, there was still plenty of activity inside the sanctuary for Karyn and Levi to be ignored.

"You do look pretty," Levi complimented with awe. Sitting, he scooted over the backpack and sat next to her on the bench. He reached inside his suit jacket and pulled out a small package then handed it to Karyn. "Here."

"What's this?"

Levi took the box and read it as if he didn't know. "Hmm. It says a cell phone." He handed it back to her.

Frowning, she wrinkled her brow. "I know that, but I have one."

"Believe me; this is purely for selfish reasons. Your excuse of 'I'm running out of minutes' is bad for a relationship. I like unlimited calling. I stopped by my wireless store and added you to my plan."

"Levi, are you sure you want a relationship with me?" Either answer would scare her. If he said yes, she would have to tell him—maybe. If he said no, she would be crushed, but her secret was safe.

"Of course," he said tenderly as he reached for her hand and massaged her fingers. His expression changed. "Listen, Karyn, I know at first I came across as a man who doesn't have it together, but each moment I spend with you, I grow stronger. Is that what's holding you back?"

God help her. She was in church. Confession was not on her plate today. Dori became fidgety, which gave Karyn time to stall.

"You must be Karyn Wallace. Hi. I'm Minister Rossi Tolliver, Levi's cousin. It's nice to meet you. If I didn't hear enough about you from Levi, Dori filled in the blanks."

Dori slid off Karyn's lap and Rossi scooped her up. His features were similar to Levi's, but everything else was a contrast. He was taller and much darker than Levi.

"Cousin Rossi, I'm hungry," Dori whined, rubbing her face with the back of her hand.

Karyn exhaled. "You all are welcome to stay for dinner. Sister Annabelle's peas and cornbread are hard to copy."

"Ah, my little sweet pea woman who loves soul food," Levi teased.

"I do, and there's plenty of food." She led the way, grabbing her backpack. She was confident they would follow. She had dodged the bullet—this time—about what was holding her back from committing to a relationship. She had a feeling that one day soon Levi was going to use his unlimited calling minutes to press her for an answer.

CHAPTER 24

Monday, Levi backed up his declaration of affection. The first boxed lunch that was delivered to Bookshelves Unlimited came with a note. Karyn's heart pounded with excitement. Just that morning she had begun to tag onto the end of her prayers, "Lord, if Levi is your will, make it work."

Two minutes after clocking out, Karyn did a speed walk to the back break room, hoping she would have forty-five minutes alone. It was not to be. As soon as she opened the door, she saw Otis, an elderly employee who was counting his days to retirement after ten years, dozing.

In the center of the table was a box of doughnuts Patrice had brought in. Coworkers couldn't stop singing the woman's praises. Maybe it was Karyn who didn't see what they saw in Patrice.

One thing Pastor Scaife reiterated to his members was to look at oneself when accusing someone else of having a problem. Although Patrice hadn't been overly friendly toward Karyn since she arrived, Patrice didn't start lashing out at Karyn until Levi showed interest.

Just that quickly, Karyn had allowed her mind to drift. Karyn claimed a chair at the end of the table. Otis wouldn't stir. He enjoyed heavy naps. Otis depended on others to wake him when his break was over.

Bowing her head, Karyn prayed over her meal. Instead of opening the lunch carton, she peeled back the flap of the envelope and slipped out the card.

> *I'm willing to take a chance. Take it with me, Karyn. I know the first of the month is busy, so just in case you can't get away for lunch, enjoy this, thinking of me. Yes to the question in your pretty little head. You'd better believe this is a bribe gift.*
>
> *Levi and Dori*

Sniffing, Karyn smiled. He had remembered the busy time at the bookstore. His gesture was sweet. She peeped at Otis before digging into her purse for her new cell phone and then punched the only number already saved in the address book.

"Thank you," she said, forgoing a greeting, whispering just in case Otis wasn't asleep.

"You're welcome."

The sound of his rich voice warmed her. Suddenly, she wasn't hungry or tired. He made her content. "Levi?"

"Yes," he practically cooed into the phone.

She struggled to find the right words. "You don't have to bribe me with gifts." She toyed with the lunch box until she opened it. "This is too much food for lunch. It had to cost—"

"This isn't about money for me, Karyn. This is about helping you make up your mind that I want you. Dori does too."

"It's about money for me. I can't afford the phone, and the lunch is a luxury."

The line became quiet. Karyn hoped she hadn't offended him. She enjoyed his attention, but she had allowed the wheels to be set in motion, and she couldn't
stop the feelings that were developing between them.

Levi still hadn't said anything.

"Well—"

"Karyn Wallace, Dori and I are in your life now. I accept you may have doubts, but I don't. I'm not wealthy,
but I am financially successful. If you need something,
I know you wouldn't ask me and you would do without,
so I'm going to have to read you like a book."

His words gave her so much comfort that she didn't
feel she deserved. She found herself constantly battling
the devil when God made her worthy to deserve any
blessing He had for her. "Levi . . ." She closed her eyes.
"I don't know what to say, but I'd better go. I'm running up your minutes."

He laughed as she disconnected.

Otis chuckled in his sleep. Karyn shook her head and
dug in.

The next four days were like déjà vu. A box came
from a different caterer with a handwritten note. Karyn
had begun to look forward to Levi's messages more
than the food.

By the end of the week, the bookstore was a zoo and
a circus, thanks to the first Friday in December com-
bined with the holiday shopping sprees. Levi was the
furthest person from her mind when she walked behind the customer service counter to retrieve customer
book orders.

"It's that time of the month, and I'm not talking
about my womanhood either," Patrice mumbled. Her

coworker didn't look like she had gotten much sleep.
If she was wearing makeup, she hadn't put on enough,
and her uniform appeared carelessly ironed.

"I have some supplies in my locker if you need
them," Karyn offered.

"I'm talking about your kinfolks," she joked with a
chuckle.

"What?" Karyn frowned, dumbfounded.

"I see Mrs. Harris coming." Patrice rolled her eyes. "I
wouldn't waste my money on those criminals. They're
probably going to die in jail anyway. But hey, they
chose to be there."

For a moment, Patrice gave her a double dose of
panic. Patrice was hitting too close to home. For Karyn,
kinfolk had three meanings: her natural family, whom
she yearned to see; the derogatory statement about
blacks who were uncouth; and mixing kinfolks and
jail in the same sentence conjured up the families that
were formed in prison to survive. Outsiders thought it
was lesbianism, and it was some of that, too, but the
women formed clusters of families with a momma,
daddy, aunties, cousins, sisters, and so on. That state
of belonging was what kept many prisoners sane from
day to day. It was a world of make-believe.

Although Karyn couldn't undo the mistakes from her
past, she preferred to keep the circumstances of her
decision in God's Book of Forgiveness. If Patrice knew
she was talking to a former convict, the woman would
probably spit in Karyn's face.

*Hold your tongue, Karyn. She doesn't know about
your past. Patrice is running off at the mouth again.*
Karyn calmed herself, only to snap. She'd had enough
of her coworker's snide remarks.

"Everyone behind prison bars isn't hopeless. Some will get out and turn their lives around."

"Ha." Patrice put her hand on her hip. "Yeah? Humph. I'd like to meet one. Criminals are stupid. Why do you think they always get caught?" She laughed at her own joke. "I would never do something stupid and go to prison."

Karyn got her emotions under control. Those outbursts, which weren't often, would blow her cover, so to speak. "Patrice, I'm sure it wasn't the goal of those people behind bars to go to prison. Be careful what you boast. God has a way of making us eat our words. Besides, without the Lord as the center of our lives, the devil would toy with our minds like a toymaker and make us commit all kind of sins."

Patrice twisted her lips. "Really? Well, I'm in my right mind and in control of my life." She began to wag her finger at Karyn. "I would not break the law under any circumstances."

Karyn just stared at her coworker. *I thought the same thing too. It just goes to show you that the devil really can make us do stuff if we don't trust in the Lord.* This time, Karyn held her tongue.

"Anyway, ooh wee. Here comes your favorite customer." Patrice antagonized Karyn then hurried away.

Shaking off the conversation, Karyn regrouped. Taking a deep breath, she gave her customer a genuine smile. "Hi, Mrs. Harris. How are you doing, today?"

"Considering I woke up this morning, I'm off to a good start. Don't you think so, baby?"

"I think so." Karyn grinned.

Karyn allowed Mrs. Harris to browse before she came to the counter with books unacceptable for prison delivery. Finally, she purchased a magazine of crossword puzzles and an extra book besides the one she always bought for Sonny.

"Three books?" Karyn lifted her brow.

"It is Christmas, you know." Mrs. Harris winked.

"I'm sure he'll enjoy it." Karyn smiled and began to ring up the purchase. She had almost totaled it when Mrs. Harris picked up a peppermint bark bar.

"Add that on, baby. It is Christmas, and I'll check my sugar later," the woman said in a hushed voice, as if her doctor were breathing down her back.

Karyn nodded. "Umm-hmm."

Once Mrs. Harris ambled out, Karyn sighed and glanced at her watch. It was a good thing Levi didn't have lunch delivered, because it would have been cold by now. Her feet were hurting from standing up at the register off and on for long periods that morning. The line was steady, as if the recession was of Christmas past.

She was past due her lunchtime. Otis was probably in the back room dozing after a satisfying meal. Karyn prayed he would wake soon. After completing another sale, the next person stepped up in line. She expected a stack of books. Instead, a boxed lunch was placed on the counter and shoved her way. Karyn looked up and saw a bouquet of flowers. She frowned. The delivery guy had gotten in line?

The flowers were removed and Levi smiled. "Sorry . I'm late, but I was busy on a site. Did you already have lunch?"

"No. I'm waiting for my relief."

"Karyn, honey, I'm sorry. My bladder doesn't work like it used to," Otis explained loud enough for Levi and a few other customers to hear. "Go on and take your lunch. When you get back, I may need to take a break."

Karyn didn't need to be told twice.

"I'll be in the café." Levi quickly left the line.

She hurried to the customer service desk to clock out before anyone could stop her. Next was a pit stop in the bathroom, where she removed her apron and washed her hands. She examined the weariness under her eyes. She patted cold water on her face and left to meet Levi.

In the café, he had her box opened. Plastic utensils were resting on napkins, and the bouquet of flowers was the centerpiece. As Karyn approached the table, Levi stood then pulled out her chair. "You look tired."

"Is that a compliment?" Karyn mocked and slid into the seat with a sigh.

"No, it's concern." He reached across the table and took her hands and bowed his head. "Lord, in the name of Jesus, we ask that you sanctify and bless our food. We thank you for Calvary and the blood you shed for our sins. Lord, I thank you for blessing me with Karyn. Amen."

"Thank you. Do you bless me when you bless your food when I'm not around?"

"Yep." Levi bit into his sandwich. "Do you work tomorrow?"

She took a sip of her raspberry tea then shook her head. "No way. I'm off, and I'm not volunteering for overtime. I want to sleep late tomorrow and—"

"Spend the day with me. Last Saturday was wonderful. Karyn, I want to introduce you to my family."

She almost choked. "Me?"

"This is a table for two. No one else is sitting here, baby. You really have brought joy into my life during the past month. I want my family to meet the special woman who has healed my wound. I'm talking about meeting them, but spending the whole day with one

Tolliver—me. Plus, Dori will be at my sister-in-law's house this weekend."

God, I don't owe this man or anybody an explanation, so why do I feel he needs one? Lord, when is the right time to tell him?

"Karyn?" He reached across the table again. "Don't be afraid."

That was easier said than done. "I am."

CHAPTER 25

The next morning, Buttercup was giving Karyn a pep talk as she twisted Karyn's hair into spiral curls. She leaned over Karyn's shoulder and peered down at her fingertips. "You sure you don't want me to do your nails? I've got these purple extensions that would go good with that turtleneck."

At times, Karyn was convinced Buttercup was color blind. Nothing on Karyn was purple. Already anxious about the day with Levi, Karyn wanted to mentally shut out Buttercup.

"Have you ever heard less is better? I agreed with you that the curls will give me a more mature look than my braid, but that's where I draw the line. I am who I am. Nothing more, definitely nothing less."

"Umm-hmm. You're going to meet the family. You've got to tell him."

"Not without Jesus giving me what to say. For so many years, I've been one of those people who—I won't say hate—but didn't like holidays. Without family, there's no joyous occasion. Then next month you're leaving. I'm scared."

"Karyn, you and I have always been honest with each other." She paused, but never stopped curling Karyn's hair.

"What?" Karyn prompted, trusting her friend's judgment.

"You're sounding like a victim! Add desperation and pitiful to your stew, but God has a reputation of coming through in the midnight hour. Always."

Buttercup was right. God had never abandoned her, even at her lowest point in prison. God had come to her through the church's ministry. She looked at her watch. Levi told her to call when she was ready to go. Karyn sighed.

"Your caseworker is even letting you get away with these last-minute special requests, but don't think they will always be granted. You know Monica can get evil when she wants to. Let me ask you, sister-girlfriend-roommate, oh saint of God, under a normal life, would Levi be the perfect man for you?"

Closing her eyes, Karyn was hesitant about admitting it. "In a fairy tale," she whispered.

"Before it goes any further, talk to Levi. If he really cares about you, he'll have an open mind and accept that none of us are perfect."

"I've given him hints," Karyn said.

Buttercup laid down the curling iron and began to rub her temples. "What were your hints? That you had to be home by ten because you'll turn into a pumpkin? Girl, you need to tell Levi the whole story. Let him decide."

"His decision would be a no-brainer. Anyone who served time in prison isn't worthy of second chances. My assumption is based on what he's already been through."

Buttercup knelt and made eye contact with Karyn. "Listen, Christ wiped your slate clean."

Karyn sniffed. "Who am I going to talk to when you're not here?"

"Try Jesus. He's on the main line. Plus, he's a good listener."

"So what do you think about her?" Levi asked his cousin with a cocky grin on his way out the door of his home. Although it didn't matter what anyone cared, Rossi knew Levi valued his assessment.

Minutes earlier, Karyn had called on "their" cell phone, as he had begun to think of his gift to her. Now, she was ready and waiting on him. Karyn was one woman he didn't want to keep waiting. He smiled as he pinched his BlackBerry between his ear and shoulder while locking his front door.

"You're a Tolliver. Of course you have good taste," Rossi complimented then teased with an old familiar line. "Does she have a sister?"

Levi let out a hearty laugh. "You're on your own, man. I can't put it into words, but this petite, unassuming beautiful bookseller caught me off guard without trying, and she's holding it, too. She just seems right for me. Of all the women who have paraded themselves in front of me in the office, at church, and other places, I find my diamond hidden in a bookstore."

"You sure you're not moving too fast?"

"I thought you would be praise dancing now that I've finally came back to life." Levi dismissed the concern in Rossi's voice. "I'm not shopping for jewelry or applying for a marriage license. Plus, Karyn's hesitation about a relationship is forcing me to hold back. That woman moves slower than me. I have yet to get the good night kiss I want."

It was Rossi's turn to release an explosion of laughs. "You are definitely losing your edge, Tolliver."

"Shut up."

"Okay, okay," Rossi said with amusement still in his voice. "So what's on tap for today?"

Levi got in his car and fastened his seatbelt. "I told her the history museum and my parents, but there's always lunch, a matinee, ice skating, shopping, art museum in between—"

"There's only twenty-four hours in a day?" Rossi asked incredulously.

"Hey, I have to give her options, but I do plan to stop by Mom and Dad's. I want them to meet her."

"Who's going to be there?"

"Just my parents. I asked Seth to come by with Tia. Karyn will love her. Who knows about Solomon?"

"Your bother is weird. That man is too quiet to be a Tolliver."

"Maybe he's adopted," Levi joked.

"He's a twin. We would have to get rid of Seth, too, and you know that's my guy. What about Jet? Are you going to introduce the two?"

"Not until our tenth wedding anniversary."

"Yeah, right." Rossi didn't impart any remarks of wisdom, leaving Levi hanging.

As Levi made a left turn out of his subdivision, he disconnected the call. Fifteen minutes later, worming his way through traffic, Levi cruised in front of Karyn's apartment building. He had barely shifted his car into park before she opened the massive front door and sashayed out. Timing seemed to be a priority for Karyn.

At least she was wrapped a little better for the cold. The curls were flowing under a knit cap. Her jacket, coat, or whatever she called her outerwear, barely came to her thighs. What he did appreciate were her jeans tucked inside black boots, which stopped at her knees.

He would have preferred to play out the suitor ideology, walking to greet her at her apartment door, not at the building's entrance. Her building didn't look shabby. As a matter of fact, it was well kept. Maybe her furnishings were sparse and she was embarrassed. Considering how long it took for her to agree to go out with him, he may have to wait even longer to see the inside of her apartment. He would even bring his own chair, he mused. One thing for sure, he wouldn't push her like she didn't push him. They had plenty of time to get to know each other.

Levi turned off the ignition, managing to get out of his car without strangling himself with the seat belt. Coming around the car, he leaped up two steps at a time to block her path. "Hi." The vapor from his breath fogged his glasses. Karyn laughed.

"How many fingers am I holding up?" she teased.

"Funny," he said as he wiped his glasses and then in one swift movement, lifted her off the ground.

She screamed, wiggling.

"Stop moving, woman, or we'll both fall down the steps. According to you, I can't see, remember?"

"I take it back. I take it back. Please don't drop me." Her laughter hinted it didn't matter.

"I have to prove I can see you clearly."

He didn't release her until they reached the passenger door, then he did so reluctantly. He helped her inside then rubbed his hands while jogging around the car. Once inside, he faced Karyn and removed his glasses. "I can see you with 20/20 vision."

Even with his eyes closed, he had a perfect vision of Karyn's features—from her eyes to her long, thin lashes. Her valentine heart–shaped lips remained his temptation. Then it was her hair brushed into a single braid.

"I need to get something out of the way first." Levi startled Karyn by pulling her into his arms and planting tender kisses on her cheeks. He took advantage of his surprise assault and delivered the exact blow to her lips. She didn't fight him, and he didn't let go until he needed to breathe.

"Ah." He grinned like a satisfied baby after a diaper change. "From this day forward, there's a new rule when you ride in my car. You have to take off your gloves. I expect your hand to be linked with mine as much as possible as I drive."

Karyn stared at him. Nothing in her expression hinted she had enjoyed his kiss. That was too bad, because he loved it. When she continued to look at him without moving her mouth, he got concerned that maybe he had offended her, but how? Then all of a sudden, one brow lifted as if she was waiting for some kind of explanation of his actions.

He cowered under pressure. "I got cheated out of my good night kiss to the princess, remember?" When she didn't answer, he whistled. His spontaneous move didn't create the breakthrough in their budding relationship he had hoped. "You're going to make me suffer, aren't you?"

Karyn shrugged. "You're the one who boasts that you can read my expressions. Oh, well." She sighed and yawned. "I guess you're losing your touch."

Levi bit his lip as his nostrils flared. "All I need is thirty seconds to regain my reputation."

"I don't take dares." She smiled although her tone was anything but amused.

"Okay, Miss Chill. Let's go, but I do need you to remove your gloves. Consider my car a no-glove zone." When he heard her snicker, he smirked. He was going to enjoy their tit for tats. Karyn did as he requested and latched onto his hand. They rode silently until Levi sparked another conversation.

"By the way, I love your hair, especially in those curls. You are truly a beautiful woman," he complimented.

"Thank you."

"But I've got to tell you, I have a miniature Karyn walking around my house with the one braid. She wouldn't let me touch it for three days. She'll be horrified to know Miss Karyn doesn't have her braid again."

"Dori's so sweet," Karyn said with such awe.

"She gets it from her father."

Karyn squinted. "I'm sure she got it equally from her mother."

"She did," Levi said without experiencing a relapse like he had done on their first date. "So, since I have a day's pass with you so to speak, are you still interested in the Missouri History Museum? I checked, and there's an exhibit on race and one about the dancer Katherine Durham. Although she died in New York, she considered East St. Louis her home for almost thirty years."

"A history buff."

Levi shrugged. "Don't get too impressed. I like to preserve the history of old neighborhoods, especially black ones. After my cousins and I rehabbed this one-story bungalow just for fun, we couldn't believe the transformation. As more of a challenge, we sought bigger projects, until finally we came up with the bright idea of going to school and later going into business. We believe restoration is preservation."

Karyn squeezed his hand. "Although I didn't know you before, I'm proud of you and what you've accomplished."

Levi felt a prick to his heart, as if a needle were tightening a suture. He choked. He couldn't get a word out.

"The exhibit sounds fun. In another life, I would've been a dancer. Now, I'm like David in the Bible and performing for the Lord."

"That's another thing that's attractive about you. You seem to focus on Christ, and you are what my life needs," he said, glancing at her before refocusing on the road. "Then Katherine Durham, here we come."

Levi was satisfied when she complied. Her hands were warm and soft, but not as soft as they would be. Christmas was coming. He would add perfumes and lotions to her list. Levi drove to Route 159 then exited on I-64 toward St. Louis.

"Did you get some rest last night?" Levi kept his eyes on the road, massaging her fingers.

"As a matter of fact, I did, once you let me off the phone."

They shared a laugh. "I told you that cell phone was for dual purposes and selfish reasons."

A half hour later, they arrived at the Missouri History Museum. The massive building stood as a gatekeeper to one of St. Louis's best known tourist attractions, Forest Park. It was boasted as one of the largest urban parks in the country, outshining New York City's Central Park. Besides the history museum, the park was a one-stop shop for a full day of free adventure: the art museum, science center, zoo, Jewel Box greenhouse, and The Muny—an outdoor theatre—skating rink, and fishing ponds.

Amazingly, Levi snatched a newly vacated parking spot near the entrance. Getting out, he walked around and helped Karyn. Once outside, she began to slip on her gloves.

Levi grabbed her hand. "I'll keep them warm."

"Both of them?" She didn't hide a mischievous grin. "How?"

"Yep. I can walk backward—" He performed a quick backpedaling demonstration.

"Stop it." Putting on her left glove, she used her right uncovered hand to take Levi's, and they sprinted for the entrance. A receptionist at the welcome desk directed them to Katherine Dunham's Beyond the Dance exhibit a few doors away.

As Karyn unzipped her coat, Levi was behind her to retrieve it. "Want me to hang it up? There's a free public coat check." He was already removing his Cardinals stadium jacket.

"Someone might steal them," she whispered.

"That would be a good reason for me to buy you a new coat." Levi wiggled his brow and adjusted his glasses, meaning it.

Karyn was different. She didn't come off as a woman who wanted something from him, which made him more determined to give her things.

She elbowed him. "I'm serious."

"Me too." He took their coats and put them on one hanger. Inside the exhibit, they strolled from one unbelievable display to another. Each showcased Dunham's elaborate costumes, which were designed and created for her by her husband, John Pratt. The scene backdrops were just as intricate.

"Wow," Karyn said as she leaned over and read one of the descriptions. "I knew she formed the first black dance company. I didn't know she added Caribbean and African movements to classic ballet."

"She was larger than life, and East St. Louis and St. Louis had her right in their backyards. People that acknowledge there's more to the Metro-East than crime. We have track legend Jackie Joyner-Kersee, Tina Turner met Ike here, plus, Miles Davis was reared in East St. Louis. It just makes sense to rebuild some communities."

Levi realized he was rambling. As soon as he faced Karyn, they were locked into that moment, until someone pounded on one of the African drums on display. Startled, Karyn jumped, and Levi wrapped his arm securely around her waist. Pulling her closer, he rubbed a kiss in her hair then guided her to the next display. When they came to the Rites de Passage, the couple lingered.

"These are the most beautiful enslaved people I've ever seen," she said, referring to the depiction of Africans crossing the Atlantic Ocean for the New World. In place of chains around their wrists, the creators used wide bands of cloth that resembled thick bracelets.

It took an hour for them to work the room. Levi would read the tidbits, and Karyn would engage them through the duration of the film clips. Both alternated between admiring memorabilia and each other.

"Hungry?" He hugged her again. It was hard for him to think when she was near him.

When she nodded, they left the room and headed for the coat check. He grimaced. Their jackets were still on the hanger. He wouldn't have minded an excuse for purchasing his-and-hers stadium jackets.

Since they were close to Washington University's campus, Levi chose Cicero's Italian restaurant nearby in the Loop in U-City, a popular hot spot for students and locals. Inside, Karyn excused herself and headed to the bathroom, rummaging through her purse. Before she opened the restroom door, she had pulled out her cell phone.

Her counselor was not in a good mood. After Monica said no twice to the abrupt change in Karyn's scheduled locations, Karyn prayed for grace. Unexpectedly, Monica had a change of heart. She okayed Karyn's lunch, but warned any other requests that day would be a mark against her. Karyn exhaled before thanking God then Monica. Karyn had to stop torturing herself. Sooner or later, she had to explain her status to Levi. Either he would or wouldn't understand. She better prepare for the latter.

Taking a few more minutes, Karyn regrouped then rejoined Levi. Once they were seated and perused the menu, they finally decided to share a hamburger-topped thin crust pizza and salads.

"You looked so stressed at work yesterday and tired. I didn't like it and I don't care for your coworker," Levi said.

She nodded. "It's the first of the month and it's busy, plus, it's December. That combination is a nightmare on my feet."

Levi reached across the table. One by one, he played with each finger. "Why do you work there?"

Frowning, she shook her head. "I need a job like thousands of other Americans. Jobs are hard to find with so many people out of work. Things will change once I graduate. God will open doors."

"I can open one door on Monday, in an office, where you will be off your feet behind a desk."

Her eyes didn't sparkle at his offer. He waited for teary, excited, and worshipping eyes. Karyn sighed and looked away. Levi expected her breath to catch in surprise. Karyn curved her lips into a smile, but she hadn't said a word.

Their waiter arrived with their orders, and Karyn didn't utter a sound. Levi reached across the table and opened his hands for Karyn to place hers. Before he said grace, he tightened his grip and leaned closer, forcing Karyn to meet his eyes. "I'm not trying to overwhelm you, but I mean every word I say. Remember that."

She nodded and bowed her head. He followed, blessing their food aloud and silently praying that God's will be done in their lives because he wanted Karyn. He needed a sign to confirm they were meant to be.

CHAPTER 26

Levi Tolliver was a prince. Karyn was convinced. The man who sat across from her had a genuine interest in trying to read her blank expressions. Levi was also a man who had survived a horrific tragedy. He had recovered from the loss of his spouse, and God appeared to have restored him.

How could she shatter his peace with her storm? Karyn imagined his response once she revealed her crime and the condemnation to prison as her punishment. First, he wouldn't believe she was capable of such a hideous act. Levi may laugh, thinking she was teasing. As the truth set in and his shock wore off, Levi would fire questions nonstop. After her explanation, he would walk out of her life forever.

Levi's goodwill gesture of offering his help to secure her a better job would mean completing a new application. The question about whether she was ever convicted of a crime was standard. To lie or tell the truth would result in rejection of her application once a background check was done. Karyn had caused their carefree mood to sour.

The earth is mine and the fullness thereof. I have cleansed your hands and you have shown me a pure heart. You shall receive blessings from me. God reminded Karyn of Psalm 24.

She smiled at God's comforting words. Without knowing the cause behind it, Levi returned her smile. His dimples winked at her. They shared their food in relative silence, leaving Levi to guess at Karyn's thoughts and Karyn to accept God's Word at face value.

Back in the car, Levi didn't say much as he drove off, heading for his parents'. Yet, he was steadfast on holding her hand.

Ten minutes later, Levi turned off a major street to a block of majestic brick houses that had to be prime property at one time. The structures had character and appeared well maintained. Once he turned off the ignition, he faced her.

"Karyn, I do apologize if I come across as overbearing. I care about you. I feel as if I want to drive a hundred miles an hour to get to a certain point in our relationship, but I need to respect that you're more comfortable cruising at thirty miles per hour."

She teared at Levi's sincerity. She reached up and massaged his jaw. "I'm just scared. You just seem too good to be true."

"You're the one," he said, his voice low and serious.

"All I ask is that you slow down to . . . maybe fifty miles per hour."

He nodded. "Okay. I'll reduce my speed, but did you know I could get a ticket for driving under the speed limit?"

"I need day by day. Okay?"

"You have it. Come on. I want you to meet my parents." He hurried out of the car then helped her out. Karyn waited while he activated his car alarm. He gave her a tight squeeze before they climbed the steep steps to a long walkway to the front door.

Before Levi's knuckle hit the wood, a fair-skinned, petite woman opened the door. She appeared to match Karyn's height.

"You must be Karyn. I'm Sharon Tolliver. I don't know why my son was going to knock. He had to know I've been peeping out the window every few minutes," Mrs. Tolliver excitedly confessed. "Come on in." She stepped back.

"Levi said you were pretty. You're beautiful," the woman complimented as she led them to a room with a high ceiling and impressive woodwork, especially around the fireplace mantel, which was huge and the focal point of the room.

The surprise was a bear of a man who stood from a sofa. He was darker than Levi, with gray hair. A full gray beard was trimmed.

"Karyn, I'm Victor. Welcome to our home." For a man who towered over Karyn, his smile was kind and his handshake gentle. He folded a newspaper and offered her the space he vacated.

Still gushing with happiness, Mrs. Tolliver edged her son out of the way. "Would you like something to eat or drink, dear? Cake, cookies, or black-eyed peas, perhaps?" She winked.

Karyn relaxed as peace and well-being seemed to descend upon her troubled spirit. She weighed her options. Two things could happen today: She could believe the scripture where it stated He who the Son has set free is free indeed, or let the devil wag his crooked finger in her face and make her feel guilty for the blessings in her life. She chose freedom.

Wrinkling her nose, she lifted a brow at her companion. Levi shrugged as he concentrated on removing her coat and hooking it on a coat rack. "Black-eyed peas? With cake and cookies? You told them."

"Of course," Mrs. Tolliver responded for Levi. "It was nothing for me to make a big pot of them for dinner. I just started early. That's all."

How many times could a person's heart melt? Levi Tolliver and family were going for a record. Karyn couldn't afford to allow the warm and fuzzy feeling to cause her to shun her responsibilities. She had to check in with Monica and give her the Tollivers' exact address. She didn't want to call her again so soon, but that was the agreement Monica had made with her the previous day. She had allowed Karyn the waiver with the stipulation to notify her once she got to her destinations.

"Do you mind if I use your ladies' room?" Karyn asked.

"Right this way," Mrs. Tolliver said, leading Karyn down a hall with a bright dome-shaped sconce near a doorway. She stopped. "While you're freshening up, I'll warm up those peas."

A few minutes later, with no drama, Karyn returned to the room, where two TV trays were set up in front of Mr. Tolliver and Levi. Karyn glanced around again. Despite the room size, it gave off a cozy feel. It had a sofa, loveseat, and a recliner, which Levi's dad was now occupying, and a couple of mismatched chairs that seemed to complement the décor.

Levi patted the space next to him on the loveseat as his mother came in with snacks and a small bowl of black-eyed peas and a chunk of cornbread. Suddenly, the food in Karyn's stomach evaporated and she was starved. She took her seat, and Levi pulled her closer. He surprised her with a kiss in her curls.

After blessing her food and taking in a mouthful, Karyn moaned her pleasure. "Umm. This is good."

"See what you missed on Thanksgiving?" Levi whispered near her ear.

Mrs. Tolliver watched their interaction with delight on her face. "Karyn, I'm not going to give you the third degree and make you feel uncomfortable. I want you to enjoy yourself and come back . . . with Levi, so we can really chat. I don't have any daughters—"

"But you'll soon have a daughter-in-law," a voice stated before a man appeared in the doorway. Another resemblance to Levi was unmistakable—a sibling, she guessed. He had the same skin color as Levi. A woman with a beautiful, engaging wide smile and expressive eyes was with him.

Levi stood and pulled Karyn up. "This is the younger of my twin brothers, Seth, and his fiancée, Tia Rogers."

Tia bumped Seth out of the way and greeted Karyn with a genuine hug. "Another woman in the house. Yes." She pumped her fist in the air. "Good."

Was everybody in his family this jovial and down to earth? They were practically accepting her at face value, just like Levi. *Lord Jesus, am I dreaming?* Karyn had to ask herself.

No good thing will I withhold to those who walk upright before me, God spoke.

For the second time that day, God made Karyn smile. Levi and Karyn returned to their seats. He scooped up the last bit of peas and deposited them in his mouth. Once he chewed and swallowed, Levi stretched his arm across the back of the sofa, inching Karyn closer.

With Tia's presence, Karyn was no longer the center of attention—briefly. Plans for Tia and Seth's nuptials took dominance in conversation. Seth said very few words, but it was evident he was enamored with Tia. That same look of adoration was reflected on Levi's face every time Karyn glanced at him. Levi's dimples were waiting to be noticed. Levi wasn't trying to mask his happiness.

"Baby, I don't care what color scheme you pick, as long as the ceremony doesn't last more than fifteen minutes, so we can get out of there. You're already making me wait a year—the torture," Seth said, shaking his head, folding his arms.

"Ah, the excitement," Tia hinted, and then she and Mrs. Tolliver gave him a serious look. Seth cleared his throat, silently chastised. Levi and his father laughed.

"You'd better learn now, son, how to bow out. Women rule." Mr. Tolliver chuckled.

"Karyn, we'll need all the help we can get with our wedding. Consider yourself invited to join in with the fun," Tia offered.

"It'll be a candlelight service," Mrs. Tolliver added.

"As a matter of fact, Macy's is having its last girls' night out bash for the year. We can sample makeup and other products. You've got to come. It will be fun."

The doorbell rang, which gave Karyn time to think of an excuse as Mr. Tolliver left the room to answer it. It was another event outside her work and church that had to be approved. He returned with his granddaughter and another woman. Dori ran into the room, heading for her grandmother, until she saw Karyn; then she made a detour.

Everyone laughed except for the new guest.

"Well, well. Who do we have here?" The woman was tall, dark, lovely, and voluptuous. She also looked deadly. Karyn swallowed. The woman stared at Karyn, expecting her to answer.

Do not be afraid. This is bigger than you. You will not have to fight this battle, but you must not back down, God spoke words from 2 Chronicles 20:17.

"Karyn, this is Jesetta, my late daughter-in-law's sister and Dori's only aunt," Mrs. Tolliver answered as Levi tensed.

"This time next year Dori will have two aunts," Tia said as she moved toward Dori and tweaked her nose. Dori giggled in response.

Levi stood. "Jet, meet Karyn Wallace, a very special lady in our lives."

Karyn also rose to her feet. From the vibes she was experiencing, it didn't appear Jet was interested in a hug or a handshake.

"Hmmm." Jet strolled farther into the room, slipping out of her coat and scarf as Karyn began to unzip Dori's jacket. "How special." She squinted.

"Very." Levi shot her a look that dared her to challenge him.

Nodding, Jet returned her gaze. She scanned Karyn from head to toe. She wrinkled her nose. "Karyn, how old are you, and what do you do for a living?"

Levi balled his fists at his side. Dori yanked on Karyn's hand for her to sit. She obliged, and Dori climbed on her lap.

"Watch it, Jet. This is not an inquest. Karyn is my guest in my parents' home," Levi warned then faked a smile. "Try not to become a party pooper."

"Oh, poo-poo," she replied with a roll of her eyes.

"I'm a bookseller at Bookshelves Unlimited," Karyn answered.

"Ooh, I love bookstores." Tia beamed.

"We know. I can't keep you out of them," her fiancé teased.

The doorbell rang again, and Mr. Tolliver left to get it. Karyn tensed, wondering who was entering the play now. Within seconds, heavy footsteps turned the cor-

ner and Levi's cousin, Minister Rossi Tolliver, stood
larger than life. He worked the room multitasking:
exchanging hugs, kissing the women, and removing
his coat.

Levi mumbled, "Might as well have gone to the mall;
everybody picked today to drop by. Who'll be coming
through the door next, Santa Claus and all of his reindeer?"

When Rossi stopped in front of Karyn, she wondered
how he would greet her. They had only met once at
church. Surprisingly, he leaned down and brushed a
chaste kiss on her cheek, mindful of Levi's censuring
eyes.

"Praise the Lord, sister. It's good to see you again."
Rossi wore the same smile as Levi's, minus the mesmerizing dimples.

Bless him, Karyn thought. His presence seemed to
deflate the devil's plot.

"What are you doing here?" Levi asked.

"Hush. Our nephew doesn't need a reason to stop by.
Who knows? Every now and then, we might need to
conduct a prayer meeting," his mother told Levi.

Rossi chuckled. "Actually, I invited myself to get a
home-cooked meal."

Leaping up as if she had been summoned, Mrs. Tolliver's eyes sparkled in delight. "Well, come on, there's
plenty in the kitchen." She rushed ahead of him.

From the corner of her eye, Karyn could feel the
daggers Jet fired her way, but she physically felt Levi's
reassurance when he drew her closer under his arm.
Levi's brother broke the ice.

"Hey, Little D, aren't you going to give your favorite
uncle a kiss, or are you going to stay with Karyn?" Seth
teased, crossing a black leather boot over his knee.

Dori shook her head, not budging. Karyn could feel the death grip Dori had on her leg. Everyone laughed except for Jet.

"So, back to the girls' night out bash. You've got to come. We'll have fun and get a chance to compare notes on these Tolliver men," Tia pressed.

"Hey, if Karyn wants to know something about this Tolliver man, all she has to do is ask me." Levi thumped his chest.

"Karyn, how did you and my brother-in-law meet?" Jet asked.

"All the particulars don't matter." He smirked. "How we met is perfect, and I'm in a perfect place right now," Levi warned. "Leave it at that."

"Jet, come taste this," Rossi yelled from the kitchen.

"I'm not hungry!" Jet seemed rooted in her spot.

"Good. You can come and watch me eat." Rossi quickly reappeared and gently tugged Jet from her perch. Hesitantly, Jet stood and left the room with Rossi.

Karyn didn't have to compare notes with Tia. She was taking her own, and from where she sat, there were no bad Tolliver guys, only a menacing sister-in-law.

CHAPTER 27

"I owe you, man, for showing up right on time at Mom and Dad's and taking Jet out of the room. I could actually feel the dark spirit swirling around her," Levi said that Sunday morning over the phone.

"Ah, cuz, I wouldn't call the kettle black. It wasn't too long ago when you were ready to bite off someone's head if they smiled too long. A shadow was cast over you."

Levi grunted. "I wasn't that bad."

"Would I lie to you?" Rossi queried.

"I have to say no, only because you're a minister," Levi argued as he headed into his walk-in closet to choose a suit for church.

"That, too, but mainly us Tollivers have each other's back."

Biting his lip, Levi nodded. He had more emotional support from his family than a person could handle. Rossi had a gift to listen and remember the smallest details. That talent seemed to always give him a heads up when they were younger.

"Karyn is doing something to me. It's as if she makes me thirsty when we're not together, and then when I see her, I have to have some point of contact, whether it's holding her hand, playing in her hair, or hugging her. She fills me up."

For the second Sunday in a row, Levi was attending Crowns for Christ. The line was quiet. Rossi was ingesting every word that was coming out of Levi's mouth. "I'm going back to Crowns for Christ today for a couple of reasons—Karyn and the preaching."

Rossi grunted. "Karyn and Karyn."

"Cut me some slack. I enjoy the teaching and preaching, but I'm a single man—not by choice. I loved Diane, but her presence is starting to fade. It's not like I want it to, but with each new day, I realize in death we do part. God left me with Dori and an overbearing sister-in-law who has good intentions. That woman bugs me with her foolishness in demanding every other weekend visitation rights with Dori as if we're a divorced couple."

"Before you mentioned Jet, you spoke of what Karyn is giving you. I bet she's clueless. So, here it goes. I've been watching and praying for you."

Levi sighed. He rubbed his face. "Karyn means something to me, and when I'm with her, I want time to stop. When I look at Dori, I want to rewind the clock. I'm still in limbo, but I'm doing better."

"Lord, it's only because of you that he has come this far," Rossi said as if God were on the other end of the phone. "I guess Karyn is good for you."

"If I was sure about her feelings, I would marry her today and you could officiate at the express ceremony, but Karyn refuses to move any faster."

Rossi whistled. "Good for her. Are you saying you're in love with her already?" he asked incredulously.

Since they had been on the phone, Levi had chosen his suit and tie. Now he was rummaging through his chest of drawers for coordinating socks. He refused to be late for service, which was an hour earlier than his church's.

"If things keep going the way they are when I'm with her, I don't see how I can help myself."

"Lord, let us pray." Rossi recited the Lord's Prayer. "Our Father, who art in heaven . . . and lead us not into temptation —and lead Levi not into temptation . . ."

"Judging by the number of sprays per second you're pumping from that perfume bottle, I'd say Levi is coming to our church again today," Buttercup teased.

"He is." Karyn beamed. Levi had phoned earlier to ask if he was invited back to listen to the Word with her.

Karyn's heart had shifted and settled in a hidden place. It's what he said next that made her believe in fairy tales, but more importantly, in God.

"I miss you," Levi had whispered.

He didn't have to prompt her to say the same words because she felt the same way. "Me too."

When they had disconnected, Karyn had tears in her eyes and a smile on her face.

A few hours later, Karyn wished she had a closet full of clothes, but that was prohibited. There wasn't space anyway, and nobody came out of prison with suitcases. She would wear her white turtleneck sweater again and her brown skirt. She finished dressing. It was plain and simple, but so was she.

She was unlike her roommate, who always had a different color fur band crowning her hair. Buttercup knew how to cram clothes in their compact living space. Today, Buttercup had enough sense to have on more comfortable footwear—low-heeled suede boots— instead of the stilettos that crushed her toes from the time she zipped them up.

"Are you happy?" Buttercup continued their conversation minutes later, stepping up on the church van. They greeted the regular Sunday crew.

"Sister Karyn, that Levi is sure a handsome fella. Do as they say on NFL: You could go all the way," was the first thing Mother Caldwell said in a bad imitation of a broadcaster before Karyn and Buttercup could take a seat. She chuckled at her own silliness. "Remember, you've been washed squeaky clean in Jesus's baptism and blood. Now, all you have to do is press toward the finish line."

"Do you really think it's deceitful that I'm withholding my past from him?" Karyn gnawed on her lips, which we re covered in gloss. She needed more *no's* to outweigh Buttercup's *yeses* to feel confident she had made the right decision.

"Listen, honey." Mother Caldwell turned to look into Karyn's eyes. She crossed her legs to reveal worn, thick pantyhose that were too big for her bony legs. She pointed a finger. "We all have a past. We have all done things we're ashamed of. God redeemed you and cleaned you up, so don't be ashamed of the gospel of Christ. Remember Romans 1:16?"

"But Mother Caldwell, I'm not telling her to wear a name badge, but we have to confide in somebody." Buttercup lifted a shoulder. "I say let it be with someone you trust." She waved her hand. "Oh, and she suffers these mood swings after a date with Mr. Tolliver."

Karyn didn't respond. She listened, but her mind was made up. Despite being tormented after each date with Levi, she was steadfast that God did damage control on the cross. She tuned them out as she reflected on the previous night.

Levi's family was welcoming. She couldn't figure out Levi's sister-in-law Jet. That woman had come across like her coworker Patrice's evil twin. Jet didn't know a thing about her, but she wasn't subtle about the fact that she wasn't trying to like her. Karyn didn't want to even think about Jet's reaction if she knew of Karyn's past.

When Karyn blinked, Halo had boarded the bus and was making himself comfortable next to Buttercup.

"My sister gets a boyfriend and she can't speak," Halo stated loud enough to reach Karyn's ear.

Blushing, Karyn reached across a vacant seat and pinched his shoulder. "Leave me alone."

Less than ten minutes later, Deacon Deacon steered the van into the church parking lot. The riders tightened their hold on the seats as he weaved around vehicles as if he were driving a compact car. With finesse, he slowed the van to a precision stop at the church's double glass doors.

As she gathered her purse to get out, Karyn peered through the window. Levi was already on the premises, waiting for her with a smile. In one hand, he clutched a single rose and his Bible. Karyn didn't see Dori; then she remembered something about Dori staying the weekend with her aunt.

As was customary, ushers posted at the doors opened them. Levi stood center stage. He nodded to Halo, who escorted Karyn in, but Levi never took his eyes off her.

"Hi," she whispered, mesmerized by his twin dimples. "You beat me here."

He wrapped her in a bear hug and muzzled a kiss in her hair while the gang from the church van witnessed his adoration.

"Levi, we have an audience." Contrary to her gentle scolding, her eyes sparkled with his outward show of affection as she elbowed him to push him away.

He loosened his hold, but grabbed her hand. "Oh, well. Good morning." He and Halo started a stare duel until Buttercup nudged Halo along to grab a seat. Halo didn't budge, defiant.

Mother Caldwell scuffled closer and with a crooked finger directed Levi down closer to her face. Karyn stilled. *Oh, Lord. What is she going to say?*

"Young man, this is your second visit here. I'm glad to see you, but my Karyn is special. She's as sweet as they come," Mother Caldwell informed him.

Levi's eyes twinkled behind his glasses. "Yes, ma'am. I know."

Halo and the others mumbled their agreement as they dispersed. This was it. Karyn's life was changing. Today marked the first time since she had become a member of Crowns for Christ that she wasn't sitting among other ex-offenders. She was moving on. Her life was moving on.

Possessively, Levi pulled her closer and headed in the opposite way, as if this was his church and he had a reserved pew. Although she noticed the rose, Levi never mentioned it.

"I missed you last night," he repeated, waving off an usher as they entered the sanctuary.

Karyn smirked, recalling the previous late-night phone call after he had dropped her off a half hour before curfew. She hadn't lied. They had fallen asleep on the phone. Thank God for Levi's unlimited minutes.

"Is Dori with her aunt?" Karyn didn't want to assume.

"Yep. I don't have to share you."

Once they came to a pew of his choosing, he stepped back and waited for her to go first. He removed her coat then his. Together, they knelt and said a prayer of thanks to the Lord for allowing them to return to the house of worship. Even in prayer, Levi's hands were linked with hers. After they sat, Levi's eyes swept over Karyn's garment. She felt self-conscious. He had seen the turtleneck last week. Her clothes consisted of thrift store bargains and hand-me-downs from the church clothes pantry.

"I see we're matching. I thought red was my favorite color, but brown is making me think twice," Levi complimented.

Band members took their position behind their instruments. Their music introduced the praise team.

"Praise the Lord for Jesus, everybody," a young woman addressed the church from behind a microphone on the pulpit. "Shake your tambourines, clap your hands, and stomp your feet. The saints are in the house!"

In harmony, they began singing Israel and New Breed's, "Here I Am to Worship." Only when Levi stood to participate did he let go of Karyn's hand. Stretching his arms in the air, Levi closed his eyes and bowed his head. Immediately, Karyn could tell he had tuned her out.

She didn't mind. There was no competition with Christ, because He would win out every time. Opting to stay seated, Karyn bowed her head and shut her eyes to meditate on the words. Her worship always included thanksgiving for freedom from prison and sin. Yes, He who the Son had set free was free indeed.

More songs followed until the music segued to Pastor Scaife speaking to the congregation. Karyn opened her eyes to find Levi preparing to sit as he wiped his face.

"Praise stimulates us, worship humbles us, but it is the fervent prayer of a righteous man that keeps us. Choir, will you sing a little of this song: 'Somebody prayed for me, had me on their minds. They took the time to pray for me. . . .'"

After two choruses, the pastor directed them to James 5:16. That's when Levi slowly presented Karyn with the rose. "Whenever you read this passage, think of me."

Affected by his thoughtfulness, Karyn could only nod. She had temporarily forgotten about the flower. He hadn't offered it to her, and she wasn't going to ask for it.

For the next forty minutes, Karyn delicately used the rose's stem as a bookmark as Pastor Scaife quoted from two other passages.

"Confess to one another therefore your faults—your slips, your false steps, your offenses, your sins—and pray also for one another, that you may be healed and restored to a spiritual tone of mind and heart. The earnest, heartfelt, continued prayer of a righteous man makes tremendous power available, dynamic in its working," Pastor Scaife explained.

There was no doubt in Karyn's mind that the rose would be an extra incentive to read her Bible. Every time she did, she would remember the sermon. God's purpose was preaching to His flock, but was the Lord talking directly to her about confessing to one another?

As the sermon came to a close, the invitation was opened for those who wanted prayer, water baptism, or someone seeking the evidence of the Holy Ghost.

After the benediction, Levi turned to Karyn. "I consider myself well fed. Hungry?"

"I am."

"Then you have an important decision to make. Have dinner with me."

She tilted her head. Karyn loved to watch him. "Tell me where we're going so I can let Buttercup know and make her jealous."

"It's a surprise." He grinned.

Karyn kept a smile in place while she cringed inside. She had to make another call to her caseworker. She was running out of favors and time.

CHAPTER 28

"Good morning," Rossi greeted his cousin that Monday as Levi swaggered into the office. Leaning back in his chair, Rossi tapped his pen on his desk as he scrutinized him.

Although Levi was humming, he didn't look totally alert as his crisp clothing would suggest. "Morn'," he dragged out and headed to the tray where their assistant placed a pot of coffee every morning.

The man didn't even have his glasses on. How did he possibly get to work in one piece? He usually never wore his contacts in the morning because of his allergies.

"If you weren't related to me, Levi Tolliver, and didn't own half the stake in this business, I'd fire you, man. We have a meeting in less than an hour with the financial advisory board. This is not the time for you to lose your common sense.

"We've worked years to get tax breaks for that stretch property in downtown East St. Louis. We've already had one delay when the crew discovered the underground city that was once flooded. Now, we could start the groundbreaking in about a month, but you already know that, Rossi reminded him."

Taking a sip from his cup, Levi scrunched his nose. "More sugar . . ." A faraway expression was frozen on his face. "Karyn's finishing up her degree in business management. What do you say about leasing her space in the old Majestic Theatre once the overhaul is complete? Of course, with a deep discount, which will be next to nothing. Since she wants to give back to the community, I want her to succeed."

Levi gnawed on his lips. Clearly, he was on a different planet, because he wasn't giving Rossi a second thought. Dismissing himself, Levi walked across the hall to his executive suite, nodding to their administrative assistant. Before Rossi could trail him, Levi backtracked.

"Or we could put her in the old Spivey Building. Since it was built in the late 1920s as the city's first skyline, I think that would be more appropriate for Karyn," Levi rambled on. "She's reaching for the stars."

Rossi eyed Levi. One thing about his cousin: Once Levi was focused on anything, he wasn't easily distracted. Unfortunately, at the moment, his concentration was misdirected. Rossi needed to divert him to the business at hand. Levi had been the one who initiated the bid. However, Rossi had to give Levi his moment of bliss. He was gaining momentum right before Rossi's eyes. Levi hadn't talked this much about Diane before he asked her to marry him.

Feeling that it was his duty, Rossi remained in spiritual guard mode so he could decipher Levi's every word. He had yet to calculate the number of times Karyn's name had been mentioned since Levi arrived at work. If Rossi had to guess, he estimated every ten words. Still, Rossi was trying to listen to God concerning Levi.

"How did Karyn get into this conversation, Levi?"

"Haven't you been listening? How much sleep did you get?" Levi taunted, seemingly annoyed that Rossi hadn't been following his thought process.

"Thanks for asking about me. I got—maybe—a little more than you," Rossi said with a heavy groan. Leaning back in his office chair, Rossi rubbed his neck and grimaced. Despite his late night, he managed to get to work on time and prepared for the meeting.

"I accepted an invitation for dinner and prayer afterward at one of our young people's houses after service yesterday. The girl was struggling through some issues and she didn't know how to approach her mother."

"What happened?" Levi gave him his full attention as he positioned himself on the edge of Rossi's desk instead of a chair, which Levi knew irritated Rossi. "This doesn't sound like it's a praise report. More like a prayer vigil."

"Five minutes." He emphasized the number with his hand. "Not even five minutes after I arrived, I saw the root of the teenager's shortcomings. I'm not mentioning any names, but the family hadn't been to church in a couple of months. Sister I'm-not-telling-you-who-she-is is a victim of domestic violence." Rossi shook his head in disgust. "I just saw Brother I'm-not-telling-you-his-name-either at midweek Bible class."

Rossi couldn't erase the image of the bruise on the mother's face and her sprained arm secured in a sling. Her husband, a well-known church leader, was not only an abuser, but an unsuccessful gambler and liar.

Levi immediately sobered. He set his coffee cup on Rossi's desk on a spot where Rossi had seconds earlier swiped a stack of contracts out of the way. "I'm sorry, man." He rubbed his hair. "I don't understand some people. Why go to church when you don't practice what's preached? And why marry a woman and beat up on her? Some animals are treated with more tender loving care than people. Speaking of which, Karyn—"

Rossi huffed. "Come on, man. Karyn again?" He gritted his teeth in frustration.

"Seriously, I think Karyn might have been a victim of domestic abuse or something."

Sitting straighter, Rossi's ears perked. "What? Why would you think that? She seems quiet, but nothing to indicate to me that she's been a victim." He frowned, recalling the first time he had met her, and then at his aunt and uncle's house. "Have you asked her?"

"No, and I don't plan to. I want her to trust me enough to tell me. I'm patient until I get tired."

CHAPTER 29

Glancing out the transit bus window, Karyn smiled. It was midweek in mid-December, and Levi hadn't missed a beat. God seemed to stir her minutes before Levi's wakeup call. Despite his attention, everything wasn't all right in Karyn's world.

God's message through Pastor Scaife's recent sermon was weighing heavily on Karyn's heart. She had to be honest with herself; Levi was probably in love with her.

When she had prayed that morning, she uttered her Bible golden text: *He who the Son sets free is free indeed.* Within her heart, she knew it was the right scripture for all situations, so why didn't she have the confidence to latch on, close her eyes, and hold tight? She was letting the devil get to her.

Levi's smile, eyes, and generosity were still lingering in her mind as the bus came to a stop and let her off at the mall. Bundling up, she practically sprinted across the parking lot to the entrance. Bookshelves Unlimited was already teeming with early morning shoppers. *Whoever would have thought that a toy store's biggest competitor would be a bookstore?* she thought, smirking to herself.

Karyn's feet were trained to go straight to the customer desk to log in. Her hands were already unzipping her jacket, but her thoughts were still on Levi and Dori.

"Is six weeks really long enough to open up and spill your secrets?" Karyn whispered out loud.

"Doesn't matter. There's no such thing as a secret," Patrice answered.

Karyn jumped, blinking. Her heart pounded. Patrice had a talent for sneaking up behind people and hearing things that shouldn't be repeated, then repeating them. Karyn hadn't realized she had verbalized her thoughts.

Patrice preyed on coworkers in their weakness. Showing a sympathetic ear, whatever Patrice took in, she diced up the information and let it out.

For the rest of the day, Karyn stayed away from Patrice and focused on customers' needs. The store's steady crowd gave Karyn a distraction from her conflicting emotions, but they would just return between shoppers. Spiritually, she seemed stronger inside the prison walls than she did now outside of them. Her strength was wavering when it came to boldly declaring God's forgiveness and keeping power.

Levi made sure that throughout the day, she would think about him—from the morning calls to the regular box lunch deliveries to curbside pickup when she clocked out, which she had already cleared with Monica. He was making her dependent on him for her happiness. That wasn't a good thing.

During her lunch break, Karyn walked into the back room and was surprised but pleased to find it empty. She needed to talk to someone and get another perspective. Buttercup's call for action plan was to tell Levi. Karyn's fellow van riders argued that Karyn dare not tell Levi, because her past was not who she was today and therefore, void. She reached for her cell phone and did what she should have done before she got caught up in her blissful web.

First glancing over her shoulder to check for privacy, Karyn then punched in the church's number. After acknowledging the secretary, Karyn was transferred to Pastor Scaife.

Once they exchanged greetings, Karyn bowed her head. To an observer she appeared to be saying grace. "I'm in turmoil. Am I deceiving myself into thinking my past doesn't matter to a man who adores me, or am I deceiving him into believing I'm a woman with no baggage?" she asked in a hushed tone.

"Sister Karyn, you are what God says you are. This trial didn't just spring up one day. It was already in the books. God already has the ending written, so trust God along the way, and let God write the script for you about what to say."

Karyn didn't say anything as she sniffed. Pastor Scaife called her name a few times to snap her back into the conversation. She released a heavy sigh.

"I could lose him."

"God can replace him." Karyn could hear a smile in his voice. "Or God could cause Levi to increase his love for you. Either way, Sister Karyn, God's purpose in your life is to save you, which He did. Anything else He decides to give us is a blessing."

Pastor Scaife continued to encourage before he prayed. "Father, in the name of Jesus, you have a purpose for Karyn's life. Not only did you forgive her, you spared her and you saved her. Lord, bless her according to your will and riches in glory. Amen."

"Amen," she repeated.

"Now, Sister Karyn, God doesn't want us worrying about anything, and I do mean anything. He reminds us of this in Philippians 4:6."

Karyn whispered "Amen" again, then disconnected. Checking her watch, she ate her lunch quickly. It would surely be for energy, because she no longer had an appetite.

"Hmmm. I wonder what secret you're keeping," Patrice taunted with a smirk as she walked into the break room.

If only she knew, Karyn thought, ignoring Patrice. Access to Karyn's employment file was so secured, no one at her job would ever know. The hiring manager was a relative of one of her church members. Besides, if Patrice knew, so would her coworkers. Thank God for that.

CHAPTER 30

Wake up and pray.

Rossi recognized the voice and did as God instructed him. At first, he drifted in and out of sleep, but he stayed on his knees for more than an hour. He began with his usual prayer requests: the safety of the military troops, the needs of the senior citizens, teachers, and homeless. "Lord Jesus, deliver Kim from the spirit of homosexuality, David from his dependency on drugs, remove Pam from adultery. . . ."

He prayed in earnest until God took possession of his mouth and began to speak in unknown tongues. A few times, Rossi heard the interpretation. Before Rossi whispered "Amen," he lifted Levi, Karyn, and Jet's names in prayer.

Watch and pray, God had spoken through His tongues.

Since the last time God had interrupted his rest, Rossi had kept his spiritual eyes open and hadn't seen the devil on the Tolliver premises, yet he would continue to be on guard. He was certain Levi was going to Crowns for Christ again this morning. Rossi would be there too.

Rossi checked the time on the clock on his nightstand: seven-thirty. He had forgotten to set the alarm; he would have overslept if God hadn't stirred him. Getting off his knees, he reached for his cordless phone.

Dori and Levi were surely up. He punched in their home number.

"I'm going." Rossi didn't wait for Levi to greet him.

"Where?"

"I'm going to Karyn's church with you," Rossi stated as he walked into his bathroom to start his bath water.

"What makes you think that? Anyway, I don't think so. Dori and I are taking Karyn out to dinner after church. Don't take this the wrong way, but four's a crowd."

Unfazed, Rossi replied, "Okay, I'll meet you there."

"I'm not saving you a seat," Levi stated defiantly.

"Did you forget that as a minister, God always saves me a seat either in the assembly or at the invitation to sit in the pulpit? Either way, there's room."

Before they hung up, Levi once again sang the praises of Karyn.

Rossi grinned as he shook his head. His cousin had it bad. It was his job to be on the lookout for the devil's mischief.

"Miss Karyn! Miss Karyn!" Dori yelled, waving as she saw Karyn step off the church van.

Karyn didn't disappoint Levi's little girl when her eyes widened and sparkled with delight. Once she entered the church foyer, she squatted and opened her arms. Dori ran into them. They squeezed each other and smiled.

Levi stood silently, waiting for his greeting. The best he got was a weak hug. "Hey, I want what she got," he protested, pointing to Dori.

"Too bad. It's reserved for good little girls," she teased. With Karyn's hair back into the single braid, she looked younger. She gave a simple sweater dress class. Dori clutched Karyn's hand as they walked into the entrance of the sanctuary with Levi trailing them.

An usher led them down an aisle. He offered them a choice near the front or on the side. Karyn choose a pew on the side, and they entered. Levi helped Karyn then Dori remove their coats then finally removed his. He laid them on the back of the seat and was the last one of them to get on his knees to pray. He thanked God for another opportunity to be in His house and with Karyn.

With praise and worship underway, Levi chanced a glance over his shoulder. He blinked at a familiar face filtering through the crowd a few pews behind him. He did come. Levi shook his head. Rossi acknowledged him with a nod then returned to his worship, singing along with the praise team. Levi smirked.

Twenty minutes later, the pastor approached the podium and adjusted the microphone. His minister's robe was red and flashed gold when the lights shone on it.

"Good morning, saints and friends." He paused and waited for their response. "It's Resist the Devil Sunday. For our visitors, this is the time we set aside to do preventive maintenance on our souls. If you haven't already, turn to Ephesians 6:11. How has your faith and endurance been holding up these last thirty days? Is your armor still sturdy? Be strong in the Lord, not in yourself or other people, but in God. Have you ever known God to lose a battle? Even when he died on the cross, He confounded the devil because He still won."

Levi leaned over and whispered in Karyn's ear. "I know some come to church expecting a financial prosperity sermon, but I've noticed for the last three Sundays, he preaches about strengthening our salvation walk."

"Oh, he does preach prosperity, but he says it's in three parts: financial, health, and soul. Pastor Scaife's philosophy is to deliver God's sheep spotless and blameless before Him. If our soul is progressing, then everything else will fall in place. I got saved through the pri—promising ministry, she explained."

Pastor Scaife drew them back in. "After you go through your armor checklist, make sure you have your oil, because you're going to need it." He closed his Bible and descended the steps of the pulpit.

"God expects you to carry oil with your armor. Don't be foolish as the virgins in Matthew 25:10. If you don't have your oil today, God has plenty in the form of the Holy Ghost. Repent and walk down the aisle. Ministers are waiting to pray for you; then if you choose to get your sins washed away . . ."

His appeal became dramatic, and people from all directions flocked to the altar for prayer. Some were led away to a side door for baptism. It took more than a half hour, but twelve souls were baptized. Four came out of the water speaking in other tongues. Not long after that, Pastor Scaife gave the benediction as he directed everyone to stand and leave a free-will offering. "Fight the good fight of faith until we meet again."

Unofficially, Levi felt like a member when someone near him made an effort to speak to him before leaving. Levi recognized another face—Halo. The buff man reminded Levi of a bouncer. He doubted if Halo wanted a moment of meet and greet. It was probably to make his presence known. The big guy was hard to miss, but size never intimidated Levi.

"I'm glad I came," Rossi said from behind him. Rossi slapped him on the shoulder and squeezed.

Karyn spoke to a few women who had gathered around her then hugged Halo to Levi's chagrin.

As the crowd thinned, Levi was about ready to leave with Karyn when something or someone stole Karyn's interest. Nosy and possessive, Levi stuffed his hands in his pockets and casually pivoted on one heel, scoping out whoever was competing for Karyn's attention.

A fair-skinned woman adorned in a mink hat and wrapped in a mink coat stood staring at Karyn. Levi frowned. Should he be concerned? Was she a threat to his woman that caused Karyn to freeze and become speechless?

Before he could get any answer, Karyn walked away in trancelike steps toward the woman. The mystery lady, in turn, left her pew to make a beeline to Karyn in more hurried steps.

Levi held his breath, trying to assess the situation and how to respond. Besides her roommate and Karyn's Sunday van riders, he knew very little about Karyn's other friends. It wasn't until after Karyn and the woman embraced that Levi exhaled. He heard a heavy sigh over his shoulder, but ignored it.

They were practically fused together as they planted kisses on each other. They released each other, scanned each other, and started the ritual again.

"Who is that?" Rossi shoved Levi as Dori ran circles around them. A minute later, a toddler joined Dori in the fun. "Are they crying?" Rossi asked, concerned.

"Let's go."

Karyn was almost hysterical in emotions when Levi scooted next to her. "Babe, is everything all right?'

"Levi and Minister Rossi," Karyn said, sniffing, "I want you to meet Nalani Wallace, my younger sister."

CHAPTER 31

"I haven't seen my sister—"

"In four years," Levi finished. "I know." He gently disengaged the sisters in order to gather Karyn into his embrace. Giving her a squeeze around her shoulders, he looked at Nalani for the first time.

"It's nice to meet you." He extended his hand "I'm Levi. That's Minister Rossi" He tilted his head. "My Cousin."

Rossi knocked Levi out of the way and accepted Nalani's hand. "It's nice to meet you."

Karyn watched as Rossi kept his eyes on her sister as if he were calculating her worth.

"And that bunch over there," Karyn said, pointing to a few of her van riders, including Halo, Buttercup, and Mrs. Caldwell, "those are my people. They not only love me, but they have my back."

They waved and one by one formed an impromptu receiving line to meet and greet Karyn's sister. Levi pulled Karyn aside to give them room.

He leaned over and whispered into Karyn's ear. "Should I be offended that your only description of me is my name?"

Karyn was too emotional to respond. Putting on her game face, she scrunched her nose at him to break the private moment he was pulling her into.

Rossi seemed to take control, dispersing the group to give Karyn and Nalani space. "Since Levi was taking Karyn to dinner, why don't you join us, Nalani?"

"Us? There is no us," Levi mumbled. "Rossi was not invited."

She was itching to be alone with her sister. Four years was a long time to be detached from the world. Before Levi, there was her family, and no one could ever replace that.

"Oh." Karyn gnawed on her lip. She faced Levi. "Do you mind if we take a rain check? I really want to catch up with my sister."

His cousin stood silently watching as if he were analyzing the situation. Rossi made Karyn nervous, as if God were exercising the gift of Knowledge through him. She hoped not. Levi deserved the truth from her—if she decided to tell him. And her "if" was growing bigger every day.

Karyn closed her eyes and gave Levi a hug. He lingered in their embrace, inhaling a whiff of her hair then kissing the crown of her head. "Woman, I'll miss you." He smoothed her cheek with the back of his finger. Karyn indulged in his touch.

"Perhaps we'll see each other again." Rossi faced Karyn. "Have a great afternoon."

The charm of the Tolliver men was in full throttle. As they walked away, Karyn claimed the nearest pew to sit and pulled her sister down with her. They squealed and hugged again like chatty teenagers.

The deacons began to turn off the main lights in the sanctuary, but the sunlight from the stained glass windows in the foyer beamed throughout the auditorium. A quiet peace filled the place. Sighing, Karyn's soul overflowed with happiness.

"I have so many questions," Nalani said. She removed her mink coat and rested it on the back of the pew.

Karyn was fascinated with her movements. The clothes on Nalani's back were a designer's. Karyn had been out of the loop too long to name the architect. Regardless, the two-piece suit with gold pearl buttons looked good on her sister.

Nalani leaned forward and observed Karyn watching her. "You remind me of a teenager." She reached out and fingered Karyn's single braid. "But your eyes tell a different story."

"And you." Karyn squinted. "You're Momma reincarnated—dainty, stylish, and confident."

Karyn guessed that, five years younger at twenty-two, Nalani was about five feet three inches without her four-inch stilettos. Where Karyn's hair was long, black, and wavy, Nalani opted for a sassy short style. Nalani Wallace had all the accessories for true diva status.

Whatever men preferred on a woman, Nalani had it from the top to bottom. Her skin was the perfect blend of beige sand, and she had an irresistible smile. Karyn didn't guess at her measurements, but was sure Victoria's Secret merchandise was sized with her in mind. She had a tiny beauty mole above her left naturally arched brow, and light brown eyes that enjoyed sunny days. Nalani hadn't lost her baby face with the high cheekbones and pointed chin.

From the looks of her mink, Nalani Wallace hadn't disappointed Senator Nathaniel and the late Lana Wallace. "You're beautiful. I wish I could take credit and say I taught you everything you know, but . . ." She swallowed and looked away. Karyn did it to herself. She couldn't blame anybody but herself for her actions.

"Hey." She squeezed Karyn's hand. "You're teaching me right now how to pick up the pieces after making a mistake. You've spiraled downhill, yet you survived prison, and I'm here to help you now."

Karyn sniffed, touching her eyes. "It's a good thing I don't wear much makeup because I wouldn't be very attractive right now."

"You'll always be attractive to me," Levi said, causing the sisters to jump.

Patting her chest, Karyn wondered how much he had heard. "You scared me. What are you still doing here?" Her heart pounded with a bout of fear.

He held up her purse and coat.

"Oh." She lowered her eyes in embarrassment. "Thanks."

"You're welcome, beautiful." He winked and whistled as he strolled away, heading toward the foyer.

She followed his movements until he, Rossi, and Dori walked out the front entrance. When she turned back to her sister, Nalani was grinning.

Nalani smirked and tilted her head in the direction of Levi's retreating figure. "Hmm. He's my first question. Does he know?"

Karyn shook her head. She didn't want to talk about Levi at the moment, so she changed the subject.

"You have no idea how badly I missed you and Daddy. One bad decision caused my freedom to be snatched away—justifiably so. The change was abrupt. Suddenly, all my rights were gone. That's when I understood that rights weren't a given, but a privilege. I no longer could choose to stay up late to watch Jay Leno. The lights went out at eight, and the only thing I could do was pray that sleep would come soon," Karyn sadly admitted, then waved her hand in the air. "I don't want to depress you."

Karyn mustered a weak smile. "So how did you find me? You stopped writing, so I figured something was going on at home . . . and you know, with Daddy's threat, I dared not call collect or write." She swallowed. "So how's Daddy?"

Nalani looked away. She stared at nothing. Next, she twisted her lips. When Nalani started fiddling with her manicured fingers, Karyn sensed Nalani was stalling.

"Karyn," she began then paused, staring at Karyn. "Daddy died . . . about six months ago."

Six months. Karyn had been released and could have been there for her sister. Tears choked Karyn's vision as her heart jumped. "Dead?" Karyn whispered. Her hands trembled. "He died," she whispered again. She covered her face with both hands. She had missed his last breath of life because she was in prison. Her father was gone. Karyn would never see him again. She could never reconcile the hurt she caused him and others. Despite her incarceration, life went on and passed away. She had missed four of Nalani's birthdays, her father's death, and no telling what else.

Whoever thought convicts had it easy with room and board needed to ask her. Prison was punishment. Just like the victims' lives were changed forever, so were the perpetrators'. Could the day get any worse? As she started another round of anguish, Karyn wished for Levi's strong arms of comfort and his solid chest for strength.

Nalani reached out and steadied her sister's hands. "Hey, let's go somewhere so we can talk. I'm not going back to that New Beginnings place. That's out of the question. I went there first and informed some woman in charge that I was your sister." She placed a fist on her hip. "The woman practically mocked me. She seemed too happy to inform me that my name wasn't on your visitor's list. Girl, I was getting ready to go ghetto on her, but another woman defused the situation. She flipped through a log and gave me this church's address. The GPS in the rental car couldn't get me here fast enough. I came here on a mission—to find my sister."

"Feisty, aren't ya?" Karyn's somber mood changed.

"You know it when it comes to my sister." Nalani grinned proudly.

Karyn chuckled. Nalani had long lashes like their mother. Her teeth were straight, the result of their dad footing the bill for braces and an orthodontist's meticulous attention.

Nathaniel Wallace—Senator Nathaniel Wallace. Karyn held in her audible sigh. The last memory of her father was his disgust that his well-bred daughter would commit such a cowardly and heinous act. From that day forward, Nathaniel Wallace withheld his affections.

"I have to call my caseworker to get her approval for a change of plans. I've pressed my luck with Levi. It's been a constant list of requests. I had no idea he planned to take me to dinner. I'm running out of excuses. Your surprise visit kept me from telling him no again. My caseworker is so sick of me bugging her for permission to change plans at the last minute. I can't afford to violate my parole for anything or anyone, but at times I felt so close to doing that."

Frowning, Nalani tilted her hand, confused. "I thought you were out."

"Yes and no. I'm no longer housed at the Decatur Correctional Center, but I'm still in the judicial system. I don't have to be in bed by eight, but my whereabouts must be accounted for at all times."

"Oh." Nalani still frowned, but handed Karyn her BlackBerry. "Make the call. I'm ready to eat."

"I have my own phone. Levi made sure of it."

CHAPTER 32

"She really must have fallen from grace with her family." Levi whistled. "Her sister looks like she has money to spare." He frowned as he stabbed his slice of meatloaf several times before taking a bite.

Rossi watched with concern for his cousin. The hearty appetite that the Tolliver men were known for had vanished from Levi. He anchored his elbow on the table and rested his chin. "Karyn catches the bus, works at a dead-end job, and is struggling to finish paying for her education."

Rossi's appetite hadn't been affected. He had already been back to the buffet station twice, but he had to get Levi to snap out of his reverie. "Hey." He used his fork to point. "You know your elbow isn't supposed to be on the table. *Aunt Jet says* it's bad manners."

Levi snarled and obediently removed it. "Yeah Aunt Jet says is as aggravating as *Simons Says*."

Rossi snickered. He knew Jet's nitpicking got under Levi's skin sometimes. Usually, Levi held his tongue out of respect for his late wife. At those times, Jet aimed at his jugular.

His joking didn't pull Levi out, so he switched back to their original topic. "I thought your Karyn was pretty, but whew . . . her sister was nice on the eyes too." Rossi nodded, sipping on his Diet Coke and eyeing Levi. He seemed too distracted to respond to Rossi's dig.

Nalani was beautiful. She was definitely a wealthier version of her sister. Wiping his mouth with his napkin, Rossi leaned back in their booth. "So, how much do you really know about Karyn?"

Levi stared in space. "Definitely not enough."

That's what I thought. Rossi didn't dare voice it.

Karyn's regular caseworker had left early due to an emergency. Her replacement implemented the rules during her shift down to the periods and commas. She would not approve of any short notices for anything, including a change of location. To Nalani's disappointment, they remained at Crowns for Christ for dinner. After the evening service, Karyn would return to New Beginnings on the van with the other riders and not in a car with her sister. Karyn was accustomed to the restrictions, but Nalani was dumbfounded, so Karyn tried to keep the mood light.

"This garlic bread tastes homemade. This is really good." Nalani took another bite.

"Judging from the way you're shoving that spaghetti down your throat, I figured you liked El Café de Crowns for Christ," Karyn teased.

Buttercup left her cozy spot next to Halo and walked to the sisters' table from across the room. She slid in beside Karyn. "Girl, I know you're happy."

Karyn nodded.

Squinting, Buttercup examined Karyn's face for any telltale signs, as if she were covering up something other than blemishes. Buttercup faced Nalani again.

"Hey, Karyn's sister, I know we met briefly back in the sanctuary. Karyn and I watch out for each other."

"Humph. More like she bosses me around," Karyn joked.

Smiling, Nalani reached across the table and tapped Buttercup's hand. "I'm glad she had you. Thank you."

Buttercup tilted her head. "Well, don't thank me too much longer, because it's almost time for me to break out the joint." She grinned, patted the table, stood, and walked back to where Halo was starting on his second plate.

Leaning over, Nalani whispered, "I like her, but she seems odd. Is she part of a Native tribe with that elaborate headband?"

"Every week," Karyn said nonchalantly.

"Huh?"

Waving her hand in the air, Karyn dismissed the distraction. "Buttercup's obsessions are another day's topic."

Suddenly, Karyn's mood turned sober. She was still digesting the breaking news that her last parent was now deceased and she had missed the opportunity to say good-bye. "What happened to Daddy?" she whispered as if not saying it aloud would not make it real.

Nalani bowed her head and played with the leftovers on her plate. She appeared uncomfortable as she met Karyn's eye. "I think he let the ups and down of life do him in. We both knew Momma's death devastated him. Your prison sentence put him over the top. He resigned from his office months after your incarceration."

Guilt set in again. Karyn sniffed and glanced around the room, ashamed to make eye contact again with a fresh batch of tears brewing.

"Daddy gave up, which made my job of helping him more difficult. He didn't want to live. His high blood pressure soared, and then he was diagnosed with diabetes. He took his medication only when symptoms surfaced. I put off college to become his caregiver." Nalani paused and sighed. "I need to ask for your forgiveness."

Karyn blinked back a tear. "Me? She squinted. "Why?"

Nalani took a deep breath and struggled to answer. "I didn't know you were released when Daddy died, but . . ." She took another deep breath. "As much as I loved you, and I do love you, I hated you."

The words stung, especially coming from Nalani. Karyn took sips of air and held it before letting some seep out. Her baby sister's disappointment was one life lesson Karyn didn't want to face. She knew evidently Nalani would react to what Karyn had done.

"I never hated anyone in my life, and I never thought I would hate my own flesh and blood sister, but at the time of Daddy's death, I was lost and angry at the world. I stopped writing when Daddy got sick, and after he died, I didn't want to talk to you. I was having a meltdown. I underwent a month of bereavement counseling. A few months later, I felt like I had regained control of my life with no one dependent upon me."

Karyn reached across the table and grabbed Nalani's hands. "Consider us even. I cut your favorite doll's hair when we were younger."

They shared a laugh.

"Well, I hope I have redeemed myself. In Daddy's will, he left everything to me. After I placed half of it in a trust fund for you, then I was ready to reach out to you only to learn you were released and on parole. The biggest blessing is you're free and I'm here for you." Nalani mustered a smile.

"Thank you for loving me." The last thing Karyn wanted was for her sister to feel bad, so she changed the subject. "What school did you attend?"

"Northwestern."

"Ah. Go Wildcats. Your major?"

"I doubled in economics and environmental science."

"Whoa." Karyn beamed. "I'm so proud of you."

"I'm proud of you, big sister. I really am, despite my actions that might say otherwise. You pled guilty to manslaughter. The prosecutors were willing to give you probation, but the baby's daddy and his nose-so-high-up-in-the-air family insisted on the maximum sentence under the law. You made no excuses, even when the medical team testified that your actions probably stemmed from postpartum depression."

Karyn remembered that fateful Sunday afternoon. It was a year after her mother had passed away. Already enrolled in Columbia University in New York, she had promised her mother that she would finish her education. It was the vow to her mother that pushed Karyn over the top.

With that as her goal, Karyn at first stayed focused and studied among the elite. Everett Choteau IV was one of them. They met a few months after her mother died, and he provided the comfort she needed. They seemed compatible, and more than once their conversation included marriage.

They were attracted to each other, but not in love—her first mistake. Her second was becoming pregnant. Everett had immediately proposed, not wanting to bring embarrassment on their families—her third mistake. When Karyn hesitated, he convinced her it would look better to marry before she showed.

With her hormones already kicking in, Karyn just wasn't so sure about anything anymore. After she said no, he stopped asking. By the time she delivered, Everett had already begun to distance himself as if the baby weren't his. Karyn suspected his family had something to do with that, since they lived their life in the public eye, and scandals were always denied.

All she had to do was get through her last semester at the Ivy League college. She loved her baby, and he was adorable, but Evan wouldn't stop crying. Karyn had changed his diaper, given him his bottle, and tested for a fever. What was wrong with him? She was stressed, and Everett's presence was minimal. When the baby wouldn't stop crying, she picked him up and held him tight until he did. Pleased that he had quieted, she put him in his bassinet and returned to her studies. When she checked on him a half hour later, he hadn't moved, and he looked funny.

Hysterical, she phoned 911, but when the paramedics arrived, it was too late. She had suffocated—murdered—her child. The Choteaus had demanded justice. Everett's father said the senator's daughter shouldn't escape prosecution because of her family's name, and nobody was above the law.

Karyn felt her sister's hand shaking her then heard Nalani calling her name. She blinked, closing the door on that chapter in her life. She had zoned out. "Sorry. I try not to think about it. When I do, I hate myself."

"You needed help. I know some people think postpartum is a made-up label for bad parenting skills, but I read up on it. I know you blame yourself, but I blame me. I always wonder what if I could have been there to help. What if Everett had been there? What if his mother or Momma had been there?"

"Nalani," Karyn said firmly, "I don't make excuses for what I did with my own hands. I don't ever want you to make excuses for me. Understand?" Karyn tried to check her anger. Her sister didn't deserve to carry her weight on her shoulders.

"Understood." Nalani nodded. "Whew." She exhaled and looked around the fellowship hall. Many of the saints had finished eating and were returning to the sanctuary for afternoon services. "So when do you plan to tell Mr. Dimpled Smiles?"

"Only God knows."

CHAPTER 33

Jet was suspicious. Her mind had been working over-time since meeting Levi's special friend. Nobody was too good to be true; Jet was convinced. Her niece had been a nonstop chatterbox about Miss Karyn, where Levi's lips seemed to be fused together.

Sitting behind her desk at work, she tapped her pen on her calendar. It was two weeks before Christmas. She still needed to shop. She squinted at an event she noted for this Saturday. It was Macy's girls' night out bash. Tia had invited her only after inviting Karyn first.

"Hmm, sounds cozy." Jet smirked. She was already devising a plan. She picked up her phone.

"Hi, Levi. This is Jet—"

"Yes, I know this is your weekend for Dori," he stated with annoyance. "You know, I really wish you'd stop demanding custody. I've never prevented you from spending time with your niece."

Jet rolled her eyes. Levi had begun to misinterpret her requests since her sister's death. "Chill, brother-in-law. Not this weekend. I'm going to Macy's with Tia and Karyn this weekend. Tia invited me. I'm really glad since she's becoming a member of the family that she's not shutting me out because I'm not a Tolliver."

Levi let her rattle on without responding.

"Anyway, will you ask Seth to remind Tia about the time we're supposed to meet? And oh, Karyn too. Or you can just give me their numbers, and I can call and finalize plans with them."

"No need. I'll have Seth remind Tia, and I'll remind Karyn." He sighed into the receiver. "Listen, Jet, Dori, and I want Karyn in our lives. We're crazy about her. Get to know her for who she is, okay? Karyn is not a man-eater, so don't treat her like one."

"Right." She twisted her lips in doubt as she disconnected the call.

Levi had relayed to Jet that the ladies were meeting at the bookstore, since Macy's was in the same mall where Karyn worked, and also that Karyn's sister was in town and would be tagging along.

At least Karyn has one, Jet thought as her heart dropped.

On Friday, Jet left work early and headed to Bookshelves Unlimited. Her excuse for arriving an hour early was to browse through the books. Truthfully, she wanted to observe Karyn. When she arrived, a worker said Karyn was in the back of the store separating customers' special orders.

Absentmindedly, Jet made her way to a biography section, which was near customer service. Karyn was coming through a door when a phone rang and she hurried to answer it. "Bookshelves Unlimited. If you want it, we've got it. This is Karyn," she greeted. Listening to the caller, Karyn answered a few questions then disconnected.

Afterward, as Karyn scanned the store, Jet ducked. With Karyn's back to the counter, Jet snuck closer as Karyn was making a call.

"Hi, Monica, I have a recreational pass for Macy's, St. Clair Square. Right. I'll leave work at six. . . ." Karyn nodded then laughed. "I'll bring back some samples. Okay, thank you."

What was that about? Jet wondered about the one-sided conversation. Jet thought the manner in which Karyn recited the information was almost akin to a terrorist plot. Jet shook her head. She was getting carried away. It was from all the counter-intelligence movies she had rented.

As Jet turned to sneak away, she bumped into a woman. She looked up, surprised. "I'm sorry. Oh, hey, Tia. What are you doing here so early?"

Tia lifted a brow. "I could ask you the same thing. I decided to buy a few books and wait in the café for Karyn and you. Then we can meet my other girlfriends at Macy's." Tia stretched her neck, glancing over Jet's shoulder. "Have you seen Karyn?"

She was saved from lying when Karyn walked between them. "Hi, ladies." She checked her watch. "It's not six yet."

"I know. Seth told you I love books. I wanted to see the new releases while I waited," Tia said then smiled.

Karyn faced Jet and waited for her explanation.

"Yeah, me too. I was considering one of the Obama books. See." Jet lifted *Mrs. O: The Face of Fashion Democracy* off the top shelf in biography. She was sure Karyn didn't want to know the truth: Jet avoided politics at all costs.

Karyn seemed to accept her excuse. Tia didn't look convinced, but kept her opinion to herself.

Tia scanned the shelves. "Karyn, recommend a book that I can put a dent into for the next hour." She looped her arm through Karyn's and the pair strolled away.

Jet used the opportunity to scrutinize Karyn's appearance. She hoped the woman was not wearing that uniform tonight, where most women would be dressed in professional or business casual attire. As usual, Tia was classy, dressed in rust suede pants and a blazer. Somehow, she had found matching boots. At least when Tia married into the family, she and Tia would have one thing in common—shopping.

If Levi was considering a replacement for her sister, Jet hoped he would have better choices. Working in a bookstore and looking like a little girl was not a role model for her niece. Jet sighed. Her brother-in-law definitely needed help in the dating department.

Bored, Jet walked in the opposite direction in search of the magazines. Although she didn't consider herself a book reader because she had enough reading materials at work, she might as well buy the book she had in her hand. Maybe Mrs. Obama would give her some inspiration.

Karyn was back behind the counter when an elderly woman walked in. The church hat she sported didn't match her drab, mismatched clothes. She was chubby with a warm face that could have easily been Jet's grandmother, who died when she was thirteen. All the women who were important to Jet seemed to die before their time: her grandmother, mother, and sister.

"Mrs. Harris, what are you doing here? It's not the first of the month." Karyn rushed to assist the woman, but was waved away.

She huffed with each step. "I wanted to send Sonny something special for Christmas."

"Did you forget that you just bought him something extra? Two shipments in one month? He's going to love you. That will be a wonderful surprise. He'll make the other prisoners jealous," Karyn chatted, beaming.

"Yeah, he says some of them get nothing." She *tsk*ed.

"It's sad and lonely. The punishment is when people on the outside forget about those on the inside."

"That will never happen. He's my flesh and blood. His pea-size brain was doing watermelon crimes, and he didn't think about the consequences, you know?'

Karyn nodded.

"Okay, baby. I'll take your suggestions about those Christian . . ."

Jet shivered. Those two talked about prison so casually that it made her uncomfortable. Jet turned toward the café to wait with Tia, who was already occupied, speaking with a well-dressed and stylish woman. Only one word could describe her: *money.*

Tia waved her over. "Jet, meet Karyn's sister, Nalani."

Nalani's eyes sparkled when she smiled as she stood. Her resemblance to Karyn was unquestionable. Her appearance was like a polished Cadillac compared to Karyn's fully-equipped compact economy car. "Hi, Jet. It's nice to meet you."

Automatically, Jet didn't like her, for no other reason than she was Karyn's sister. *God, what is happening to me?* When did she start to dislike people she didn't know? She was turning into someone she couldn't stand.

Friday evening was turning out to be full of surprises. First, there was Karyn. The first time she met her had been at Levi's parents' house. Jet's first impression was that she was pretty and simple. The second time was a few hours earlier. In her store uniform, she looked tired and simpler. That was not the woman Jet planned to mingle with from cosmetic counters to lingerie tables to hat racks.

Karyn clocked out and went into a back room. She came out fifteen minutes later with a makeover.

Reluctantly, Jet admitted this Karyn Wallace was attractive in her stacked-heel leather boots. Her pants were good quality wool, and her sweater neckline was trimmed in faux fur—maybe. Karyn's earrings even seemed to be an upgrade. Maybe Karyn wasn't after Levi's money.

Tia seemed to hit it off with Karyn and her sister, which made Jet feel like an outcast. The trio joined forces with Tia's other girls from her sorority. Jet had to give the entire group credit. On more than one occasion, the women, including Karyn, had pulled her into their conversations.

Although Karyn was nothing less than friendly to her, Jet wasn't quite convinced that Karyn was suitable for Levi. For that cause, she needed to hang back and watch. One oddity was that Karyn kept glancing at her wrist watch. Why? The second, Karyn seemed to avoid another woman who wore long braids topped with some sort of headband. She was fashionable in an amateur way. When the two observed an item, they scurried away from each other as if they didn't want to be seen together.

Jet frowned. That was it: Karyn was a homosexual. She was going to have to be the bearer of bad news to Levi.

Instead of enjoying herself, Jet was becoming exhausted monitoring the two. She really hadn't wanted to come anyway. Also, the closeness and love between Karyn and her sister made Jet sad.

Who could fill Jet's emptiness? More importantly, was Karyn really stitching the gash in Levi's heart? At one time, Levi's anguish seemed to be as great as hers, but not since Karyn had come into the picture.

About 9:30 P.M., the gang wanted to leave. Karyn needed to get home, and Tia wanted to see Seth. Without her niece to fill her loneliness, Jet drove away in her luxury vehicle to a big empty home.

Forty-five minutes later, Jet pulled into her driveway and sat with the motor running. She didn't park or activate the garage opener. People who didn't know Jet thought she had everything: car, home, and cushy job. Some thought she was a man-eater because she didn't suffer fools or men who lacked confidence. As far as forming friendships with women, the effort wasn't worth it. Friendships were fragile—they were easily broken and painful to suture. Not so with a sister. The petty cat fights between sisters over clothes and such could never erase the bloodline, the bond, and forgiveness that always followed.

Sighing, she opened the garage door and drove through. Once inside her immaculate, twenty-five-hundred-square-foot house, she began to flip on light switches. Now that she was home, she thought about calling Levi with her suspicions, but then thought against it.

"I'm losing my mind. There's nothing wrong with that woman—a little strange, but normal."

Less than an hour later, Jet had dressed for bed and was brushing her teeth when the phone rang. Spitting out the toothpaste and barely rinsing, she hurried to answer it. She checked the caller ID: TOLLIVER.

"Hello?" She sat on the bed and brought her knees up to her chest. She wasn't getting off the phone any time soon.

"Did you have a good time with Karyn, her sister, and Tia?"

"Yes, Rossi. You know you don't have to call and check up on me so much. I'm not suicidal anymore. You just don't understand how it feels to lose someone. I hope you never have to experience that."

"God knows, Jet. I'm going to say this with the authority of God: One morning, you'll awake and it will be a new time in your life. You will move past this, and God will restore what you've lost."

"Ha! A new sister. I'd like to see that miracle."

Rossi snorted. "He's known as a miracle worker."

CHAPTER 34

A few days later, stretched out on his sofa, Levi didn't allow his cell phone to complete the first ring.

"You're late calling me, woman," Levi teased with a smile as he glanced at his watch. The time never mattered to him, as long as he and Karyn talked as much as possible throughout the day and before they closed their eyes at night.

"Poor baby," she taunted him.

"I would be jealous, but I know you've been catching up with your sister. I'm happy just to see you happy."

"Thank you for understanding, Levi. I'm sorry if I've been neglecting you. Nalani has one semester left at Northwestern, so she'll return to Chicago next month. I hated to see her go back to the hotel where she's staying."

"I know you wish your apartment was bigger for an extra guest," Levi guessed, since Karyn had never invited him inside.

"Umm-hmm. We've been cramming in every second. Levi, you don't know how glad I am she found me."

Confused, he frowned. "Found you? Right, like you were lost. I'm just sorry you couldn't mend fences with your father before he died."

Levi could have kicked himself. He had seen how devastated she was after learning her dad had passed away. Whoever said a man couldn't multitask was wrong. Since he had become highly addicted to Karyn, he could listen to her sweet voice, read the expressions across her face, and feel her moods. And Levi had been attentive as Karyn recanted what Nalani had told her. He heard her sadness and experienced the pain. He loved reading her facial expressions; they proved the honesty behind everything she told him.

Thinking fast, he changed the subject. "Since you don't care if I missed you, I'll use my secret weapon. Dori asked about you today." He grinned. Levi knew that would pull at her heartstrings.

"I love that little girl."

Closing his eyes, Levi could imagine Karyn's smile and genuine look of adoration. "Hmm. What about her old man?" He rushed to keep her from saying anything. "Save your response until we see each other this weekend. Do you have any plans for Christmas?"

"Besides spending it with my sister, no."

"Good. Consider you and your sister guests at my parents' home."

After a few moments of hesitation, she thanked him. She muffled a yawn.

Levi took the cue. "Hey, I know it's late. We better get some rest. Karyn?"

"Yes?" Her voice softened.

"Listen, baby, I know we pray together sometimes, but I'm going to do one of my cousin's spontaneous numbers. I just feel led that we should pray. Okay?"

"I would love that."

Of course she would. That was one thing he adored about her. Karyn thrived on their quick prayers. Anchoring an elbow on his knee, he bowed his. He heard the amber pop in the fireplace as he gathered his thoughts. "Father, in the name of Jesus, we thank you for Calvary, thank you for my blessings, and my joy in the morning. Lord, I ask you to bless Karyn and her sister. Lord, show us the way you've destined for us. Cover her with your blood in all that she does. Thank you. Ame—"

"No, Levi. It's my turn. Jesus, you know my shortcomings, yet you blessed me with a wonderful man who I know loves me even though he hasn't said it. Thank you for bringing him into my life. Lord, let me be worthy to receive your blessings." Her voice cracked as she sniffed. "I love you, Jesus."

"Amen," they harmonized.

"Karyn, let me be the first to go on record and say I do love you. I know it's not romantic over the phone, but when I see—" There was no telling how he would react. He might lose control, so he stopped.

She sniffed again. "I love you, too, Levi."

"I know. Good night, baby."

Levi woke the next morning still reminiscing about his conversation with Karyn. The vibes were still there. The chiming of his doorbell cut into his daydream. Dori's shouts of jubilee at the possibility of company made him get up to answer it.

"Daddy, somebody's at the door." She pulled at his hand. "Come on, Daddy, before they go away."

Whoever was on the other side had no intention of leaving with the insistent chiming. Levi opened the door, and Dori screamed her delight.

"Uncle Seth! Hi, Miss Tia."

Seth bent and scooped up his niece. Tia tickled her stomach.

"What are you two doing here? Dori and I were going to finish Christmas shopping."

Tia grinned. "For Karyn?"

Dori nodded. "She has lots of presents from me and Daddy."

"Really?" Tia lifted a brow as Levi ushered them in the door then shut it.

Levi took their coats but didn't bother to hang them in the closet. With little care, he discarded them in a nearby chair as his brother and Tia headed to the fireplace. Dori broke away and ran into her room. Within minutes, she returned, dragging a stuffed animal Jet had recently bought her.

Tia *ooh*ed and *ahh*ed over the toy to Dori's delight. Seth's gaze followed his fiancée with love. Levi watched their interaction with a little jealousy. If Nalani weren't in town, Karyn would be with him. He had never gotten the opportunity to show her where he lived, and in almost two months, she had never asked. Now that they had officially professed their love, things would change and their relationship could move at a faster pace. Thank God.

When Tia settled on the sofa, Dori claimed one side of her, and Seth stole the other. Levi sat back on the other sofa and stared. "So, what's up? Oh, pardon my manners. Do you want something hot to drink or a snack?"

They shook their heads as Seth stood. "Come on, Dori. Show your favorite uncle your room."

Dori jumped off the sofa, grabbed his hand, and led him away. "Uncle Solomon is my favorite uncle." She laughed, giggling at the game they always played.

Levi eyed him with suspicion before looking at Tia. His future sister-in-law had brought so much life and energy to the Tolliver family. Plus, she would be the daughter his mother had longed for, but if he and Karyn continued on the same path, Sharon Tolliver would get two daughters.

Leaning forward, Tia glanced over her shoulder then lowered her voice. "I wanted to talk to you about Karyn."

Instantly, Levi stiffened as if braced to react. "Why? What's wrong? I just talked to her not long ago." Levi was getting up to get his car keys.

"Sit down, Tolliver." She laughed. "I wanted to give my two cents from a woman who is marrying into the family. I like her. She's down to earth and pretty and has the sweetest spirit. I know I don't have to sing her praises, because you know all that. I didn't have a chance to meet Diane, so I can't compare the two, but I do know Karyn is perfect for you and for Dori."

Grinning, Levi relaxed. "You gave me a serious moment of high blood pressure." Levi's heart continued pounding. "Don't you ever do that to me again. I loved Diane and will always miss her, but she gave me Dori. Karyn . . ." He took a deep breath. "What can I say? The most important thing is that Karyn's mine."

Jumping up from her chair, Tia leaned over and patted Levi's knee. "Good. My job is done. I just wanted to give you a woman's perspective."

"You're late. Momma gave me that the first day she met Karyn, and as close as Jet is to Dori, no other woman has made it to the top of Dori's list."

"Good, because I asked her to be in my wedding."

Levi snickered. He knew there was a reason he loved his future sister-in-law. "What did she say?"

"Oh, I guess it all depends." Shrugging, Tia shouted over her shoulder. "Seth, baby, you ready to go?"

What kind of answer was that? Levi also stood. "Depends on what?"

"You." Tia wagged her finger. "Don't mess this up, Tolliver. I get good vibes about her."

Seth came out of Dori's bedroom. "Not quite, T. Dori and I are having a tea party," he said, feigning seriousness. His eye-rolling revealed he needed rescuing.

Tia laughed first, and then Levi joined her. Stepping around the coffee table, Tia looped her arm through Levi's. Together, they strolled to Dori's room. Levi shook his head. As the only grandchild, Dori had all of them wrapped around her finger.

In Dori's bedroom doorway, Levi noted the layout. Seth returned to the floor, twisting his long legs in an Indian style at a colorful plastic table. At more than six feet, his body and legs would crush Dori's children's furniture. Stuffed animals were situated on both sides of the table as invited guests.

Tia concealed her laughter as Dori unsuccessfully tried to steady a miniature party hat on Seth's head. Levi wasn't so discreet.

On the table in front of Seth was a tiny saucer. Seth turned and looked at them with the cup to his lips and his pinky posed. "Tea, anyone? Herbal or black?"

Levi and Tia collapsed on each other as they bowled over laughing.

CHAPTER 35

The mood was somber inside Karyn and Buttercup's living quarters.

"I was hoping your sister was coming to break you out of this joint at the same time I was escaping," Buttercup said, wrapping her micro braids around a hot curler.

For the past fifteen months, Buttercup had been a resident at the transitional women's center, and she had met the requirements to be released—at times, barely. She had saved more than the mandatory thirty percent of her weekly paychecks, had steady employment for more than a year, and had earned a raise. She had obeyed all the center's rules, except for the over-the-limit accumulation of personal belongings—headbands—but her counselor had looked the other way as Monica had with Karyn.

Karyn's soon-to-be-former roommate had secured a small but furnished one-bedroom apartment a forty-five-minute bus ride from New Beginnings. Buttercup had signed a one-year lease, believing she and Halo would be married soon.

The next few weeks would be bittersweet for Karyn. Buttercup had been a good friend. Karyn's next roommate would begin her cycle of starting anew, while Karyn would begin her countdown of the months before she left.

"I'm going to miss you," Karyn said with a soft sigh. "In less than thirty days, you'll be gone."

"You'll be right behind me in six long, excruciating months." Buttercup grinned. "Hey. Your sister is a jewel. She didn't have to set aside that money for you."

"I know," Karyn agreed.

"She could've been like some people and written you off because you're an ex-felon." Buttercup stopped curling her hair and turned around. With a fist positioned on her healthy hips, she tapped her house shoe on the wood floor. "Run this by me again, the reason you can't move in with her."

"Because . . ." Karyn stretched out on their couch. "She's staying in university housing. That's not considered a permanent residence by the state." Karyn squeezed her lips to keep from pouting. "Once she sublets an apartment near here so she'll have somewhere to stay besides in the hotel, then I'll be able to get weekend passes so I can visit her."

"At least you have access to money from your trust fund. Girl, do you know how much damage we can do at the thrift stores? Forget that. You don't even have to wait until Macy's has a sale. You could create your own."

"That money is going to be a blessing as a deposit on the loan for our business." Karyn began to loosen her braid since Buttercup had agreed to wash her hair after she finished with her own. "And, as you know, that money will not void my parole. I still have to hold down a job to complete it. And believe me, that's my goal."

"Because of Levi Tolliver," Buttercup stated.

Karyn didn't answer.

Taking the hint, Buttercup resumed curling her hair. "Humph. A low-paying job with crazy employees—"

Karyn held up her finger. "Just one."

"Yeah, right. Okay, back to Levi. When do you plan to tell him?"

"Who said I was?"

"See, you must think me and everybody on the church van is stupid, because even they know you will, even if you don't think so. As you know, Mother Caldwell has reversed her decision of telling Levi. Now she's keeping a tally on how many of us think you'll break soon. She's guessing on the first of the month—perfect way to start the new year, she says. Deacon Deacon has already been wrong twice. He thought you would cave in after the church sermons."

A couple of times, Karyn was close to confessing everything she had done since kindergarten. She also contemplated celebrating the year with a clean slate, especially since Levi had been upfront with her on their first date about his pain, anger, and his struggle to move on—not first date material, but the honesty was there from the beginning.

Buttercup didn't skip a beat. "Brother Brad Pickle picked the twentieth because he used to run numbers, and Halo—my honey—is praying never. And you know he's one praying hunk."

Outnumbered, Karyn shook her head. "What's the prize?"

"For Mother Caldwell, the satisfaction of being right."

"What about the others?"

"The satisfaction of Mother Caldwell being wrong."

They shared a laugh.

"You're going to tell him?"

Karyn huffed. "Buttercup, why do you keep harping on this? I'm not obligated to tell him. My sins are in my past, and I have the scriptures to back me up."

Buttercup yanked on her braids as she tried to de-tangle her curler. Once she accomplished the task, she used the hot appliance as a pointer. "Wrong. You're not obligated to tell your neighbor, teacher, car salesman, or store clerk, but the man you love? He's in à different category. When you love each other, you share secrets, faults, and fears. You know what the Bible says about perfect love. First John 4:18 says it casts out all fear."

"What if I lose him?"

"God's got an answer for that too." Resting her curler on the sink, Buttercup crossed the short distance to the couch and forced Karyn to sit up. "I don't have the correct answer." She sat next to her. "Listen. There is nothing worse than losing our freedom—nothing. Scratch that. Going to hell is irreversible. If Levi wasn't so important to you, you wouldn't be this tormented."

Tears streamed down Karyn's face. She was torn be-tween two emotions: being mad at Buttercup because she was speaking the truth, and being mad at But-tercup because she and Halo had both overcome the same issue—incarceration. There would never be any judgmental spats between them.

Karyn closed her eyes and leaned her head back until it rested on the wall. Buttercup wrapped her arm around her shoulders. Karyn had anticipated roadblocks once she was released; falling in love with a good man who was also the victim of crime wasn't one of them.

Buttercup squeezed her a few times. She untangled her arm from behind Karyn's back then checked her watch. "Ooh, if I don't get to bed soon, my skin cells—" Buttercup paused, realizing she was getting carried away with her beauty regimen. "One final question: Does Levi have perfect love?"

Karyn had just closed her eyes when one popped open. "Is this a trick question? Only God has perfect love for us."

Buttercup shrugged. "Then trust God's perfect love to give you peace, regardless of how much of a jerk Levi acts."

"Hey." Karyn jumped up. She balled her fists, ready to fight. "Levi is not a jerk!"

Buttercup grunted. "Then I guess he'll have to prove it."

CHAPTER 36

Jet cleared her desk in preparation for her end-of-the-year two-week vacation. She wanted next year to be different for her. It was time to make peace within. Although she wasn't a churchgoer, Jet had to have faith that justice was served for her sister.

Lifting her phone off the console, Jet made the decision to make the first step toward healing. She punched in the number to Tollivers Real Estate and Development. Once the receptionist answered, she was transferred immediately to Levi.

"Hey, Jet. What's up?" he answered.

"Levi," she said, swallowing. She was a strong, independent, successful black woman. Her mantra had always been that she didn't need anybody, but she had been wrong. "I'm ready for closure. Will you go to a crime victims' grief counseling with me, please?"

Levi was speechless. Jet knew she had caught him off guard with her request. Initially, he and Jet had balked at the idea because Diane's death was still too fresh. At least Levi had attended once, maybe twice.

"Will you?"

"Yes," he choked. "Yes, Jesetta, I will go."

"Thank you." Jet relaxed as they chatted a few more minutes before signing off with "Merry Christmas."

Closing her eyes, Jet inhaled deeply as if she were repeating a yoga technique. "A new year and a new beginning." She opened her eyes with a slight smile. If only she had a song in her head, she would hum it.

She was about to shut down her computer when, against better judgment and contrary to her declaration of moving on, she decided to pull up the story about the grocery store massacre. It had become a yearly ritual. Hopefully, it would be the final time she would reread line by line the names of the victims.

The news articles always made Jet cry, not only for her sister, but the families whose lives were shattered by the senseless act. "I love you, Diane," she whispered. She continued the self-torture by Googling the website that listed all inmates, including those convicted for the shooting, with their whereabouts and status.

From there, Jet started to feed her curiosity as she plugged in random names: herself, Rossi's, Levi's, co-workers. When she typed in the name Karyn Wallace, Jet's heart stopped, her mouth dropped, and her eyes bucked. She blinked in disbelief. It had to be a joke. She didn't actually believe she would get a hit.

A Karyn Wallace had a registration number. This Karyn Wallace—a black female, age twenty-six—was released earlier in the year. Could she be the same one? If only she could see a picture. Jet was on a roll. She pulled up picture after picture, but those were current inmates. She didn't have a social security number to get a police check. Was Levi's Karyn an ex-con? Did he know? If so, what was he thinking?

There was only one way to find out. It better be a coincidence, because Jet would not allow her niece to be around any type of criminals. It was three days before Christmas, and Karyn Wallace had to be at work. Jet signed off her computer and snatched her purse out of her desk drawer then locked it. Her adrenaline was pumping.

She glanced out the window. The snow was steady and heavy, but it didn't matter. Her vehicle had front wheel drive, and she was going to put it to the test. All bets were off for her to seek counseling if Karyn Wallace #176410-456 was the same one disguised as a bookseller.

Criminals didn't deserve second chances. Two of the gunmen in Diane's killing were on parole at the time of the murders. "Evidently, they weren't reformed." Anyone who served time in prison wasn't trustworthy.

Suddenly, Karyn's face was plastered on the person who pulled the trigger and killed her sister. Did Levi and everyone else know and didn't tell her? Jet now saw Karyn's face on one of the shooters. How many Karyns with a 'y' had the last name Wallace and had served time in prison? If she couldn't get her hands on the people who killed her sister, Jet would be satisfied with any ex-con as a stand-in.

Neither the snow nor other shoppers at St. Clair Square deterred Jet from completing her mission. She would confront Karyn and respond accordingly. In the parking lot, Jet made her own parking space, taking liberties with a handicap spot. Turning off the engine, she grabbed her purse and got out. Briefly forgetting about the hazard of snow, she almost slipped.

"Karyn, for your sake and safety, I hope there are thousands of Karyn Wallaces in prison." This was one of those times Jet wished she had bought a gun. Her steps were angry as she cleared the mall entrance. She made a beeline for Bookshelves Unlimited.

She searched the store as if her eyes were a scope on a rifle. Once she locked in on her target, she kept walking, not so gently moving customers out of her way.

Jet was within feet of Karyn, who was helping a couple, when she halted, causing someone behind her to trip. Jet was rigid. "Karyn, do you have a minute?" she said in a tone that let Karyn know it was in her best interests to make a minute.

"Hi, Jet. I don't now, but if you want to wait in the café, as soon as I get a break, we can talk." Karyn turned back to the couple.

That was akin to brushing her off, which infuriated Jet. "No, you are going to talk to me now, hussy. Have you ever spent time in prison?" Jet waited for the flinch in Karyn's brow like on the TV shows when someone lied. *Nothing.*

"What? Jet, I'm working, if you don't mind." Karyn dismissed her.

Jet reached out to grab her at the same time a security guard snatched her. "Let me go! Let me go!" Jet started to fight back. Another guard hurried to assist. The pair managed to drag Jet out of the store. One was already radioing for backup. *Great.* She was going to jail. She didn't want a record and to have her picture posted somewhere like a criminal.

Within minutes, a patrol car sped to a stop in front of the mall entrance. The red and blue lights were spinning.

Two more officers jumped out and raced through the doors. Jet was still struggling to free herself as a crowd gathered.

"What seems to be the problem, Jim? What do we have? Another shoplifter?" A tall and skinny officer demanded.

The cop was black. The situation could go two ways. She could plead she was "Shopping While Black" and she was targeted by the white officers, and she might get some sympathy; or he could be colorblind and treat her like the very criminals she despised.

"I don't know if she's on drugs or drunk, but she marched into the bookstore and threatened a worker."

"Assault, huh?" the same officer stated as if it were an open and shut case.

Since Jet had an audience, she decided to give them a show—big mistake. Screaming at the officers was not the way to be heard. The next thing she knew, she was in the backseat of a patrol car and charged with peace disturbance and resisting arrest.

A half hour later, Jet found herself in a Belleville Police jail cell. Weren't they supposed to read her Miranda rights or something? She blamed temporary insanity for her predicament. Once she calmed down and thought how ridiculous the accusation was, she could have kicked herself. Karyn didn't look like she had it in her to hit a squirrel in traffic.

She called Rossi to post bail. "You know I'm good for the money," she rambled on as he yelled and kept asking her to repeat herself. Surprisingly, he didn't seem surprised.

After two hours of the nightmarish ordeal, she was released. Outside the police station, Jet fell into Rossi's arms and cried like a baby. He hugged her and let her vent.

"I already prayed for you, Jet, after you called. You'll be okay. Come on. I'll take you to your car and then I'll trail you home. I know how this ended, but I'm a little curious how it all began."

Jet was grateful Rossi didn't ask another question. The short, humiliating ride was done in silence. He didn't play the radio. Even the snowfall had stopped. It was her curtain call to a bad day.

When Rossi parked next to her car, she mumbled her thanks and got out. A parking ticket under her wipers didn't faze her as Rossi got out and cleaned her windows. Once she was inside her car, Jet laid her head on the steering wheel. She needed counseling. She needed God. She needed a drink.

Rossi honked. Jet jerked up. Rossi was back in his car, waiting. Her hand shook as she fumbled to insert her key into the ignition. She adjusted the heat then drove away from her attempted scene of a crime.

She also opted for silence on her drive home. Jesetta Hutchens was once a really nice person, she thought, but the years after her sister's death had taken a toll on her.

Rossi continued to trail her as she turned into her subdivision. She waved good night as she rolled into her garage and let down the door. Snatching her designer purse off the passenger seat, she dragged it out of the car along with her body and headed inside.

She deactivated the alarm and began her routine of flicking on the lights. She kicked off her shoes and dumped her coat on the kitchen floor, an uncharacteristic behavior for a neat freak. She jumped when her doorbell rang.

Going to the door, she checked the peephole—Rossi. Jet groaned. Didn't he know she just wanted to climb in bed and hide under the covers? Determined, he laid his thumb against the bell. Taking a deep breath, Jet reluctantly unlocked the door. He strolled in without an invitation.

Rossi seemed even taller than his six foot five height now that she was barefoot. An unreadable expression on Rossi's dark, rich skin caused Jet to hold her breath. She was certain he was about to unleash his wrath. She didn't ask to take his coat, but that didn't stop him from removing it anyway and taking the liberty of going into her kitchen. He stepped over her coat on the floor.

"Where's your coffee?" he asked over his shoulder as he opened and slammed cabinet door after door in search of it.

"I don't drink coffee."

"One of us is going to need it." With his hand on the refrigerator handle, he paused, asking permission.

Crossing her arms, Jet rolled her eyes as she leaned against the doorjamb. "Why stop now? Help yourself."

He did. Grabbing a pitcher of punch, he found two glasses. He poured both of them a drink.

Rossi downed the contents. He grabbed the pitcher and poured a second. Pulling out a barstool from the counter, he collapsed on it. Rossi wiped a hand over his face and bowed his head. "Jesetta whatever-your-middle-name-is Hutchens, start from the top and tell me when you lost your mind."

Taking a deep breath, she paced the floor as she told Rossi of her suspicion that Karyn was a criminal. "I saw her name listed in an inmate registry."

"You mean you saw a similar name. You can't jump to conclusions like that. Plus, why are you still visiting that federal prison site as if you're one of those addicts bookmarking porn sites?"

Whether Rossi intended it to or not, his chastening shamed her. She sobbed and slobbered like a drunkard as she explained the chain of events. Rossi didn't interrupt, but each flinch was a silent reminder of the error of her ways.

Once she had emptied her heart, she braced herself for Rossi, the cousin of her brother-in-law, or Rossi, the youth minister, to respond.

"First of all, I'm going to pray for you."

She should have known, the preacher man.

"Jet, this has gone on long enough. I've been praying for you for so long. About three this afternoon God told me to pray. I didn't know who or what for, but I obeyed.

"I doubt the Karyn you found online is the same woman. You said there was no picture. You didn't rationalize this. You could have caused Karyn to lose her job, making false accusations like that. Plus, when did you become so enraged that you're going to hit somebody? You're one temper away from becoming delusional. You can't lash out on other people for no cause, or even if a person gave you a cause. Stop this behavior! As far as I know, Karyn hasn't said an unkind word to you. Don't you know God protects his saints?"

"Not my sister," Jet reminded him as she flopped on an opposite barstool.

"Jet," Rossi spoke softly, reaching across the table and covering her hand. "God was with her at the time of her death. Those who die without Christ feel the sting of death. Diane was not one of them. For the saints of God, it's different."

Rossi stood and walked back into the living room. He returned to his seat with a small Bible he must have carried in his coat pocket. He flipped through the pages until he found a passage. "In 1 Corinthians 15, there are several scriptures I like to read.

"*So it is with the resurrection of the dead. The body that is sown is perishable and decays, but the body that is resurrected is imperishable, immune to decay. It is sown in dishonor and humiliation; it is raised in honor and glory. It is sown in infirmity and weakness; it is resurrected in strength and endued with power. It is sown a natural physical body; it is raised*

*a supernatural body. There is a physical body. There
is also a spiritual body."*

Jet didn't want to hear this, but she found herself
listening anyway.

"We only know one part of what Diane experienced
that night. You need to know the other part. In verse
forty-five . . ." Rossi continued reading.

Jet held up her hands. "Rossi, I appreciate the Bible
like anybody else on a Sunday morning, but come on.
It's late. Can you just get to the point?" she pleaded.

Rossi smiled. "Sure. As a minister, I do tend to get
carried away. I'll just skip to verse 51: *We shall not
all fall asleep in death, but we shall all be changed or
transformed. In a moment, in the twinkling of an eye,
at the sound of the last trumpet call. For a trumpet will
sound, and the dead in Christ will be raised imperishable. . . . O death, where is your victory? O death,
where is your sting?* You can read it for yourself."

Her eyes drooped. "I don't have to. I'm sure you've
read the whole thing to me."

"I didn't, but the bottom line is Diane is all right. It's
us living folks down here who are trying to get our act
together. Now, I know you're tired. Walk me to the door,
and I repeat, don't ever act like that again. You've got too
much class, and you know it. Clip the claws, tomcat."

She stood with her shoulders slumped. "I guess I
got carried away with my imagination. Wait until Levi
hears about this." Jet groaned. "He may disown me."

At the door, Rossi laid his hands on Jet and prayed.
He kissed her on the cheek and walked out. "Lock up,"
he ordered then got in his car and drove away.

She owed Karyn an apology—maybe. It depended on
her mood, and she still would like an answer.

CHAPTER 37

Rossi drove away from Jet's house without playing his radio. He needed some quiet time to reflect on her ridiculous ramblings. A few minutes later, he was cruising on Interstate 64 toward downtown St. Louis to his condo. Sighing, he tried to concentrate on his driving. Thankfully, the roads were in good condition.

It didn't take long before he recalled a moment earlier in the day. God had called out to him. It had been faint, but forceful. Many times, God spoke to him at home alone, seldom at the office around others.

Once his spirit confirmed that it was indeed God, Rossi locked his office door. Returning to his desk, Rossi folded his hands and began to pray in a restrained manner that wouldn't cause his assistant or Levi to break the door down in alarm. He shivered. Rossi could feel in his spirit that something was about to happen. It seemed as if some demons were about to stir up dust and leave a trail of devastation. "Lord, have mercy on us." Even after Rossi left the office and headed home, his heart had remained troubled.

If Jet's ridiculous suspicions proved to be right, the fallout would be greater than even he would be able to console. Levi was in love with Karyn, and she didn't fit the stereotypical female ex-con, whatever that was.

Jet's accusations were far-fetched. The question was if Rossi should mention the incident to Levi. Rossi frowned then glanced in the rearview mirror before getting in the right lane to exit the interstate. "Lord, I've been watching and praying. What is going on?"

Keep praying, God replied.

In two days, Levi's family would be gathered at his uncle and aunt's house. Rossi hadn't planned on stopping by, preferring to spend time with his own Tolliver clan, but something told him his presence would be needed. In the meanwhile, he would keep an eye on Jet about getting some type of counseling from a professional or his pastor.

"She did what? Aw naw," Buttercup said, cracking her knuckles and rolling her shoulders. Adjusting the headband she wore at night to keep her braids neat, she jumped in place as if she were about to enter the ring.

"I knew she was trouble when I saw her watching us at Macy's girls' night out bash. And I thought the only person I had to watch out for was you, so I wouldn't violate my parole by associating with my ex-con roommate outside church and our living quarters. I should have kept my eyes on her. You want me to have a talk with her?" Buttercup grinned. "I sized her up. We're about the same height, and maybe the same size. I may have her about ten extra pounds. That would work in my favor."

Karyn gnawed on her lip, shaking her head. "No, Sister Sanctified. You're busting out this joint—your words, not mine—next month. Talk about hostile fire. I wonder what set her off. It's a good thing security was right behind her. She was going to hit me. I may be short, but I'm a survivor. What happened to all the wisdom you've been imparting to me the last few weeks?"

"I threw it out the window at the sign of trouble." Buttercup slouched. "I have to learn to be an over-comer and not let the devil bait me."

"Excuse me. Bait you? I was in the middle of the crossfire." Karyn gawked.

"You better tell Levi real soon before that crazy woman does you bodily harm."

"It looks that way, doesn't it?" Karyn stood to go into her bedroom. "I'm going to call Nalani, get her take and see what she thinks I should do; then I might call Pastor Scaife and ask him to pray for me, then—"

"Girl, if you call anybody else, you might as well put it on a billboard. Your sister is going to say what I said: Jump Jet."

"I'm going to ask Pastor Scaife to pray for you too."

Once in her bedroom behind closed doors, Karyn collapsed on her bed. "What happened to my plan?" Why did she foolishly convince herself she was strong enough for a relationship?

When you are weak, I am strong, God spoke.

Karyn rolled on her stomach and cried. She was going through her second round when her cell phone rang—Levi. It rang again. Did he know? Was that why he was calling, or was it to make sure she got home safely since he couldn't pick her up and Nalani was back in Chicago to take care of business before Christmas? Sniffing, she stopped guessing. Collecting her thoughts, she answered with a smile. Of course, it was their nightly chat.

"What's wrong?" Levi's voice was strong and concerned.

"Nothing."

"I thought when two people love each other they don't lie to each other."

Why did he say that? Is Levi talking about my past?
His tender, sincere words started another round of
tears. The deeper she inhaled, the more she cried. Levi
was saying something, but her mind didn't compre-
hend.

Buttercup busted through her door with her headband on crooked. "What's wrong with you?"

Karyn tried to shush her, pointing to her cell phone.

Buttercup frowned. "I told you I sleep light," she
mouthed and backed out of the room, closing the door.

"Karyn, Karyn, you're scaring me. I'm on my way."
Levi didn't sound as if he was bluffing.

"No, wait!" She panicked. The staff wouldn't open
the premises this late for visitors or residents anyway.
"I just had a bad day at work."

"Patrice is really starting to bug me. I'm getting tired
of her messing with my baby—"

"Surprisingly, Patrice has been nice to me lately."
Karyn chuckled, ready to defend in her honor through
her tears.

*Tell him the real reason before Jet gives him her
own version,* her mind prompted her. A headache began brewing as she thought about what to say.

"Oh." He exhaled. "At least my heart rate is returning
to normal. I hear a smile. I don't like you working that
low-paying job. What upset you?

Karyn wanted to pour out her soul to him just as she
had drained herself of tears. "My heart is heavy, but I
feel better." She closed her eyes.

"Well, I don't. Since you've come into Dori's and my
life, I can't be happier. I want the same happiness for
you. I've seen a glimpse of it since you've reunited with
your sister. Haven't I earned a place in your heart to be
a trusted confidant to share your burdens?"

Now Karyn felt miserable. Levi meant so much to her. Maybe that's why she was hurting so bad, because she hadn't confided in him. Taking a deep breath, Karyn changed the subject and started inquiring about her favorite person—Dori. Sooner or later, Karyn would have to make a decision: Tell Levi, or leave him before his look of disdain killed her.

Evidently, he didn't know about Jet showing up at her job and whirling accusations at her. *Maybe,* Karyn thought, *I'll wait and see if Jet really knows something.* With the upcoming holidays, Jet wouldn't be able to find out much for a week or so. That gave Karyn a little more time.

Usually she fell asleep after talking to Levi, but she couldn't. She did the one thing that was tried and true: She slid to the floor to pray. "Lord Jesus, I know you're a God of second chances. I know you go after the lost sheep that I am—the ones society would say they don't need anymore; but, God, you love the underdog. Even after the first murderer, you loved Cain and put a mark on him so others wouldn't touch him. You redeemed Saul and changed his name to Paul to work for you. The thief on the cross asked to be remembered in paradise, and you did just that. Lord, you gave me a second chance at life. Is it too much to ask for love?" She took a deep breath and whispered, "Amen."

Levi couldn't sleep. Something or someone had upset Karyn. All kinds of scenarios were running circles in his head. He dozed off and on throughout the night. On Friday morning, his wakeup call to Karyn was twenty minutes early.

"Hello," Karyn answered after a few rings. Her voice was drowsy.

"What was last night all about?" Levi demanded, forgoing his normal sweet words.

Karyn's sigh was heavy. "I just don't know if I should say anything . . ."

Levi was a patient man to a certain point, but he was already grouchy from lack of sleep. "Baby, you know you can talk to me about anything."

She seemed hesitant. "Can I really? I mean about anything?"

He nodded as if she could see him, and took a deep breath. His body tensed, bracing for something he wasn't going to like. "Yes, anything, baby."

"Jet came—"

"What!" Levi shot up in bed. "What has she done? I told her if she—"

"Levi, please calm down. That's why I didn't want to say anything, because she's your sister-in-law."

He peeled off the covers and stepped out of bed. Levi stomped back and forth in his bedroom, rubbing his head. Retaliation was already in planning stage. Levi was mad.

"I guess I can't talk to you."

Taking a deep breath, he calmed down as he wiped his hand over his face. "You can. I'm sorry. Please tell me. I'm calm."

"Are you sure?"

"Yep." Levi closed his eyes.

"She came storming into my job, mad about something, demanding I stop what I was doing. Jet could see it was a madhouse. She became so upset. Mall security guards took her away—"

"What!" Levi practically roared. He didn't need to hear another word. Yesterday, Jet admitted she needed help.

What made her flip? Lord, help me not to kill my late wife's sister, because I am on the verge of doing bodily harm, he said silently.

"Levi, something is wrong with her. I'm not a professional, but I can see she's hurting."

Right. He heard every other word Karyn was saying, but he had no intention of being so generous. Levi crossed the room to pick up his glasses. Once they were on his nose, he glanced at his clock. He needed to talk to Jet before he got to work rather than later. "She didn't lay a hand on you, did she?"

"No. I'm fine, but just a little shaken up and embarrassed that it happened on my job. I want to reach out to her, but—"

"I'll take care of it," he said firmly. He was already heading to the bathroom to shower. Good thing Dori was staying with his parents until Christmas.

"Levi, I don't know if that is a good idea."

He assured her that he wouldn't go ballistic when he confronted Jet, but he could tell she didn't believe him. "Karyn, you are so important to me. I will not let anyone, and I do mean anyone, disrespect you."

"I believe you," she responded softly. "But right now, I just want to hear you pray for me, for us, and for Jet."

That all sounded good, but Levi wanted to have some choice words with Jet before he had to repent. "You better start the prayer, baby, and I'll join in."

Levi was distracted through the short prayer. He disconnected quickly. He had business to take care of before he got to the office to take care of his other business.

***

Less than a half hour later, Levi was gripping the steering wheel as he sped to Jet's subdivision and her house. Getting a ticket would be the least of his problems. Jet's neighborhood was so quiet; a person never knew if a resident was home or not with the driveways empty.

Levi parked and got out of his car. Although the snow was under an inch, he did slip on a slick spot before making his way to her porch. Levi didn't bother with the doorbell; he pounded on her door until his fist bruised, and then he leaned on the doorbell. He pulled out his cell phone and called her home and cell number.

She was dodging him. Taking a deep breath, he spun around and headed back to his car. "You can run, but you can't hide." He would hunt her down after work.

"Not now, Rossi." Levi ordered minutes after he walked into his office.

"I think you might want to hear this. I had to bail Jet out of jail last night," Rossi stated.

"Why?" he snarled and balled his fists. "That may be the safest place for her right now."

"What are you talking about?" Rossi squinted. "So you know why, don't you?"

Levi nodded, not trusting himself to say anything inappropriate in front of his cousin's minister ears.

"Levi, Jet is in bad shape mentally. She needs counseling, medication, and most importantly, Jesus.

"I am beyond sick of her. If I could divorce my sister-in-law, I would over that stunt she pulled at Karyn's job." Levi stuffed his hands in his pockets and paced his office.

"You know this happens every time she visits that inmate location site at the end of the year. She was plugging in names—"

The phone interrupted Rossi from finishing. It was Jet. "I need to take this," he said, dismissing Rossi as he touched the screen to answer the call.

"Jet, you have lost your mind. Karyn is off limits. It's a good thing Rossi bailed you out, because I would have left you there." He wasn't interested in her explanation, and he continued to rant. After he ran out of steam, he disconnected the call.

After a few minutes, he bowed his head at his desk and prayed. "God, please help me to be sorry for everything I said to Jet, but I meant it."

CHAPTER 38

"Beginning today, behold all things are new for you," Pastor Scaife preached to his congregation at the Christmas service on Sunday morning. He lifted a finger. "That is if you believe in Jesus's birth, death, and grand resurrection. If you're expecting something on the surface, open the presents under a tree, but if you want something with an unlimited warranty, Jesus is your man."

Nalani nudged Karyn and whispered into her ear, "The option is a no-brainer."

Karyn nodded.

"Use this day as an opportunity to be more Christ-like," he said. "First things first: You should have joy today. If you can get it and keep it, then you'll have peace."

"Okay, I'm getting the message." Nalani smiled at Karyn. "His encouragement is so tangible every time I visit."

"Does that mean you're ready to repent and be baptized?"

Nalani shook her head. "Not quite. I'm not totally convinced."

It was as if Pastor Scaife heard Nalani. "Are you totally persuaded to follow Christ? This is a free will group. You must decide to come on your own."

Folding her arms, Nalani gave Karyn a smug look. "See."

And Nalani meant what she said. The short service came to an end, and Nalani didn't make a move from her seat until after the benediction. Still, Karyn was grateful. Nalani's flight had been on time from Midway, her rental car had been waiting, and she was already dressed for church. Nalani drove to Karyn's building in a legally record time.

"Karyn, there was no way I was going down to that altar knowing that I'm ready to whip up somebody for messing with my sister."

"Nalani, you can't fight my battles."

"How do you know? I would have given Jet a run for her money. I wish I had been in town when that you-know-what decided to act a fool."

There were things about Nalani that hadn't changed since they were teenagers: She was stubborn, had a quick temper, and believed in the cause—whatever it was at the moment.

"What I want is for my sister to follow me to Christ. I'm living the best example that I can." Karyn just needed to hold it together. She had been praying since she talked to Levi yesterday.

Karyn was afraid to find out if he had spoken to Jet and what happened. She feasted on today's sermon and felt as if she had left a spiritual spa. She was rejuvenated with joy. If she needed to, she would go head to head with the devil. *Bring it on!*

Less than forty minutes later, Karyn and Nalani weren't far away from his parents' house in the city. Levi called for the fourth time, wondering about the whereabouts of the

Wallace sisters. When Nalani turned the corner, Karyn saw Levi standing near the curb in front of his parents' house as a doorman.

Despite his hat, coat, and gloves, he shivered as the car came to a stop. He opened Karyn's door first and wrapped her in a smothering bear hug. The coldness on his cheeks was evidence that he had been outside a while. Levi kissed her with desperation, as if he hadn't seen her in weeks instead of yesterday, when he came up to her job to see with his own eyes that Karyn was okay physically and mentally. He stole another peck with no regard for Nalani. Afterward, he spoke and nodded to her sister.

"Merry Christmas, Nalani. It's nice to see you again."

Nalani laughed as she activated the alarm on her SUV rental. Levi escorted the sisters up the stairs to the porch. Dori was standing in the doorway, grinning and waving at Karyn.

Karyn relaxed. She hoped the incident wouldn't put a damper on the holiday. Karyn wondered if the rest of Levi's family knew what Jet had done, or if they believed Jet's suspicions. Either way, she was determined to have a Merry Christmas, especially after the sermon Pastor Scaife had preached.

Inside the house, after removing her coat, Karyn knelt and hugged Dori. She *ooh*ed and *ahh*ed over her ever-green-colored velvet dress and white tights, which had already accumulated a few smudges. As she greeted everyone, more than one of Levi's family members commented how she and Levi were matching with red turtlenecks. Even his quiet brother did. The compliment seemed to kick Levi's dimples into overdrive.

More than once, Levi stole her away to a spot under the mistletoe. She giggled. Even Seth's twin Solomon seemed to be in a jovial mood.

Up until that point, the day had been whimsical. Not even an hour later, after everyone had exchanged pleasantries, it appeared the devil called Karyn's earlier bluff when the doorbell rang and Jesetta Hutchens walked into the living room, appearing larger than life wrapped in her mink coat. Gifts were dangling in her arms.

Karyn groaned inwardly as Jet smiled at everyone. Dori screamed her delight at seeing her aunt and the presents she was bearing.

Karyn sucked in her breath. She wasn't sure if Jet was going to try to finish what she started the other day, or if another personality was going to rear its head. Levi felt her stiffen, and he tightened his arm around her while casually using his free hand to sip his punch.

"Jet will apologize. If she even breathes on you too much, she's out of here." He lifted a brow. There weren't any dimples forthcoming. Levi was serious.

Karyn gave him a tentative smile. How she longed to know what words were exchanged between Levi and Jet. To break eye contact with Levi, Karyn glanced at Nalani, who was chatting with Solomon as if they were old friends.

Jet offered Levi's family kisses and hugs. She halted when she faced Karyn. Jet squinted as if she were making a decision. "I'm sorry for my actions the other night, Karyn. Please forgive me?" Jet lowered her lashes.

Although Karyn was obligated to forgive, she remained wary of Jet. "Yes, I do."

Nalani made her presence known, coming to stand next to Jet. "Merry Christmas, Jet. Remember me?" Nalani gave a camera-ready smile, but it was obvious to Karyn it wasn't genuine.

"Hi, Nalani," Jet said softly.

"Aunt Jet, Aunt Jet, come see what I got for Christmas."

Jet turned to her niece and allowed Dori to drag her away. "This isn't over," she practically hissed.

"It's just the beginning," Karyn mumbled. *Without a test, there's no testimony,* Karyn reminded herself. *Lord, you do have my back on this, don't you? Please.*

CHAPTER 39

Levi didn't miss anything. Depending on the day of the week, it wasn't unusual for Jet to have her claws out, but she was making a mistake if she thought Levi was going to sit back and let her put them in Karyn. That's what Levi had reminded her this morning. However, he watched Jet's interaction with Karyn with great interest. He chuckled at his sweet little woman's reaction to Jet as if she were silently communicating, *Bring it on.*

The other day when he had gone to Jet's house after work, Rossi insisted on coming to serve as a buffer. Within minutes of Levi's temper flaring, Jet had broken down and apologized profusely for her behavior. She seemed embarrassed to discuss what had prompted her to snap. The storm that Levi had brought with him to her house fizzled. Levi empathized with her vulnerability.

"I'll apologize to Karyn," Jet had said.

"Jet," Rossi instructed her, "more than anything you better attend that crime victims' grief counseling session you mentioned to Levi before you destroy yourself."

"I haven't made the appointment yet."

"Do it," the Tolliver men had said in unison.

She had frowned. "How did you know? Should have figured my big-mouth brother-in-law would have said something to the family preacher." Bowing her head, Jet took a few minutes before meeting Levi's eyes. "I'll apologize to Karyn. I know I'll see her on Christmas at your parents' house." She cleared her throat and her voice had become stronger. "Apologizing doesn't mean I'm okay with her trying to take Diane's place. I believe I have the right to be suspect of any woman in my niece's life."

Levi had been a minute away from threatening Jet when Rossi shook his head not to take Jet's bait. Rossi must have recognized it as a defense mechanism to mask her breaking point. Levi had backed down. Before leaving her house, they hugged and patched up the past twenty-four hours. He walked out of her house, leaving Rossi behind to pray with her.

Levi took a deep breath and refocused on the present when the doorbell rang and heavy footsteps introduced a new guest. Rossi entered the living room with small gifts packed neatly in a red plastic crate.

"Merry Christmas, family, for Jesus is born," he said, reciting his standard holiday greeting.

Levi frowned. Christmas was a time when his family house-hopped, visiting relatives, but Rossi was a bit early. Each preferred spending most of the day with their respective parents.

Rossi made his rounds, delivering small tokens as gifts. He hugged Levi's mother and Tia and then shook hands with Levi's twin brothers and his father. When he stopped in front of Levi, he planted a slender box that probably was a tie on his lap; then Rossi pulled out a box for Karyn.

Levi lifted a brow and pointed. "What is that?"

"It's not for you, chump," Rossi taunted then grinned at Karyn. "Merry Christmas, sister."

Karyn looked from Rossi to Levi. "Oh, I wasn't expecting—"

"Shhh. That's the best part of a gift. We never expect it. Enjoy."

The simplest things affected her. Every minute with Karyn humbled Levi. Nalani was Rossi's last stop, and he lingered. He seemed enthralled with the other Miss Wallace as he handed Nalani a card, which Levi guessed was her gift.

When Levi glanced at Dori, from the corner of his eye, he noticed Rossi mouthing to Karyn, *I'm praying for you.* Levi frowned. What was that all about? If anybody was going to do any whispering, his name would be Levi, not Rossi Tolliver.

"I would've thought all the gifts under the tree would be opened by now," Rossi said after he returned to the living room from hanging his coat in the closet.

"Basically, we have. The rest are Karyn's," he said loud enough to break up the private conference between Karyn and Nalani.

"Mine?" Karyn splayed her fingers on her chest. Surprise was evident on her gorgeous face before she glowed. She was a vision sure to visit him in his sleep. Her hair— not curls or braid, but straight—swept her shoulders. Her stature might be petite, but her curves would tempt a man—him. Her legs were encased in the sheerest stockings he had ever seen.

Nalani didn't try to mask her delight. Levi earned an ally. There was no mistaking their sisterhood. Both had the same facial structure. The younger sister was taller, but not by much. Nalani's hair looked like she had it purposely cut short.

"It's like a wedding shower," Sharon Tolliver said as she sat back in her reclining sofa sectional. Crossing her feet at the ankles, she grinned. "I stopped counting at twenty gifts, Karyn."

Levi didn't voice it, but the scene did remind him of bridal showers he had seen on sitcoms and commercials as he stared into Karyn's eyes. Reaching for her hand, Levi tugged her closer to the decorated tree, which touched the eight-foot ceiling.

Tia elbowed Seth. "Take note, honey, because whatever Levi got Karyn, I want one too."

Everyone laughed as Seth grabbed her around her waist and pulled her into his lap. He whispered something in her ear and laughed.

"Don't you think you went a little overboard?" Karyn said in a hushed tone meant for Levi's ears.

Nalani whispered through clenched teeth, "Just say thank you, girl."

"Can I talk to you for a moment?" Karyn looked up into his eyes.

Squeezing her hand, they strolled into the marble-covered foyer. Levi guided her to a cozy window seat hidden under a set of stairs that climbed to the second floor. "Is this enough privacy?" He grinned mischievously, stealing a kiss. Karyn's response was a tender brush of his lips. "Now, what would you like to say?" He pulled her closer.

"I have a small gift for Dori and even a smaller one for you." She lowered her lashes. "I wasn't expecting so much generosity."

Even with the additional funds Nalani had given Karyn after the sisters reunited, his woman still lived modestly. He teased her chin with a finger and lifted her face. "Karyn, those gifts are from my heart, just like yours. After I bought the first gift, I thought I was finished until I saw something else. Is it my fault that

I think of you all the time? If it will make you feel any better, I can return them."

"And stand in a long, non-moving return line? Nah, I can't put you through that. Come on," she teased, dragging him back toward the living room. "I can't wait to get started." She clapped her hands in mock applause.

Levi laughed and allowed her to lead the way. Once in the doorway, Levi clapped. "Okay, folks, I've talked her into it. Let the fun begin."

Cheers erupted throughout the room. Karyn was the main attraction.

Dori left Rossi's side to sit on the floor with Karyn, who entertained his daughter by ripping open the wrapping paper and screaming her delight at the gifts she suspected were Dori's ideas: a Tiana doll from Disney's *The Princess and the Frog* movie, a kangaroo stuffed animal, striped stocks, and more.

Between the choruses of laughter, Jet mumbled snide comments, which everyone ignored—except Levi, who shot her a warning glare. Karyn opened her last gift, which was a tennis bracelet. Standing, Karyn hugged Levi, then Dori, as everyone pitched in to gather the discarded wrapping paper.

"Does anyone have energy left to go ice skating at Steinberg Rink?" Rossi assisted Nalani and Jet to their feet.

"I may live in the Midwest, but I'm not one for staying outdoors for any type of activity in December," Jet stated, shivering.

"I'm with you, sweetie." Sharon waved her hand. "How about hanging out with me, Jet? We can deliver my home-baked cookies to the other Tolliver households."

She shrugged. "Okay."

"I haven't been ice skating since I was a little girl," Karyn said. She grimaced, glancing at Nalani. "I don't know." Karyn grabbed her purse. "I need to use the bathroom."

"I guarantee you, I won't let you fall," Levi yelled after her with a double meaning.

When she returned, she briefly whispered to Nalani then relaxed. Karyn smiled at Levi. "Okay. What are we waiting for? Let's go."

They piled into Nalani's rented SUV. Dori sat in her booster seat, which Levi had retrieved from his car. She quickly occupied herself with her handheld electronic game Rossi had given her. Levi and Karyn sat on either side of her. As Nalani drove, Rossi sat in the passenger seat and gave her directions to nearby Forest Park, where the rink was located.

"Are you having a good time?"

Karyn looked at Levi with adoration. "You have no idea how happy I am right now."

With little traffic, they arrived at the rink in record time and rented skates. Once they were on the ice, Rossi coaxed Dori to skate with him and Nalani, giving Levi free time with Karyn. Levi hadn't determined if his cousin was doing him a favor or using his daughter as bait with Nalani, as he had done with Karyn.

"I apologize for my sister-in-law. I'll keep her in check."

Karyn covered Levi's lips with her hand. "Shhh. She apologized and now I want to move on"

"You amaze me with the amount of charity in your heart for people. That's why I went ballistic on Jet."

"Today has been so beautiful, and I don't want to complain, because you've been so good to me."

"Did you enjoy your presents?"

She nodded, chuckling. "Yes, all twenty-seven of them."

"The jewelry box? The house shoes, the bracelet . . ."

"Yes, all of them."

When Levi leaned in to kiss Karyn, a skater zoomed by, causing Levi to lose his footing and fall. Rossi barked out a laugh in the distance as Karyn smirked, helping him up. He would be aching later, but once he remembered how he got hurt, he would smile through the pain.

CHAPTER 40

Buttercup's moving-out-moving-on-and-getting-gone party was winding down at New Beginnings. In three days, by the time the clock struck midnight to announce another year, Buttercup's stay would be a memory.

"Girl, I hope you get a sane roommate like me." Buttercup grinned, adjusting her gold headband, which matched her pantsuit, another over-the-limit outfit.

Karyn wouldn't trade Buttercup for anyone in the world. She had been her voice of reason—and insanity when it came to her beauty experiments. She walked to the buffet table and poured more punch then helped herself to some finger sandwiches. Karyn was starved, having to work through her break because the bookstore was bombarded with customers making returns or cashing in their holiday gift cards.

Refusing Levi's offer for a ride home, Karyn had insisted on taking the bus home. She feared that if Levi knew about Buttercup's party, he would have expected an impromptu invitation. His curiosity would be piqued once she explained men were not allowed inside unless they were family.

"At least soon you'll be able to ride off in the sunset," Karyn said with a sigh.

"It could be that way with you, too, if you talk to Levi. Look how he stood up for you with that Jet woman."

She smiled. "He did, didn't he? But families can kiss and make up. Girlfriends can be cut and replaced." She paused and pointed her finger at Buttercup. "This conversation is about you, not me. Now, the parole board did grant you and Halo permission to get married, right?" One thing Karyn wouldn't miss was Buttercup's soapbox on Levi.

Grinning, Buttercup folded her arms. "Yes, indeedy. The ex-felons can wed. Thank God we don't have to get the okay to have babies," she said dryly.

"It's the price we pay for breaking the law." Karyn sighed. Once a felon, always an ex-felon, or so they say. That would never change.

"I know what you're thinking. We can't worry about what labels society puts on us. We just have to roll with it." Buttercup held Karyn's eye contact. "Repeat after me: *While we were yet in weakness, powerless to help ourselves, at the fitting time Christ died for the ungodly . . .*"

Karyn finished quoting Romans 5: 6–8 with her friend.

"Ah, now, don't you feel better?" Buttercup grinned. "Back to Levi. You are going to tell him, right?"

"Yes!" Karyn filled her mouth with gourmet meatballs. Buttercup was wearing her down.

"When?"

"I'm counting down the days. When the time is right," Karyn mumbled, still chewing as Buttercup trailed her to a cozy chair.

Buttercup twisted her lips in doubt. "I don't believe in perfect timing; or at least it never worked for anyone behind bars who committed a crime. We still got caught."

***

It was a good thing Karyn stuffed her face the night before, because she would be fasting the entire day. After getting out of bed that morning, she stayed on her knees a little longer, crying out to God for wisdom to deal with a situation where she wouldn't walk away the biggest loser.

At work, she meditated on everything that God had spoken to her since dating Levi. She recalled scriptures about salvation. She was determined to stay focused on God throughout the day.

It didn't take long for Satan to tempt her with Patrice. Karyn was helping a toddler put a jigsaw puzzle together when Patrice called her aside because besides the manager, there were no other employees on the sales floor.

"You know that new girl they just hired?" She didn't wait for Karyn to answer. Patrice leaned in closer. "She has two kids, and this is her first job off welfare . . ."

Karyn said nothing.

Patrice continued. "I can't believe they just let anybody work here." She frowned in disgust. "I hope we won't have any baby momma drama up in here."

Karyn walked away, shaking her head. She refused to fill her mind with petty gossip, but rather something positive, as she had read the other day in Philippians 4.

Late afternoon, as Karyn was near the home stretch of her fast, God led her in an unexpected direction. She blinked, afraid of his request. Her spirit seemed to pound.

Clocking out, she took her final break. "Lord, I believe this is your will, although I don't understand why me. I ask your blessings for being obedient." She whispered "Amen" and took a deep breath.

"I might as well get this out of the way." She hit Levi's speed-dial number on her cell phone.

"Yes, dear." He answered almost immediately with his standard greeting, almost cooing in her ear with his baritone voice. He never made her feel as if she were disturbing him.

"Hello, Levi." Smiling, she swallowed. She loved him so much. "I need a favor," she said tentatively.

When he chuckled, she imagined his dimples. "You've got it. What's up?"

"I would like Jet's number, please."

"Karyn, I would give you the moon or anything else within my power. None of your requests would be turned down, but this one? My sister-in-law is not in a good state of mind right now. The holidays have always been hard for us without Diane. This year, it has been particularly rough for her, probably because I have you and she has nobody. She's becoming a pro at pushing people away." He exhaled. "Babe, this will have to be my first official no."

When Karyn didn't say anything, Levi's voice changed to a slight edge. "Wait a minute. Has she said anything to upset you again?" His questions were nonstop.

The Lord had told Karyn to reach out to Jet, that she was His priority. Jet was His lost sheep right now. *Minister to her*, God had instructed her. She prayed Jesus would fill her mouth with the words, because as far as she was concerned, she wanted to avoid Jet at all costs.

Karyn's pleading didn't seem effective. Finally, she repeated what God had told her. Then reluctantly, Levi agreed, but only after confirming he was still picking her up from work.

Disconnecting, it was Karyn's turn to take a deep breath.

Tapping in Jet's number, Karyn's heart pounded in fear of the impending conversation. "But I trust you, Jesus," she whispered repeatedly.

"Hey, Levi," Jet answered. "When did you get a new cell number?"

Caller ID. "This isn't Levi, Jet. It's Karyn." She waited for the surprise to sink in. She didn't offer that this was her cell number. "Do you have a few minutes to talk?"

"I've already apologized. Let's leave it there. I'm not looking for friendship. What else is there to talk about?"

"How about you storming into my workplace, whirling accusations at me in front of my customers? It might not be the corner office, but it's still my income."

Karyn had to get that off her chest. *God forgive me,* she asked. "I don't want to be your enemy."

"Just answer the question, Miss Karyn," she said, mocking her niece's voice. "Are you a criminal?"

"Why would you even ask me that?" Karyn wondered what the basis of Jet's suspicion was. Karyn refused to add fuel to any fire Jet was trying to light. Had she taken her suspicions to Levi? He hadn't treated her differently.

Lord, what is this woman up to? And why did you send me?

"Let's say I have my reasons. Now answer the question," Jet insisted.

"No, I'm not." And that was the honest to God's truth. She had been redeemed. "I would like for us to be friends—"

"I pick my friends, not the other way around. I'll do a background check and get back to you." *Click.*

Karyn released her breath. This would be her first test as an ex-felon when someone learned she was on parole. She didn't know what would be her final grade, but she would pass with or without Levi.

CHAPTER 41

Jet hung up, disgusted with herself. She had just walked through the garage door from bargain shopping. It had been a fairly good day. As a matter of fact, it was good therapy. When her cell rang, she answered it—still in a good mood—assuming it was Levi. When she heard Karyn's voice, her mood turned sour. It had been an instant transformation. The woman rubbed her the wrong way. How many times would she have to apologize to her to stay in Levi's good graces? To calculate the number would be exhausting.

Karyn initiated an olive branch, but something within Jet kept her from reaching for it. Before Diane's death, she had more smiles, friends, and dates. In the last four years, she felt she had aged ten.

"I'm just not friends with anybody," she mocked herself. "I believe in checking people out." She groaned as she remembered disconnecting without saying goodbye. Levi would definitely disown her for that one.

Jet had to get to a grief counseling session fast. Rubbing her temples, she reached for her phone again. This time she called Levi. She should have been dialing Rossi for prayer. He stomach whined for attention, but she ignored its demand.

Levi answered almost immediately. "Hey, Jet."

"I talked to your little woman friend." That came out the wrong way. Plus, it was a bad choice of words.

He practically growled into the phone. "What did you say to Karyn? If you upset her—"

"I called her a criminal." She cringed. Honesty wasn't always the best policy. She was digging herself into the Grand Canyon.

"You called her what?" Levi's roar practically vibrated the phone in her hand. "What is wrong with you? I knew it was a bad idea to give her your number. Karyn is a peacemaker. Haven't you ever heard of *blessed are the peacemakers?*"

Jet gritted her teeth. Did Levi expect her to answer in the middle of his tirade? She did remember hearing something like that as a child.

"You've got to stop building grudges against every woman I date."

"Technically, Karyn is the first one that lasted more than a month."

"Technically you're right, which might tell you something. Karyn is the sweetest woman I've met since your sister. I haven't done a good job of holding my tongue with you, and you're not making it easy. Diane would be crushed by the way you're acting."

Jet imagined the slap and covered her face with a hand in shame. She walked the few steps to her kitchen table and collapsed in a chair. She twisted a large portion of her natural long mane in a tight ponytail and let it go.

"I know. I know. I'm starting not to like myself."

She glanced around her spotless kitchen as she waited for his answer. It was equipped with every accessory a homeowner could desire, but Jet wasn't content. She felt her life was empty. If she could adopt a sister as wonderful as Diane had been, she would do it in a minute.

"I know you love Karyn and so does Dori. If you love her, I want to at least like her, but I can't, Levi. I feel like you are cutting your ties with me because of her."

"Jet, only one woman could force me to cut ties with you." He paused. "That's you. You're pushing me away, and once I get to a certain point, I don't know if I'll come back. Face it, Jet. Karyn will be part of my future. It's up to you how you handle it."

She had been given the ultimatum. Jet had to try to get along with Karyn. At least to be cordial. "Do you think she'd mind going to the grief counseling session for crime victims with us? Maybe she'll learn I'm a victim of circumstances and I'm trying. She did say she wanted to be friends."

"I'm sure she won't mind. Karyn is a good listener and great comforter. She is as genuine as it gets. "

"Okay. Thank you. I love you, brother-in-law."

"And I love you too, sister-in-law."

Jet bowed her head. She hadn't asked in a while, but that didn't stop Levi or Rossi from always offering. "Will you pray for me?"

"I know that took a lot of strength for you to ask. Can I get Rossi on the line?"

She nodded before she whispered, "Yes."

In less than a minute, Jet was on a three-way with the Tolliver men. Closing her eyes, she didn't join in, but listened as she silently asked God to do something for her soon.

Levi was drained after he and Rossi prayed for Jet then themselves. He couldn't get too angry with Jet, because he understood exactly how she felt and what she was going through.

God had sent the perfect healing balm into his life: Karyn. He clicked off his flat screen TV, which was on a basketball game that was watching him instead of him watching it. Scenarios ran across his mind as he wondered what Karyn and Jet had discussed besides Karyn seeking friendship and Jet rejecting it.

He was restless while Dori was occupied in her bedroom, playing with the jungle of Christmas presents. Removing his glasses, Levi rubbed the bridge of his nose.

His cell phone rang again. It was Rossi. He answered, "Yeah."

"Just thinking about Jet."

Levi exhaled. "I know, but at least she asked for prayer."

"That's saying a lot," Rossi said. "I think I'll swing by her house later after I finish mentoring the Temple brothers. They've been out of jail for two weeks, and I'm determined to keep them out." He released a frustrated sigh.

"Well, they have to want to stop shoplifting. They made a choice." Levi shook his head. What a waste of life. "You know, as private as Jet is, I'm surprised she would ask that Karyn come along."

"Maybe this could be the beginning of a great sister-friendship."

Nodding, Levi grinned. "You may be right. I never thought of that, Minister Rossi."

CHAPTER 42

Saturday evening, sitting crisscross on twin double beds, the Wallace sisters faced each other on New Year's Eve. After indulging in their suite's Jacuzzi, they were wrapped in thick cotton white robes, courtesy of the Renaissance St. Louis downtown hotel. Room service had just delivered fruits, chocolates, sparkling grape juice, and pastries, and a parole officer had just checked on Karyn's whereabouts.

"Ah, I missed this," Nalani said with a fake slur as she sipped juice from her crystal goblet.

Karyn laughed at her sister's silliness. "You couldn't wait for that first New Year's that you could legally drink to get drunk."

Nalani had a mischievous glint in her eyes. "Yeah, and that night I puked nonstop. I could've saved myself the trouble."

"Served you right." Karyn nodded as she admired their luxury accommodations. It included two bouquets of flowers, courtesy of Nalani, who had splurged on renting ball gowns for their private party, movies, and stocking up on board games.

Ever since they were young, the Wallace household would hold a contest to see who could stay up all night. Usually, the next morning their house would be a wreck for the maid to clean, and their sleep stations would be any spots where they could hide for a catnap without losing the contest.

"You know, I don't know if I could have survived what you've been through," Nalani admitted as she uncrossed her legs and adjusted three rows of overstuffed pillows to rest her back.

Karyn had avoided an in depth discussion about her life behind bars with Nalani. With Levi in the picture, their conversations were always gloss-overs as far as Karyn was concerned. Tonight they wouldn't have to hold back any thoughts or emotions. They were sisters, and their bond would always remain.

God bless her caseworker. Monica granted Karyn a thirty-six-hour pass that began the previous night on Friday because of the holiday. Honestly, Karyn was surprised her counselor approved the hotel location, which was against the rules. It was only because other staff members were attending a party in the downstairs ballroom. That gave the sisters plenty of time for a long, uninterrupted heart to heart.

Her other heart, Levi, wasn't too happy about bringing in the New York without her. He vocalized his displeasure more than once. Karyn recalled Levi's puppy dog expression when she informed him any phone calls would not be answered until she checked out of an undisclosed hotel.

"The last few months had been about you, me, and Dori spending time together. At midnight, I wanted to begin it with you and me," he had said.

The night with Nalani had been a truthful alibi. She would have nowhere to go after they celebrated the New Year. As long as she stayed at New Beginnings, the rules applied, which meant the ten o'clock curfew would be enforced.

Levi was the most unselfish man Karyn had ever met. He was willing to deny his happiness to make hers possible when she asked for his understanding while she rebuilt a relationship with Nalani.

"Will it make you happy if I give you this space?" He had inched closer to her lips. They had been outside Karyn's doorsteps at the time after she had worked a day shift and Levi had given her a ride home.

She could hardly breathe. "Yes."

"Consider it done," he whispered then kissed her tenderly and slowly. Later that night, her lips still tingled when she went to bed.

Smiling at the memories, Karyn lay back on top of the rich burgundy comforter made of jacquard silk, and crossed her arms behind her head.

"I see you practically glowing. Since you just zoned out on me, that could only mean one thing—you're thinking about him," Nalani teased and laughed.

"Who?" Karyn feigned cluelessness. This night was not about her and Levi. It was a long overdue sisters' night out. She refocused. "To answer your question, I didn't think I would survive after I was sentenced to prison. At that point, I really didn't care about what happened to me. Who would have ever thought I would cause the death of anybody, no less a child—and to make matters worse, my own child—and go to prison. I keep replaying that dark day in my head, even though I know I can't bring my baby back."

Turning on her side, Karyn faced Nalani. "You had every right to hate me. I became the big family disappointment. So much responsibility was shifted on you with Daddy. Although I'm hurt that you didn't notify me of Daddy's death, I realize that I'm not entitled to anything. I'm just so glad you don't hate me anymore."

"I didn't hate you for what you did, because deep down inside, I knew it was an accident and nobody could ever convince me differently—the media, family, or so-called friends." Nalani gnawed her bottom lip. "The hate I felt is hard to explain. Maybe it was my moment of rebellion. I just wanted to grieve alone. I had no right to withhold the notification of Daddy's death from you. For that, Karyn, I am truly sorry. God took away our mother. In a way, Daddy took his own life through negligence, and your freedom was taken away. I had to get myself together mentally to deal with your incarceration, prepare for your pending release, and help you salvage your life after prison. After taking care of Daddy . . ." She paused and looked at Karyn, "I just wasn't strong enough to have to take care of your needs. I am so sorry."

She waved her off. "Nalani, your confession just proves you're human like me. I appreciate your honesty. Your words stung, but I needed to know of your hurt. I'm just so happy that you love me so much to want me back in your life."

The sisters were quiet, caught up in their own thoughts, until Nalani reached over and plucked the largest chocolate-covered strawberry off a tray for her eating pleasure. After popping it in her mouth, she shrugged. "I figured God, Momma, and Dad only gave me one sister—you. I knew you before that happened. I knew your heart, not the things the reporters were saying. We slept in the same bedroom, ate at the same kitchen table, and attended the same school. You were my hero because you always made good decisions."

Karyn teared up. "Not that time. An innocent, helpless baby, who I birthed into this world, died at my hands. That stuff happens to other people, not me—a senator's daughter," she mocked, sniffing.

Getting up, Nalani scooted Karyn over so she could stretch out in the bed with her. "I hadn't heard of postpartum depression before, and it can be prevented if diagnosed and treated early. The bottom line is you are my sister. I don't know how not to love you, even at the moments I hated you, if that makes any sense. Even if you became a prostitute, I would still love you."

"What! Of all things, a prostitute?" Karyn swiped a pillow, scooted back to have some distance, and aimed for Nalani's head. She retaliated, so a pillow fight ensued. Karyn was getting the best of her sister when Nalani begged for mercy.

"Okay, okay. How about a drug dealer?" The blow came to Nalani's chin before she called for time out. "Hey, it's ten-thirty. We'd better get dressed."

They scurried off the bed and ran to the closet. As soon as they cracked the mirrored door, lace and taffeta peeked out. For the next hours, the two of them would be dancing with the stars from movies they had rented: *White Christmas*, black holiday musical *A Diva's Christmas Carol*, comedy *While You were Sleeping,* and their favorite, *Rudolph's Shiny New Year.*

Once they were dolled up, they put in one video after another, from waltzing to ballroom dancing to salsa. They laughed as their movements were restrained in the contraptions.

"Hey, it's almost time," Nalani said with excitement.

Karyn checked as they scrambled to refill their goblets with sparkling grape juice. Nalani pointed the remote at the flat screen to the channel broadcasting from Times Square. With their glasses raised to the TV, they joined in the countdown. "Five, four, three, two, one!" they shouted and looped their arms and sipped out of each other's glasses.

"Happy New Year." Karyn hugged her sister.

"Happy New Year to you. I'm pulling for you and Levi and little Dori, but if I were you, I'd watch my back with Jet."

"You just had to sneak Levi's name in there, didn't you?"

"You told me not to mention his name last night. It's a new day and a new year. Levi, Levi, Levi," Nalani teased.

When a brief knock at the door interrupted them, they checked the time and then Karyn proceeded to open the door. As expected, her counselor strolled in and performed a quick inspection.

"Okay, Karyn, everything looks fine. Stay out of trouble, and Happy New Year's," Monica said and left.

As soon as the door closed, Nalani pointed her finger at it. "I know you will be glad when that checking up on you stuff is over." She folded her arms in a huff.

"I'll be glad when the rapture comes. I have really made a mess of my life down here. That's for sure."

"You are not the only one who has ever done anything wrong."

Karyn nodded. "I know. Listen, let me change the subject. Speaking of Levi, he called me with the oddest request."

"Really?"

"Remember the other day when I tried to reach out to Jet? That phone call didn't go so well. I guess God didn't prep her spirit for me, but left me on hold. Whew."

"I don't even know why you wasted your time," Nalani said as she worked to get out of her ball grown.

"It was God's idea, not mine." They took turns unzipping each other's dresses. "Well, Levi said she sounded pitiful after she snapped at me. To make a long story short, she is ready to get help. She's going to a crime victims' grief counseling session. She asked Levi to ask me to go with her."

Nalani eyed her sister suspiciously. "I wouldn't fall for that in a New York, Chicago, or L.A. minute."

"I guess she wants me to see she's trying."

"And you believe that?"

"I don't know what to believe right now. I do know God is in the plan, so I might as well put my blindfold on and listen to His voice to lead me."

"Humph. With dealing with that girl, I would take NoDoz to keep both eyes open." As Nalani slipped out of her dress and wrapped the robe around her, she climbed back on top of her bed. "Karyn," Nalani spoke softly, "it's a new year. When are you going to tell him? How can your love grow when he doesn't know everything?"

Pacing the room, Karyn avoided eye contact with her sister. "Every time I think I know the answer, doubt kicks in; but with God as my witness, before January is out, Levi will know the truth."

"And the truth will set you free. Isn't that how it goes?"

"Yes, and free indeed."

CHAPTER 43

Karyn changed from her uniform into her turtleneck sweater dress, black tights, and leather boots. She added a few more clothes to her closet, mindful of the center's clothing limit and the capital needed from her trust fund for her joint business venture. For the third time in months, Karyn had asked to get off early—another exception to house rules. She was past pressing her luck.

It was the end of the first week of the New Year, and Jet's first session was less than two hours away. It had to be in a safe location during daylight hours for victims to feel secure. As Karyn neared the mall entrance, Levi was posted at the door, waiting for her. As soon as their eyes made contact, he stood taller and his dimples saluted her.

"Hi." He kissed her cheek at the same time, removing the backpack from her shoulder. "Thank you for coming along. I'm hoping this will help Jet move on. Rossi's meeting us there."

Karyn froze. "Oh, is this a family affair? Maybe I shouldn't go."

Levi shook his head. He ushered her to his car and made sure she was strapped in before pulling off. "One thing you have to know about my cousin: Since he's the oldest, Rossi thinks he's in charge of everything, and being a minister in the family has privileges. Plus, he's really worried about Jet. We all are. As you can see, the grief is eating away at her. Losing her only sister was devastating for her, me, and the family."

"I understand. I wouldn't wish that on anyone. Nalani is all I have, and we lost contact for four years. I was living in a prison." There, she'd dropped the first hint. Subtle, but she would build up from there.

A red light caught them at Lincoln Trail. A young black woman, no older than twenty, seized the opportunity to approach cars, asking for a donation in exchange for miniature bags of cookies and chips. Karyn began to rummage through her handbag.

Levi tapped on the steering wheel, ignoring the beggar as she came to his window. He glanced at Karyn to keep from looking at the woman. "What are you doing?"

"Looking for some money."

"No telling what they do with that money," he stated with little sympathy.

"Levi, it's the grace of God that's it not me—or you—standing there." She pointed to the intersection then tapped her chest with her thumb. "I'm lucky I'm not hoping for someone to have mercy on me in order for me to survive."

He stared at Karyn, trying to read her expression. "Woman, you have a heart of gold." He reached for his wallet in his back pants pocket, but the light flashed green. A car behind them honked, forcing Levi to drive away. The crestfallen look on the woman's face tugged at Karyn's heart.

She didn't know that woman, but she knew of another church's ministry that focused on former gang members, drug addicts, and others who were saved off the streets and in a rehabilitation program. Their keep for a bed and hot meal every night in the church-sponsored housing was to hit the street every morning and peddle their wares of candies, cookies, and other treats. The participants would turn the majority of the funds over to the ministry.

Suddenly, Levi pulled to the curb, activated his hazard lights, shifted his gear into park, and got out. Without restraint, he slid out his wallet. Turning around, Karyn watched as the beggar eagerly skipped to Levi. Without much fanfare, Levi handed her a folded bill and sprinted back to the car.

"I love you," were the first words out of Karyn's mouth. He was the one with the heart of gold. It was so easy to fall in love with him.

"I love you too, my conscience." He smacked a kiss on her lips, then checked his rearview mirror and proceeded to drive off. "She said, 'God bless you,' and I said 'He already has.' " Levi chuckled, winking at Karyn. "You are good for me. You humble me."

"Thank you for doing that. That woman is probably in a shelter, and that's one way she has to earn her room and board."

"No, thank you for teaching me. I forgot your church is heavy into the outreach ministry."

"Yes, I'm proud to say I'm a member of Crowns for Christ. We focus on prison ministry, the homeless, and low-income families."

Maybe if I keep saying prison *that will open the door,* she hoped. Looking out the window, she added, "It's God who takes care of the sparrows in the air and His people below."

They rode in silence the next fifteen minutes, until they reached Berryman Bank at the intersection of North Illinois Street and Frank Adams Parkway. Levi parked and walked around the car and assisted Karyn.

Karyn glanced around. "We're going to be late, aren't we, by stopping at the bank?"

"Actually, the victims of crime group that Jet contacted meets here. The owners of the bank allow them to use their executive conference room. I guess with cameras and a security guard, this is safe for them. Another agency rents space in a school or hospital."

Levi nodded at the massive brick structure. "They didn't spare any expense on the architectural design. It definitely stands out. Come on." He squeezed her hand. "I don't see Jet or Rossi's SUV yet. I know he had to meet with a potential client in our new East St. Louis development."

He turned and stared at her. "You're awfully quiet. Are you all right with this?"

Karyn swallowed. Actually, she wasn't okay. Her caseworker advised her against it. Monica didn't think Karyn was ready to come face to face with victims' pain, but she relented and cautiously, against her better judgment, gave Karyn a pass to go.

"I don't want to be here. I guess I'm facing my fears."

A third hint. Ask. Ask, Levi, what I mean, Karyn silently challenged him.

He leaned closer as Karyn's heart pounded. "Baby, I already suspected, but I was waiting for you to confide in me, because I didn't want to pry. You've been a victim of domestic abuse or something, haven't you? The signs have been there: slow in trusting again, a secured building, and—"

Huh? Where did Levi get that idea? Just as she was about to correct him with bigger hints, Jet drove into the parking lot and honked. Rossi trailed her.

"It's okay. We'll talk later after this." Levi smacked a kiss against her lips.

Rossi had gotten out of his vehicle then walked over to open Jet's door. Karyn couldn't hear their conversation, but one thing was for sure, it appeared he was coaxing her.

Finally, they all walked into the bank and the security guard directed them to the elevator. On the second floor, there was plush carpet, wood and brass features on the wall, and a few steps away from them was a set of mahogany double doors with Board Room carved in bold scripted lettering led them to their final destination.

Before opening the door, Rossi reached for Jet and Levi's hands, which left Karyn no choice but to latch on to Jet's hand. "Let's say a quick prayer. Father God, in the name of Jesus, please heal the broken spirits in that room and set the captives free. We thank you for your grace and promise, in the name of Jesus."

The prayer ended with choruses of "Amen," including Jet's mumble.

Levi took a deep breath. "Ready?"

Everyone nodded as he slowly opened the door for Jet and Karyn to enter. There were already a handful of people gathered around a massive long table, where pitchers of water and platters of fruits and snacks rested.

The setup appeared to be for anything else—a business meeting, a committee meeting, or a PTA meeting—not an uncensored discussion on death, crime, punishment, and pain. It also was a flashback, reminding Karyn of standing before the parole board. Its members held a stake in her fate: release or remain imprisoned.

The participants were ethnically mixed. Crime doesn't discriminate. Four women refused to make eye contact

with them. Two men gave tentative smiles. Karyn conjured up various scenarios: Did the two men represent
losing a wife like Levi, or were they there to support a
wife who was robbed, or did they have children who
were murdered?

A tall woman—anyone was taller than Karyn's five
feet two—stood. She appeared to be in her sixties, judging from the gray strands that overtook the black in her
hair. When she cleared her throat, the group stared at
the newcomers, curiosity mixing with suspicion. If the
woman was the moderator, she blended with the others in her very casual attire of a white blouse and blue
jeans.

"Welcome, everybody," she said as Karyn and the others took a seat around the table. "Let's start by introduc-
ing ourselves and letting others know if this is your first
time here." She nodded at Rossi, who was still holding
one of Jet's hands.

"I'm Minister Rossi Tolliver. I'm here to support my
relative. This is my first time."

That was probably the easiest way to describe the
cousin-in-law of Jet's late sister, Karyn thought.

"My name is Annie Coleman. My husband was killed
when a burglar broke into our house while we were
sleeping. My husband went to investigate." She paused
and struggled to finish. "My husband was shot dead.
It's been two years, and I'm still living at what police
called the crime scene."

The introductions continued; some revealed their
circumstances, and a few remained withdrawn. Although Levi was attending for Jet's sake, Karyn wondered if he would take advantage of the opportunity to
further his healing. He did when it was his turn.

"My name is Levi Tolliver, and my wife was killed during a robbery attempt, execution-style, for no reason. I've been living in a limbo for four years between anger and helplessness. Nothing seemed to move me along until this pretty little lady beside me came into my life." He turned Karyn's hand inside and kissed her palm. Whatever else he was going to say, he choked, shaking his head. Rossi slapped him on the back while Karyn massaged his hand.

The moderator intervened. "It's okay. We're here to listen. Do you need more time?" she asked as a few others around the table sniffed. They nodded with empathy.

After a few moments of strained silence, the moderator nodded for Jet to proceed.

Jet began with a shaky voice. "His wife," she said, pointing to Levi, "was my younger sister. My only sister." Choking on her words, Jet paused to recover. "I was mad four years ago, and I'm still mad now. Her unexpected, senseless killing makes me afraid every time I walk into a twenty-four-hour grocery or convenience store. I wonder what was going through my sister's mind when thugs ordered her and the others to line up. I'm afraid to be in my house alone. I turn on all the lights. Now, lights are my bed companions. I cling to the Tolliver family because I'm afraid. They are all I have."

When Jet took a deep breath, Karyn wiped at her own tears. She could feel Jet's pain.

"I'm mad because all of those murderers aren't in prison. There's still one sorry, inhumane person out there, walking around alive and free. I want them all to die and be tortured before taking their last breaths. I want them to look me in the eye and tell me why my sister's life wasn't important and theirs are." Jet shook her head. She was visibly drained. "I'm angry. I'm scared, and I'm dying while I'm living."

Her emotions were so raw that tears began to spring forth from faces in the room. Even the men were reaching for tissue. Levi reached over Rossi and squeezed Jet's hand.

By Jet's depiction, Karyn seemed to relive the scene in a grocery store she had never stepped foot inside. She could feel the sensation of fear, trembling in their bodies. Her mind raced to devise a plan to escape imminent death.

Suddenly, Karyn's mind jumped to enemy lines. She was on the same side as the demon-led executioners, not seeing lives worth living at any cost. Falling into the vortex, Karyn began to sob as she tried to escape the transferred guilt. She screamed, "No! It was an accident." She shook her head back and forth. The tears obstructed her view, her breathing became labored. "I'm so sorry. I didn't mean to kill him."

Near hysterical, Karyn snatched her hand from Levi's and leaped from the table, knocking over her chair. She ran out of the room as if tigers were chasing her.

Karyn had almost reached safety when strong arms wrapped around her waist to restrain her. Levi turned her into his embrace.

"Shhh. I shouldn't have asked you to come. I know it's overwhelming and depressing. That's why I didn't return after the first time." He rocked her in his arms with an easy rhythm.

Karyn had stopped shaking as she returned to the present. She was still fighting to regulate her breathing when Levi's concerned face came into view.

"It's okay, baby."

The moment had come. She had to tell Levi, and for the second time in her life, she would suffer the consequences for her actions. Barely composed, Karyn stepped out of Levi's strong embrace at the same time Jet stalked out of the room—like the tiger chasing her. Jet appeared as dazed as Karyn felt.

Taking a deep breath, Karyn gathered her courage. She was not a coward. The loving concern locked on Levi's handsome face made her question her next statement. "Levi, I didn't pull the trigger that killed your wife, but I did kill someone—"

A slap struck Karyn's face. She screamed in pain as she began to lose her balance, but Levi moved quickly, shielding Karyn and steadying her on her feet. His other hand reached for Jet's throat as he growled like an animal. Rossi got in the middle of the ruckus.

Levi's nostrils flared in anger. "What is wrong with you?" He made another step toward Jet, loosening his hold on Karyn, but Rossi continued to block his path. "Are you crazy, woman?" he shouted at Jet then turned to examine Karyn's face. He grimaced.

The moderator came out into the hall. "Is everything all right? I know it got pretty emotional in there." Waiting for a response that never came, the woman gnawed on her lip. "Take whatever time you need to calm down, and rejoin us if you want." She stepped back in the room and closed the door.

Before Levi could resume his retaliation, Rossi had a strong grip around Jet and dragged her away to increase the distance. That didn't stop Jet from trying to claw her way to her prey.

"Jet," Rossi commanded forcefully, "calm down. Why did you do that?"

She didn't answer him, but screamed at Karyn. "You murderer! Take that for every victim left behind. Go back to jail and pass it on to the people who killed my sister."

The sting began to tingle on Karyn's face. Flinching, she refused to cry. The scripture about turning the other cheek must have been a misprint. She didn't want to give Jet any ideas. Karyn's petite size was no match for Jet's plus-size figure, but if push came to shove, she wouldn't go down without a fight. The throbbing increased. Jet's handprint had possibly reshaped Karyn's face.

"Jet!" Levi shouted, growling. "I'm one breath away from smacking my first woman. I advise you to step back before I make it happen. Karyn didn't kill anybody." He turned his attention back to Karyn. Hesitantly, he touched her face, careful not to cause further pain.

"Levi, I did commit murder."

Frowning, confusion plagued Levi's expression "What are you saying, baby?"

Sniffing, tears betrayed her. Karyn whispered, "I served—" She stuttered then hiccupped. "I served . . . four years in the Decatur Correctional Center for involuntary manslaughter. I have five more months on my parole."

"You . . ." Jet lashed out with profanities, fighting to free herself from Rossi's stronghold, but Rossi had her caged in. "I asked you if you were a criminal, and you lied and said no!"

Emotionally drained, Karyn walked around Levi, who still shielded her from Jet. Keeping a safe distance from her, Karyn returned to the room to retrieve her coat and purse. She avoided eye contact with the others, almost certain they had overheard the entire conversation and they would stand in line to release their venom.

Fearing a mob like attack, Karyn hurried from the room, ignoring the stunned trio outside in the hall waiting for her.

The elevator opened and a different security officer stepped out. "Is everything okay up here? Somebody reported hearing angry voices."

Jet was about to prove the officer's query when she opened her mouth, but Rossi clamped it shut with his hand.

Karyn headed for the elevator. Levi didn't move to stop her. *He who the Son has set free is free indeed,* shouted in her mind. Well, she had put that scripture to the test.

The officer held the elevator doors open for her. She was about to turn the corner when she chanced a look back. They were rooted in their place, watching her escape.

"Jet, I'm not a criminal," Karyn shouted from a safe distance. "I'm a sinner saved by grace." She ordered her legs to start moving, hoping a cab would be her chariot waiting to whisk her away. If not, a long bus ride home didn't sound bad.

"Karyn," Levi yelled, "what happened?" It wasn't a query. It was a demand.

She froze then pivoted around. "I smothered my infant son." This time, Karyn stepped in and allowed the elevator doors to close on the love story of her life.

CHAPTER 44

What just happened? Levi's mind filled with questions as his eyes blurred at Karyn's retreating figure. Karyn did what? His Karyn? He closed his eyes and pushed the glasses back up his nose. He dared not glance at Jet or Rossi. Confused and disgusted with his judgment of character, he turned and stormed in the opposite direction of the hall.

"Levi, are you okay?" Rossi's voice was low, his words hesitant.

Wasn't it obvious? That was the most stupid question he had ever heard. *No, I'm not okay.* He contained his roar. How could he answer when his mind was still numb?

"Cuz?"

"Not now," Levi barked over his shoulder.

What kind of cruel joke was the devil playing? Levi found the stairwell exit and forced it open with a bang. He collapsed on the steps. Removing his glasses, he closed his eyes and hung his head. He wanted to call Karyn a liar. There was no way she could have done what she said. There was no way she could have served time in prison. The inmates would have devoured her.

Lord, what did I do to deserve this? If he didn't have Dori to consider, he would lose his mind. Evidently, Jet had been in her right mind when she called Karyn a criminal.

Be not distraught. I will bless you, God spoke.

At that moment, Levi felt he couldn't believe what anybody said anymore, including God. Instead of one wound in his heart, he now had two. With only his car keys and no coat, he stood and marched down the stairs to the first-floor lobby. Rossi would get his things. If not, Levi would buy a new coat and new life, if both were for sale.

He didn't care what people thought as he braved the cold elements to get to his get-away vehicle. Levi thought about kicking his tires or having a temper tantrum on the hood of his car, but then he rethought that.

"I am so through with women," he muttered as he tried to disarm his car locks; instead he sounded his panic alarm. "Great." He kicked his high-performance Goodyear tire anyway.

He gritted his teeth in aggravation. Once Levi was inside his car, he indulged in a boxing match with his steering wheel. "I must be blind, stupid, desperate, a fool, an idiot." He paused, attempting to conjure up more words to describe his state of mind, which couldn't compare with Job's in the Bible after losing his property and children. He could understand why Job's friends told him to curse God and die. Levi was hurting, but he wasn't that stupid.

Closing his eyes, Levi inhaled deeply. He opened them and stared out the window at an audience watching him from inside the bank. He scanned the sky. The sun would be setting soon on the chilly evening. He wondered about Karyn. Where was she and how did she get there? Was she dressed warm enough? He bowed his head and asked the question he wasn't man enough to find out: What was she feeling?

"Lord, you did give, and then you took away twice, God?" he questioned. He needed to talk to Karyn. If she was a shoplifter, he could simply watch his wallet. Any other nonviolent crime he could forgive, but killing an innocent child—what was she, a monster? Levi craved the answers, but deep down, he doubted it would make a difference.

"What a slap in the face of Diane's memory." Maybe Jet was right to slap Karyn, but he couldn't bear to witness that scene again. He pounded the steering wheel. His wife had been murdered. What did he do, fall in love with a murderer. *I've lost my mind, God.*

Levi felt empty. Karyn filled his life suddenly, and just as quickly, she had deflated it. Snatching off his glasses, he pinched the bridge of his nose. His eyes watered, but he refused to be a sissy and cry. He refused. As angry as he was for Jet's ballistic behavior, he was madder at the woman he loved. How could she?

A rebellious tear slid down his face. His and Karyn's relationship was over, but who ended it, or was it a mutual understanding?

In the distance, his cell phone rang. In his head, Levi wanted the caller to be Karyn, so he could reject her. His heart demanded that he kiss and make up. How does one make up after this devastating news? He grabbed the phone and read the ID—ROSSI.

He didn't feel like being psycho-spiritually analyzed. He turned the ignition, forcing himself to reshuffle his life and go pick up Dori. She was his sole focus and lifeline.

Love covers a multitude of faults, God spoke.

"That's a lot of faults," Levi said angrily.

Forgive so your sins may be forgiven, God spoke again.

After a heavy, frustrated sigh, Levi responded. "Okay, I'll forgive, but I can never forget this."

I forgive you every time you ask. I forgave you as I hung on the cross, then God said nothing else.

CHAPTER 45

So, that's what all the intercessory prayers have been about, Rossi concluded. Jet had been on to something, and Karyn's disclosure confirmed it. He loosened his hold on Jet, but still restrained her with one arm. For the past five minutes, he had been quietly coaxing her to calm down. He didn't feel like bailing her out of jail again for assault with a deadly weapon—her body. Jet's sista hips would have crushed Karyn.

Moments earlier, he had watched Levi, who stood speechless and motionless. When oxygen was restored to his lungs, he moved unsteadily on his feet as he walked aimlessly until he found a door to escape. Clearly, Levi needed help, but Rossi probably would offend him to offer it.

Jet, on the other hand, was near hysteria trying to break out of his bear hold. Rossi had to practically drag her with him as he returned to the room to retrieve their belongings, including Levi's. Within minutes, Jet's energy was zapped as she slumped against him while he guided her to the elevator.

What Rossi wanted was to get Jet to the nearest emergency room and ask a doctor to admit her for mental observation. When he glanced at her again, he felt she was no longer a threat, but a sedative wouldn't be a bad idea. Too bad he wasn't a medical doctor to prescribe it.

In the parking lot, Rossi bypassed Jet's car. He would be the designated driver. Before he drove to her upscale neighborhood, he detoured to a CVS pharmacy. He asked the pharmacist to suggest a non-prescription sleep aid.

Less than thirty minutes later, Rossi pulled into her driveway and parked. "Do you have a remote on your keychain?"

Jet nodded, but didn't make an effort to get it.

"Ah, will you use it so we can go inside?"

She scraped the bottom of her purse, located her ring of keys, and then pushed the remote button to open the garage door. Rossi drove forward and helped Jet out, and she followed him at a snail's pace. The beeping started as Rossi watched Jet ceremoniously flick on her lights. Rossi now understood that habit stemmed out of fear after Diane's death.

"I prefer you put in your code, because I'm not Henry Louis Gates, and President Obama will not invite me to the White House for a beer if I try to explain my way out once the police come," he said, referring to the mixup with the Harvard professor and the Boston officers who responded to a call for a possible break-in as Gates was trying to enter his own house.

She did as instructed.

Her kitchen was gleaming white, with splashes of colors thrown in here and there—the same tidiness as when he was there a few weeks ago. Rossi stuck his head in the living room, then in the formal dining room, checking needlessly for anything suspicious. Jet's physical house was in order, but her mental and spiritual house were in disarray. He had once told her that.

"It's not of my choosing," Jet had balked, referring to her sister's death.

Rossi didn't respond to her sudden rambling. He chose to pray silently rather than to ignite the rage swirling within her.

Walking to the cabinet, he grabbed a glass, turned on the water, and filled it. Opening the pharmacy bag, Rossi pulled out Jet's over-the-counter medicine. He read the instructions and twisted off the bottle cap.

"Here—two of these should calm you down. Take a short nap. I'll be here, and we can talk afterward." She didn't resist his orders.

Jet wandered down the hall and disappeared into a room. When Rossi heard the door close, he exhaled and slid into an uncomfortable chair. It was too dainty for entertaining. The chair had to be a show piece only. He rubbed his face and let his head fall back. "Lord, why am I the one who's supposed to hold things together?" Rossi didn't expect God to answer, and He didn't either.

He had a brain freeze on the last few hours of events: Jet admitting her paranoia, Karyn confessing her past transgression, and Levi's lack of a reaction—that was the scariest for Rossi.

As if he were assembling a device or something, the pieces were starting to fit. Karyn attended Crowns for Christ, a church dedicated to prison ministry. Karyn worked a job she seemed more than capable of owning or managing. Then there were Karyn's Cinderella outings with early check-ins that Levi had complained about a few times. His cousin hadn't connected the dots, but neither had he.

"Okay, Lord, what's the game plan now?"

Silence.

Shaking off his jacket, Rossi anchored his elbows on his knees then dropped his face in the palms of his hands. "Karyn killed her baby?" he whispered.

He thought about Levi. Had he calmed down? Pulling out his BlackBerry, Rossi speed-dialed Levi's number. It went straight to voice mail.

The accusation seemed far-fetched. It didn't seem possible that she was capable of causing injury to anyone. He wondered how Karyn was holding up. Clearly, it wasn't easy for her to hear the angst of victims, even though she had paid for her crime in full. Rossi sighed. He scanned his address book for Nalani Wallace's number. There was no argument that Nalani loved her sister. That's why he wasn't surprised when she gave him her number for emergencies when they were skating on Christmas day.

If this wasn't an emergency, then what was the definition? Sitting in Jet's pristine house with the ticking of an antique grandfather clock to entertain him, he took a deep breath. Rossi never took pleasure in being the bearer of bad news. How was Rossi to know he would have to call Nalani so soon?

He selected her number and waited for her to answer. She didn't. Her sultry voice recording greeted him.

"Nalani . . ." He paused. Surely as close as the sisters were, she knew. "This is Rossi. You may have already spoken with Karyn; then you must know she told Levi about her time in prison. If you didn't know, I'm sorry to be the one to tell you. It was an ugly scene. Both of them are pretty upset. Call me as soon as you get my message." He clicked off. They both had a job to do, and the mission didn't seem easy for either of them.

His cell vibrated. He checked the ID, hoping it was Levi. It wasn't. "Nalani?"

"Yes? Who is this?" she asked.

"This is Rossi." He sighed. "Levi knows about Karyn. She told him. The truth came out, but I don't know if she planned to tell him."

"Of course she planned to tell him," Nalani snapped.

Rossi sat straighter. He was not about to get into it with another woman that day. "I don't doubt that, but it couldn't have come at a worse time. It was a big mess. I just wish I had known."

"Karyn's past is hers to share as she wills, not to be threatened to confess. She loves Levi."

"He loves her, too, but this isn't a simple misunderstanding to overcome."

"Well, I'd better call my sister, then. I'll be back in town as soon as possible."

Hitting the OFF button, Rossi dropped his head. If he could retire from the ministry at the age of thirty-three, he would, but the choice wasn't his. Fortunately or unfortunately, God chose him—not the other way around, praise God.

"For many are called, but few are chosen." He recited Matthew 22:14.

Less than an hour later, Jet stumbled out of a room. She didn't look any better after the nap. As a matter of fact, she appeared worse.

"Rossi," she said, startled. "I forgot you were here." Rubbing her head, Jet frowned. "Did I kill her?"

"No."

"Too bad." Jet spun around and retreated back down the hall toward her bedroom.

CHAPTER 46

Where was a cab when a person wanted to make a fast getaway? Karyn walked past a few bus stops just to put some distance between her and them—Jet, Minister Rossi, and . . . Levi. In hindsight, Karyn wished she had taken Nalani's offer to buy her a car, but no, Karyn wanted to use the money in her trust fund to go toward her business venture. Not to mention the fact that her driver's license had expired while she was in prison, and she would have to start from scratch with the test again.

At a bus stop, Karyn relived the last five minutes before her life ended for a second time. Sitting on the bench, Karyn allowed the tears to flow. She wanted to be cried out by the time she made it back to New Beginnings, which would take two bus rides.

"I knew this was going to happen. I'm not naïve to believe it would have turned out any other way." Where was her testimony? She endured the test—barely. "God, you knew about this, and like Job, you had confidence that I could pass this trial, but from where I'm sitting, I don't think so."

Moments like this, Karyn needed Buttercup—her humor, her scriptures, her pep talk—but she had moved on with her life and out of the women's transitional shelter. Although Buttercup had completed her parole, Karyn hadn't finished hers, and to communicate with a convicted ex-offender was forbidden. "Forbidden." She twisted her mouth at the bitter taste the word implied. "Love is forbidden."

She stood and boarded her first chariot home. If Jet's handprint didn't have Karyn's face red, then her swollen eyes and red nose were a silent hint to bus riders not to ask if she was okay. Clearly, she wasn't. She loved Levi, and for no other reason than being Cinderella for two months, it was worth every moment she had with him.

When Karyn stepped off the first bus to wait to transfer to another one, she looked at her phone. Although the group moderator had requested everyone turn their phones off, Karyn had put hers on silent. Parolees had to be accessible at all times. She groaned, knowing she had to advise her caseworker that she would be returning to the center early and on public transportation.

There were three missed calls. She had hoped they would be from Levi. Did she have the emotional strength to talk to him as an enemy and not the man she loved?

They were from Nalani, and she hadn't left a message. With a seven-minute wait for the other bus and the temperatures dropping, her sister's voice would warm her emotionally. First, she called the caseworker. The woman wasn't happy about the change in plans, but Karyn didn't lose a brownie point. Next was her sister.

"Karyn!" Nalani answered.

"What's wrong?" Karyn's heart dropped at Nalani's hysterical tone. She pushed her debacle on the back burner as her concern grew for her sister.

"Well, there are several things, and they all involve you."

"Levi? How did you know?" Karyn frowned.

"Let's say a bird didn't tell me. His cousin, Minister Rossi, called me."

"Why would he do that? I didn't know he had your number. Did he say how Levi's doing?"

"If he did, I don't remember. My concern is you. I gave Rossi my number weeks ago and asked him to call me if something was wrong with my sister. That was a good move on my part, considering my sister didn't call me," Nalani scolded.

Closing her eyes, Karyn replayed the scene word for word, and then Jet's blow and Levi's response. "You should've seen the hurt on his face."

"No, I should have seen the look on Jet's face after I returned her slap." She mumbled profanities.

Karyn had to convince Nalani not to drop everything in Chicago and fly to Fairview Heights to leave her trademark on Jet. Karyn had to snicker at her younger sister's feistiness, but that wasn't the direction Karyn wanted her to go. Since their reconnection, Karyn wanted to be the example for Nalani to come to Christ.

"You sound just like Buttercup."

"Girl, I am so mad. I'm more deadly than Buttercup, because I don't have a record yet," Nalani said, fuming.

"Believe me, you don't want one." Ironically, Karyn calmed her sister while downplaying her own emotional breakdown.

"Okay, okay, but you better pray for that Jet woman, Karyn, because no one goes after my sister. You weren't responsible for her loss. I was going to drive down on Saturday, but you know what? I'm booking a flight for tomorrow. I'm not waiting until the weekend."

"Nalani, I'll be all right."

"I know you will. You've survived so much more. What's that saying? This too will pass. Frankly, I was hoping for . . . never mind. I believed Levi really cared about you, but it takes a special man to love a special woman who has baggage. And all women do."

"What do you know about a special man and baggage?" Karyn teased.

Karyn marveled at how Nalani skillfully swapped personalities. She smiled, forgetting Nalani could turn on and off the different sides of her temperament. Her talent could earn her a future Oscar nomination.

"Well, you can always move back home. Levi was your only reason to stay."

"And Chicago is my reason to stay away. I can see the headlines: The late Senator Wallace's daughter has been released from prison, blah, blah. That's okay. There are too many bad memories. I'll visit, but I don't want to plant roots there again."

"Oh, so Fairview Heights doesn't have bad memories?"

"Actually," Karyn said, "the good outweighs the bad. I've got a great support system through my church. Believe it or not, my heart will bounce back, and there is a third reason. I can't walk away from my business venture with Halo and Buttercup. We've been saving as much as we possibly can from our low-paying jobs for Crowning Glory. A church member submitted our paperwork for a small business loan for minority owners. Hopefully, we'll hear something soon.

"We have great plans. It won't be just our livelihood, but we would give back to other ex-felons who need a haircut or shampoo for that job interview. I've worked hard on that business proposal. Even Levi was impressed . . ." Karyn shrugged. Levi didn't matter anymore.

"I want you happy. If you want to move to Kentucky, we'll move. If you want to stay there, I'll move there, but we're staying together."

Karyn sat quietly, thinking about another chapter in her life. She tried to justify not telling Levi, tricking herself into believing they wouldn't get past the first date. When Levi poured out his soul to her, maybe it was God's cue for her to walk away instead of hanging around to hurt him more.

"I don't care what that Butternut roommate of yours says. You didn't owe him an explanation of your past. We all make mistakes."

"Wait a minute. Weren't you the one who told me to tell him a few weeks ago?"

"Like I said, we all make mistakes." Nalani laughed and despite the dry humor, Karyn chuckled.

She admired her sister. Nalani was so strong-willed, independent, and most of all, despite what Karyn had done, Nalani still loved her—the sinner she was and all. Defying their father, Nalani had written Karyn, but urged her every time not to respond.

Then, Nalani had delayed her education to single-handedly care for their severely depressed and health-comprised father. Nalani was the woman Karyn had once thought she would become. "I love you," she whispered as her bus turned the corner.

"I love you too. We'll get through this—together."

Sighing, Karyn felt better. "I know. I've got to go. My public chariot is here."

"You need a car!"

"Bye." Karyn shivered. Her sister was right.

Feeling better, Karyn managed a smile as she boarded the bus. She didn't want to be like Rosa Parks, so Karyn headed to the back of the bus. The Lord dropped a familiar church song in her heart: *I'm yours, Lord. Try me out and see, see if I can be completely yours.*

Twenty minutes later, Karyn opened the door to the New Beginnings shelter. Her counselor stopped her at the desk.

"Hi, Karyn. I need a urine sample. We have new house guests, and as you know, we'll have to show them we mean business," she said, enforcing the random drug testing for all residents. As Karyn walked closer to take the cup, Monica squinted. Evidently, Jet's handprint was ingrained on Karyn's cheek.

"What happened?" Monica asked as she pulled Karyn near a light. She peered through her glasses, angling Karyn's face.

"I got slapped," she answered with humiliation.

"I see that. You know your involvement in any kind of altercation could violate your parole."

The reminder. Every moment was a reminder—Mrs. Harris's monthly purchase for her grandson, the slap from Jet, her living quarters. How could Karyn forget she was on parole? The staff was kind to its temporary residents, but once the law was laid down, it was enforced without mercy.

After Karyn rehashed the evening, Monica grabbled for some comforting and encouraging words, but nothing helped. Karyn only wanted to do one thing—cry; but first she would apply a cold towel to her face. She would pray later. There would be plenty of time in the future.

"I'm so sorry, Karyn. I didn't think it was a good idea, but you were adamant about going. The helplessness victims feel is raw. It doesn't matter whether you committed a crime against them or not. You represent an uncontrollable person who broke the law and therefore, part of a whole problem. It's not going to be easy, but you will go on and live a normal life. Now," her counselor said, holding a Dixie-sized cup, "I still need a urine sample."

Karyn nodded and took off her coat before complying. Afterward, she counted the steps as she climbed the stairs to the third floor. Unlocking the suite, she longed for Buttercup's presence. She headed for the bathroom. Turning on the light, she peered at her face. Jet had large hands and long fingers. The redness on her cheek proved it.

She grabbed her face towel and made a cold compress. Back in the bedroom with the light from the bathroom as her guide, she lay in the bed with her clothes on. As she stared at the dark ceiling, Karyn's mind floated back to the day that changed her life. She chided herself for believing in fairy tales.

Mentally exhausted from recalling past wounds, Karyn drifted off to sleep, but not before remembering Levi's face—his twin dimples, brown eyes, and tenderness every time she caught him looking at her. Although she would miss her happiness with Levi, the absence of Dori's smile would crush her the most.

Saturday morning, Karyn woke to the commotions of a new roommate, Jay—Jalisiana. The woman was shorter than Karyn, and judging from first impressions, Jay needed whatever services Buttercup would give her for free. Before she could get out of bed and use the bathroom, Karyn learned Jay's life story, age, and her score on the GED test, as well as how much time she spent for larceny and picking locks.

"Girl, what happened to ya face?" Popping a tiny piece of gum that wasn't meant to be popped, Jay stood inches in front of Karyn. Her large, dingy eyes scanned Karyn's face. They widened as if they were magnifying glasses that had discovered a piece of lint. "Did you cut her?"

Karyn shook her head. "No," she said softly. "Jesus would have wanted me to turn the other cheek."

"Humph." She stepped back and put her fists on her little-girl hips. "Jesus never got slapped like that."

"No . . . he was pierced in his side, whipped on his back, and was fitted with a crown of thorns."

"Girl, that's deep." She walked back into her newly assigned bedroom. "I'm going to take a nap now. I'm a light sleeper, so try not to make that much noise."

Karyn's day went downhill from there. Nalani was juggling her school schedule and trying to sell the family house, so she wouldn't be able to get away for another few days. Karyn wished she was on the schedule to work—anything but staying in the shared living quarters, watching television. Jay complained about the muffled sounds from the TV, until finally Karyn put the volume on mute. She hadn't registered for spring classes. Now Karyn wished she had.

After leaving three messages, Karyn finally received a return call from Pastor Scaife. While Karyn was pouring out her heart and accepting prayer, Jay got up and strolled into Karyn's bedroom, coming out with a bar of soap. She was clearly violating two house rules: no borrowing, and no entering another's bedroom.

On Sunday morning, Karyn locked her bedroom door, thankful she didn't really have any valuables except the music box Levi had bought her as one of many gifts for Christmas. The tennis bracelet she cherished never left her sight or wrist except when she showered.

Karyn changed her mind and unlocked her door. She walked back inside and eyed the miniature music box. She would stuff it in her purse, even if she had to dump everything out to make room.

The church van was waiting when Karyn walked out of the building. That was a first. She and Buttercup had always been ready. Her Sunday attire was a dark dress and boots. It matched her mood. Her face bore only a faint bruise, thanks to some makeup tricks Buttercup had taught her.

She took a deep breath as she stepped up into the van. The thrill she felt in the presence of the saints of God was gone.

"Child, you okay?" Mother Caldwell asked before Deacon Deacon had shut the doors. "Pastor Scaife called me last night and told the prayer warriors to start praying for one of our own. I was on my knees for an hour, mainly because it took me a while to get up, but it was worth it, baby. God was speaking to me something fierce through His holy tongues. I figured He knew what you needed."

"Thank you," Karyn said, collapsing on the seat Mother Caldwell patted next to her. "It hurts so bad." She clutched her purse, mindful of the treasure inside. "It was another crime that I couldn't get away with either. I did nothing to stop him from falling in love with me."

Mother Caldwell adjusted her hat then folded her arms. "God cleans up real good. The Lord has the final say-so in our lives, not the devil."

"That's right, Mother," Deacon Deacon yelled over his shoulder from the driver's seat. Karyn closed her eyes. She couldn't get to church fast enough to hear God's message.

After two more stops, the van pulled into Crowns for Christ's semicircular drive. Buttercup was standing out in the cold, wrapped in a poncho with her arms folded. Her headband was a faux fur. Guarding Buttercup's side was Halo. Since Buttercup no longer rode the bus, he didn't either. Halo had purchased an old clunker.

They were officially engaged after the controlling authority—aka parole board—approved of their union. Although their debts had been paid, society could rest at night because Big Brother would always be watching them; and private-run prisons were praying for a mess-up so they could return as confined guests at their facilities.

Neither Buttercup nor Halo looked too happy as they craned their necks, trying to see inside the van. When Deacon Deacon opened the door, Buttercup and Halo were ready to storm the van.

"Wait right there, you two. Everybody will disembark my cruise liner in an orderly fashion."

Consenting, Halo pulled Buttercup back, speaking to the riders as they got out. Karyn trailed Mother Caldwell. As Deacon Deacon assisted Mother Caldwell down, Halo reached for Karyn's arm.

Buttercup blocked her entrance. "Okay, what happened?" Buttercup wore a game face, and surprisingly, all her makeup was the same shade.

"I'm mad at you," Karyn said as she tried to walk past her.

"Me?" Buttercup asked incredulously.

"Yeah." Karyn pointed. "First, you were right, which makes me mad. Second, you deserted me, and I have a ghetto roommate who is a career lock picker, and this makeup is not hiding this bruise well enough."

"What bruise?" Halo spoke for the first time. His hands balled into fists. "I just need a name and a description." He separated his legs in a military stance.

Buttercup smacked Halo in the chest with the back of her hand. "I thought you left your thug days behind. I've got this." She pointed to herself then turned to Karyn. "Who?"

Karyn shook her head. She didn't doubt her friends meant business, but some things weren't worth going back to prison.

In the sanctuary, Pastor Scaife preached from Romans 8. It was a familiar passage, but the only phrase that kept ringing in her ear was verse 35: *Who shall ever separate us from Christ's love? Shall suffering and affliction and tribulation? Or calamity and distress? Or persecution or hunger or destitution or peril or sword?*

CHAPTER 47

A week after his life shattered for the second time, Levi welcomed Jet's scheduled weekend with Dori. They hadn't spoken since Karyn's revelation, and that was fine with him. He left the task up to Rossi to make sure Jet was okay. It was bad enough he couldn't stop thinking about Karyn, but after today, it would be the last time he would talk about her.

"Levi, I—" Jet opened her door before Levi could leave a fingerprint on her doorbell.

He held up his hand. Levi didn't know what side of the fence Jet was on that day: Was it "I told you so" or "I'm sorry I acted a fool"? Either way, Levi didn't want to hear it.

Levi bent and hugged his daughter good-bye. "Have fun with your auntie."

"Okay, Daddy." Dori grinned and began slipping the backpack stuffed with her clothes off her back.

Levi tightened his coat collar around his neck. He started to walk away.

"Levi," Jet yelled from the doorway.

Out of courtesy and respect, he spun around. Huffing, he waited.

"I'm sorry."

For what? Slapping Karyn? Trying to warn him, or for his hurting? Levi didn't want to know the answer. Nodding, he struggled to accept her apology, only be-

cause it was the Christian thing to do. Levi continued
to his car, which he left with the motor running in her
driveway, and drove away. Destination: his parents'
house for a family meeting he had requested.

Traffic on I-64 into St. Louis was backed up, which
made Levi impatient. He wanted to get this ordeal over
with. A half hour later, he ambled through Victor and
Sharon's front door, his heart heavy and aching. He
was the last to arrive.

Tia, his twin brothers, and his parents were lounging
around the living room, laughing. Tia held court, regal-
ing them with tales of outlandish weddings. He would
be the party crasher as the bearer of bad news.

His father and Seth's conversation had slipped into
debating stats for the upcoming Super Bowl. As expected, Solomon sat among them quietly, seeming uninterested, but his expression betrayed him. Levi knew
Solomon caught every word. The oldest twin liked to
keep people guessing what he was thinking. It worked
to his advantage because usually their assumptions
were off.

Seth looked up. "Oh, you're here. Take off your jacket,
man, and get comfortable."

Levi frowned. Was he not the one to call the meeting? They didn't know this was Karyn's wake before
he buried her name forever. Levi sighed and collapsed
on the couch without removing his jacket. Closing his
eyes, Levi willed for this moment to be quick and pain-
less.

Opening them, Levi exhaled and faced them. "I'm
going to cut to the chase. Karyn and I are no longer seeing each other."

"We figured as much," Seth said nonchalantly as he
crossed his ankle on his knee. "Tia and I agreed it's
probably your fault."

Surprise jerked Levi forward. "My fault?" Fury built inside the pit of his stomach. His nostrils flared. Levi was ready to back up his bark with a bite. "Do you have any idea what she did?" He found no pleasure in telling them Karyn was a murderer.

"It doesn't matter. It's always the man's fault. That's what Tia tells me all the time." Seth winked at his fiancée and she reciprocated with a lifted brow and a smirk.

Evidently his brother and future sister-in-law enjoyed making up after a disagreement. That wasn't an option for him, so Levi refocused. "I'm sure you'll side with me on this one."

Tia waved her hand in the air. "Please. I've already talked to Karyn."

"Really?" Levi's interest piqued, he sat straighter on the sofa. His heart pounded, wanting to hear more. "And what did she say?"

"Put it this way: Your name didn't come up." Tia shrugged.

What was the topic of discussion? Did Karyn tell Tia the gory details and why she did what she did? His questions were endless.

"Well, what is it, son?" his mother asked, linking her hands and breaking into his reverie.

"Levi," Vincent said. His father wasn't a patient man.

Three, two, one. "Karyn served time in prison for killing her baby." Levi exhaled and braced for impact. Their gasps were synchronized as they delayed their outrage and onslaught of questions.

Mouths dropped open and eyes bucked. Suddenly, they quieted as if a vacuum had sucked the life out of the room. Their expressions were frozen and they stared at Levi as if there would be a punch line to follow. Even the sunshine beaming through the sheer curtains paused. Levi wouldn't be surprised if they stopped breathing—he had, the moment Karyn admitted it.

"What?" Seth jerked his head and frowned. "Come again?"

"Why?" Tia asked. She scooted to the edge of her seat.

"When was this?" His father's question hinted that he didn't believe a word of it.

Levi punched the couch. "I don't have all the answers. Does it matter?"

"It might." Solomon spoke for the first time.

His mother's brows knitted in concern. "Are you sure? That's just not possible," Sharon's voice faded. "Is this hearsay, or do you have evidence of this rumor?"

"Come on, Mom. It's not like I do background checks on my dates."

"Maybe you should. Women are the fastest growing prison population." Solomon rolled out the stats from the Rolodex in his head. As a detective, his brain was priceless. He was an all-facts man, very little emotions. "That's too bad, because her sister seemed . . . interesting," Solomon added to everyone's dismay. His compliments were few.

Levi huffed. The timing was all wrong for Solomon to be interested.

"Karyn?" Sharon stated in disbelief as she stared past Levi. "She did what?"

Tia shuddered as her eyes glazed over. Seth automatically had his arms around her. He gently squeezed her shoulder. Tia composed herself and whipped out her cell phone.

"Who are you calling?" Seth asked.

"Karyn," she answered, annoyed.

Levi held his breath, hoping Karyn would answer. Whether she did or not, Levi only heard Tia say before disconnecting, "Let's do lunch."

His father stood to his intimidating height. After a few paces, he walked out of the room. Victor was a thinker. Levi would pay money to eavesdrop on his thoughts.

"She doesn't look like a criminal," his mother rambled as she tried to convince herself.

When his father returned, they waited for his speech of wisdom. His frown, blinks, and grimaces revealed he was still digesting the story. Victor took a deep breath. "As Christians, we're commanded to show compassion. Beyond that, I don't know what to say. Where is my nephew when I need him?" Victor was clearly flustered about Rossi's absence.

Tia cleared her throat. "You know this is not making any sense, Levi. Evidently, Karyn needs a friend. I don't know what she's been through, but I feel in my heart that I'm no better than her when Christ judges us."

"Come on, Tia. Being noble is one thing, but murder? How can you ignore that? All I know is I'm keeping my daughter as far away from Karyn Wallace as possible," Levi stated, gritting his teeth and balling his hands into fists. "Maybe she's a pedophile and set her sights on Dori." Levi cringed at his last statement, but with the new revelation, he couldn't rule out any scenarios.

"Levi." Tia stood at the same time his father walked out of the room again. "You're talking about Karyn like she's demon-possessed."

"Stay out of it, babe," Seth warned from his seat with a failed attempt to pull her back down.

Tia defied her fiancé. "Levi, don't you love her? Is it superficial or rooted? Don't make a judgment call yet. Your brother better not desert me over any of my past transgressions."

"How did I get in this?" Seth balked with confusion. He looked at Levi for answers.

Levi groaned. This was getting out of control.

Before Tia could continue her inquest, Seth stood and dragged her away to the kitchen, which left only his mother in the room.

Levi took a deep breath and walked over and collapsed beside her. "Mom, what are you thinking?"

Sharon reached over and rubbed his jaw. Tears were in her eyes. "I can't think. What are you expecting me to say?"

"I don't know. I expected you to be outraged and screaming and calling her a child killer."

"Somehow, I think you've already done that, but those things are playing in my mind like a marquee." Sharon paused, distracted by leftover Christmas decorations on a nearby table. She stared at them before meeting Levi's eyes. "If she were on drugs, I would be alarmed, but . . . maybe she suffered from some chemical imbalance like postpartum depression or something. I really don't know."

"That's what I was thinking, Mrs. Tolliver," Tia said, rejoining the debate after breaking free of Seth's entanglement.

"Call it what you want, but no normal mother would ever harm her child. She'll get no sympathy from me. I can't overlook that," Levi told them as his brother reluctantly returned to the living room. "Seth, what do you have to say about it?"

"Absolutely nothing." Seth eyed Tia.

Levi needed one person on his side to say he had done the right thing. The loss of Karyn was different from Diane. Where Diane's absence had left one gigantic hole in his life, Karyn's exit was a pint-size hole that made it impossible to plug the leak. They hadn't talked, and it wasn't because he disconnected her phone service—though he thought about it. Neither had he taken Dori back to the bookstore. He diverted her attention to anything, even a camping trip in their basement, but every now and then she wished Miss Karyn was with them.

"You need answers. You want me to talk to her?" Solomon offered.

"No!" everyone said in unison, knowing Solomon's talk meant fierce, unmerciful interrogation.

CHAPTER 48

Monday morning Levi entered his office. From his outer appearance, he was dressed for work: starched oxford shirt, suspenders, printed tie, polished leather shoes—everything to look like a man in charge of his world. What people couldn't see was the void, the loss of companionship, the loss of contentment in knowing Karyn was a phone call away when he couldn't see her. He had to play the part and convince people—mainly his cousin—that he was all right.

Levi walked passed Rossi's open office as if he were in a hurry, on a mission to take care of some important business. He had almost made it when Rossi called out to him.

"Hey, got a minute?"

Grunting, Levi backtracked to the doorway. "Nope, I'm really busy."

"Great. Have a seat." Rossi pointed to a chair in his office and didn't wait for Levi to comply. "Crews have broken ground, and they expect the renovation on the old Majestic Hotel will be done in four phases. We're getting calls now about leasing space."

Levi nodded. Good, business as usual.

"We're booking up fast. It seems a lot of people want to see the area regain its luster. A bakery wants in, a women's dress shop, a bookstore . . . speaking of bookstore . . . ah, are we still holding a space for Karyn? "

"No." Levi didn't have to think about it. "It's supposed to be Tolliver Town, not Criminal Corner."

"That was nasty and uncalled for." Rossi shook his head. "And we're cousins. Anyway, I've done a little research. Did you know that criminals—as you call ex-offenders—were responsible for archiving the Freedman Bank records in Utah, giving a lot of us folks—African Americans—a way to trace our family roots? Plus, there is a business near downtown St. Louis that hires former inmates to give them a second chance at starting over. The customers love what the owner is doing and support the shop religiously," Rossi said too smugly for him.

Levi twisted his lips and pushed his glasses higher on his nose. "Listen, man, nobody is going to want to be a tenant next door to ex-felons, felons, or whatever they call people with a criminal record. No one is going to feel safe shopping with them around. We're here to make money, not run a rehab neighborhood."

Rossi aimed his pen at Levi and fired. He missed. "Look, I'm getting really tired of this dark cloud you're carrying with you. What do you want from Karyn?"

"An apology?" Levi didn't know.

"Listen, man, nothing and no one on this earth is perfect, including you and me.

Rossi leaned back in his leather executive chair and rocked. He toyed with his mustache. "I haven't been where you are sitting. I haven't found love, lost love, and found it again, but I happen to be a one-of-a-kind man who believes in fairy tales. I would let her know I love her in spite of, and I can't live without her because of, propose, and marry before my lust takes over."

Levi wasn't amused. "If I can move on after Diane as hard as that was, I can move on after Karyn." Did he sound convincing? Levi didn't believe a word he had just said.

"I love you, cousin, but you better drop the attitude. Put yourself in Karyn's shoes." Rossi tried to console him.

"Ah, wrong size. I would never harm anybody, especially my child."

"Be careful, Levi. You're boasting. Without the Lord, we don't know what we would do. It's by the grace of God that we are what we are today. Don't ever forget that."

"Rossi, don't take this the wrong way, but I find it hard to believe a woman would do that."

"Do you need to get counseling from our pastor?"

Levi snarled. "Why should I make an appointment to get counseling when you give it to me without me asking?"

A few hours later, Rossi closed his office door and made the call. "We've got to do something," he said as soon as Nalani answered.

"We," she snapped.

Rossi held in a chuckle. Karyn and Nalani were two feisty little women. "That's right. Your sister and my cousin. Let's meet when you're back in town. You wouldn't dare talk bad to a minister face to face, would you?"

"Umm-hmm." She chuckled. "Actually, I'm in Fairview Heights now. I have a few hours before Karyn gets off work."

Rossi suggested they meet for lunch at the Mississippi Grill in East St. Louis near their construction site.

Arriving first a half hour later, Rossi secured a table. There was no mistaking when Nalani sashayed through the door that she and Karyn were sisters, but Nalani had a sweet sassiness that was appealing. She admitted she didn't have Christ in her life, but she wasn't opposed to it either.

"At the moment, Karyn's my priority," she had informed him more than once when he tried to witness to her.

That had given Rossi two missions: work with her about Karyn and Levi's situation, and preach the gospel of Jesus Christ to her without a pulpit, to show her the benefits of salvation.

Standing, Rossi placed a kiss on Nalani's cheek. He waited for her to be seated, and then sat across from her.

"You look pretty." He complimented her choice of purple.

She smiled that same Karyn-smile and winked. "You don't look bad yourself. Suits and ties become you."

A waitress came to their table, rattled off the late lunch specials and gave them a few minutes to think about it. They ignored the menus.

"How's Karyn?" Rossi asked.

"How do you think she is? She's devastated. I'm not a praying woman, but I haven't stopped praying for my sister. Men!"

Rossi leaned closer. "She should have told him, Nalani."

She lifted an arched brow. Her lips tightened as if she were puckering for a kiss. Her expression was a reminder a kiss wasn't coming. "The only confession my sister needed to do was to the Man upstairs. That was her past. That's not who she is today."

Being combative wouldn't solve anything, he told himself. "Does she love him?"

"Humph. I hope not for much longer, because it's killing her."

"Well, imagine how betrayed my cousin must've felt. He loses his first love to a murderer, and then he chooses his second love, who is—"

Nalani's chest heaved. Rossi could tell she was ready to attack. *Lord, help me to choose my words.*

"His second love is what, Minister Tolliver?" Inching up from the table, she leaned into him, inches from his face. A challenge blazed from her eyes, and Nalani clinched her teeth. Her paws—manicured nails—were in a position to attack.

He might be a minister, but he was still a man, and a woman bold enough to invade a man's personal space was asking for some attention. Oddly, he wanted to spar with Nalani, but this wasn't Rossi and Nalani's battle.

"Okay, Nalani. I like your sister, but maybe if she could call and explain to—"

"Forget it. Excuse my English, but she ain't going to do it. If she tries, I'll hurt her. She deserves better. Any man who loves his woman is on her side whatever the reason."

Rossi raised his finger. "A good woman who says she loves her man will confide in him and trust him with her heart."

Nalani leaned back and folded her arms. "I heard somewhere that if a person takes one step, God will take two. In this case, Levi better make some big leaps, because my sister has less than three months on parole, and then we're out of here." She flicked her thumb as if she were hitchhiking. "Chicago is out, but there's always Miami, L.A., Phoenix, even Oregon."

"Oregon?" Rossi kept from chuckling. "Are there any blacks in Oregon?"

"There'll be two."

Time was running out for Karyn and Levi. God didn't have to tell Rossi to pray. He already was.

CHAPTER 49

After the fiasco from the crime victims' grief counseling session, Jet opted for private counseling. Hearing about other people's sorrow and pain was too overwhelming for Jet. The one-on-one proved to be better. They were empowering her to release and manage some of her anger. Also, she did feel like a hero after exposing Karyn's dirty deed. Clearly, Karyn had no intent of telling Levi, so Jet had stopped Levi from making a big mistake.

Once the shock of Karyn's confession wore off, Jet Googled Karyn's name, adding key phrases like "prison," "infant," and "murder." She applauded the *Chicago Tribune's* news coverage on her family history, Karyn's ambitions, and her relationship with the baby's father. It appeared the senator's daughter had it all and blew it.

Reading several media source accounts, Jet learned more about Karyn before her fall—tumble—from grace.

Since her brother-in-law hadn't been in a talkative mood lately, she confided her findings to Rossi.

"I commend you for seeking individual counseling for your depression, but whatever dirt you have uncovered on Karyn, leave me off your list to share the information," Rossi had told her.

His rejection didn't faze Jet. She still felt vindicated that she had been right about Karyn.

Stretching, Jet spun her chair around from the large window behind her desk. Jet shut off her daydreaming. She smiled with contentment about her progress.

As a mid-level manager in the corporate lending division, Jet's main responsibility was to oversee small business loan requests. It was almost the end of the month, and all files needed to be closed, stamped with a yea or nay. She pulled up the monthly list. Out of three hundred and something applications, Karyn Wallace's name popped out.

"What does she want now?" Jet hissed as her good mood began to disintegrate.

Clicking on the file, Jet absorbed herself in reading the ten-page document. The plan was thorough and the profit projections were in line, but the mission of assisting offenders in assimilating into society after prison translated to a bunch of dangerous low-lives running loose. It was not her idea of protecting the community. Plus, Karyn wanted dibs on one of Levi's current redevelopment properties. "No way."

Without blinking, Jet denied the loan request and forwarded it to the department's supervisor to generate a standard rejection letter. Grinning, she signed off her computer and grabbed her purse out of her desk drawer. She was going home to celebrate by opening up a bottle of wine. She would toast to her sister's memory.

Karyn was happy but not surprised to get the phone call from Tia Rogers. Levi's future sister-in-law was a classy woman who seemed genuine and easygoing. What would always endear Karyn to her was that she saw the goodness in her and wanted to count Karyn as a friend.

The next afternoon, Tia met her at the bookstore. She browsed while Karyn finished with a customer.

"Are you ready?" Karyn startled Tia, who was turning pages in a romance book.

"Yeah." Tia chuckled. "It doesn't take me long to get caught up in a story. Let me pay for this first."

Karyn stopped her. "Let me treat you." She smiled. Her offer was a testimony that Karyn was thriving within her means. She actually had spare money from her meager salary. She refused to splurge on the hundreds of thousands of dollars in her trust fund that Nalani had handed over to her.

"Okay. I'll spring for lunch."

"That's a plan." Karyn clocked out for her forty-five-minute lunch. Tia, wearing heels, and Karyn, keeping pace in comfortable flats, hurried to the food court. They bypassed any food vendors that sounded healthy and chose super-sized slices of pizza from Sbarro and two bottles of fruit juice.

Once they found a seat, Tia joined hands with Karyn and prayed. "Father, in the name of Jesus, we thank you for our meal and the fellowship. I especially thank you for bringing Karyn into my life. As you bless me, please bless her. Amen."

Opening her blurry eyes, Karyn met Tia's with a smile. Tia held up her hand. "Let me take a bite first." She did, closing her eyes and moaning her delight. "Ahh. Now, the first rule to our lunch date is not to mention *him*. Agreed?"

Nodding, Karyn helped herself to a taste. They chatted about Tia's wedding, how Dori was faring, and Karyn's sister. After they consumed their pizza, Karyn folded her arms on the table.

"I would still love to have you in my wedding," Tia said.

Karyn looked away. At one time, she would have been honored, but now, to be in a Tolliver wedding without Levi in her life was wrong. She couldn't do Levi like that. "I'll send a gift."

Tia didn't push her into changing her mind. For that, Karyn was grateful and respected Tia more.

"Okay, since we aren't discussing *him*, I'm sure *him* told you about me. Aren't you curious?" Karyn asked.

Tia drained the last of her juice from the bottle. "I am, but it's real important for us to have an honest relationship before talking about something from our past. It's like showing a stranger your scar from gallbladder surgery."

Karyn and Tia laughed.

"Seriously, Karyn, let me prove myself as your friend."

This blew Karyn away. She had never met anyone like Tia. She choked on emotions. "The only thing I can say is I want to be like you when I grow up," Karyn joked.

"Too late. You're older than me if you're dating *him*." She grinned. Tia leaned closer and whispered, "It's not too early for me to share a secret with you. Please don't tell anybody."

Karyn didn't know what to expect. "O—okay," she stuttered. Karyn was honored to be considered as a confidant.

Tia exhaled and glanced around to make sure she couldn't be overheard. "Seth has the ugliest feet I've seen on a man. We went swimming—"

Karyn almost fell out of the chair laughing. Tia joined in the fun. "I couldn't ask for a better friend."

"Me either." Tia winked.

They finished lunch and Karyn returned to work. *Him* was the farthest thing from her mind, but the closest to her heart.

On Sunday after worship service, Sister Ivy, who worked at the bank, gave Karyn, Buttercup, and Halo the bad news. There wasn't a saint in the church that Sister Ivy hadn't helped in some kind of way when it came to loans: educational, home, or small business.

"I don't understand it. I really thought you had a good chance. I tweaked the application myself, but Miss Hutchens is a stickler for detail. She sees problems in an application that we overlook. You all will get letters in the mail probably tomorrow or Tuesday. I waited until after service to tell you. I'm so sorry. I'll pray the Lord will open another door."

Sister Ivy fought back tears as she hugged each of them. With nothing more to say, she picked up her purse and walked out of the sanctuary as two of her children ran behind her.

The group crumbled into the nearest pews from the aftershock. Halo was the first one to cry out to God. "Lord, your Word says if we walk right before you, no good thing will you withhold. We've done that, Lord. . . ." His voice faded in defeat.

"That was our dream. Our mission is to be self-sufficient and help someone along the way." Buttercup's words choked. "God, please don't forsake us." Buttercup covered her face as her shoulders shook. "This is what kept me going at that call center sweat shop, knowing I would be starting up our business. It's gone."

Karyn was already crying on the inside. In a few minutes, she would be bawling. Nalani slipped next to her and squeezed her hand.

"What do we do now? We don't have a backup plan," Karyn whispered. She had yet to blink. "What could we have done differently? I didn't touch that trust money so we would have collateral."

"I've been fasting all week, praying that God will make a way for us." Halo was too much of a man's man to cry, but he turned his head and sniffed. He rubbed his eyes before looking at Karyn again. "What caused this Miss Hutchens to reject it? The clientele alone couldn't be it, and no one knew that it was the brainchild of ex-felons."

"Wait a minute. Miss Hutchens at First Freedom Bank?" Karyn groaned.

"What?" Buttercup looked hopeful through her tear-stained face. Halo stopped massaging her shoulders.

"What, Karyn?" Halo repeated, staring.

"Sis?" Nalani chimed in.

"I think Jet's last name is Hutchens, and at Macy's girls' night out bash, I overhead a woman ask Jet how things were going at the bank where she once worked. I didn't hear the name of the bank though."

The trio gasped. Halo's nostrils flared, Buttercup's eyes twitched, and Nalani shot up and hurriedly grabbed her things. The mood went from sober to energized with a call for action.

"Where are you going?" Karyn asked.

"I've got to step outside this church so I can curse. I just want to know if Jet's fingerprints are on that application literally."

Buttercup shook her head. "Let her go. If God hadn't saved me, I would join her, but we have to stay on the Lord's side in this."

"I'm sorry, Halo and Buttercup. I'm sure she turned our proposal down because of me. My relationship with her brother-in-law was doomed from the beginning. I really messed things up."

The lights flickered in the sanctuary, indicating dinner was ready to be served in the fellowship hall. Buttercup reached out and rubbed Karyn's arm. "Don't blame yourself for this."

Karyn looked away, allowing her eyes to adjust to the light from the stained-glass dome in the ceiling. "I expected whatever I had done years ago not to matter." Karyn stood. "Come on, let's go next door to eat."

"You better go and get your sister before she curses out the wrong person," Buttercup suggested.

CHAPTER 50

Monday morning, Jet was in her office when the supervisor from the lending department interrupted her.

"I'm sorry, Miss Hutchens. I have a woman who insists on seeing you about a loan application that was denied," Claudia Ivy said. Her demeanor betrayed her words. Claudia didn't appear to be the least bit apologetic.

Jet hadn't been at work an hour, and already this was the third interruption. Not all were Claudia's fault, but very few rejection appeals showed up on her desk. "Which loan? We receive hundreds a month," Jet said, annoyed.

"The Crowning Glory proposal."

Claudia had made Jet's day. Nodding, Jet welcomed a calculated breath then concealed a victorious and satisfying grin. She rested her pen on a pile of papers and shrugged. "Sure. I have a few minutes." Jet leaned back in her leather chair and waited for the fireworks to begin.

Expecting Karyn, Jet was disappointed when her sister sashayed in. Most men might have considered her face pretty and curves appealing, but her petite body was no match for Jet's plus-size African hips. A few times, she was compared to the once popular movie character Foxy, played by former actress–turned author Pam Grier. It definitely wouldn't be a fair fight.

Jet smirked at Nalani's glare.

Nalani positioned her fists on her waist. "You've got a lot of nerve. I don't believe in coincidences. There was nothing wrong with my sister's proposal. I'm financing a large portion of her business, so you better have a good reason for rejecting her application. As a matter of fact, I don't even want to hear it. Just prepare for a showdown." She dropped her arms and wiggled her fingers as if she were a cowgirl ready to draw her gun.

Yawning, Jet lifted her pen without breaking eye contact. "She's a criminal. There are others ahead of her, so she can take a back seat. Our bank doesn't hire felons; neither do we loan money to them."

"Karyn's debt is paid in full."

"Once a criminal, always a criminal in my book," Jet said.

Nalani stepped closer to Jet's desk. "Listen, Chaka Khan . . ." It wasn't the first time someone made a comparison between Jet's long, natural hair and that of the former entertainer. "Don't get me confused with my sister. I believe the bigger they are, the harder they fall theory." She pounded a fist on the desk and leaned forward. "I've got people in high places ready to take you down."

Jet laughed. "Yeah, I know. Jesus, right?"

"I don't need Jesus for something I can take care of myself." She stepped back from Jet's desk.

"You've wasted enough of my time. I have qualified loans to approve." Jet dismissed Nalani as she tapped on her keyboard.

"You"—Nalani pointed—"might want to rethink your decision and okay that Crowning Glory proposal. I'll file so many complaints against you and this banking institution there will be a waiting list of plaintiffs ready to testify about any past discriminatory practices."

"I don't think so."

"You'll eat your words, and I hope I'm there to feed them to you, and that Karyn is beside me to wipe the corners of your mouth." Nalani scooped up her purse and left.

CHAPTER 51

Levi told himself he was running out of excuses. Dori's questions had become unrelenting about Karyn's whereabouts. Sooner or later, he could no longer avoid taking Dori back to the bookstore. First, he had to bring closure between him and Karyn. He loved her . . . but he wanted to hate her. What kind of Christian admitted that?

Above all things have intense and unfailing love for one another, for love covers a multitude of sins. God whispered 1 Peter 4:8.

He swallowed as he glanced at his desk calendar. Valentine's Day was a week away. If things had been different, Levi would have proposed. He didn't need years for a long courtship. Practicing Christians could only hold out so long for intimacy, and shacking up wasn't God's or his style. But that didn't matter now. The grief session that was meant to heal wounded souls had forced the truth out of Karyn.

What made Karyn do it? How could she do it? Would she have ever told him she did it? The questions had nagged him since day one, but pride kept him from asking her. He had refused to take the first step until now. They either had to have closure or reconciliation.

Even Tia verified she and Karyn had lunch, but divulged no further details. The look on her face warned him not to ask. Seth had seconded the motion.

Closing his eyes, Levi silently prayed and asked God how to proceed. He waited, but God's voice was still. Levi had always treated Karyn with adoration. He admitted that regardless of the strife between them, he should not withhold his kindness. He still loved her.

Picking up the phone, Levi punched in the number to the florist in the mall where Karyn worked. He ordered a dozen roses and asked that a note be attached: *Can we talk? Dinner tonight. Please call me. Levi.* He requested an immediate delivery and waited.

A few minutes later, Levi second guessed himself. *Have I lost my mind?* He should be disgusted at the sight of Karyn. Instead, he longed to see her.

The call he expected didn't come as soon as he had hoped. When an hour passed, he followed up with the florist and was told the delivery had been made. Levi continued to wait. Then, ten minutes before four o'clock, his phone rang.

Levi checked his ID. He didn't recognize the number, but the name. Karyn was no longer using the phone he had purchased for her.

He didn't bother with a greeting. He wanted to hear her voice despite his conflicting feelings. "Karyn." He didn't realize his heart was pumping harder.

There were a few moments of awkward silence before she responded. "Thank you for the flowers, but I can't go out to dinner with you. My center has a new residential facility director. She came from a halfway house environment where there isn't much flexibility. As of a few weeks ago, New Beginnings' rules will be strictly enforced with no exceptions."

Words like *halfway house, enforced, residential* had never been part of their conversations before. Levi didn't even realize that her apartment building was a women's residential center. He was dumbfounded; he didn't know how to respond. Should he converse normally or ask questions about her lifestyle? He wasn't going to get any answers by talking to himself.

"I'm sorry, Karyn, for the way I responded," he whispered. He didn't know what else to say.

"I'm sorry, too, Levi. I guess we were just passing through each other's lives. Just know that God can wash away any sins, including mine." She took a deep breath and exhaled. "I know you haven't brought Dori to the bookstore because of me. Don't stifle her reading abilities. She's very smart and will make you proud one day. If you can hold off for a few weeks, I'll no longer work here, so you can bring her back then. I wish and pray nothing but God's blessings for you."

"What do you mean?"

"I have a new job. I start in two weeks."

Why did relief settle over him? A new job was good. Karyn deserved better. At least she wasn't moving to another city, or God forbid, losing her freedom again. Then again, she wouldn't give a notice. The authorities would just take her away. "Karyn, I—"

"Listen, I've got to go. Take care, and give Dori a kiss and hug. You don't have to tell her it's from me."

She disconnected, and Levi felt a prick. The bleeding had begun again. This time he might bleed to death, because there was no way he would subject himself to falling in love again.

A week later, Karyn had dressed for an evening out for Valentine's Day. This time last year, she didn't think about being anyone's valentine. Freedom, food, clothing, and shelter were her immediate needs.

***

Then a few months ago, Karyn would have been looking forward to a night out with her handsome prince—Levi Tolliver. *But life goes on,* Karyn reminded herself. God had promised her salvation, not necessarily happiness while on this earth.

She returned her mind to the task at hand, getting ready. She put her hair in a ponytail, smoothed her red sweater dress, and inserted the tiny earrings through her lobes.

Her new cell phone her sister bought her rang as she slipped into her boots. The church van would pick up her and any other ladies who wanted to attend Crowns for Christ's special event. As part of their community outreach, the church treated any woman to dinner who would otherwise be alone on special days, especially Valentine's Day.

The women would be showered with roses, a teddy bear, bath toiletries, and chocolate. A few times, men had tried to attend, but Pastor Scaife nipped that in the bud. "Brothers, unless you're here to serve our lovely sisters, then you can't come in," he had insisted.

Karyn's pastor and First Lady Doctor Winnie Jordan Scaife sacrificed their romantic evening together to serve others. Karyn would never think about going to another church. They fed her soul and were the best example of Christ's love for the outcasts.

Recognizing Nalani's number, Karyn mustered a smile. It was bittersweet to know a Tolliver was flying to Chicago on this day to have dinner with a Wallace. It was just the wrong couple. Maybe God's plan was for Minister Rossi and Nalani, and she and Levi were just tools used for someone else's happiness. Karyn strained her brain power, wondering when the two had become that close.

Nalani argued it was a business meeting. Karyn didn't believe it. Maybe she would see a fairy tale after all.

"So, has Rossi made it there yet?"

"He's in the limo now and on his way."

"Happy Valentine's Day," Karyn said softly and disconnected the call.

CHAPTER 52

Rossi didn't practice lying to people, himself, or God. He was in Chicago to see Nalani for various reasons. As far as he was concerned, Levi would not dominate their conversation.

What was a forty-five-minute flight on a Wednesday afternoon to see a beautiful woman on Valentine's Day? Rossi enjoyed Nalani's sense of humor and energy. Too bad they were on opposing teams—Tolliver vs. Wallace.

Rossi knocked on her door with a dozen red roses in hand and a miniature box of chocolate-covered strawberries. When Nalani opened the door, his mouth dropped. Seconds later, he didn't give himself time to study the garment's details and the gold choker that graced her neck. Her earrings reminded him of teardrops, and her smile was contagious. Rossi suddenly wondered how the beauty of God's angels would compare to her. "Good evening." He forced the words out of his throat.

"Minister Rossi." Her eyes sparkled as she gave him a sweeping inspection.

"Nalani." He nodded. "Although God's ministry is always with me, the title is in church. Please call me Rossi. I'm the fourth one in my family."

"As you wish. Let me get my cape."

As the driver stood outside the limo waiting for the couple, Rossi remained outside Nalani's door, waiting. Temptation was on the other side, and Rossi wasn't going to cross over.

In the limo during the ride to Sixteen, one of Chicago's most elegant restaurants located in the Trump International Hotel & Tower, they exchanged small talk. Both steered away from mentioning their relatives.

Once they were seated at the restaurant, Rossi looked out the window and admired the exceptional view of Lake Michigan. They decided on the Valentine's Day buffet and chatted throughout their meal. His dinner companion was charming, beautiful . . . and scheming. Rossi had just swallowed his last bite of cheesecake, which Nalani insisted they share, and picked up their conversation about Jet's inference with Crowning Glory.

"So what exactly are you saying?" he asked her.

"Do you know who I am, Rossi?"

"You're Nalani Wallace—or do you have a secret identity I should know about?"

She snickered and tapped a shimmery red polished fingernail on their white tablecloth. "No, and I don't have a criminal record, if that idea is floating in your head. Karyn and I" —she patted her chest—"come from a long generation of political families, which means, despite my father's death, I still have some connections with senators who enjoy the role as my godfathers."

"Again, what are you saying, Nalani? I like things plain and simple. I don't care for reading between the lines."

"Fine. I don't care about Levi backing out of a verbal offer to my sister in your new development. I also don't care about Jet's rejection of a good proposal because she's evil. Any bank would accept Karyn's plan; but I happen to want Jet to make the sole decision to reverse her decision. It could mean her job or the bank's reputation."

Rossi couldn't believe it. Nalani was calling Jet evil, which was true sometimes, but the pretty creature sitting across from him seemed as if she could pull evil tricks out of her bag too.

"Ah. The cat's got the minister's tongue. It's simple, Ross," she said, having the nerve to shorten his name. "Either you talk—or pray, if you want—but it's in Jet's best interest to reverse her decision on the Crowning Glory proposal, or I'll ask one of my godfathers to launch an investigation into the bank's dealings with minorities. You know, discrimination is bad for business. Whether the allegations would prove to be true or not, the publicity will be priceless."

"More mango Sprite lemonade?" their waiter asked, approaching the table. When they didn't respond, he walked away.

Rossi leaned forward and Nalani met him halfway. "This battle is not yours or mine; it's the Lord's." He summoned the waiter back with his hand. "Check, please."

"You'll never guess who called me," Karyn said to Nalani as they walked out of the mall after leaving the bookstore. It was days after Valentine's Day. Nalani tried to make it a habit of coming to Fairview Heights every weekend, especially since Buttercup had moved and Karyn was no longer dating Levi. Nalani had said it was her way of reminding Karyn that she was never alone.

"President Obama," Nalani guessed.

"Yeah, right." Karyn laughed as they sprinted across the parking lot until Nalani sped ahead in an impromptu race.

Seconds later, Karyn bumped the side of the car as if they were playing a game of tag. "How did you beat me in those stilettos? So, guess." She panted as Nalani deactivated the car alarm.

"Just tell me," she said as they got in the car.

"Levi Tolliver."

Nalani grinned as she turned the ignition. "Hmmm."

"We spoke for a few minutes. He invited me to dinner. Thank God I couldn't go because it was last minute. I can't bear to see the look of disgust again that flashed on his face last month."

Karyn sighed as she glanced out the window. "I prepared myself for society's rejection. That's a piece of cake compared to Levi's."

The true blessing in her life was restoring her relationship with her sister. Once her parole was finished, she could freely fellowship with Halo and Buttercup without waiting for Sunday service.

"At least I can look forward to starting a new job." Karyn played with her gloved fingers, something Levi would not allow if she was in his car. She took a deep breath to shake the memories.

"Are the three of you giving up on Crowning Glory?"

Karyn shook her head. "We just agreed to hold off before we submit it somewhere else."

"I don't know. Maybe things may turn around with First Freedom Bank."

Grunting, Karyn twisted her lips as she turned down the interior heat. "I doubt it with Jet at the helm of business loans." Karyn thought of Jet as being one of God's lost sheep. She had to keep praying for Jet, whether Levi was in her life or not.

"Stranger things have happened. Now, back to Levi. He's had time to think about what he's giving up. The ball is in Levi's court. Will he run or pass?"

"Those options don't seem to be a win-win situation for me."

"Good point. I'll think of another analogy."

CHAPTER 53

As the days skipped on, Levi's mind had a will of its own. When he tried to focus on family or work, his traitorous thoughts returned to memories of Karyn. To make his life more miserable, Tia purposely wasn't speaking to him, Dori's behavior had become increasingly rebellious, and Rossi would just shake his head when he looked at him. His parents hadn't said much, leaving him to speculate what they were thinking.

Questions were swirling in his head like an annoying mosquito. So far, nothing held Levi's attention—not assisting Dori with some ridiculous preschool homework that Dori already knew the answers, or LeBron James's antics on the basketball court against the Indiana Pacers.

"What's the matter, Daddy? Are you sad because you miss Miss Karyn too?"

It was more complicated than a yes or no. At the moment, it wasn't good that Dori was a perceptive child. "I'll be happy when we finish your homework. This is hard, but you're really smart, because these are all right."

She beamed, looking so much like Diane. Levi's heart pricked again. Life was a gamble, and he had yet to have a winning hand. He had to wonder if God had taken His eye off what was going on in his life. Did He not have mercy?

Dori was asleep when Levi started to pace the floor in his bedroom. He kept checking his watch. It was almost ten o'clock, and Cinderella had to be in. At 10:05, he closed his door. He counted to three to gather his courage. He had to talk to her. "Okay, Tolliver. Just do it."

She answered before the call transferred to voice mail. He opened his mouth, but nothing came out.

"Hello, Levi." Her greeting was soft and tentative.

"Karyn." He used his professional voice, as if he were speaking with a client. Forget it. It was too much work to act detached. *Silence.*

"I expected you to disconnect this phone. That was nice of you that you didn't."

Well, if that didn't make him feel like a jerk. "Thank you for answering it. It was a gift for you. It used to be our lifeline," Eventually, once he decided their ties were permanently severed, he would have turned off the phone service.

"For your selfish reasons, remember?"

He smiled and chuckled with her.

"After we broke up, Nalani bought me a BlackBerry." She paused. "I was afraid to use this phone, knowing your disconnection was more about us than the phone."

She was right. "Listen, Karyn. I know we parted on bad terms . . ." He waited for her to agree, but she left him hanging.

"Anyway, I'm sorry to use this phone again, but I lost my battery charger for the BlackBerry, and I plan to buy another one when I get paid."

Still frugal despite the money her father left behind. He doubted Karyn would ever live beyond her means in her lifetime. "I have so many questions."

"And I have answers," she said softly, "if only you had asked."

"You never gave me the opportunity," Levi scolded, but at least he was getting somewhere. He relaxed his tense body and crossed his bare feet at the ankles when he lay on top of the bed. "I can't imagine you in prison, but I can't imagine you doing what you said you did."

She sighed. "Prison is like living in outer space. There are no surprises, sunrises, or sunsets. The correctional officers are the alarm clocks. Up at seven, beds made at eight. When we bless our food and say, 'For the nourishment of our bodies,' it's not an understatement. The food is tasteless and sometimes room temperature before it hits your mouth."

If he were confined, he would probably die of starvation. For Levi, a warm meal was a phone call away for delivery, or less than thirty minutes to his parents' house. "How did you fill your days?"

"Work or school. Federal law requires all inmates without a high school education to study for their GED. Otherwise you work."

"Hard labor?"

"Not really," Karyn said with a sigh. "I had to cook, clean, whatever they wanted me to do under the watchful eyes of armed correctional officers. Sometimes they were the biggest threat if you made them mad. We earned anywhere between thirty and ninety cents a day."

"What?" Levi's mouth dropped in shock. "Dori's allowance is more than that. What could you do with that pittance?"

"If I stretched it, I'd buy necessities like deodorant, socks, toothpaste, and other personal items."

Levi closed his eyes. He couldn't visualize Karyn in a lineup or posing for a mug shot. "Were you scared, baby?" Levi released the compassion.

"At first, yes. Inmates, whether male or female, usually try and sometimes they succeed in retaliating for the death of a child. Believe it or not, crimes have a tier system in prison. Violence against children isn't cool among criminals. I side with them, although I was a perpetrator of such an act.

"Some of the older inmates took pity on me and adopted me as part of their family. That gave me some protection. Because of my size, I was their baby girl. I had a mother, father, aunties, and sisters."

He didn't want to think about her participating in homosexual activities. "Were you . . . you know . . . ever raped?"

"Oh, no. Those women were like extended families. They became my play momma, play aunties. You know how everybody in the neighborhood was your cousin growing up? That cluster combated the isolation from the outside. Even God said man should not be alone. Prison is lonely.

"That didn't mean there weren't some scary people in there. One lady was a cannibal. Thank God I didn't share a cell with her."

Levi swallowed. *I guess it wasn't a picnic for her and others.* Levi had lived emotionally secluded for four years until Karyn filled his life.

"One unspoken rule was to never say you're innocent—which I wasn't—because everybody in there insists they were framed. The golden rule is to keep your mouth shut."

She explained the ten o'clock curfew at the women's transitional housing. "It doesn't take much to violate parole. My whereabouts have to be accounted for every minute. Changes of plans are frowned upon. I could have lost privileges or been sent back to jail every time I asked to go somewhere with you."

"The phone calls in the bathroom," he stated.

"Yes, but I had fallen in love with you, and I wanted to be with you. I'm sorry. Hold on," she said, covering up the phone. "Jay, I'm in here."

Levi heard a muffled voice in the background.

"Who was that?"

"My new roommate, Jay. She did petty theft until she mastered picking locks, then she progressed to burglaries, home invasions, and other stuff. One house rule is to stay out of the other people's bedrooms and not borrow anything. This little freedom is going to her head. Some ex-offenders can't handle making choices, because they've been institutionalized for so long. Plus, she's missed a few curfews."

"Maybe she should. Evidently, she's back to her old tricks. Has she taken anything of yours—the gifts I bought you?"

"Nothing important. My shampoo or some fingernail polish Buttercup left me. Except for the maximum number of outfits allowed, Nalani took everything back to Chicago with her. When she comes to visit on the weekends, I tell her what to bring. The music box I take with me everywhere."

The music box. He remembered purchasing it. The globe with a woman dressed in African garb, balancing a container on her head. When twisted, the figure began a circular dance to "A Ribbon in the Sky." She touched his soft spot for the second time during the conversation. Now, it was time for him to get real answers.

"Levi, I wouldn't wish prison on anybody."

He grunted. "Well, I do. Anytime a person brutally murders or takes a life, they'll never change."

"I've changed," she argued, raising her voice. "Some of us make mistakes—bad ones. People think because we're confined, we get state- or government-financed room and board, a free education—"

"I'm sorry, Karyn, but some folks should never get out."

"Let me break it down for you," she snapped. "Prison is not a country club. Being released is not a hotel guest checking out as if nothing ever happened. My sin did happen, and for the rest of my life, authorities and society will monitor me until the day I die because of it. Ex-offenders have to prove we're worthy of forgiveness with man. Praise God, He's more gracious."

They had never had an argument when they dated for a few months, but that was before he knew her history. It would always be a sore spot between them.

Levi leaped up in bed. No, she was not putting him in his place. "I think victims of crime have a right to ask for forgiveness, restitution, and anything else. To hear you practically defend criminals makes me regret—"

"What, Levi?"

"You know what, Karyn? You're like a beautiful vampire who sucked all the life out of me and left me to die. You're killing me with this righteous-victim attitude. Did you, or do you have any remorse for what you did?" Levi couldn't believe he had stooped that low to ask that. She didn't have to respond for him to know his words had hurt her.

"Yes, yes, I did, but I'm not going to keep apologizing for something God already forgave me for. I'm a new creature, and people can accept that or reject it. Either way I'm free."

"I'll be in touch," Levi said, gritting his teeth as he pushed the OFF button on his phone. Karyn Wallace was going to make him run to Walgreens and buy a high blood pressure monitor.

"I'm fine, Jay," Karyn explained to her new roommate after Jay had picked Karyn's locked bedroom door to check on her. Once Jay backed out, Karyn rolled over on her stomach then cried herself to sleep, repeating, *He who the Son set free is free indeed.* The devil was a lie. She had been set free.

March first was Karyn's last shift at Bookshelves Unlimited. Throughout the day, she had taken deep breaths to inhale the aroma of new books, sneezed from the dust that laced shelves of old books, and took liberty with the free refills of the café's lattes.

She teared at the upcoming new phase in her life. The job had given her a second chance. Crowns for Christ had given her the first then helped her stay focused. Levi was her third chance—to show she could love again. Karyn's ultimate goal was to be a productive citizen, as well as a productive saint of God.

By late afternoon, Karyn grew concerned as she kept watching the door for her last glimpse at her favorite customer—Mrs. Harris. As the crowd thinned, Karyn took another patrol of the aisles, admiring the kids' section where she had entertained many children with story time and met the man who she didn't deserve, but then neither did he deserve her.

The staff had given her a going away party. Patrice, who had been out sick, feigning she hurt her back while lifting a heavy crate of books—a task she left for others—sent a card that said she would miss her. Karyn had shaken her head. Patrice often never said what she meant, so even in leaving, Karyn wondered at the truth behind Patrice's remarks.

Karyn was about to clock out for lunch when Mrs. Harris teetered through the door with the aid of her cane. She wore a bright smile and a church hat, of course. The elderly customer had made her day. She was about to go and assist her when she felt her skin tingle.

"Do you want to have children again?"

The voice was unmistakable. Karyn's heart crashed against her chest, her breathing missed a beat, and she trembled with unthreatened fear as she pivoted on her heel. She came face to face with Levi: the glasses, the mustache, the dimples, and the tortured expression. She inhaled his fresh scent. Since that disastrous day, Karyn had tried to be strong and not harp on things she couldn't have, but looking into his brown eyes made her wish for them anyway.

"Of course I want children," she whispered. *But only with you,* she thought.

"Good. Go out with me, Karyn," he said without breaking eye contact. "Tonight," he demanded in an eerie calm.

Karyn squinted. "If I were to go, will we be on opposing teams?"

"No. I have other plans."

What plans? Karyn searched his face for clues, but couldn't read between the lines. She missed him so much. The center's director already had every woman's schedule set in stone for a week. "You'll have to change them."

CHAPTER 54

"Mom, Dad, how do you feel about Karyn re-entering my life, knowing that she committed a horrible act?" Levi asked his parents the same night he would have taken Karyn out to dinner. He needed their validation that he wasn't making a bad decision.

"Son, I have to tell you, the news disturbed me. I can't imagine that sweet young lady doing something like that, but it appears that she has reconciled with her past." Victor glanced away, squinted at nothing, and then met Levi's stare. "The question is, can you handle her past?"

"I don't know." He groaned, rubbing his head. Levi had been trying to find the answer to that since he picked up the phone and ordered flowers. He honestly didn't know what he was setting in motion.

Levi waited for the response from his mother, who had a soft spot in her heart for Tia and Karyn.

"I guess we never know what a person is capable of doing. In the back of my mind, I wonder what would keep her from doing it again. What caused her . . ." Sharon frowned. "What were the circumstances? I think even if I had the answers, it wouldn't answer my unvoiced questions."

Levi had those same fears. If he could salvage their relationship, it would no longer be about him, but Karyn and God would be their center. "I love her. If I can convince her to give us a second chance, would you accept her?"

"If you love her, we will also. Pray and see how God directs you," his father said.

"Do you think it's a slap in Diane's face?" Levi had to ask, although he didn't know if their answers would change how he felt about Karyn.

Sharon smiled. "No I think Diane would be rejoicing that Karyn came to Christ."

"Thanks." Doing what mothers do best, it was as if her words had kissed his wound to make him feel better.

Levi waited impatiently for the next week to end so he could take Karyn out to dinner and celebrate her new gig as an accounting clerk at Emerson, Watts & Turner in Belleville. A staffing agency that had a track record of placing ex-offenders in temp-to-hire positions had recommended Karyn. He didn't realize how much grace Karyn's counselor had given her when they dated.

His heart bled for the things that went wrong in Karyn's life and the consequences she endured. He openly cried as Karyn retold the story of how she stole her son's life.

"God had chastened and comforted me, but He also reassured me that as imperfect as I am, if I dare follow His instructions, I'll be made perfect." Karyn paused and whispered, "I believe Matthew 5:48."

"I admire that you know your scriptures." He respected that she didn't try to use them to justify what she did.

"His Word was the only thing that kept me from self-destructing. Many times I thought that killing myself was the only way out."

From that confession, every conversation with her became enlightening. He and Karyn spoke every night, using the cell phone he had originally purchased for her. They came to an understanding that Levi may not ever fully understand Karyn's actions, but she made a believer out of him that people did change, and some prisoners could be rehabilitated.

Friday evening at seven, Levi stood on the porch outside New Beginnings and rang the bell. Although Karyn explained to him that no men were allowed inside, it didn't keep him from picking up his date at the door.

"You scared me," Karyn said, startled when she opened the door. "I thought you would be waiting in the car."

"I've waited long enough to see you. Here." He handed her a rose. "Will you be my Valentine?" he asked, although the holiday had passed weeks ago.

Blinking back tears, Karyn nodded. She reached up to hug him, and he crushed her to him. "I've missed you. I've missed you."

"Me too. The phone calls don't do it for me." After engulfing her in a bear hug, he guided her down the stairs to his car. "Well, we better hurry, Cinderella, since I know what time your chariot will turn into a pumpkin."

Twenty minutes later, they were seated at Andria's Steakhouse, because Levi wanted to start their first date over.

"So, how does it feel to know everything about a person on the first date?" he asked as they ignored their menus.

"I'm relieved."

"Good, so let's skip the preliminaries. We're back together again—you as my baby and me as your man. Agreed?"

"Yes." Her answer was barely audible, but his heart heard it.

When their server came, Levi sent her away.

Levi reached across the table and took Karyn's hands. Turning them over, he examined them. "You know, I've never thought your hands were soft enough." He let them go as he retrieved a travel-size tube of Victoria's Secret Love Spell lotion, highly recommended by Tia, from inside his jacket.

Squeezing a generous amount into his palm, Levi rubbed his hands together then recaptured her hands, linking his fingers through hers. Meticulously, he manipulated the lotion until he was satisfied that her every pore was nourished and moist to his liking.

Karyn's eyes sparkled as they did on their first date. Makeup emphasized Karyn's brown eyes. He didn't know cosmetics could give his woman an Asian allure from eyeliners. Her lips were outlined, glossy, and tempting. Her hair wasn't dolled up in a mass of curls as it was the first night, but gone was the single braid that enticed Dori. It swept straight down her back. Karyn was the epitome of a strong black woman. She had fallen from man's grace, but the grace of God had pulled her up.

"You know, when we get married and you become pregnant . . ." Levi tightened his grip on her hands to keep her from retreating. "I'm going to be scared for you. I'm being honest, Karyn, because I want complete honesty and openness from you. I promise you I will never, ever abandon you again."

She blinked several times, displaying a bewildered expression. Leaning closer, he smiled. "Meet me half-way."

She did. "Are you proposing to me?" she whispered with a touch of awe as she came close enough to kiss him.

"I am." Levi's nostrils flared in a challenge. He silently dared her to say anything but the answer he wanted to hear.

She looked unimpressed as she grunted. "Can't you do better than that?"

Levi smirked. "You tease. As a matter of fact, I can." Reaching inside his breast pocket, he pulled out a velvet ring box. Getting up, he came around the table and bent before her. Staring into her brown eyes made him forget the lines he had rehearsed.

Clearing his throat, he gathered her left hand. He kissed the inside of her palm before turning it over. "Karyn Wallace, you are the strength to my weakness. You are the beginning of my restored blessing. Marry me, so we can weather the storms together. I love you with a mended heart, and if you say no, I'll have a very disappointed daughter at home."

Tears fell as Karyn nodded. "Levi," she whispered. "I love you and Dori so much. Yes."

Clapping and whistles filled the room.

Karyn jumped and looked around at familiar faces: his family, her van riders, Nalani, and Rossi were close by. "You set me up?"

"Yep, and I'm not ashamed." Laughing, he opened the box, lifted the ring, and slipped it on the correct finger. He sighed with relief.

Buttercup paraded to their table as Levi stood, but Dori raced by her to get to Karyn with her arms stretched out.

"Miss Karyn, Miss Karyn." Dori squeezed her neck tightly.

Karyn held on as a tear slid down her cheek. There was no doubt in Levi's mind that his family was complete.

Cheers erupted as Levi joined the pair in a group hug. His competition was with Dori to smother Karyn with kisses.

"Of course, I'll do your hair for the wedding," Buttercup said, fluffing Karyn's hair as if Karyn had asked.

The restaurant owner moved the group to a small banquet room to continue their celebration. More Tollivers were there to greet Karyn.

Levi looked to his father, who held back from the others. When he nodded, Levi smiled. Sharon nudged Karyn to the side for a private moment. Levi couldn't read lips, so he discreetly walked closer.

"Karyn, I've been a very good mother. I want to be a great mother-in-law to you. Be patient with me. Most of all, don't ever think that I don't love you. Your past is hard for me to digest, but I'm asking God to help me not judge."

"Mrs. Tolliver, I don't know what all Levi has shared with you about my past, but I live every moment berating myself for what I did. During those times, God steps in, reminding me that my sins are forgiven."

"Mine too," Sharon said, hugging Karyn.

Levi took that as his cue to head to the buffet table. Their server had been in on the proposal and helped in its preparation.

When Levi turned around after stacking two plates with sandwiches, vegetables, and other finger foods, he paused. Tia was engaged in a lively conversation with Karyn, laughing and hugging. Dori stood guard at Karyn's side. Levi rested his shoulder against a nearby wall and watched, placing their plates on a nearby table. He loved Karyn and wanted her happy. From the looks of his family, it appeared they were going to assist in making that happen.

Nalani lifted a glass and tapped it with a spoon.

"Attention, everyone." She smiled. "I have an announcement." The noise hushed as they waited. "To add to this joyous occasion and to follow in my big sister's footsteps, I've"—she paused and scrunched her nose at Rossi, who had his arms folded—"I've decided to get baptized. I want to experience the confidence she has in God's forgiveness."

Rossi was the first to clap. Others joined in. Another round of congratulations floated around the room. Karyn hurried to Nalani and crushed her in a hug. Riders from the church van encircled them. Some lifted their hands in the air in praise.

Levi strolled to Rossi. "I'm assuming you were instrumental in Nalani's decision?"

Rossi slipped his hands into his pants pockets. "I hope so."

In step, the cousins walked toward the sisters.

"I guess I'm attending Crowns for Christ again this Sunday to be a witness." Rossi congratulated Nalani.

"Oh." Nalani frowned. "Make it next Sunday. I've got some pending business."

CHAPTER 55

News traveled fast. Jet couldn't believe Levi had actually asked Karyn to marry him. "What was he thinking?" she hissed as she sat behind her desk on Monday. So far this morning, nothing was going her way. She had received a surprising e-mail from her boss's boss. He issued immediate changes in the review process for new business loans, beginning with the one she recently rejected and had celebrated—her decision to turn down Crowning Glory.

"It's important we are viewed positively . . . Our image is our business . . ."

First Freedom Bank CEO Richard Harvey had practically scolded her in his memo. Jet rolled her eyes as she scanned the rest of the e-mail.

A knock at the door interrupted her disgruntled moment. Her administrative assistant entered. "Miss Hutchens, a Miss Wallace is here to see you. She says you spoke to her a few weeks ago.

Great. Karyn's here to rub it in my face, Jet silently fumed. "I'm really busy. Ask her to make an appointment." She dismissed the woman and returned to her work on her desk that she wasn't doing. Less than a minute later, Nalani strolled in without knocking.

"What are you doing here?"

Nalani shrugged. "Glad you asked. I came to feed you as you eat your own words, remember? Sorry Karyn isn't here to wipe your mouth."

With her nostrils flared, Jet fired darts at Nalani.

"No, seriously though . . ." Nalani helped herself to a nearby seat and crossed one leg over her knee and began to swing it. "I came to say thanks in advance for approving my sister's loan."

Jet responded with profanities. "It appears, according to my e-mail, I have no choice. You sicced Senator Coleman on me. Talk about corruption in high places. All of a sudden, Senator Coleman became very interested in Crowning Glory's concept. The senator seems to be brainwashed into believing this could be a model program for other communities. Who would have thought he and Mr. Harvey played golf?"

"Really?" Nalani looked surprised.

Jet snarled at Nalani's mockery. "Maybe not now, but I will have the last word. Now get out!"

Glancing at her watch, Nalani stood. "You're right. I really do have to get going. Karyn needs help planning her wedding." She headed for the door then whirled around. "Ta-ta." She waved.

Jet wanted to strangle Nalani. Jet had an unblemished performance record at the bank. Thanks to Karyn's cronies, it could be blemished because of her judgment call.

Nobody was worth Jet losing her job. Karyn would run up against other brick walls. She counted on it.

A week or so later, Karyn called Jet, wanting to meet for lunch at McDonald's. Jet laughed. McDonald's? She didn't eat at McDonald's unless she had Dori. Jet was about to decline when she decided, why not? Maybe she could have the last word after all. Jet accepted.

"I can't believe Levi is replacing my sister with a criminal," Jet said over a grilled chicken sandwich days later. She didn't try to lower her voice, not caring if nearby patrons heard their conversation.

Karyn slowly laid down her fork and wiped her mouth. "Jet, if you've never made a mistake or committed a sin against God, raise your hand," Karyn challenged.

Jet did just that. She lifted her arm high in the air with an attitude to match. "You committed the unthinkable, deplorable act. It definitely was a shortcut to hell. Now you're taking the little family I have left. I don't care how much you repent. Do you actually think God feels your life is worth living?"

"*With loving kindness have I drawn thee,*" Karyn mumbled. "Love covers a multitude of faults," she added.

Karyn took a deep breath and bowed her head. She felt an overwhelming yearning to get through to Levi's sister-in-law. "Jet, God died on the cross to save me. When Cain became the world's first murderer and killed his brother, God still loved Cain and put a mark on his forehead so no harm would come to him. Today that mark is Jesus' blood. I'm covered and protected. Sin is sin, big or small. They all will take you to hell. The Bible says he who has committed no sin lies to himself."

"If I wanted preaching, I'd speed-dial Rossi," Jet spat then quieted as if the fight had seeped out of her. Her voice was above a whisper. "We'll never be friends." Grabbing her jacket, Jet stood and stormed away, leaving Karyn to throw away her trash.

CHAPTER 56

The following Sunday, Karyn witnessed her sister's surrender to God as Pastor Scaife made the altar call.

"I don't fully understand what changes God will make in my life, but I'm curious enough to find out. I'm sure you'll help me," Nalani whispered to Karyn as she scooted out of the pew then boldly walked down the aisle to the waiting ministers posted in front of the pulpit.

Less than fifteen minutes later, Nalani and a few other candidates were dressed in white—from a swimming cap on the head to thick socks on their feet. They lined up for their descent into the pool for baptism and the conversion of their souls.

A minister, also dressed in white, lifted his hands. "My dearly beloved sisters, with the confidence we have in the blessed Word of God, concerning His death, burial, and grand resurrection, I indeed baptize you in the name of Jesus, which the Bible says there is no other name to be saved, for the remission of your sins. Amen."

As Nalani and the others were submerged, Karyn and her van riders cheered the loudest and rejoiced the hardest. Minister Rossi, who was also in attendance, lifted his hands in praise.

Throughout the day, Nalani would briefly praise God, speaking in unknown tongues. Once she closed her eyes, Karyn could tell she was savoring the experience.

Before the night was over, Nalani made a confession. "I baited Jet earlier this week. Although I knew I had made up my mind to get baptized, I was determined to rub in her face the decision she was forced to make on giving you that loan for your business. I realize I shouldn't have done that. Do you think God forgave me the minute I repented of my sins before I was baptized?"

"Yep." Karyn paused. "But you know, to fulfill your role as a Christian, you're going to have to ask for her forgiveness."

Nalani was silent as she frowned, twisted her lips, then nodded. "I ain't that saved yet."

Karyn chuckled, but Nalani wasn't laughing. Thank God Nalani would be surrounded by people, including her, who would set an example of Christ-like living.

After completing her parole a few months later, Karyn moved out of New Beginnings and temporarily in with Tia, since she was beating Tia to the alter. When Karyn shut the front door of the center, she closed a badly written chapter of her life.

The sun warmed her face, birds danced from one tree branch to another, and Levi was a short distance away, leaning against his parked car, awaiting her like he was a limo driver. When he saw her walk out the door, he sprinted up the steps and jogged down the short pathway to meet her.

"Ready?" There was no condemnation in his voice, just pure love.

"Yes." Karyn teared as Levi gathered her few belongings, then escorted her to his getaway car, as Buttercup would have described it.

"It's over, Karyn. Your past is sealed and your life goes on." He opened her car door then put her things in the trunk before he got inside. He smiled at her before he drove off.

Karyn glanced out her window at the passing scenery. Levi grabbed her hand and squeezed. "How is it possible to have so many blessings and be scared?" she whispered in a trance.

"Sweetheart, I know blessings can sometimes seem overwhelming, but the Tollivers are here, Nalani is here, and your friends at church are here to help you in any way."

"I just don't want to make any mistakes this time around," Karyn confessed.

"Now unto Him that is able to keep you from falling . . ." and to present you faultless before the presence of His glory with exceeding joy"

Karyn recited the remainder of Jude 1:24 with Levi. She smiled. "You know, I think I can make it."

"Good." He lifted her hand to his lips and brushed a kiss on it. "Now I really need you to refocus, because in thirty days you'll become the wife to Levi Tolliver and the mother to Dori." He smirked. "Can you handle that?"

Happiness filled her heart. "Is that a challenge, Mr. Tolliver?"

"Only for me, because I dare to make you happy. Now, where would you like to go and have breakfast?"

She no longer had to stick to a pre-planned schedule or ask for permission when things changed at the last minute. Squeezing her eyes shut, Karyn yelled, "Anywhere! I'm free!"

CHAPTER 57

Karyn was minutes away from becoming the first Tolliver daughter-in-law.

"Welcome to the family. We Tolliver wives will be a force to be reckoned with," Tia stated, although her wedding to Seth was six months away. Sharon Tolliver had warmly congratulated Karyn moments earlier, before an usher summoned the mother of the groom.

Tia exchanged air kisses with Karyn before she left the dressing room normally reserved for choir members to take her place in the processional as her bridesmaid

Karyn faced the mirror again and blinked at the image. Her headpiece was a crown adorned with pearls with a short veil. Her wedding gown, a soft champagne color with layers of lace and organza, was a perfect fit from a secondhand store. Instead of white pumps, Buttercup insisted Karyn wear fuchsia stilettos, which were the latest craze.

"Trust me on the shoes. This is your fairy tale, Cinderella," Buttercup said, "because here is your happy ending." She gave Karyn a loose hug. "Now, remember: Hold your head high and step with a purpose to give your curls a slight bounce." As Karyn's matron of honor, Buttercup hurried from the room to get in position.

Karyn shook her head to test the curls. Briefly, she wondered how Halo was faring as one of Levi's groomsmen. He never smiled around Levi. Halo had said it was to keep Levi on his feet, knowing Halo was watching his every move.

Nalani sniffed as she approached her sister. "This is it. I love you."

"I know." Karyn swallowed to rein in threatening tears. "You will never know how much I love you for being in my corner these past years. There is no one like you, and I'm so blessed to be your sister."

"The honor is all mine. See, I got baptized because of your example, and I witnessed the evidence of the Holy Ghost experience. Oh," Nalani said, flustered, "I better go before Levi comes looking for you." She kissed Karyn, adjusted the straps on her tea-length bridesmaid dress, and glided out of the room.

Alone, Karyn took a deep breath to relax. Suddenly, she felt a pat on her dress. She had forgotten about Dori. She knelt and adjusted the fresh flowers delicately woven into Dori's single braid. "Yes, sweetie?'

"Do I have to leave? I don't wanna."

Karyn frowned. "Why? What's the matter?" Karyn clasped Dori's hands and chuckled at the white glitter fingernail polish Buttercup had applied that morning.

"I want to walk with you, because Daddy said he wouldn't be able to take his eyes off you. That way Daddy can look at both of us."

God, I don't deserve the two blessings you are about to give me, but I thank you. Karyn swallowed so she wouldn't tear up. "Okay," she whispered.

"When the minister tells Daddy he can kiss you, can I kiss you too, Miss Karyn?"

"Absolutely, but you can't call me Miss Karyn after we kiss."

"Oh." Dori covered her mouth, worried. "Can I call you Miss Mommy?"

She tweaked her nose and smiled. "You don't have to call me Miss anything."

Dori jumped up and down in glee, spilling flower petals and a white envelope from her basket.

"Dori, be still. You want to look pretty for Daddy, remember?" Karyn reached down and picked up the envelope. Her name was scribbled across it. "Who gave you this?"

"Oops. Daddy told me to give it to you, but I forgot."

As Karyn opened the envelope and slipped out the card, Deacon Deacon, not only the church's van driver, but an aspiring organist, struck the first keys of "Wedding March" off key; then Deacon Deacon sailed through it.

> *Karyn, I promise you my undying love, my unwavering faith in you, and my fierce protection of your heart. I'm honored to be your husband. Come to me.*
>
> *Levi*

"Hurry, Miss Karyn, there's the *du-du-du-du* music."

Laughing at Dori, Karyn allowed her soon-to-be stepdaughter to drag her out of the room. Together, they began their coordinated steps down the aisle.

Karyn's beauty captured all of Levi's senses when she first appeared in the doorway with Dori. Levi had grown concerned when Dori hadn't come out as planned. All kinds of scenarios swirled in his mind. He started to sweat.

It seemed as if Rossi could read his thoughts. "Chill, Tolliver. Nobody wants you but Karyn."

Levi started tapping his foot when it appeared Karyn was either taking baby steps or had stopped moving. He contemplated taking off down the aisle, but Rossi crushed his shoe on top of Levi's.

"Don't worry. It's patent leather. It won't leave any footprints or dull the shine," Rossi whispered.

His cousin's diversion ended when Karyn was a few feet away.

"She looks like an African princess," Levi stuttered.

"Close your mouth, man, and go get your woman," Rossi urged with a slight shove.

Levi hurried to Karyn's side and lifted her in his arms. There were pockets of chuckles and sighs in the audience.

"Let me down. You're not supposed to carry me until the honeymoon." Karyn giggled as she held on tighter.

"Watch me," he said defiantly, then planted her in front of Pastor Scaife, who shook his head. "We're ready, sir." Levi was so charged he gave the minister a salute.

"Oh, boy," Rossi softly joked.

Pastor Scaife read a short passage from the Bible then nodded for them to recite their own vows. "Sister Karyn."

"Levi, although I'm speechless at the magnitude of your love for me, I promise to cherish that love by honoring you, being your strength when you're weak, following your guidance, and forsaking all others for you."

A tear dripped from her eye. Levi reached under the veil that stopped at her nose to catch it. Then it was his turn.

"Karyn, thank you for agreeing to share the rest of your life with me. I will cocoon you with protection, love, and honor. . . ."

When Levi choked on more words, Pastor Scaife took advantage of the pause and pronounced them husband and wife. "Brother Tolliver, you may now greet Sister Tolliver."

The pastor stepped back, giving Levi free rein to kiss his wife as the cheers, snickers, and claps exploded around him. His kiss was thorough, tender, and it would have been longer if it were not for Dori calling his name as she yanked on his pants leg.

"Daddy, I need to kiss Miss Karyn so she can become my mommy." His daughter was almost hysterical. "Come on, Daddy. You're taking too long."

Levi lifted his daughter with one arm. With Dori in the center, Levi and his new bride bestowed kisses on their daughter. "It's official. We're a family."

CHAPTER 58

Months later . . .

A crowd swelled around the restored Majestic Theatre, one of three historic sites in downtown East St.
Louis. It was the ribbon-cutting ceremony for the
grand opening of Crowning Glory. Levi squeezed
Karyn as she stood poised to unlock the door.

"Ready?" he whispered.

Taking a deep breath, Karyn swallowed. All her
dreams had come true. She stared into her husband's
eyes. Moisture blurred her vision. "Yes and no."

"Come on, babe. What's going on in that beautiful
little head of yours? By the way, you look pretty today,
Mrs. Tolliver." He massaged her back, coaxing her to
talk to him.

"After I was released, I thought I could conquer the
world just on my faith—"

"You conquered me," he whispered against her lips.

"But if this grandiose plan doesn't work, it could be a
disaster for your professional reputation."

"We know that's not going to happen. We have the
backing of Senator Coleman, civil leaders, and endless sponsors. I signed on to your dream the day I fell
in love with you. God opened the door that no man or
woman can shut."

Karyn fingered his bottom lip then kissed him until the mayor of East St. Louis cleared his throat. Levi stole one more smack.

"We're ready." Levi grinned.

Earlier, Jet made her presence known with a small group of protestors. Levi was about to confront her when Rossi waved him off as he headed to defuse the situation. Not long after that, cheers, whistles, and applause drowned them out until they dispersed, while a couple of community leaders gave speeches before the ribbon-cutting ceremony.

Karyn, Buttercup, and Halo posed for the media then turned the lock, signaling that they were open for business. True to their word, Crowning Glory offered limited free services, employed two barbers who were former convicts, a manicurist from the local community, and two certified masseuses. Six hairdressers were on board, with Buttercup as the head stylist, and Karyn would be the business manager, keeping Buttercup, who served time for forgery, away from the checks, cash, and credit cards. Halo would serve as their one-man security when he wasn't filling in as a barber or tending to the maintenance of the shop.

Tia strolled in as their first customer, followed by other Tolliver family members. Pastor Scaife stated he needed a haircut, and First Lady Scaife needed a touch-up. Friends from Crowns for Christ Church were steady customers all day.

Everybody *ooh*ed and *ahh*ed about the décor of soft pastel–colored walls accessorized with daring dark furniture selections. The contrast was stunning.

After an hour of doting, Tia and Levi's mothers happily paid for their services and were about to leave, until Halo stopped them at the door.

"One moment, ladies. Our services are not complete without your token."

Posted at the door, Dori discarded one of the home-baked cookies donated by the church to dig into a big box. From under a pool of tissue paper, she uncovered a miniature gold rhinestone tiara with the store's logo. "You have to bend down, Grandma. You're too tall."

Mrs. Tolliver did as Dori instructed, and Dori carefully positioned the tiara on her hair so as not to mess up her hairstyle. "You get this too, Grandma." She handed her a scroll, which Mrs. Tolliver unwrapped. A scripture for every day of the week was printed on it. "Thank you, baby."

"You're welcome, Grandma, but don't lose your crown, because you won't get a new one. You have to bring it back with you. Right, Mommy?"

Karyn nodded.

The shop remained busy until the close of the business day. Karyn was about to be the last to leave when Levi stopped her.

"What's wrong?" she asked tiredly.

"One person forgot to get pampered," he stated.

Shaking her head, Karyn knew that wasn't possible. Every customer had been served, receiving personalized attention. "Who?"

"You." He twirled her around to guide her back to the area for foot massages and pedicures.

"Do you even know what you're doing?" She giggled.

"Consider it on-the-job training."

CHAPTER 59

Another month later . . .

Levi walked through the kitchen, removing his tie after he shut the garage door. He hugged Karyn then looked at his daughter.

"Hi, Daddy."

"Hi, sweetheart." He kissed the top of Dori's head as she finished her homework at the kitchen table.

Turning back to Karyn, he scanned her pretty figure then locked in on her face. "You look tired. Was the shop busy today?"

She nodded and mouthed, "I need to talk to you."

Levi lifted a brow. "Now?"

Karyn shook her head. "After dinner."

Levi had an uneasy feeling. "I don't think so." He reached for Karyn's hand and led her out of the room. "We'll be right back, Dori."

"Okay, Daddy, but if you kiss Mommy too long this time, I might get hungry," she said without looking up at them.

"I won't."

In their bedroom, Levi closed the door and guided Karyn to a lounger. He knelt beside her. "Baby, what's wrong?"

When tears began to fill Karyn's eyes, Levi panicked. "What?"

Without answering, Karyn got up and went into the bathroom. Levi was unsure if he should follow. Immediately, Karyn returned with a colored strip. He held his breath. Did that mean what he thought it meant? Her expression gave no clue as to how he should respond.

Standing, he asked, "Is that what I think it is?"

She nodded.

"Yes! We're going to have a baby." He grinned, pumping his fist in the air. "Yes." He hurried to Karyn and wrapped her in a hug. He had lifted her off her feet when Dori opened their door without knocking.

"Mommy, Daddy, I'm hungry. See, I told ya you kiss too long." She skipped out of the room as Karyn sniffed.

For a few seconds, he held Karyn while she cried. "What if I hurt my baby again?" Karyn finally asked.

Levi frowned. He hadn't thought about that.

CHAPTER 60

A baby. Family, friends, customers, and former van riders were ecstatic. Even strangers seemed to smile at them for no known reason. The body of Christ immediately added them to numerous prayer lists. At the shop, it wasn't unusual for some customers to gather for a brief impromptu group prayer on Karyn's behalf before leaving the shop.

"God gave me my assignment weeks ago," Rossi told Levi and Karyn over the phone. "We're going to pray the devil off his seat."

The couple sought counseling with Pastor Scaife, since Levi had decided to change church membership. Levi bought every book he could find on postpartum depression and stayed up late at night, surfing the web for information.

"Baby, did you know you have a greater chance of suffering from postpartum depression again?" he had mumbled with almost a defeated sigh as he lay next to her. He seemed to shake it off. "Well, without a test, there is no testimony." Those had become their words of encouragement to each other.

One Friday evening, Karyn was at home while Levi surveyed a new job site. Jet had Dori for the weekend. The devil seemed to wait when she was alone to tempt her with fear. During those times, Karyn would pray until, sometimes, she cried.

The doorbell rang. Karyn wasn't expecting any visitors when she looked through the peephole. Smiling, she opened the door.

"Come on in, Mom Tolliver." The women embraced.

"I hope you don't mind that I stopped by," she said, removing her coat as they walked through the foyer to the living room.

After taking a seat, Mrs. Tolliver patted Karyn's hand. "I want to share something with you."

"Sure." Karyn was glad for the company.

"When I was pregnant with Levi, I didn't experience the jubilation I had expected based on what I had heard from other new mothers. I was miserable. I had an extended period of morning sickness. It seemed as if it never was going to stop. I kept waiting and waiting for the 'happy about having a baby' moment. It never came. I couldn't wait to deliver. Once I did, my mood didn't change.

"I became withdrawn. My mother and friends said it was nothing more than the baby blues, but I just didn't feel right." She frowned as if she were trying to understand it too. "Levi was a handsome little thing and a good baby, but I just felt overwhelmed."

Karyn closed her eyes. She understood overwhelmed very well.

"When I delivered the twins, I would've given them up for adoption if I thought Victor would've let me." Mrs. Tolliver wasn't smiling. "But I had a good husband, like you. He didn't complain about my mood swings. He loved me despite it all, like Levi loves you.

"Karyn, I'm telling you this because I'm wondering if I suffered from some form of postpartum depression. I bought that book by Brooke Shields. Even the rich and famous aren't exempt from suffering from it. I didn't realize that the baby blues describes mood swings for about two weeks, and anything longer—up to two years—could be signs of postpartum depression. I had no idea there was a name for what I was experiencing."

Compassion. That's what Karyn saw in her mother-in-law's eyes. Karyn sniffed to keep from falling apart. "Thank you for telling me that, because I'm so scared. I'm mustering as much faith as I can, but I'm scared."

Mrs. Tolliver opened her arms, and Karyn scooted over and fell into them, sobbing. The woman stroked her hair. "I'll be beside you every step of the way. The Tollivers will be your support system. Plus, your sister and that Butternut woman, I guess she won't stress you out."

Karyn laughed at the mix-up on Buttercup's nickname. "God sent her to me when I was released. She was my sanity and satire. It wouldn't be the same without her."

Weeks later, Karyn and Levi met with a highly recommended psychologist who specialized in postpartum depression. To Karyn, the doctor appeared too young to know anything. Dr. Lee Hayes manifested his wealth of knowledge as he responded to their every question.

"Mr. and Mrs. Tolliver, it's very important to know that a prior diagnosis of postpartum depression doesn't mean it will recur."

Out of the corner of her eye, Karyn saw Levi physically relax. When Dr. Hayes held up his finger, Levi stiffened.

"But . . . Mrs. Tolliver does have a higher chance of suffering from the illness after subsequent pregnancies. You"—he paused and pointed at Levi—"need to watch for symptoms."

In hindsight, Karyn had already learned them. Levi, on the other hand, said he ached and prayed for her.

"It's genetic if one or both parents have experienced depression. Poor appetite or overeating could be a sign of stress or a feeling of being overwhelmed. Fatigue, poor self-esteem, helplessness—"

"Wait a minute," Levi interrupted. He eyed her before carefully phrasing his question. "Dr. Hayes, that sounds like every woman I know on a given day. Even our daughter shows bouts of self-esteem issues."

Dr. Hayes nodded. "Fair enough, but if Karyn—Mrs. Tolliver—would begin to feel her life is worthless, she begins to blame others for her condition, which would basically be you." He didn't crack a smile. "If she begins to talk incoherently about ending her life or the baby's, those are red flags."

Levi reached over and squeezed Karyn's hand then massaged her fingers. "That's not going to happen."

The doctor nodded. "I agree. With weekly therapy and medication and prayer, your wife will be fine. The most important thing is not to compare her experience to that of your friends, mothers, or others during her pregnancy. Don't put too much pressure on her that would make her feel like she has to be a superwoman, superwife, or supermom."

Dr. Hayes paused and studied Karyn. "Incidentally, I understand you're a stepmom. How are you adjusting to that role?"

"I'm not." Karyn thought Levi was about to pass out from shock, so she clarified her answer. "I'm adjusting to being a mom. We do not use the term *step* in our household. I've never been this happy in my life." She glanced at Levi, and she had never seen him look so relieved.

Levi escorted Karyn to every obstetrician and therapy appointment. More than once she complained he was overwhelming her by trying not to overwhelm her.

"Levi, I promise if I feel anything out of the ordinary, like using a pan as a flying saucer at your head—okay, that wasn't funny—I won't hide it from you. Our baby and our happiness are too important to me."

That earned her a kiss. "Good answer, Mrs. Tolliver."

Her smile was brilliant in return. "Okay." She stretched her arms behind her head while she lounged in a recliner "The baby wants some strawberry sherbet."

Soon the first wave of the Tolliver maternity squad reported to duty. Karyn had barely begun to show when hot dinners were delivered, errands were run, and Karyn was ushered away to girls' night out events.

On subsequent visits to Dr. Hayes, Levi was tempted to take copies of Karyn's answers to the same questions he asked them during every appointment.

One night, about five months into the pregnancy, when Levi came home, Karyn ran him a tub of bath water. She poured a little of her bubble bath in it as a joke. He complained he'd rather his wife smelled good. He was a man's man.

Afterward, he climbed into bed, where Karyn was snuggled under the covers, waiting for him. He smothered her with tender kisses and hushed words of love.

"How you feeling, baby?"

"Nervous."

"Remember, without a test there is no testimony."

EPILOGUE

The fireworks exploded on July 4 as the Tollivers welcomed Levi Dennis Tolliver, Jr. into the world at seven pounds and three ounces. Gifts, calls of congratulations, and visits were constant. Levi didn't leave Karyn's side throughout the twelve-hour delivery. So as not to break the cycle of bonding, he was determined to spend the night in the hospital room on a cot.

"Levi, you're not going to be comfortable. Go home and get some sleep. I have the nurses here to help me," Karyn said in wasted breath.

He twisted his body to get comfortable. His face told the story that it was useless. "It's not about that. I don't want to be home without you, even if I don't get any sleep."

Every few hours, the nurses returned to the room to check Karyn's vital signs or for the baby's feeding. Levi didn't stir. Karyn and the nurse exchanged smiles.

For the next months, the Tollivers kept their word. Tia, who was getting married in a few months; Nalani, who had relocated permanently to the Metro East; Buttercup, Mrs. Tolliver, and even Mother Caldwell circulated a sign-up sheet for shifts.

Karyn didn't have to lift a finger. They cleaned, cooked, and watched LJ during the day so Karyn could take naps.

When Buttercup and Halo weren't working at Crowning Glory, they came and washed and shampooed Karyn's hair.

Acting as a nurse's aide, Buttercup would arrive with a clipboard and ask questions. "Good evening, Mrs. Tolliver." She would grin and wrinkle her nose. "Any feelings of depression or sadness?"

"Nope." Karyn beamed, rubbing her baby's back.

"What about irritability?"

"Only if you keep this up."

"Humph. You know I'm not scared." Buttercup rolled her eyes and smacked her lips. She looked down at her checklist and scribbled. "It must be your hormones raging out of control."

"Thanks to my family and friends, that isn't happening. Levi has a maid come in twice a week. Mom Tolliver cooks meals. You make sure my hair is curled and nails painted—at least you mastered that. Rossi makes sure I'm covered under daily prayers, and Tia and Nalani are my fashion gurus to make sure I'm stylish even if I'm lounging around the house. I say I'm covered with blessings from the crown of my head to the soles of my feet. I am so blessed."

BOOK CLUB QUESTIONS

1. Why did Karyn feel she didn't owe Levi an explanation about her past?

2. What was Rossi's mission in the book?

3. Who should be Rossi's love interest? You MUST e-mail the author your answer: pat@patsimmons.net.

4. Talk about Jesetta. Could you relate to her emotions, or was she too far gone emotionally?

5. How did you view ex-offenders before you read the story? Did the book change your view of the life of ex-offenders? Why or why not?

6. How much do you know about postpartum depression?

7. Is there a sin or act of crime you couldn't forgive? Be honest.

8. Women are the fastest growing prison population. Why?

9. Talk about someone you know who is a victim of crime, or a recent story in the headlines.

10. Talk about Tia's interaction with Karyn.

11. Discuss Nalani's determination to confront Jet before she knew she was getting baptized. Would that classify as presumptuous sin?

AUTHOR BIO

Pat Simmons considers herself a self-proclaimed genealogy sleuth. She is passionate about researching her ancestors and then casting them in starring roles in her novels. She has been a genealogy enthusiast since her great-grandmother died at the young age of ninety-seven years old.

She describes the evidence of the gift of the Holy Ghost as an amazing, unforgettable, life-altering experience. She believes God is the Author who advances the stories she writes.

Pat has a B.S. in mass communications from Emerson College in Boston, MA. She has worked in various media positions in radio, television, and print for more than twenty years. Currently, she oversees the media publicity for the annual RT Booklovers Conventions.

She is the award-winning author of *Talk to Me,* ranked #14 on the *Black Pearls Magazine* list of Top 50 Books in 2008 that Changed Lives. She also received the Katherine D. Jones Award for Grace and Humility from the Romance Slam Jam committee in 2008. Pat is best known for her Guilty series: *Guilty of Love, Not Guilty of Love,* and *Still Guilty. Crowning Glory* is her fifth novel.

Author Bio

Pat has converted her sofa-strapped, sports-fanatical husband into an amateur travel agent, untrained bodyguard, and GPS-guided chauffeur. They have a son and daughter.

Pat's media appearances include: KMOV-TV, St. Louis; The Best of STL, St. Louis; *St. Louis American Newspaper*; WFUN 95.5 FM, St. Louis; *Ferguson Times Newspaper*, Ferguson, MO; Heaven 1580 AM, Lanham, MD; WCLM, Richmond, VA; ArtistFirst Radio Network, Alliance, OH; Blog Radio Network; WKKV 100.7 FM, Racine, WI; and WHPR-FM, Detroit, MI.

To keep up with the latest on Pat Simmons, please visit her at www.patsimmons.net.

Author's note about Crowning Glory.

In 1987, a shocking news story made national and St. Louis headlines. Seven employees who worked at one of the defunct National Supermarkets were shot; two survived. I will never forget that story or some of the victims. One was a sixteen-year-old male who worked as a bagger and had dreams of becoming a surgeon. Another was a cashier close to retirement. It was this horrific crime that was the backdrop for Jet's anguish.

On June 28, 2008, Jimmy Brand's murder didn't make national headlines. Television and newspapers carried the story of yet another senseless crime that shattered lives. Unlike the grocery store, he wasn't gunned down in a public place. The crime scene was at the front door of his home. During an interview, his wife, Ella, whispered she might not ever get over the senseless act.

It is my desire that we reach out to survivors and all victims of crime, for their lives are forever altered.

Urban Christian His Glory Book Club!

Established January 2007, *UC His Glory Book Club* is another way to introduce Urban Books' imprint, Urban Christian, and its authors, to the literary world. We are an online book club supporting Urban Christian authors by purchasing, reading, and providing written reviews of the books that are read. *UC His Glory* welcomes both men and women of the literary world who have a passion for reading Christian-based fiction.

UC His Glory is the brainchild of Joylynn Jossel, Author and Executive Editor of Urban Christian, and bestselling Christian author Kendra Norman-Bellamy. The book club will provide support, positive feedback, encouragement, and a forum whereby members can openly discuss and review the literary works of Urban Christian authors. In the future, we anticipate broadening our spectrum of services to include online author chats, author spotlights, interviews with your favorite Urban Christian author(s), special online groups for *UC His Glory Book Club* members, the ability to post reviews on the Web site and amazon.com, membership ID cards, a Yahoo! group, and much more.

Even though there will be no membership fees attached to becoming a member of *UC His Glory Book Club,* we do expect our members to be active, committed, and to follow the guidelines of the club.

Urban Christian His Glory Book Club

UC His Glory members pledge to:
- Follow the guidelines of *UC His Glory Book Club.*
- Provide input, opinions, and reviews that build up, rather than tear down.
- Commit to purchasing, reading, and discussing the featured book(s) of the month.
- Agree not to miss more than three consecutive online monthly meetings.
- Respect the Christian beliefs of *UC His Glory Book Club.*
- Believe that Jesus is the Christ, Son of the Living God

We look forward to the online fellowship.

Many Blessings to You!

Shelia E Lipsey
President
UC His Glory Book Club

**Visit the official Urban Christian His Glory Book Club website at www.uchisglorybookclub.net

Notes

Notes